力得文化
Leader Culture

滿分名師的教學密笈

U0077394

突破新多益

800

輕鬆戰勝新多益、突破自我

首度公開名師自身第一次考新多益就拿滿分的備考方式
如何在短期的學習中突破新多益分數瓶頸
迅速增加**200**分**UP**的秘訣

洪子健 ◎著

- **突破重點1** 針對國人在新多益考試中常遇到的問題所量身打造的考試攻略
- **突破重點2** 只是「多記單字、多背文法」不足以拿到高分,而是用英語母
  語人士的學習法,自然地學會單字及文法
- **突破重點3** 詳盡分析新多益7大題型,利用題型小練習,找出學習盲點,
  立即掌握解題要領
- **突破重點4** 附外師專業錄製美英澳三國口音MP3
- **突破重點5** 針對不同口音,有詳細的「聽力要訣」解析,輕鬆拿高分

MP3

作者序

在民國 91 年的三月初，決定報名參加月底的新多益後，得到友人相助贈送三本新多益官方考題。花了兩禮拜的時間熟悉了一下考試型態與方法，在應考前就覺得新多益其實不難啊！聽力就是加了英國腔和澳洲腔，而自己在美國工作多年，連最難的印度腔可以聽懂，英、澳腔算什麼。再來是閱讀，說真的考的文法基本上國中都教過，而單字高二左右程度就可以應付，閱讀唯一的特點就是題目多而已，只要閱讀能力夠，根本不會是問題。

考完當時就知道兩題聽力、兩題閱讀沒把握，回家 Google 了一下知道其中一題文法對了，也就是說我拿了滿分（新多益聽力一般而言可以錯五題左右，閱讀一般可以錯兩題還是滿分）。當時覺得新多益其實還蠻簡單的，如同前一段所提的，新多益也就是聽力就是加了英、澳腔，文法只是國中文法，單字其實也只有高二左右的程度。當時只覺得叫我考幾次聽力都可以滿分，而閱讀上面十次裡面至少有八、九次可以拿滿分，那時只覺得奇怪，怎麼大家會考不好？

後來有機會到 HiTutor 擔任英文老師，尤其是以新多益考試為主，以及另外在中國科技大學教授新多益課程。以我在 HiTutor 的新多益教學經驗，學生基本上都進步一百五到兩百以上，一些遵照我所講授的技巧和方法來認真準備的學生，進步的幅度更不止兩百！在跟些好友聊過，還有自己的教學經驗裡漸漸地了解了為什麼台灣學生和上班族新多益考不好，甚至就算花錢補習效果都不好的原因。

在我的 FB 粉絲專頁『跟 TC 學英文』裡面，也有網友要我介紹一些新多益的書籍，說實話市面上的新多益書籍雖然很多，卻沒有一本能讓我覺得值得按讚的，有些甚至差到讓我想按爛。陸陸續續也有幾位

HiTutor 的學生問我，有沒有考慮寫一本新多益的書？其實以新多益考試而言，最重要的是念英文的方式和解題目的方法。台灣學生和上班族在新多益考試上會面臨撞牆情況，最主要的原因正是因為唸英文和解題目的方法都錯了！在沒有解決這個問題之前，念再多本的書、補再多次的習，只會讓你花更多的錢，然後再一次一次地撞牆，撞得頭破血流，卻絲毫見不到成效，一般市面上的新多益書籍，也沒能指出這點！

在跟倍斯特合作出版了留學達人英語通以及合著了簡報英文後，我主動地跟倍斯特提出希望出版這本新多益高分秘笈，針對台灣考生所面臨的問題來設計題目，用來教大家如何正確、有效的唸英文、學習英文以及準備新多益，進而在新多益考試上拿到高分的方法和重點。我只是指出在那面又高、又硬的牆旁邊，其實有一扇門，你可以打開那道門，完全不需要撞牆，就可以輕鬆跨過新多益門檻拿到高分。

出版這本書，除了讓大家能夠在新多益奪取高分外，其實我更希望讓大家了解到正確的英文學習方法：就是把文章念出來、念到要有FU，千萬不要硬背單字，千萬不要去背文法規則，只是要教大家如何打開旁邊的那道門，輕鬆地穿越英文障礙，學好英文。

推薦序

　　跟 TC 老師合作的三年間，TC 老師除了本身具備新多益 990 分滿分的硬底子，在教學上，更有他獨到的方式。首先，TC 老師聲音宏亮，非常具有感染力與熱情，我們是線上教學的產業，老師的聲音就是他所傳達的表情，透過一條網路線，讓學員彷彿看到老師在眼前上課，毫無距離感。其次，TC 老師非常了解新多益考生的程度差距和需要改善的能力。舉例來說，老師會先研究新多益考生目前的程度，以及期望達到的程度，這中間的差距，因人而異，不論是四國口音、聽力技巧、詞彙能力、文法、略讀和精讀技巧、句子改述到閱讀速度等等，TC 老師都能依照學生的情況做準確的判斷，知道如何幫助新多益考生達到期望程度，並告訴學生，該花多久的時間，做足哪些準備。這一系列的「診斷」，不僅讓學生有心理準備，更是訂定了明確的目標和方向，不會再有「心慌慌」的症狀。

　　本書的特色除了清楚陳述上述的要點，更在每一個 PART 之前，詳細說明本篇須掌握的重點以及準備方法，經過 TC 老師娓娓道來，深入的說明加上 TC 老師式的講述方式，彷彿聘請到一位高手到府授課。例如講到聽力，老師建議「自己先念過，然後不看稿子的聽」，並大聲疾呼『腦子裡不能出現中文！』；而閱讀部分則強調語感的培養，在書中有大量的闡述。

　　所謂學習無捷徑，新多益官方曾經公布一個統計，若要從新多益 200 分進步到新多益 730 分，個人自修學習的時間高達 1850 小時，若經過專業有系統的引導，可以大大地縮短學習時數，也讓學習更有效率，而 TC 老師的指導和他所出的書籍，就是您最佳的選擇。

HiTutor 線上教務

Claire H.

編者序

根據美國 ETC 在 2012 年全球多益報告中指出,台灣該年報考新多益有 26 萬 4563 人次,平均分數為 539 分,創下新低。

許多平均分數在五、六百的新多益考生在本書作者:洪老師的短期課程中,成功地突破了新多益 800 分的門檻,進步超過 200 分以上。

本書與其他新多益相關書籍不同的地方,我們沒有很多回的『擬真試題』,但是有絕大的部分都是在教您如何看懂題目,正確答題。作者指出在他的學生中有許多英文程度並不像他們自身覺得的有那麼不好,而是沒有找對方法學習。一昧地背單字及文法並不能解決問題,書中有針對台灣地區的考生,甚至是中文母語人士,提供最合適的學習方法,及確切地指出學習盲點。還有以大量的語感練習來讓讀者學會最接近英語母語人士理解題目及解題的方式。

編輯群

目次 CONTENTS

Part 1 新多益測驗滿分名師的教學密笈

新多益測驗資訊分享站

TOEIC 的 全 名 是 New Test of English for International Communication（新國際溝通英語測驗），在臺灣一般稱之為「多益」，而在中國，則稱為「托業」。而 New TOEIC 稱為新多益，新版與舊版的不同是在於聽力測驗中，新多益考試有加入英、澳口音。

這是一個專門為母語非英語的人士所設計之英語能力測驗；測驗的分數能反應出受測者在國際職場環境中以英語與他人溝通的熟稔程度。

新多益是目前全世界最大也是最受歡迎的職場英語能力測驗，不光是企業界用新多益作為公司員工的英語能力測驗標準；各大專院校、一些國際及展覽的主辦單位也都以此來評定相關人員的英文能力。根據官方統計，光是在 2012 年，全球就有超過七百萬人報考新多益測驗，並在 150 個國家中有超過 14,000 家的企業、學校或政府機構使用新多益測驗，同時在全球超過 165 個國家施測，是最被廣泛接受且最方便報考的英語測驗之一。

為了更貼近實際職場與生活環境的需求，目前的 New TOEIC 測驗作了以下的改變：
1. 聽力方面 – 面對各種英語發音是否能對答如流的能力
　　(1) 題目長度增長
　　(2) 連鎖題組方式呈現
　　(3) 美 / 英 / 澳 / 加等口音

2. 閱讀方面－受測者是否有整合句子與段落內容的能力

　(1) 題目長度增長

　(2) 以「段落填空」取代挑錯題

　(3) 閱讀測驗型態更新 → 對多篇文章的關連性理解

 新多益測驗方式

分「聽力」、「閱讀」兩部分進行；在測驗開始之前，受測者約花費半個小時填寫個人資料及問卷，測驗進行中不休息，真正待在考場裡的時間約為兩個半小時。以下為新多益測驗的題型說明：

聽力測驗－測驗時間為 45 分鐘，分四個大題，共 100 題。

大題	內容		題數
I	Photographs	照片描述	10 題
II	Question-Response	應答問題	30 題
III	Short Conversations	簡短對話	10 組 30 題
IV	Short Talks	簡短獨白	10 組 30 題

閱讀測驗－測驗時間為 75 分鐘，分三個大題，共 100 題。

大題	內容		題數
V	Incomplete Sentences	句子填空	40 題
VI	Text Completion	段落填空	4 組 12 題
VII	Reading Comprehension	閱讀測驗	
	*Single Passage	* 單篇閱讀	7-10 組 28 題
	*Double Passage	* 雙篇閱讀	4 組 20 題

 新多益測驗內容

1. 一般商務－契約、談判、行銷、銷售、商業企劃、會議

2. 製造業－工廠管理、生產線、品管

3. 金融／預算－銀行業務、投資、稅務、會計、帳單

4. 企業發展－研究、產品研發

5. 辦公室－董事會、委員會、信件、備忘錄、電話、傳真、電子郵件、辦公室器材與傢俱、辦公室流程

6. 人事－招考、雇用、退休、薪資、升遷、應徵與廣告

7. 採購－比價、訂貨、送貨、發票

8. 技術層面－電子、科技、電腦、實驗室與相關器材、技術規格

9. 房屋／公司地產－建築、規格、購買租賃、電力瓦斯服務

10. 旅遊－火車、飛機、計程車、巴士、船隻、渡輪、票務、時刻表、車站、機場廣播、租車、飯店、預訂、脫班與取消

11. 外食－商務／非正式午餐、宴會、招待會、餐廳訂位

12. 娛樂－電影、劇場、音樂、藝術、媒體

13. 保健－醫藥保險、看醫生、牙醫、診所、醫院

 新多益測驗分數計算

New TOEIC 測驗是以總分（含聽力＋閱讀）10~990 分來表現受測者的英語能力，依測驗成績有五種等級的證書：金色證書（860~990分）、藍色證書（730~855 分）、綠色證書（470~725 分）、棕色證書（220~465 分）、橘色證書（10~215 分）。

 新多益測驗考試時間與報名方式

1. 新多益測驗時間（New TOEIC 官網）
   http://toeic.com.tw/tests_info.jsp

2. New TOEIC 測驗報名費用為 NT1,500 元，報名方式有「網路報名」、「通訊報名」與「臨櫃報名」等三種，報名流程與詳細說明：
   http://www.toeic.com.tw/toeic_news_pub.jsp?type=8

Part

新多益測驗滿分
名師的教學密笈

1

Unit 1 新多益高分密笈

前言

在解釋新多益如何能考高分的秘笈之前，我想先提一下台灣一般的英文學習方式，而這造成了哪些問題？再來我解釋一下為什麼這些問題，會造成台灣考生在新多益考試時面臨撞牆的困擾，也就是再怎麼準備、再怎麼補習都沒什麼效果，台灣學生的新多益成績就是僵在某個點上面。

在台灣是怎麼樣學英文的

記單字的正確方法

在學校裡只要在文章裡看到單字，第一個反應就是查字典，然後把所有單字的中文意思都寫在單字下面。不信嗎？看看你以前的英文課本，是不是在課文的單字下面都寫上中文意思。或許你會問了，那難道還有其他方式嗎？當然有！而這也正是我會撰寫這本書的原因了。請先看看以下的一句簡單例子：

The candidates need to be fluent in English.

台灣學生看到這句裡的 fluent，不懂就立刻查字典對吧！其實根本不用查字典，先簡單的判斷一下：fluent 在這句話裡的意思，是好是壞？既然一定要 fluent in English，那 fluent 一定是好是對吧！然後想想，英文很好以中文而言，你會怎麼說？他的英文很？？（流利……對吧？），那你說

fluent 的意思會是？沒錯就是流利！

接下來台灣學生又會怎麼做？當然就是 fluent 流利的、fluent 流利的、fluent 流利的，開始背這個單字，沒錯吧！這難道不對嗎？單字不背怎麼記得住？我告訴你這才真的是錯得離譜！

讓我教你一個簡單、有效真正能記住單字的方法。再次用前面的例子，當你猜出 fluent 的意思以後，instead of 一個英文、一個中文 fluent 流利的、fluent 流利的，這麼的硬背，你應該再把這整句話再念一次：The candidates need to be fluent in English. 然後念一下 fluent in English、fluent in English 最後把 fluent、fluent、fluent 念三次，你説是不是對 fluent 這個字就有 FU 了？你説是不是容易多了？不用硬背，對 "fluent" 這個字就有印象了，也容易記住了。

如果你有些單字需要記起來，最有效的方法是，上網找例句。找出一些好的例句，然後念例句，利用例句裡面你對那個單字的 FU，把那個單字記住，例如前面所舉的 fluent in English。

以準備新多益而言，又該怎麼記單字呢？如果你買了一些新多益單字書，裡面只是把單字一個英文、一個中文的列出來，把那本書丟了不要用。如果每個單字都附些例句，念一下書裡的例句，看看是不是能對那個單字有感覺、有 FU？如同 fluent in English 裡的 fluent 一樣。如果能有 FU，把例句多念幾次，讓你的腦子消化一下，這個字絕對好記多了。如果你根本沒買任何所謂的新多益單字書籍，那更好，把書裡所有的文章與句子，念個幾遍，尤其裡面有你不認識的單字的文章和句子，更要多念幾次。只要作者寫的文章、句子夠好，你就很容易對那些字有感覺，就能幫助你不需要硬背的記住單字。

學文法正確的方式

單字講過了該講文法了。還記得你怎麼學文法的嗎？拿起你手邊的文法書或是上網查幾個英文文法名詞，例如關係子句。基本上都是以中文來解釋，甚至把文法寫成規則或是公式，好心一點的舉個一兩個例句，最後一定是考試練習。你應該有印象吧，看這些文法規則和例句以後，好像有一點 FU，問題是試著寫練習題時，往往又出問題了。就算練習時沒什麼沒問題，一到考試卻又會搞混了，選不出正確答案對吧。

其實學文法跟記單字的基本方法都一樣：念例句。用例句來對單字產生 FU，利用那個 FU 來記住單字。文法也一樣多念例句，把例句唸到有 FU，就可以很自然地把文法輕鬆地學起來。我就先用以下的例子先做個簡單的說明：

In the final - - - - - -, Mr. Chen is not a popular leader because he is too stingy on his staff.

(A) analyst

(B) analysis

(C) analytic

(D) analyze

文法大師這就說了：in the (final) - - - - - - 後面要加名詞，尤其是前面有個形容詞 final，所以答案是 (B) 名詞 analysis。

我的建議是把以下的例句多念幾遍：

in the final **analysis** 最後的分析

He is a financial **analyst**. 財務分析師（注意一下 analyst 的正確唸法是：A-na-lyst，重音在最前面的 A。）

an **analytic** model 分析模型（注意一下這個字的發音是 a-na-LY-tic）

We need to **analyze** the market condition first. 分析市場情況

把上面的四句多念幾次，是不是可以直接把答案唸出來。你會需要去辨別哪個情況需要動詞？哪時候要名詞？哪些狀況需要形容詞嗎？在這本書裡有更多的例子，讓你能夠把四個答案念一下，選那個念的最順的選出來就是正確答案，就對了。

再來你是否注意到，裡面好像有個單字不是很熟悉？沒錯，就是 "Mr. Chen is not a popular leader because he is too stingy on his staff." 裡面的 stingy 這個字，記得前面説的不要急著查字典，先再一次念這句子：

Mr. Chen is not a popular leader because he is too stingy on his staff.

然後猜猜 stingy 這個字是好是壞？既然 not popular，那可以推測，"stingy" 一定不會是好事！猜完後才去查字典，知道是吝嗇、小氣的意思，再回來念一次：

Mr. Chen is not a popular leader because he is too stingy on his staff. too stingy on his staff 是不是對這個字就有 FU 了，也容易記了！

死背單字、文法所造成的問題

單字面

先說背單字好了，大家應該都有印象，念書時一、二十個單字或許可以硬背起來，五、六十個就開始難了，兩、三百個單字就開始出現背了就忘、忘了再背，背得很辛苦的慘狀，對吧。更討厭的是，就算背起來了，考試還是會出問題。就以以下的考題為例：

We - - - - - - prompt service to all of our customers.

(A) provide

(B) hold

(C) send

(D) offer

看到題目後感覺真是太棒了，四個單字我都背過而且都還記得。(A) 提供 (B) 擁有、抓住 (C) 發送、寄 (D) 提供。這下可傻眼了 (A) 和 (D) 都一樣是提供！許多我教過的，只要是精通背單字的學生，不管程度高低沒有例外，對 provide 和 offer 這兩個字的差別，幾乎都不知道！你單字背得很熟、很厲害，結果發現 provide 是提供，offer 也是提供，背起來了卻又傻眼了，難道兩個都可以？

回到我一直強調的例句，先把一下兩句分別念個幾遍。

We **offer** prompt service **to** all of our customers. (offer... to)

We **provide** all of our customers **with** prompt service. (provide ... with)

是不是連想都不用想，輕鬆地把答案選出來。

文法面

再來聊聊文法，大家應該都學過以下這個，最基本的文法規則：
現在式時態在主詞第三人稱單數時，動詞要加 s。

結果考試的時候，就需要先看看時態是不是現在式？然後要判斷主詞是不是第三人稱？然後看看是不是單數？最後終於知道動詞需不需要加 s。

連我看了都累，更不用說考試時你需要花多少時間，來根據文法規則一條一條得來判斷，花時間能選出正確答案還好，更慘的是往往在花了一堆時間後，卻還經常判斷錯誤，真是賠了夫人又折兵。連這個最簡單國一就學過的文法都會如此，更不用說其他更難的了。

你應該會問了，就以這個主詞第三人稱單數，現在式動詞要加 s，又應該怎麼學？其實很簡單，回到我一直強調的例句。先把以下的兩個例句，分別念個幾遍，念的時候記得要把粗體字大寫的 s 唸出來。
The candidate**S** need to be fluent in English.
The candidate need**S** to be fluent in English.

多念幾次你就可以自然的發現，candidate 和 need 只能有一個，也一定會有一個，需要加 s。有了這個 FU 以後，不管怎麼考，都可以把答案很順利地唸出來，根本不需要按照文法規則來判斷。

最後談談硬背單字，只重文法的教學，所造成的最大壞處：超級差的閱讀能力。有許多英文老師都怪到學生頭上，叫你背單字你不背，難怪文章看不懂。這點謬論這其實不用多解釋，以下是大家都經歷過的。把文章的句子裡的每個單字，都查出來了、寫上去了，結果整句話卻還是看不懂！！

單字都查了、文法也都教了，文章卻還是看不懂。說實話台灣的英文老師，在要求背單字、教文法之時，什麼時候問過學生，是否把文章看懂了？把文章看懂從來都不是教英文的重點，難怪大家的英文閱讀能力都不好。

為什麼新多益成績就是會撞牆

前面說了台灣學英文時，最強調的就是一個英文、一個中文的背單字，辛苦就算了，更大的問題是沒有效率，背了就忘、忘了又背，應該是大家都經歷過的過程。而大家都不知道的是，這個壞習慣竟也造成了大家聽力測驗上無法拿高分的困擾。這點也是在我教授許多學員的新多益課程後，發現的。你或許不相信，請看我的解釋。

不管是看課文還是念句子，大家養成的習慣是：一見到單字根本不會去管剩下的句子看懂了沒，立刻就拋下一切去查字典。結果在聽力考試時，一聽到有哪些字沒有完全聽懂，就立刻去回想那個字是什麼意思？結果這句沒聽懂就算了，連帶下一句原本可以聽懂的，也沒聽到、注意到。

我常跟學生講，聽力只有一次機會，沒聽懂就沒了。最重要的是專注在你聽懂的部分，而這個最重要的聽力技巧卻因為看到單字立刻查字典的壞習慣，反而要多次練習才能改正。我相信有許多學生還不知道這個壞習慣，或是不知道如何改掉。更不用說新多益加了英、澳腔讓你有更多的單字聽不出來。你是不是只要有幾個字沒聽出來，就自然而然的整句聽不懂，結果其實很簡單的聽力，大家都考不好了。

單字部分，我建議是以例句的方式作為輔助，以多念的方法。硬背單字的結果往往會造成單字沒法記牢，大多是模糊的印象，更不用說一些拼字相近或是意思類似的字，根本搞不清楚，單字會考的好才怪。如果是以記憶句子、多念的方式，能夠加深對單字的印象，也能自然而然地學到這個單字在句子中的用法。

同樣的方式也能用在文法的學習上，但在台灣，教英文文法時，喜歡用中文説公式、講規則，結果是大家用公式和規則來解文法，從句子裡判斷是要選動詞、名詞、形容詞還是副詞？動詞需要加 ing 還是 ed？如同前面所説勞心又勞力，花時間又沒效率。我的建議是應該以多閱讀及反覆念的方式，以類似我們學母語（中文）的方式，加上歸納出的文法規則為輔，才能最有效地學好英文。

新多益閱讀考試的特色

新多益閱讀共有 100 題，其中 52 題單字與文法，48 題閱讀測驗。而閱讀測驗裡面又有四個大題是雙篇文章的閱讀測驗，也就是這四大題有八篇文章，連同前面九篇的單篇閱讀（以多益出版的八份官方考題為例），總共有十七篇文章。測驗閱讀的測驗時間是 75 分鐘要寫完 100 題，也就是三分鐘寫四題。其中有將近一半（48 題）是閱讀測驗，包含十七篇文章，你説時間夠不夠？如果你在文法題目上面，用傳統的文法教學來判斷答案，浪費時間又沒效率，再加上將近一半考題的閱讀測驗，我保證絕對寫不完。單字硬背容易忘，文法規則花時間，閱讀能力又不好，難怪大家新多益考不好，而且怎麼補習都一樣。考了幾次以後，新多益成績就撞牆了，怎麼撞都突破不了那塊隱形的天花板。

在我教授的新多益課程中，許多學生因為我所教授的正確準備方法和考試技巧，而在短期內將新多益成績提高超過兩百分，而同時在那期間，也感受到了台灣人新多益考試的問題後，決定出版這本書，指出正確的新多益準備方向，介紹給大家那道牆邊的門，讓你輕鬆地突破困境，拿取新多益高分。

聽力應試技巧

各類的英文考試總是以聽力與閱讀兩大類為主，新多益也不例外。第一部分的聽力以四種類型（Part 1, 2, 3, 4），來測試考生的英聽能力。第二部分分成三類，前兩種（Part 5, 6）考單字與文法，而最後的 Part 7 就是一般所謂的閱讀測驗。其實準備英文考試不管是英檢、新多益、托福、雅思或是 GRE、GMAT，都應該培養兩種技能：考試技巧和英文能力。

台灣一般的教材還有補習班，往往只重視能力而忽略技巧。先強調一下，我這裡所講的考試技巧，跟一般補習班所說的完全不一樣！先耐著心繼續看下去。你可以看看坊間所有的英文考試書籍還有補習班，都在強調背單字與學文法對吧？

你會問：背單字、學文法難道不是要培養英文考試能力？這難道有錯嗎？你一定聽老師說過要把單字都背好、文法都學完，才能看懂句子、搞清楚文章。說實話從小到大，有哪次的英聽測驗，你能把每個字都聽懂？哪次英文考試你每個字都認得？沒有吧！如果真的是把單字都背好、文法都學完才可以，那不是不用想考高分了。而這正是我強調的考試技巧，如何在沒能聽清楚每個字的情況下，聽懂文章進而選出答案？如何在有單字的情形下看懂句子，明瞭文章來輕鬆的解題？這樣的考試技巧是不是每種英文考試都用得上？而且說實話這種技巧才是輕鬆學好英文的最大關鍵。加強英文能力，只能幫助你在考試裡面拿到某個不錯的分數，如果你想在英文考試上拿高分，沒有考試技巧真的很難。

在同個等級的英文考試裡，聽力測驗的考題與文章絕對比閱讀的簡單。所以相對而言，培養聽力的實力，也就是讓自己聽懂內容就比較重要了。然後在有些單字、片語聽不懂的題目裡，再用考試技巧來選出答案。相反的閱讀測驗裡面，單字、片語還有又臭又長的句子，就多很多了。所以在閱讀測驗上面，學會在有單字、片語看不懂的情形下，把文章看懂的考試技巧就相對的重要了。回到新多益考試，聽力裡面加了大家不熟悉的英、澳腔，既然聽力測驗首重培養實力，那學會聽懂英、澳腔絕對是刻不容緩的事情。不過話說回來，再怎麼練習英、澳腔，我敢保證考新多益聽力時，你還是會有些字聽不出來，所以聽力考試技巧，也就是在沒能聽懂每個字的情況下聽懂句子、文章，進而選出答案也就更加重要了。

本書在聽力上面，先教大家如何練習聽懂英、澳腔，接著教大家如何在有些字沒聽出來的狀況下，選出答案。文法上面則強調語感的培養，平常念多了、念順了，在考試時簡單地把念起來最順的挑出來，就對了。在最短的時間裡選出正確答案，而在閱讀上面，則著重在教大家如何簡單、有效的透過句子與文章來記住單字，以及怎麼的在有單字的情況下，看懂文章。讓你不管是聽力還是閱讀，都會讓你能夠增強考試技巧、培養英文能力，進而在新多益考試取得高分。

最後我要提出使用本書，一定要遵守也是最重要的規矩：
絕對不要在你不懂的單字下面，寫上它的中文意思！

就以先前所舉的例子：
The candidates must be fluent in English

在台灣幾乎所有的學生都會在 fluent 這個字先畫底線，然後在線下面寫出中文：流利的、流暢的。你可以在 fluent 下面畫底線，好讓自己知道不認識這個字，但是**絕對不要在 fluent 下面寫中文**！

有需要的話，另外準備一本筆記本，專門用來寫出所有單字和它們的中文意思，**絕對要用另一本**。前面我說過，要念一下 fluent in English、fluent in English 再把 fluent、fluent、fluent 念三次，你自然就會對 fluent 這個字有 FU 了，也可以輕鬆地把這個字背下來。

但是有可能你過幾天後看到文章裡的這句話，如果你把中文意思直接寫在字底下，你會覺得已經記住這個字，然而事實上你是看到了中文的：流利的、流暢的才能了解 fluent in English，其實並沒有真正的記住 fluent 這個字，等到考試碰到這個字，又忘記了。如果 fluent 下面沒寫中文意思，因為沒有中文的提醒，你才會知道是否真的記住了。如果忘了，你就需要再次把 fluent in English、fluent in English 再把 fluent、fluent、fluent 念三次，再次的培養你對這個字的 FU，讓你加深印象的記住這個字。沒有把中文意思寫在字底下，才能真正讓你清楚，是否真的對每個單字真的有印象、真的記住了？所以一定要遵守這個規矩：絕對不要在你不懂的單字下面，直接寫上它的中文意思。

基本聽力練習

聽力最重要、最重要的練習方式，不管是美國南方腔、英國腔、澳洲腔甚至是最難聽懂得印度腔，通通一樣，就是自己把原文先念過，確認念過就懂，然後不看原文的聽，我保證你可以聽懂。試試以下這個圖片題的例子：

（為了讓你習慣只聽不看，所以以下練習題目會以倒放方式呈現）

Step 1　先試著聽整題考題 Track 01

Look at the picture marked number 1 in your test book.

(D) The cellphone is next to a television.
(C) A woman is using the cellphone.
(B) The cellphone is on top of the day planner.
(A) The cellphone is on a chair.

以百分比而言你覺得聽懂多少？

Step 2　再來請你

先念 (A) 的句子

The cellphone is on a chair.

再來聽 (A) Track 02

念完 (B)

The cellphone is on top of the day planner.

再來聽 (B) Track 03

念一下 (C)

A woman is using the cellphone.

再來聽 (C) Track 04

念 (D)

The cellphone is next to a television.

再來聽 (D) Track 05

Step 3 接下來四個答案一起聽 Track 06

Step 4 是不是發覺完全聽懂了！記得不論是什麼腔，通通一樣，就是自己把原文先念過，確認念過就懂，然後不看原文的聽，我保證你可以聽懂。

Step 5 請看中譯

請看試題本上標號第 1 題的照片。

(A) 手機在椅子上。

(B) 手機在記事本上。

(C) 一位女士正在使用手機。

(D) 手機在電視旁邊。

如果你都已經聽懂英文了，會需要以上的中文翻譯嗎？話說回來，如果需要中文翻譯才能選出正確答案，那你的聽力會考的好嗎？

解析：當你聽懂四個答案後，就可以輕鬆地選出此題的答案為 (B)。但是先前提到了考試技巧也很重要，以此題而言，雖然簡單，卻也可以用作為練習考試技巧的例子。三個錯誤的選項裡，只要你聽到 (A) 裡面的 chair，(C) 裡面的 woman 和 (D) 裡面的 television，而圖片裡並沒有看到任何的 chair, woman 和 television 就算你沒法完全聽懂，還是可以判斷出這三個不是正確答案，想想如果你聽不懂 (B) 裡面的 the day planner，結果讓你專注地去想 the day planner 到底是甚麼意思，是不是反而讓你沒法去聽 (C) 和 (D) 的答案？不去想聽不懂的，而是專注在聽懂的部分，是不是很重要？

其他聽力練習以及針對新多益各部分聽力考試的準備技巧，稍後在本書，我會另外用考題來解釋、說明。但是在這裏，有個聽力考高分的重點，我一定要提！在你考聽力時，腦子裡絕對不能出現中文，只要考試腦子裡想到任何中文，新多益聽力絕對考不高！或許你會問，這很難吧。其實只要練習的方式正確，要你的腦子只出現英文其實很簡單。只要用這本書後面所講的方法練習聽力，你的腦子就會自然而然的摒棄中文。在你學會在聽力上能適時拋棄中文思考之後，聽力上面的練習就該分兩部分：『聽力能力』與『聽力技巧』。

所謂的『聽力能力』，就是把手邊的題目練習到把整句還有整篇文章，不管是哪種腔調都能完全聽懂。新多益聽力達到三百五、四百分之前，這永遠是首要的工作。而練習方式就是前面講的，就是自己把原文先念過，確認念過就懂，然後不看原文的聽。只要多加練習，聽力能力是很容易進步的。再把本書即將在後面介紹的聽力 Part 3 和 Part 4 的考試技巧學會以後，聽力拿到三百五、四百分絕不是難事。

在你聽力成績達到四百以後，練習『聽力考試技巧』就是更重要的下一步了。說實話，如果考試技巧沒練好，你很難在四百上面有很大的進步。這裡的聽力技巧強調的就是：聽不懂的部分完全不要管，只專注在你聽懂的部分，由你聽懂的來判斷出答案。

為什麼這是高分需要的技巧？想想看在哪次的聽力測驗裡，你可以聽懂每個字、每句話？更何況新多益還特地加了大家不熟悉的英、澳腔，短期間內，或許有機會習慣英、澳腔，卻不可能讓你聽懂所有的英、澳腔。我自認為聽力很強，連印度腔都能懂，在考試時還是有幾個字沒聽出來，何況是一般的考生。

在練習聽習慣英、澳腔，聽力達到四百左右時，就要練習聽力考試技巧：聽不懂得完全不要管，只專注在你聽懂的部分，由你聽懂到的來判斷出答案。我常跟聽力不錯也就是聽力已經超過三百五、四百分的學生講，在複習寫錯的聽力題目時，**千萬不要立刻去看原稿**。自己先試著多聽兩次，**專注在聽懂的部分，練習一下從聽懂得部分來判斷出答案**。初學者和聽力需要加強的學生則是，直接先念原稿然後回來聽。為什麼需要如此完全相反的練習？因為聽力好的學生，只要看到原稿，絕對可以聽懂，在看過原稿後，就完全沒法練習這個，只專注在你聽懂的部分的技巧了。每次新多益聽力考試都會有些字聽不懂或聽不出來，沒法只專注在你聽懂的部分，想考高分就難了。記得在你按照我最早的，念過原稿然後回來聽之後，聽力成績進到某個程度卻卡住以後，就要練習這個技巧了。以我的經驗，大概聽力單項成績三百五到四百分左右。如何練習這種聽力技巧，請看本書後面的聽力章節。

除了以新多益相關書籍來練習聽力以外，網路上多的是練習英、澳腔的網站。舉例來說：http://www.bbc.com/ 以及 http://tv.australiaplus.com/，都是很棒的英、澳腔練習網站。那裏有許多相關的連結與資料可以運用。如果你沒太多時間去瀏覽，我建議直接看以下的兩個連結：http://www.bbc.co.uk/worldservice/learningenglish/general/englishatwork/ 和 http://legacy.australianetwork.com/livingenglish/episodes.htm。

這兩個連結的好處是，它們把一個完整的故事分成許多 episodes，讓你可以一小段、一小段的練習聽力。Australia Network 的內容相對比較簡單，但是多了一些不必要的文法解釋。我的建議是聽懂就對了。BBC 的連結讓你可以輕鬆的下載所有 episodes 的語音稿和 mp3 檔案，花點時間把這兩個連結裡的資料拿來做聽力練習，英、澳腔絕對會變得很容易。不過一定要記得一點，絕對不要邊看原稿邊聽，有任何內容聽不懂，找到相關原稿，自己唸出來然後遮住原稿來聽語音。

當然網路上還有更多的資源，例如：YouTube 和 http://www.ted.com/。去找你有興趣的主題來練習聽力，不要只是把新多益練習侷限在參考書籍裡，用自己喜歡而且有興趣的主題資料來練習，絕對更是事半功倍。

閱讀應試技巧

首先我要強調一下，閱讀技巧不是只能用新多益模考試題才可以練習，事實上隨時都可以練習增加你的閱讀技巧與速度。我常跟學生強調，網路上英文文章多的是，隨時都可以用你喜歡的文章來練習閱讀。讓大家學會閱讀技巧。根據研究顯示，大量的閱讀除了能增加閱讀的速度及技巧之外，還能大幅度的提升你的字彙量及文法觀念。但根據我個人的教學經驗來看，重要的是改變你一直以來的閱讀習慣，以達到以大量閱讀來增進英語力的目的。

我就以『掌握NEWS關鍵字』這本書裡面的一篇文章作為範例，告訴你英文文章應該怎麼讀，首先我會把整篇文章一段、一段的呈現出來，希望你不論懂不懂，先試著自己看完，然後才看我的解釋，還有絕對不要先查字典！先用這個方式看完以下的幾段文章，後看我的解釋，體會一下我所介紹的閱讀方法。每一段文章都自己先看一次，記得不要查字典。不管是不是看的懂都一樣，想辦法不要查字典的讓自己看完，然後才看我的解釋。這麼一段、一段文章的練習，我保證你會有很大的收穫。

閱讀小技巧

Step 1→先讀完英文句子

Step 2→以上下文去推敲出不懂的單字的意思（請參照下段解釋）

Step 3→查字典

Step 4→再讀一遍句子，多念幾次，自然有 FU

 練 習 一

Globalization is a development process of an increasingly integrated global economy marked by free trade, free flow of capital, and the tapping of cheaper foreign labor markets.

先依照上述的閱讀小技巧中的 Step 1，將這句英文完整的讀完，看過以後，再來看看我的解釋。其實這句話很簡單，如果將後面的相關資訊刪除的話，我們可以得到這一段的主要意思只是 "Globalization is a development process." 如此而已！

而是什麼樣的 process？由文中可得是 a process of integrated global economy，假設你不知道 integrated 這個字，這時候，依照 Step 2，以上下文推敲的方式，先想一下這句話：

『一個把 global economy（全球經濟）integrated 起來的 process。』

感覺一下這句裡面 integrated 有可能的意思，然後才是 Step 3：查字典。

在了解 integrate 這一個單字是「整合」的意思之後，請遵照 Step 4，把這句：

"a development process of an increasingly integrated global economy，integrated global economy"

多念幾次，自然就會對 integrated 這個字有 FU 了。

後面的 "marked by free trade, free flow of capital, and the tapping of cheaper foreign labor markets"，你可以看成："an increasingly integrated global economy (which is) marked by free trade, free flow of capital, and the tapping of cheaper foreign labor markets"

也就是說這個 integrated global economy 有三種特性（marked by），分別為 "free trade"，"free flow of capital"，還有 "the tapping of cheaper foreign labor markets"。

我相信有許多人不知道 tap 這個字，先不要急著查字典，先依照上述的方法試一下

Step 1 → 讀完句子

"the tapping of cheaper foreign labor markets,"

Step 2 → 以上下文推敲字意

感覺一下 tap, tapping 這個字的意思，及以其上下文 "tapping of cheaper foreign labor markets"（tapping of 便宜的外國勞動市場），是不是感受到 tapping，有可能為「取得、獲得」之類的意思？

Step 3 →查字典

知道 tapping 有為「取得、獲得」之意。

Step 4 →再讀一遍句子，多念幾次，自然有 FU

然後再多念幾次 tapping of cheaper foreign labor markets 是不是就可以對 tap 有 FU，而且也容易記。

最後把這段文章再念一次：

Globalization is a development process of an increasingly integrated global economy marked by free trade, free flow of capital, and the tapping of cheaper foreign labor markets.

你就可以完全看懂這段文章了！

The International Monetary Fund identified four basic aspects of globalization: trade and transactions, capital and investment movement, migration and movement of people, and the dissemination of knowledge. Different kinds of environmental challenges are also linked with globalization.

這裡的 International Monetary Fund 如果你知道，很棒，但不知道其實影響也不大，反正都大寫，便可以得知，應該是個專有名詞，也推測出是某種的國際組織。

而在這一段文章中提到，這個 IMF identified globalization 有四個基本的 aspects "four basic aspects of globalization"，你覺得這四個 aspects 中的 aspect 的意思會是什麼？如果還不清楚，先讀完句子後，依上下文推敲字意，再查字典，就會知道 aspect 為「方面、觀點」之意。

再回過頭來把這一句：four basic aspects of globalization 念個幾次，對 aspect 就會有 FU 了，也容易記了。

還有 identify 這個字如果不認識，再念一次：the IMF identified four basic aspects，IMF 這個組織 identified 四個基本的 aspects 感覺一下 identify 以後才去查字典知道是識別、確認的意思以後，再念一次：the IMF identified four basic aspects 是不是就有 FU 了，也容易記了。

接下來看看文中剛剛提到的，有四個方面（aspects），那是哪四方面呢？由文章中可得是 "trade and transactions"，"capital and investment movement"，"migration and movement of people" 以及 "and the dissemination of knowledge" 這四項。

先以看懂文章的觀點來看，transaction 不懂沒關係，知道 trade 就 OK。如果不知道 capital，明白 investment 就沒問題（investment movement）。
不認識 migration，懂得 movement 就行了（movement of people）。
dissemination 沒見過，反正就是 knowledge 的 dissemination。

把這四點多念幾遍，然後在查字典前想想 transaction 跟 trade 在一起，

capital 跟 investment 在一起，migration 跟 movement 在一起，意思應該相近吧。

查完字典後，你會發現 transaction 確實可以當「交易」的意思，investment 的意思就是需要資金（capital）的「投資」，人類的移動叫 movement；而動物則是 migration，接下來再把 trade and transactions, capital and investment movement, migration and movement of people 多念幾次，絕對能會加深你對 transaction, capital 和 migration 的印象，更會幫助你記住這些字。

最後這個 dissemination 查完字典後知道是散播、宣傳，回頭來多念幾次 the dissemination of knowledge，dissemination 這個字就簡單了。最後的一句 Different kinds of environmental challenges are also linked with globalization. 如果有單字不懂，同樣的先念個幾遍，感覺一下甚至猜一下它的意思，然後才去查字典。各種不同的環境挑戰也跟 globalization 有關。

練習三

In response to the comments of the chairwoman of Taiwan's opposition Democratic Progressive Party (DPP) – Tsai, Ing-wen, Ma said that the DPP's notion of globalization was "globalization without mainland China," thus highlighting the differences between the two parties and their understanding of globalization.

這句最前面的部分其實很簡單，只是 in response to the comment of Tsai, Ing-wen 如此而已，其他的只是說明：蔡英文的職位是 DDP 民進黨主席，而民進黨是反對黨，所以 opposition 當然就是反對，把國民黨的 opposition 民進黨多念幾次，自然的就把 opposition 記下來了。In response to 蔡英文的 comment，response 當然就是反應、回應。DDP globalization 的 notion 就是不包含中國的全球化（globalization without mainland China）你說 notion 是不是有觀點、看法的感覺？念個幾次 DPP's notion of globalization was "globalization without mainland China," 就會對 notion 有 FU 了。很明顯馬英九就是在強調，國民黨對 globalization 的 notion 跟民進黨不同，不就是 highlighting the differences between the two parties and their understanding of globalization。

練 習 四

In the past couple decades; globalization had mostly benefited the world economies. The general stance is that the benefits of globalization outweigh the economic and social costs by providing GDP growth in several underdeveloped regions. Relatively speaking, developing countries also become wealthier based on per capita GDP growth rates. Benefits to economic development, international trade, and standards of living are obvious as the outcome of globalization.

既然這篇文章講的是全球化，那 globalization had benefited the world economies 裡的 benefit 應該是好事。你可能已經知道 benefit

的意思,不過我這麼講也讓你更有 FU 了對吧!

接下來的 stance 查字典是立場、態度,在這裡當看法、觀點可能更恰當。那你會需要再加一個看法、觀點的意思來背 stance 嗎?千萬不要,看法、觀點這個意思,是因應這裡的中文翻譯而來,英文上面就是 the stance 這個說法,只要你能在英文句子裡面明白 the stance 就夠了,至於它的中文翻譯,那要看前後的中文意思而定。千萬不要為了各種不同的中文句意,來背英文單字。

that 以後的部分意思看的出來嗎?其實只是 the benefits outweigh the economic cost and social cost,而 by providing DFP growth in several underdeveloped regions 只是用來解釋 benefits outweigh the cost 的因素和做法。而後面一句則是說明發展中國家(developing countries),因為 per capita GDP 的成長而更有錢了。你或許會問那 GDP 和 per capital GDP 是什麼?其實就算你不懂也沒關係,只要知道那是經濟學名詞就夠了。這裡的 GDP 是 Gross Domestic Product,國內生產毛額,而 per capita 就是人均、平均每人。如果不是學商的,不知道真的沒關係。

最後一句 Benefits to economic development, international trade, and standards of living are obvious as the outcome of globalization. 你知道如何簡化嗎?其實只是 Benefits **to economic development, international trade, and standards of living** are obvious as the outcome of globalization. 灰色字體只是說明哪三方面的 benefits:economic development 經濟發展,international trade 國際貿易,standards of living 生活水平這三點。

練 習 五

However, experts argued that it is the world's most advanced economies which had mostly benefited from globalization, leading to a widening global gap between the rich and the poor. Studies showed that Finland, Denmark, Japan, Germany and Switzerland had become the largest beneficiaries of globalization. Germany had gained an extra two trillion euros in GDP, an average of 1,240 euros per person, per year since 1990.

前面一段強調 globalization 的好處，這一段的第一個字就是 however，很明顯的，這裡要說壞處了。Most advanced economies 在 globalization 裡面得到最多的利益（had mostly benefited from globalization），下一句說五個國家是最大的受益者。（如果你不認識其中的幾個國家根本沒關係，只要知道都是國家就夠了。）下半句說了，因為（經濟進步國家得益較多），有錢和沒錢國家間的 gap 就變大（widen）了。最後以一些數字來說明自 1990 年後，德國在 globalization 裡面得到多少好處。

練 習 六

While globalization generated an average fifteen hundreds euros annual per capita income gain in Finland, in developing countries such as China, Mexico, and India, per capita income rose by less than a hundred euros. From these numbers, it is clear that globalization tends to widen the gap between the rich and the poor in the international community.

這段的第一句或許很長，架構卻很簡單。只是 while A, B. 也就是 while A 這件事發生了，B 這件事也成形了。A 是 globalization generated an average fifteen hundreds euros annual per capita income gain in Finland，B 是 in developing countries such as China, Mexico, and India, per capita income rose by less than a hundred euros。只是再度強調 while 芬蘭得到每年（annual）平均（average）fifteen hundreds euros 這麼多好處，中國、墨西哥和印度這些 developing countries 卻只有不到一百歐元。最後下個結論：從這些數字看來，可以清楚看出 globalization tends to widen the gap between the rich and the poor in the international community 如果 gap 這個字不清楚先查一下字典知道是：間隔、缺口、差距的意思以後，把 globalization tends to widen the gap between the rich and the poor 再把 widen the gap 念個幾次。整句就只是：全球化只是擴大了國際社會裡窮國與富國的差距（widen the gap between the rich and the poor）。

 練 習 七

Nevertheless, despite its low per capita income growth, mainland China is among the winners of globalization. Since the introduction of economic reforms in 1978, mainland China has become one of the world's fastest growing countries. As of 2013, it became the world's second-largest economy, and it is also the world's largest exporter and importer of goods. Mainland China is also a member of numerous formal and informal multilateral organizations, including the WTO, APEC, and the Shanghai Cooperation Organization.

在新多益的考試當中，偶爾會考副詞的選擇，英文裡副詞很多，同樣的不要硬背。就以這裡的 nevertheless 為例，前面一段講的是 globalization 的壞處，在 nevertheless 後面接的是 despite its low per capita income growth, mainland China is among the winners of globalization。簡單來說中國是贏家，顯然句型是 globalization 的壞處尤其是對窮國的壞處（其中包含中國），然後接 nevertheless，中國是贏家。是不是就可以感覺出，nevertheless 有點像 however？幾乎所有的副詞，都可以從文章裡的前後句義，感覺出它們的意思，然後再把句子多念幾遍，就可以輕鬆的把它們記下來了。如同這裡的，globalization 對窮國的壞處，nevertheless，中國是贏家。Nevertheless 後面接的是 "despite its low per capita income growth, mainland China is among the winners of globalization."。簡單的講就是 despite low income growth，中國是贏家。

同義，再把這句：despite low income growth, 中國是贏家。多念幾次，你就可以很自然地把 despite 這個字記起來。更重要的是，你還可以知道 despite 的用法。這裡我先打住，等到單字文法部分，再仔細說明所謂的 despite 這個字的用法，這可是新多益考試的重點。接下來的：Since the introduction of economic reforms in 1978, mainland China has become one of the world's fastest growing countries. 架構也很簡單。Since 這部分很簡單，只是 since the introduction in 1978，什麼樣的 introduction？ introduction of economic reform（經濟改革），如此而已，後面應該很容易吧！中國成為世界成長最快的國家（之一）。

接下來的：As of 2013, it became the world's second-largest economy, and it is also the world's largest exporter and importer of goods. 也不難，以2013而言中國成為世界第二大經濟，也是世界最大 goods 的進、出口國。可千萬不要把 good 當好的意思來看，goods 的進口和出口，如果不知道查一下字典原來 goods 是貨物、商品，是不是就可以把 the world's largest exporter and importer of goods 看懂了？記得不要硬背 goods（要有 s）：貨物、商品，把 the importer of goods 還有 the exporter of goods 多念幾次絕對比較有效。

Mainland China is also a member of numerous formal and informal multilateral organizations, including the WTO, APEC, and the Shanghai Cooperation Organization. 這句應該可以看的懂吧。numerous 基本上從 number 變來的也就是很多，multi 很多的、lateral 側面、邊邊，所以 multilateral 就是多邊的。後面的 WTO, APEC, Shanghai Cooperation Organization 正是各種各樣的 organizations（組織），如果你不認識以上所講的任何一個單字，把整句話多念幾次就對了。

Yet again, now mainland China sees the downside of globalization. Years of rapid economic growth had brought various social problems, and mainland China is launching a series of reforms trying to solve these problems.

前一段講了許多全球化對中國的好處，這裡一開始就是 Yet again，Yet

在這裡只是用來表示語氣的轉折，所以看到這裡，就能知道，顯然是要開始説壞處了。Yet again, now mainland China sees the downside of globalization. 中國大陸看到 globalization 的 downside 真的是壞。後面這句先看前半段：Years of rapid economic growth had brought various social problems 經濟的快速成長帶來了各種各樣的 social problems。在 and 後面則説：mainland China is launching a series of reforms trying to solve these problems. 中國正在 launching 一連串的 reforms，試著要 solve 這些 problems。前面提到了 1978 年的 economic reform，所以 reform 應該看的懂，launch 一些 reform 要 solve 這些 problems 你覺得 launch 除了開始、發動外，還會有其他的意思嗎？

看完了以上的文章和我的解釋之後，是不是對閱讀有點信心了？相信我，看懂文章真的不難，而事實上，新多益的閱讀測驗文章有八、九成都比這篇簡單，除了少數幾篇甚至少數幾句以外，真的很容易看懂，除了新多益相關書籍以外，你更需要多看一些英文文章，以前的高中教科書還有雜誌，都可以用來練習閱讀能力。只是要記得，用我這種閱讀方式，不要輕易的查字典，不管有沒有單字，試著把句子看懂，把單字的意思根據前後的句義先猜一下，對整段甚至整篇文章有所了解才是最重要的，單字、文法真的不是那麼重要，只要多加練習，閱讀能力的提升真的沒那麼難。

Part

新多益
考試的準備

2

聽力測驗準備

聽力的準備

前面提到了練習聽力，最重要的不是反覆一直聽，而是自己先念過，然後不看稿子的聽。不管你聽的是英國腔、澳洲腔還是美國腔，用這種方式多練習，你的腦子自然而然地就會聽懂這些腔調了。

還有在考聽力時最重要的一點就是，腦子裡絕對不能有中文！因為只要出現中文，你的思考就會變慢，因為你多花了點時間聽懂了這一句，下一句根本沒時間聽。讀者看到這裡或許會問，根據新多益官方網站，考試所考的包含美、加、英、澳四個腔調，為什麼這裡只提美、英、澳三個？事實上美國和加拿大因為地緣關係，基本上腔調差異不大，一般台灣學生都熟悉美國腔，自然對加拿大腔不會有大問題。澳洲原先是英國殖民地，算來跟英國腔系屬同源。但是因為澳洲獨自處在南半球，因為地緣關係時間久了，慢慢演變出自己的腔調。所以英、澳腔間的差別會比美、加腔間的大多了。但是事實上英國各地的腔調也有差別，英格蘭、蘇格蘭、威爾斯和北愛爾蘭間各有差異。或許你會想這下完了，哪那麼多時間把所有腔調聽懂？但是說實話只要你把這本書裡的英、澳腔聽懂，我敢講腔調的問題就小多了。

當然我也鼓勵你到前面章節所提的 http://www.bbc.com/ 以及 http://tv.australiaplus.com/ 去多練習一下英、澳腔，記得自己先念過然後聽，英、澳腔真的不難聽懂。說到這裡我要強調一下幾個字的英澳腔，這幾個字的特點是，英澳腔和美國腔間有蠻大的不同，如果沒有特別注意，你很可能會聽不出來。我在聽力課時也一定會特別說明這四個字：either, neither, laboratory 還有 advertisement。你特別要注意的是前兩個字的音要發成：EYE-ther 和 nEYE-ther，我常跟學生講，從今天起你要念：EYE-ther or 和 nEYE-ther nor，讓自己習慣這兩個字的英國腔。

再來是 laboratory, 大家應該都很清楚美國音是：LA-bo-ra-to-ry，重音在 LA，你要注意的是英澳腔變成：la-BO-ra-to-ry，重音在 BO 而不是同樣的 advertisement 美國腔是：ad-ver-TISE-ment 而英澳腔則變成：ad-VER-tise-ment 甚至會變成 ad-VER-se-ment 中間的 tise 聽起來更像 se 而已。有興趣的讀者，可以到雅虎奇摩字典裡去聽聽看，兩種口音間的差別。這幾個字如果沒有特別注意，英澳腔講出來你根本就聽不懂在說什麼。當然本書中會特別用這些字來當練習。

練習聽力最重要的第一步就是自己唸，唸完後立刻就懂，腦子裡完全不需要中文，在這本書裡，我還是會依照台灣以往的聽力慣例，提供中文翻譯，但是中文翻譯不會立刻出現在英文語句的旁邊，會間隔一點距離，盡量養成大家直接了解英文，真正有問題時才去看中文翻譯。而且你要清楚一點，中文翻譯只是讓你參考用的，最終目標還是那句老話：『自己唸，唸完後立刻就懂，腦子裡完全不需要中文。』

1.1 新多益 Part 1 照片描述聽力測驗的準備

第一部分的看圖聽力考試的準備方式，跟一般的聽力考試有些不同。首先在這部分所碰到的每個單字，絕對不能硬背，反而是要以圖像方式呈現在你的腦海裡面。

舉個簡單的例子來說聽到 tiger 這個字，腦海裡應該浮現以下的這個圖。

聽到 flamingo，腦海裡應該浮現以下的這個圖。

你或許會問為什麼？如果你聽到 tiger 先想到老虎，然後腦子裡才出現圖像，你的反應是不是比較慢？這部分考的是圖像，等你腦子想到這張圖，可能第二句已經播放出來了，你也就沒時間聽第二句了。在 Part 1 圖片題裡，如果你的腦袋還得再轉換一下才能想到正確的圖片，這只會讓你的判斷更加遲緩，還沒能聽懂這個答案時，下一個答案已經講出來了，慌亂之間會讓你沒時間選出正確答案。

另外我再舉一組更實用的例子：two glasses of water 和 two pairs of glasses。看以下的兩張圖，你立刻會明白這兩者間的差異，不需要去想哪個是玻璃杯？哪個是眼鏡？如果你要先想清楚是玻璃杯還是眼鏡，你的理解速度是不是就慢了？而且很可能影響你聽下一句對吧！

現在就盯著上面的圖念一下：two glasses of water，然後盯著下面的圖念一下：two pairs of glasses。是不是腦子裡完全不需要中文就可以聽懂了？

washing the dishes VS rinsing the plates

這裡的 washing 就是所謂的洗，而 rinsing 嚴格來說是用水沖洗。不過說實話，新多益不會考到這麼細，要你分辨 wash 和 rinse 的差別。

stirring the coffee VS sipping the tea VS drinking the water

這裡的 stirring 就是用攪拌咖啡，sipping 是小小口的喝，而 drinking 就是喝，這應該沒問題吧！

watering the garden with a hose

基本上就是用 hose 來 water the garden 所以 hose 就是水管，如果你不知道，沒關係！把這句話：watering the garden with a hose 多念幾次就會有印象、有 FU 了，根本不需要硬背。

mopping the floor VS brooming the stairs VS sweeping the hall way

以上三句基本上都是掃，mopping 用 mop：拖把，brooming 用 broom：掃把，而 sweeping 就是掃，用 mop 或是用 broom 都可以説成 sweeping。

關於單字，尤其是 Part 1 的單字，如果有那些不懂，我的建議是到 google 去用圖片搜尋，然後看著圖片念那個字。舉兩個簡單的例子來説明：

warehouse 這個字如果不知道，用 google 圖片搜尋把 warehouse 打上去藉由搜尋出來的圖片加深你的印象。同樣的你也可以用圖片搜尋 an office clerk，利用圖片幫助你記住單字。

聽力小練習

接下來請聽以下這句：

 Track 07

聽得懂嗎？如果聽不出來先念一下：

Workers are entering the laboratory with protective goggles.
（工作人員帶著護目鏡進實驗室。）

認識 goggles 這個字嗎？用 google 圖片蒐尋找一下『protective goggles』是不是就懂了？然後再聽一次：

 Track 07

但是總有些例外，前面提到了 either or 和 neither nor，記得要念成 EYE-ther or 和 nEYE-ther nor，這裡的 laboratory 也是另一個要注意的字，美國腔念成：LA-bo-ra-to-ry，而英澳腔卻成為：la-BO-ra-to-ry，重音變了。還有已經提過，還是新多益必考單字：advertisement，美國音是：AD-ver-tise-ment，而英國音是：ad-VER-tise-ment，差別還蠻大的。以下是這兩個字的發音：

 Track 08

laboratory 美 ['læbrətɔːri] 英 [ləˈbɒrətri]
advertisement 美 [ˌædvərˈtaɪzmənt] 英 [ədˈvɜːtɪsmənt]

注意到沒？我們一般學到的是：LA-bo-ra-to-ry，而你聽到的是：la-BO-ra-to-ry。前面說過了，英澳腔只要你自己念過，就算是美國腔，基本上都能聽懂。

以下介紹一些 Part one 常見的單字，有些我提供了圖片增加你的印象，
記得借助 Google 圖片搜尋來幫助記憶，千萬不要硬背。

stairs railing, stairs handrail
就是這個

scarf
就是這個

以下當你的 Google 圖片搜尋作業，讓你體會一下圖片搜尋的好處。請分別搜尋

1. building a fence
2. tents
3. lighting fixtures
4. pedestrians
5. utensil 還有 dinner utensil
6. vase 還有 flower vase
7. cupboard 還有 kitchen cupboard
8. smiling 還有 smiling at each other

接下來三個一起找：racks, shelves, cabinet。記得，如果在你的新多益模擬試題中，尤其是 Part 1 裡有不認識的單字時，應先利用 Google 圖片搜尋，還有需要時才去查字典，最後記得盯著圖片念單字。例如你現在就可以盯著 racks, shelves, cabinet 的圖片，邊看圖邊念 racks, shelves, cabinet。真的很容易有 FU 對吧！

以下講解一些不是那麼容易用圖片了解的單字：

table cloth VS clothes/clothing:

這裡的 table cloth 是桌布、cloth 是布、clothes 和 clothing 才是衣服。新多益的測驗中，是不會在圖片裡展示 clothes，然後答案裡用 cloth 來欺騙你是正確答案，只是我覺得還是把這點小差別搞懂比較好。Beverage 這個字指的是各種飲料，有時也包含酒精類的飲品。

along the street VS across the street:

簡單的說是：一個沿著街（along the street）、一個是（穿）過街（across the street）。如果以方向表示的話，在東西向的街道上，沿著街（along the street）則也是東西向；而（穿）過街（across the street）則是南北向。

deck VS dock:

這兩個字容易搞混，我的建議是多念幾次："house deck, lake dock / port dock（看你的喜好）"。

還有 deck 在英文裡除了房子的木板平台外，還可以是船上的甲板，只是當在新多益考試裡面，deck 當船上甲板的機會不大。

merchandise VS goods

最後介紹一下兩個在新多益考試上面，意思一樣的字：merchandise 和 goods。這兩個字都當作商品、貨物。

1.2 新多益 Part 1 照片描述小練習

Track 09

Now Part 1 will begin.

1. Please look at the picture marked number 1 in your textbook.

(D) She is talking to her colleague.

(C) She is looking at the computer.

(B) She is wiping the screen.

(A) She is making a phone call.

2. Please look at the picture marked number 2 in your textbook.

(D) He is buying some drink from a vending machine.

(C) He is purchasing some juice with a cell phone.

(B) He is fixing the machine.

(A) He is paying for the meal.

Part3

(A) He is cleaning the walls.

(B) He is mopping the floor.

(C) He is sweeping the street.

(D) He is carrying a broom.

4. Please look at the picture marked number 4 in your textbook.

Part2

(A) The man is teaching the woman how to dance.

(B) They are dancing on a street.

(C) They are practicing on a dance machine.

(D) They are trying on new outfits.

3. Please look at the picture marked number 3 in your textbook.

Part1

5. Please look at the picture marked number 5 in your textbook.

(A) Different kinds of bread are displayed on the shelves.

(B) They are talking to each other.

(C) The sales clerk is helping the kid with a purchase.

(D) They are lining up for check out.

6. Please look at the picture marked number 6 in your textbook.

(A) They are discussing what to eat for lunch.

(B) One man is raising his hand.

(C) They are taking a rest in the employee lounge.

(D) One man is standing up from his chair.

7. Please look at the picture marked number 7 in your textbook.

(A) There is a lamp beside the bed.
(B) She is removing the bed in a hotel room.
(C) She is doing room service.
(D) The customer is leaving the room.

8. Please look at the picture marked number 8 in your textbook.

(A) People are waiting for their suitcases.
(B) The briefcase is under inspection.
(C) The luggage is on a baggage carousel.
(D) There is no one around the check-in counter.

9. Please look at the picture marked number 9 in your textbook.

(D) She is using a telescope.

(C) She is enjoying the scenery of the ocean.

(B) She is making a movie.

(A) She is taking a photo.

10. Please look at the picture marked number 10 in your textbook.

(D) Two geishas are sitting on the floor.

(C) The guests are leaving the room.

(B) The musicians are singing.

(A) The geishas are dancing.

考過後覺得如何？接下來是原稿和詳解。我想強調一下，就算你這些題寫得不錯，我還是希望你看一下我的解釋，因為裡面可能會有一些對你有幫助的考試技巧。還有，如同我先前所解釋的，每題考題的中文翻譯不會立刻放在每題試題下面，十題的中文翻譯會一起放在最後面，希望你能養成不看翻譯的習慣。

1. (A) She is making a phone call.
   (B) She is wiping the screen.
   (C) She is looking at the computer.
   (D) She is talking to her colleague.

   很明顯答案是：(C) She is looking at the computer. 而 B 裡面的 wiping the screen 就是拿布擦拭螢幕。(D) 如果你不認識 (D) 裡面的 colleague 很簡單，就是 co-worker。

2. (A) He is paying for the meal.
   (B) He is fixing the machine.
   (C) He is purchasing some juice with a cell phone.
   (D) He is buying some drink from a vending machine.

   (A) paying OK 但是 paying for meal 錯了，(C) purchasing some juice OK 但是 with a cell phone 錯了，答案是：(D) He is buying some drink from a vending machine. 不知道的話 vending machine 多念幾次。

3. (A) The man is teaching the woman how to dance.

(B) They are dancing on a street.

(C) They are practicing on a dance machine.

(D) They are trying on new outfits.

(A) 兩人一起跳，看不出誰 teach 誰；(B) dancing OK 但是 on a street 不對；(D) trying on 試穿 outfit 在這裡就是衣服；答案是 (C) They are practicing on a dance machine.

---

4. (A) He is cleaning the walls.　　(B) He is mopping the floor.

(C) He is sweeping the street.　　(D) He is carrying a broom.

(A) 不用看；(C) sweeping OK 但是 the street 錯了；(D)broom 不對，答案是 (B) He is popping the floor.

---

5. (A) Different kinds of bread are displayed on the shelves.

(B) They are talking to each other.

(C) The sales clerk is help the kid with a purchase.

(D) They are lining up for check out.

(B) 沒有 talking to each other；(C) 沒看到 sales clerk；(D) 沒人 lining up，答案是 (A) Different kinds of bread are displayed on the shelves. 展示在架上

---

6. (A) They are discussing what to eat for lunch.

(B) One man is raising his hand.

(C) They are taking a rest in the employee lounge.

(D) One man is standing up from his chair.

(A) discussing 似乎 OK，但是應該不是 discussing what to eat；(C) 完全沒有 taking a rest 而且 employee lounge 員工休閒室，也不對；(D) 只有一位 standing 但不是 standing from his chair 答案是：(B) One man is raising his hand.

----

7. (A) There is a lamp besides the bed.

(B) She is removing the bed in a hotel room.

(C) She is doing room service.

(D) The customer is leaving the room.

這一題要特別注意，新多益會有這類圖片裡面有人的題目，重點是偶而正確答案卻是背景裡的事物，跟圖片裡的人毫無關係。(B) 其他OK，removing the bed 錯了；(C) room service 客房服務錯了；(D) 顯然是 maid 不是 customer；答案是 (A) There is a lamp besides the bed. 確實有個 lamp besides the bed。

----

8. (A) People are waiting for their suitcases.

(B) The briefcase is under inspection.

(C) The luggage is on a baggage carousel.

(D) There is no one around the check-in counter.

(A) 沒看到 people；(B) 沒人在做 inspection；(D) 顯然不是 check-in counter；答案是 (C) The luggage is on a baggage carousel. 如果不知道，看圖片就明白 baggage carousel 了，順道提一下，

carousel 就是遊樂園裡的旋轉木馬。

---

9. (A) She is taking a photo.
   (B) She is making a movie.
   (C) She is enjoying the scenery of the ocean.
   (D) She is using a telescope.

(B) making a movie 錯；(C) enjoying the scenery 勉強，但是 ocean 絕對錯；(D) telescope, no way。

---

10. (A) The geishas are dancing.
    (B) The musicians are singing.
    (C) The guests are leaving the room.
    (D) Two geishas are sitting on the floor.

首先，我敢保證這張圖片裡的藝妓 geisha 絕對不會出現在新多益的考試裡，但是這題卻有個很重要的用意：有些時候圖片裡會出現一些你不認識的東西或物品，這時不需要驚慌，只要有心理準備正確答案裡可能會有些你不熟悉甚至不認識的單字或片語。聽到了就直接忽略，完全不需要去管這些不懂的單字或片語，專心注意在你聽懂的部分。(A) dancing 錯；(B) musician 和 singing 都錯；(C) guests 完全沒看到；答案是 (D) Two geishas are sitting on the floor. 因為 sitting on the floor OK。

你可以注意到在這十題的解釋裡面，我盡可能只用答案裡的英文，盡量避掉 key words 的翻譯，我想你應該知道我的用意，但是不能免俗的我還是提供了考題的翻譯。

1. (A) 她正在打電話　　(B) 她正在擦拭螢幕
   (C) 她正看著電腦　(D) 她正和同事聊天

2. (A) 他在付餐費　　　(B) 他在修機器
   (C) 他正用手機買飲料　**(D) 他從販賣機買飲料**

3. (A) 男士在教女士跳舞　(B) 他們在街上跳舞
   (C) 他們在跳舞機上練習　(D) 他們在試穿新衣服

4. (A) 他正在清洗牆壁　　**(B) 他正在拖地**
   (C) 他正在清掃街道　　(D) 他帶著一隻掃把

5. **(A) 各種不同的麵包在架上展示著**　(B) 他們在互相交談
   (C) 店員在幫忙小孩買東西　(D) 他們正排隊等著付帳

6. (A) 他們在討論著午餐吃什麼　　**(B) 一位男士正舉著手**
　　(C) 他們正在員工休閒室裡休息　　(D) 一位男士正從椅子上站起來

7. (**A) 床邊有盞檯燈**　　　　　　(B) 她正在把張床搬出去
　　(C) 她正在做客房服務　　　　　(D) 顧客正離開房間

8. (A) 人們在等行李　　　　　　　**(B) 行李箱受檢中**
　　(C) 這行李箱在（行李）轉盤上　(D) 登記櫃台完全沒人

9. (**A) 她正在講電話**　　　　　　(B) 她正在拍電影
　　(C) 她正享受著海景　　　　　　(D) 她正在用望遠鏡

10. (A) 藝妓正在跳舞　　　　　　　(B) 音樂家正在唱歌
　　(C) 顧客正離開坊間　　　　　　**(D) 兩位藝妓正坐在地板上**

1.3 新多益 Part 2 應答問題聽力測驗的準備

準備重點

教新多益時我都會跟學生強調，Part 2 有兩個一定要 follow 的重點：

● **聽起來很像題目的答案一定錯**

請聽以下例題 Track 10

(C) I am really hungry.

(B) Yes, please.

(A) I can try it here.

Would you like to try some ice tea?

是不是聽起來感覺答案 (A) 跟題目有點像？所以絕對不要選 (A)！因為聽起來很像題目的答案一定錯。如果有題目沒能真正聽清楚，憑著你的感覺把聽起來像題目的答案刪掉不選就對了。

以上講的是考試技巧，但是聽力能力的培養更重要，請你念一下題目和答案的原稿。

Would you like to try some ice tea?

(A) I can try it.　　(B) Yes, please.　　(C) I am really hungry.

接下來請你閉著眼睛聽這題的英、澳、美腔。　　🎧 Track 11

(C) I am really hungry.

(B) Yes, please.

(A) I can try it.

Would you like to have some ice tea?

是不是都可以聽懂了？

以上題目的翻譯是：

Q：想喝杯冰茶嗎？

　　(A) 我可以試試看。　　　　(B) 是的，麻煩你。　　　　(C) 我真的很餓。

● **題目前幾個字，特別是第一個字，一定要聽懂**

在應考時，如果前面一題聽不懂題目或是一時恍神沒聽到答案，不要浪費時間把最像題目的答案去掉後，閉著眼睛選剩下的就對了，然後集中精神聽下一題。因為題目前幾個字，特別是第一個字，一定要聽懂！新多益 Part 2 的基本問答題就是 wh（when, where, who, which, why, what and how）問題，尤其是 wh 問題，如果你沒聽到第一個字是 where、who 還是 when，基本上這題就毀了，所以一定要記住應考 part 2 時，如果一時不知道答案，不要選聽起來像題目的答案，不要浪費時間挑剩下的就對了，然後好整以暇的準備聽下一題的題目。　　🎧 Track 12

(C) I am meeting with your group.

(B) Every Monday at 3.

(A) It's in conference room 2.

Where is the weekly group meeting?

如果你沒聽到第一個字 where，這題是不是就毀了？而且這題只要聽到第一個字 where，就可以答題了對吧，再試一題： Track 13

(C) We had a great time.
(B) At Hilton Hotel.
(A) December 21st.
When is the company year-end party?

同樣的第一個字 when 一定要聽到，這類的 wh 問題是新多益必考題。在考 Part 2 時，讓自己有時間靜下心聽下一題，絕對是關鍵。接下來當然是練習聽懂題目加三個答案。

先念一下原稿：

Where is the weekly group meeting?

(A) It's in conference room 2.

(B) Every Monday at 3.

(C) I am meeting with your group.

翻譯是（我希望你不要看翻譯）：

Q：每週的週會在哪裡？

　　(A) 在第二會議室　　**(B) 每週一三點**　　(C) 我會和你那組開會。

接下來閉著眼睛不看稿子的聽聽看（為了加強讀者對各種腔調的適應力，以下會有三種不同的腔調組合） Track 14

(C) I am with your group.

(B) Every Monday at 3.

(A) It's in conference room 2.

Where is the weekly group meeting?

再念下一題的原稿：

When is the company year-end party?

(A) December 21st.

(B) At Hilton Hotel.

(C) We are going to have a great time.

翻譯是（我希望你不要看）：

Q：公司年終晚會是什麼時候？

(A) 12 月 21 日　　(B) 在希爾頓飯店　　(C) 晚會會很讚

接下來閉著眼睛不看稿子的聽聽看 Track 15

(C) We are going to have a great time.

(B) At Hilton Hotel.

(A) December 21st.

When is the company year-end party?

接下來請你試試幾題基本的 wh 問題 Track 16

1. When was the last time you went to Mount Fuji?
(A) For three months.
(B) Two years ago on a business trip there.
(C) I am going to Fujifilm.

2. When do we have to send out the final report?
(A) Not until 5 PM this Friday.
(B) Nancy is in charge of it.
(C) You need to send out a hard copy report.

3. How are we going to the airport?
(A) We'll take the 2 PM flight to Tokyo.
(B) Tony will drive us there.
(C) Right after lunch.

4. Where are you going for the New Year holiday?
(A) I am going to take the MRT.
(B) Hualien, to be with my family.
(C) We'll leave on Sunday.

5. Why did Mr. Novacek call the hotel?
(A) He was in the lobby.
(B) The hotel has no vacancy.
(C) To confirm the reservation.

回答得如何？是否能全部聽懂？接下來把以下的原文念念看：

1. When was the last time you went to Mount Fuji?
   (A) For three months.
   (B) Two years ago on a business trip there.
   (C) I am going to Fujifilm.

2. When do we have to send out the final report?
   (A) Not until 5 PM this Friday.
   (B) Nancy is in charge of it.
   (C) You need to send out a hard copy report.

3. How are we going to the airport?
   (A) We'll take the 2 PM flight to Tokyo.
   (B) Tony will drive us there.
   (C) Right after lunch.

4. Where are you going for the New Year holiday?
   (A) I am going to take the MRT.
   (B) Hualien, to be with my family.
   (C) We'll leave on Sunday.

5. Why did Mr. Novacek call the hotel?

   (A) He was in the lobby.

   (B) The hotel has no vacancy.

   (C) To confirm the reservation.

再聽 一次

然後閉著眼睛再聽一次： Track 16

如果沒法一次聽懂五題，就一題、一題的分開念過以後再聽。如果其中有一、兩題沒法一次聽懂，就把那題的題目和三個答案一句、一句的念，然後一句、一句地聽，我保證你可以聽懂，當然最後還是需要一整題連題目和答案的聽。這部分的練習最終目標，不只是你能夠選對五題答案，而是要你能一口氣的把五題裡面的每個句子都能完全聽懂！

題目中譯

1. 你上次去富士山是什麼時候？

   (A) 三個月　　　　　　　　　**(B) 兩年前出差時**

   (C) 我正要去富士軟片

2. 什麼時候要送出總結報告？

   (A) 本週五五點前　　　　(B) 由 Nancy 負責

   (C) 你需要送出紙本報告

3. 我們要怎麼去機場？

　　(A) 我們會搭兩點的班機去東京　　　**(B) Tony 會載我們去**

　　(C) 午餐後出發

4. 新年假期你要去哪？

　　(A) 我會搭捷運　　　　　　　　　　**(B) 花蓮跟家人團聚**

　　(C) 我們週日出發

5. 為什麼 Novacek 先生要打電話給旅館？

　　(A) 他人在大廳　　　　　　　　　　(B) 旅館已經客滿了

　　(C) 確認我們的訂位

 wh 問題進階練習

讀者把前面五題練習完後，可能會覺得聽力好像沒那麼難嘛！這裡我要稍稍潑點冷水，前面五題是最基本的 wh 問題，以下的題目就有些變化了。

請你試試： Track 17

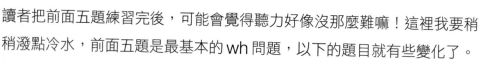

1. When does the movie start?

　　(A) Let's go to a movie.

　　(B) Let me go online and check the website.

　　(C) I have something to do this afternoon.

2. How would the project be financed?
(A) The government will sponsor it.
(B) The company is financially sound.
(C) We should be able to get the project done on schedule.

3. Who is going to revise the report?
(A) I don't think it has been assigned.
(B) It must be done by Friday.
(C) The manager has been really busy lately.

4. Why didn't you tell us you majored in finance?
(A) I didn't officially get the degree.
(B) I read the books mostly in the library.
(C) I need to get the job done quickly.

5. How about going for a coffee break?
(A) I drink coffee every day.
(B) We can try it tomorrow.
(C) That's a great idea.

回答得如何？是否全部答對？接下來同樣的先**念一下以下的原文**：

1. When does the movie start?
   (A) Let's go to a movie.
   (B) Let me go online and check the website.
   (C) I have something to do this afternoon.

2. How would the project be financed?
   (A) The government will sponsor it.
   (B) The company is financially sound.
   (C) We should be able to get the project done on schedule.

3. Who is going to revise the report?
   (A) I don't think it has been assigned.
   (B) It must be done by Friday.
   (C) The manager has been really busy lately.

4. Why didn't you tell us you majored in finance?
   (A) I didn't officially get the degree.
   (B) I read the books mostly in the library.
   (C) I need to get the job done quickly.

5. How about going for a coffee break?

    (A) I drink coffee every day.

    (B) We can try it tomorrow.

    (C) That's a great idea.

再聽一次 & 題目中譯

然後閉著眼睛再聽一次： 🎧 Track 17

翻譯是：

1. 電影什麼時候開演？

    (A) 一起看電影吧   **(B) 我到網站上去看看**   (C) 我今天下午有事

2. 這個計劃的錢從哪來？

    (A) 政府會贊助   (B) 這公司的財務狀況很好

    (C) 我們應該可以如期完成這計畫

3. 是誰負責修訂計畫？

    (A) 應該還沒指派吧   (B) 週五前一定要完成   (C) 經理最近很忙

4. 你怎麼沒跟我們說你主修財務金融？

    (A) 我沒有正式拿到學位   (B) 我多數在圖書館看書

    (C) 我要趕緊把事做完

5. 喝杯咖啡休息一下如何？

    (A) 我每天喝咖啡　　(B) 明天可以試試　　**(C) 好主意**

解析 ◯

注意到沒？這類的題目和答案，有兩個特點：要不單字艱深了一點，要不就是答案沒那麼直接而是會轉彎。

以第一題來說，題目問的是 when，考生會直接地想聽到關於時間的答案，結果沒想到答案竟然是：Let me go online and check the website. 跟時間一點關係也沒有！這也是我對部分新多益書籍和一些補習班老師稍有微詞的地方，有些書、有些老師會告訴同學先設想好答案，聽到 when 就設想時間，聽到 who 就設想人，聽到 where 就設想地方，請大家**絕對不要這麼做**！這麼做只會影響到你對難一點的題目的答題，只會讓你無法取得高分。聽力考試絕對不要去設想答案，聽力考試只有一個目標：把題目和答案聽懂。只有這樣才能答對這類的答案會轉彎的題目。

再來是第二題，題目裡有個字：finance，答案裡出現另一個字：sponsor，這兩個字說難不難，但也不是簡單的字，在聽力上面這類的字就算難題了。Finance 這個字你只要記住一件事：finance 跟錢有關，所以 personal finance 就是財務、資金，而 government finance 就是財政、財源，finance 跟錢有關，是不是就容易記住了？而 sponsor 這個字就更容易記了，看這題的題目 "How would the project be financed?" 和答案 "The government will sponsor it."。錢要從哪來？政府會 sponsor。那你說 sponsor 的意思會是？

再給你一個例句：

Coke is sponsoring the Olympic Games.

可口可樂 is sponsoring 奧林匹克。

sponsor 除了贊助還會是其他意思嗎？接下來把這兩句再多念幾遍：

The government will sponsor it.

Coke is sponsoring the Olympic Games.

你說 sponsor 這個字還需要硬背嗎？

接下來的第三和第四題也是類似的狀況，基本上答案都轉了一兩個彎，結論就是，把題目和答案都聽懂就不會有問題了。

再來就是需要個別提出來的最後一題，這題雖然一開始是 how 但是整個句子基本上不是個問句，而是個提議，"How about going for a coffee break?"（喝杯咖啡休息一下如何？）所以答案就是接受或是拒絕提議，回答方式跟一般的 wh 問題完全不同，這類問題還有以下其他的問法：

Why don't we buy some flowers instead?

What about Chinese food for lunch? Would you like to join us for dinner?

甚至最直接的 "Let's go for a movie."。這類的題目最重要的就是聽出來這只是提個 suggestion，只要能聽出來是個 suggestion 就簡單了，要是不清楚題意，就很難答對，因為答案只是簡單的接受或是拒絕。例如：That's a great idea. I'd love that. Sounds good to me.

如果是拒絕的答案則會說的比較委婉，例如：Sorry, I am busy. Sorry, I already have plans.

或是提出另一個選項，例如：I prefer Japanese 用來回應 What about Chinese food for lunch?

比較難一點的拒絕答案則是：I'd like to finish this section first. After I get this part done. 之類的。

多練習一下這類的題目：Why don't we..., How about..., What about..., Would you like to... 應該就沒問題了。

Yes/No 回答練習 ○

介紹完 wh 後，接下來講第二大類的 yes/no, 否定問句和附加問句。先說明一下最簡單的 yes/no，**請試試以下的例子：** Track 18

1. Have you seen my cellphone?
   (A) The cellphone is mine.
   (B) I've never seen it before.
   (C) On the table, next to the remote control.

2. Are you going to Mr. Arnold's welcome party?
   (A) Sure, I will not miss it for the world.
   (B) It should be Jack's job.
   (C) The party is over there.

3. Can you help Mr. Johnson with his report?
　(A) I will, right after finishing up mine.
　(B) He should be helpful.
　(C) I saw him this morning.

4. Are you going to the farewell party for Mr. Park?
　(A) I saw Mr. Park yesterday.
　(B) Farewell, my friends. I'll miss you.
　(C) Sorry, I have something to take care of.

試著開口說 ◗

接下來請你念以下的原文：（就算你全部答對還是要念一下，除非你已經把每個字都聽懂，完全沒有遺漏。畢竟練習到完全聽懂，你才能有萬無一失的把握。）

1. Have you seen my cellphone?
　(A) The cellphone is mine.
　(B) I've never seen it before.
　(C) It's on the table, next to the remote control.

2. Are you going to Mr. Arnold's welcome party?
　(A) Sure, I will not miss it for the world.
　(B) It should be Jack's job.
　(C) The party is over there.

3. Can you help Mr. Johnson with his report?

    (A) I will, right after finishing up mine.

    (B) He should be helpful.

    (C) I saw him this morning.

---

4. Are you going to the farewell party for Mr. Park?

    (A) I saw Mr. Park yesterday.

    (B) Farewell, my friends. I'll miss you.

    (C) Sorry, I have something to take care of.

再聽一次 & 題目中譯

然後不看原稿的再聽一次：　Track 18

翻譯是：

1. 有沒有看到我的手機？

    (A) 這手機是我的

    (B) 我從沒見過這手機

    (C) 就在桌上遙控器旁邊

---

2. 你會去 Arnold 先生的歡迎會嗎？

    (A) 當然，就算需要排除萬難我都會去

    (B) 這應該是 Jack 的工作吧

    (C) 惜別會就在那裡

3. 你能幫 Johnson 先生寫報告嗎？

(A) 弄完我的以後就會幫　　　(B) 他應該可以幫得上忙

(C) 我今天早上才看到他

---

4. 你會去 Park(朴) 先生的惜別會嗎？

(A) 我昨天才見到他　　　(B) 朋友們再見，我會想念你們

(C) 抱歉，我有事要忙

 否定問句 / 附加問句練習 ○

簡單的練習過後要來聽聽難一點的了，否定問句以及附加問句。我先用以下的例子說明這些問句間的差異和共通點。

Are you a student?

⇨ Aren't you a student?

You are a student, aren't you?

⇨ You aren't a student, are you?

以上四句問法不同，但回答的方式卻都一樣，基本上就是：

Yes, I am a student.

No, I am not a student.

在中文裡卻不是如此回答的。我舉一個例子：你沒去昨天的演唱會嗎？是啊！我忙得沒時間去。或是：誰說的，我去了。英文針對問題本身的

是否回答。而中文卻順著問話者的語氣回答。所以針對新多益考試這類的問題，不要去管 yes 或是 no，只要專心聽懂答案是否回答問題，不要去管答案裡面是 yes 還是 no，這樣的問題，就會變得簡單了。先來試試幾題。 Track 19

1. Don't we need some new chairs in the lobby?
(A) Yes and I already ordered some.
(B) No, Mary is the new chair person.
(C) Yes, they need to be fixed.

2. You really enjoyed the movie, didn't you?
(A) Yes, I like to move in tomorrow.
(B) No, Monday at nine.
(C) Yes, especially the action scenes.

3. Aren't you excited about the new CEO?
(A) He was born in California.
(B) Actually, I am a bit worried.
(C) Any exciting news lately?

4. You don't want to transfer to the new branch office, do you?
(A) With my family living here, certainly not.
(B) The tree has too many branches.
(C) No, next week would be the deadline.

答得如何？是不是比前面的題目難一點？同樣的，先**把以下的原稿念一遍**。

1. Don't we need some new chairs in the lobby?
   (A) Yes and I already ordered some.
   (B) No, Mary is the new chair person.
   (C) Yes, they need to be fixed.

2. You really enjoyed the movie, didn't you?
   (A) Yes, I like to move in tomorrow.
   (B) No, Monday at nine.
   (C) Yes, especially the action scenes.

3. Aren't you excited about the new CEO?
   (A) He was born in California.
   (B) Actually, I am a bit worried.
   (C) Any exciting news lately?

4. You don't want to transfer to the new branch office, do you?
   (A) With my family living here, certainly not.
   (B) The tree has too many branches.
   (C) No, next week would be the deadline.

再聽 一次

然後不看原稿的再聽一次 Track 19

是不是可以完全聽懂，而且題目也變得容易了？就像我前面說的，在同個等級的英文考試裡，聽力測驗的考題與文章絕對比閱讀的簡單。所以相對而言，培養聽力實力也就是讓自己聽懂內容就比較重要了。以新多益而言，其實它的聽力測驗程度上而言並不很難，難的只是新多益專有的英澳腔，只要你能掌握本書所介紹的正確練習方法，學會聽懂英澳腔，新多益聽力真的很容易。

題目中譯

翻譯是：

1. 大廳是不是需要些新椅子？

   (A) 是啊，我已經訂購了　　　(B) 不，Mary 是新的主席
   (C) 是，椅子該修了

2. 你真的很喜歡這部電影，對嗎？

   (A) 是，我想明天搬　　　(B) 不，週一九點
   (C) 是，尤其是那些動作場景

3. 你對新的 CEO 不感到興奮嗎？

   (A) 他在加州出生　　　**(B) 事實上我有點擔心**
   (C) 最近有什麼令人興奮的消息

4. 你不想被調到新的分公司，對嗎？

(A) 我家住這裡當然不想　　　(B) 這棵樹有太多分枝了

(C) 不，下禮拜截止

 否定問句/附加問句練習 ⭘

接下來，再介紹另一種 part 2 聽力裡面對台灣考生而言比較困難的考題，也就是以下的：間接問句以及 A or B。先講比較簡單間接問句，先來三個例子：

Do you know where they are going?

Can you tell me where the supermarket is?

Do you think we have enough chairs?

這類的問句一般用在比較不熟的朋友或是陌生人，感覺上比較 polite 一點。也因為如此，這類問句的重點都是在後半部，前面只是一些比較客氣的説法而已，除了前面的例子以外，還有以下的：

Could you tell me...?

Would it be possible...?

Is there any chance...?

Do you have any idea...?

I'd like to know...?

Would you mind telling me...?

不管是任何形式，你只要聽懂後半部，而且注意，三個答案裡哪個正確的回答了後半部的問題，就是正確答案。**來試一下：** Track 20

1. Do you know when the bus would come?
   (A) The bus stops right here.
   (B) In ten minutes.
   (C) I can drive you to the airport.

2. Could you tell me why he is in such a good mood?
   (A) His daughter studying overseas just came back.
   (B) I am fine, thank you.
   (C) You can tell me.

3. Do you happen to know where my notebook computer is?
   (A) Your note is needed for the meeting.
   (B) I just saw it. It's on your desk.
   (C) Mine is right here.

4. Would you mind telling me when the department store will open?
   (A) The party will start at 10.
   (B) Sorry, I have no idea.
   (C) I need time to think about it.

試著開口說 〇

答得如何？有把握嗎？**接下來先念一下原文：**

1. Do you know when the bus would come?
   (A) The bus stops right here.
   (B) In ten minutes.
   (C) I can drive you to the airport.

2. Could you tell me why he is in such a good mood?
   (A) His daughter studying overseas just came back.
   (B) I am fine, thank you.
   (C) You can tell me.

3. Do you happen to know where my notebook computer is?
   (A) Your note is needed for the meeting.
   (B) I just saw it. It's on your desk.
   (C) Mine is right here.

4. Would you mind telling me when the department store will open?
   (A) The party will start at 10.
   (B) Sorry, I have no idea.
   (C) I need time to think about it.

然後不看原稿的再聽一次 🔊 Track 20

是不是可以聽懂了，題目也比較簡單了。

翻譯是：

1. 你知道巴士什麼時候會到嗎？

(A) 巴士在這裡會停　　　　**(B) 十分鐘內**

(C) 我可以載你到機場

---

2. 能否告訴我他心情為什麼這麼好？

(A) 他國外留學的女兒剛剛回國　(B) 我很好，謝謝

(C) 你可以打電話給我

---

3. 你是否知道我的筆記型電腦在哪裡？

(A) 這會議需要你的筆記　　**(B) 我剛看到在你桌上**

(C) 我的就在這兒

---

4. 你會介意告訴我百貨公司什麼時候開店嗎？

(A) 慶祝會在十點開始　　　**(B) 抱歉我不知道**

(C) 我需要時間想想

A or B 問題練習

再來是比較難的 A or B，這類的題目一開始就像一般的 yes/no，但是在問句結束前加一個 or 再給一個選項，結果原來的 yes/no 變成了 A or B 二選一，而答案不出以下的情況：選 A、選 B、兩者都 OK 或是提出其他選項，答案裡絕對不能有 yes 或是 no。

或許你會問這聽起來不難啊！問題是，因為這類的題目基本上是 yes/no 加上 or 另一個選項，所以會比一般的題目還要長，而且你的腦袋必須及時反應出是哪兩個選項，A 是什麼、還有 B 是什麼，才能立刻選出正確答案。一樣的**先來幾個練習題：** Track 21

1. Are you available on Monday, or Tuesday?
(A) We'll be paid on Tuesday.
(B) Monday would be more convenient for me.
(C) Yes, I am leaving Monday.

2. Do you want to go grocery shopping now or later?
(A) Yes, I enjoy shopping.
(B) Let me write down the things to buy first.
(C) No later than 2 o'clock.

5. Do you want the whole team to meet at the front entrance of the Municipal Train Station or do you prefer the East Gate?
   (A) How about the West Gate? It's more convenient.
   (B) The East Gate just renovated recently.
   (C) I like Gatorade.

4. Would you like to eat out tonight or just reheat the lunch leftovers?
   (A) Either way is fine with me.
   (B) No, I don't like being leftover.
   (C) Tonight's weather is great.

3. Will you stay on for one more year or retire at the end of this year?
   (A) Yes, you are too young to retire.
   (B) All four tires need to be realigned.
   (C) I need more time to think about it.

試著開口說

如何？是不是有些難度？同樣的先**把以下原稿念一次：**

1. Are you available on Monday, or Tuesday?
   （所以基本上問題變成：Monday or Tuesday）
   (A) We'll be paid on Tuesday.
   (B) Monday would be more convenient for me.
   (C) Yes, I am leaving Monday.

2. Do you want to go grocery shopping now or later?
   （問題變成 shopping now or later）
   (A) Yes, I enjoy shopping.
   (B) Let me write down the things to buy first.
   (C) No later than 2 o'clock.
   （雖然問題裡的 shopping now or later 聽來簡單，但是答案轉了個
   彎，也就變難了）

3. Will you stay on for one more year or retire at the end of this year?

（one more year or retire this year 還有這題問句變長了，相對的也就難一點了）

(A) Yes, you are too young to retire.

(B) All four tires need to be realigned.

(C) I need more time to think about it.

（這題不只題目難了，答案的彎轉的還更大，你要能選得出來，新多益聽力成績不會太差。）

---

4. Would you like to eat out tonight or just reheat the lunch leftovers?

（如果你能聽出來：eat out tonight or reheat the leftovers 就很棒了。當然只要你能注意到 eat out tonight or reheat 其實也就夠了。）

(A) Either way is fine with me.

(B) No, I don't like being leftover.

(C) Tonight's weather is great.

（英澳腔的 either or, neither nor 還記得嗎？）

5. Do you want the whole team to meet at the front entrance of the Municipal Train Station or do you prefer the East Gate?

（這題最長，相對的也最難，如果全部都聽懂當然很棒，但是只要你能立刻抓到 at the front or the East Gate 也就夠了，這就是我強調的，腦筋要轉的夠快要能捉住重點。）

(A) How about the West Gate? It's more convenient.

(B) The East Gate just renovated recently.

(C) I like Gatorade.

（結果是其他建議，當然得說個理由）

再聽一次 & 題目中譯 ○

然後不看原稿的再聽一次 🎧 Track 21

翻譯是：

1. 你週一有空嗎？還是週二？

　　(A) 我們週一會收到錢　　　　**(B) 週一我比較方便**

　　(C) 是的，我週一出發

2. 要現在去買蔬果嗎？還是晚一點？

　　(A) 是，我喜歡採買　　　　**(B) 我先寫下要買的東西再說**

　　(C) 兩點之前

3. 你會留下來再做一年還是年底退休？

(A) 是的，你退休太年輕了啦　　　(B) 四個輪胎都需要校正

(C) 我需要點時間想想

---

4. 想要出去吃晚餐還是就把午餐剩下的飯菜熱一下就好？

(A) 我都可以　　　　　　　　(B) 不，我不喜歡被孤單的拋棄

(C) 今晚的天氣很棒

---

5. 你要隊伍在火車站正門集合還是在東門？

(A) 西門呢？西門比較方便　　　(B) 東門剛剛整修過了

(C) 我喜歡喝開特力

記得反應要快，立刻抓住重點是 A or B，這類的問題就容易掌握住了。

 肯定句問題練習 ◯

最後要講的重點是肯定句，也就是說題目一開始的問題不是問句，而是個肯定句。這類的題目難就難在你根本無從預測答案是什麼樣的情況，所以最好的方式就是盡量聽懂三個答案，記得要注意一點，如果有些聽不懂，專注在你聽懂的部分。**請試試以下的例子：** Track 22

4. This is much tougher than I originally thought.

(A) It couldn't be any easier.

(B) Do you need any help?

(C) I can go there with you.

3. VP of marketing visited us last week.

(A) I am going to be there.

(B) Did you talk to him about next year's advertising campaign?

(C) I am going to pay him.

2. He really knows what he is doing.

(A) We are lucky to get him to work for us.

(B) You should be doing it.

(C) He needs our help for sure.

1. Today sure is hot.

(A) The soup is too hot for me.

(B) Tell me about it.

(C) Leave it here for a while and it would cool down for sure.

(C) It should be easy to identify the best case.

(B) Vivian is chosen as employee of the month.

(A) With so many excellent candidates to choose from, I am not surprised.

5. They are having a hard time picking employee of the year.

![試著開口說]

碰到這類的肯定句問題，是不是覺得答案真的可以有多種變化？說實話你不會有時間去想這題是 yes/no，那題是肯定句。就是把題目聽懂，然後不設定任何假設的選出正確答案。接下來，**請念一下原稿。**

1. Today sure is hot.

(A) The soup is too hot for me.

(B) Tell me about it.

(C) Leave it here for a while and it would cool down for sure.

(B) Tell me about it. 是個很口語的說法，意思是：你說的沒錯。而這題還可以有很多種答案，例如：

Let me turn on the air conditioner. You can turn the temperature setting a bit lower.（打開冷氣機還有調低溫度設定。）
You can open the window and let some cool air in.（開窗通風）
都是合理的答案。

2. He really knows what he is doing.

(A) We are lucky to get him to work for us.

(B) You should be doing it.

(C) He needs our help for sure.

3. VP of marketing visited us last week.

(A) I am going to be there.

(B) Did you talk to him about next year's advertising campaign?

(C) I am going to pay him.

4. This is much tougher than I originally thought.

(A) It couldn't be any easier.

(B) Do you need any help?

(C) I can go there with you.

(B) 這個答案算是最順的答案，但是還有其他可能的回答，例如：

You still need to finish it on time.（還是要準時完成）

甚至像轉了幾個彎的

Now you know why you were picked for the job.（現在你終於知道為什麼挑你了吧！）

這類轉了幾個彎的答案，正是新多益聽力高分甚至滿分的關鍵題。

5. They are having a hard time picking employee of the year.

(A) With so many excellent candidates to choose from, I am not surprised.

(B) Vivian is chosen as employee of the month.

(C) It should be easy to identify the best case.

再聽一次 & 題目中譯

然後不看原稿的再聽一次 Track 22

是不是覺得只要能聽懂，不管什麼樣的題目都會變簡單。

翻譯是：

1. 今天真的很熱。

(A) 這湯太燙了

(B) 可真沒錯（Tell me about it. 是美國人常說的口語，意思就是你說的沒錯）

(C) 把它放在那兒一陣子待會就會涼了

2. 他真知道他在做什麼？

(A) 還真幸運有他來幫我們做事

(B) 這事是你該做的

(C) 他肯定需要我們幫忙

3. 行銷副總上禮拜來了。

(A) 我也會去

(B) 你跟他談過明年的廣告活動嗎？

(C) 我要付錢給他

4. 這比我原先所想的難多了。

(A) 這再簡單不過（It couldn't be any easier. 直翻：不可能更簡單）

(B) 你需要幫忙嗎？

(C) 我可以跟你去

5. 要他們挑出年度最佳員工還真難。

(A) 這麼多優秀的候選人，我一點也不意外

(B) Vivian 被選為本月最佳員工

(C) 挑出最佳方案應該很容易啊

最後再強調一次，一個在 Part 1 和 Part 2 都很重要的考試技巧。當你聽到每個答案時就立刻判斷是對、錯、還是沒把握。在你聽力程度越來越高之時，尤其要注意，只要沒有十足把握，那個答案就列入沒把握、不知道，然後把你的筆直接點在那個答案上面，專心聽下一個答案。舉例來說，如果答案 A 沒聽清楚或是不知道，就把筆點在 A，接下來聽 B，假設 B 你知道是錯，筆還是點在 A 繼續聽 C，由你對答案 C 的判斷來決定要選 A 還是 C。尤其是 Part 1 有四個答案，這技巧更重要，可不要在聽完四個答案都挑不出來以後，忘了剛剛沒把握的答案是 A、B 還是 C，記得筆永遠點在沒把握的那個答案上面，這樣的慘劇就絕不會發生在你身上。

1.5 新多益 Part 3 簡短對話和 Part 4 簡短獨白的準備

準備重點

我先簡單的說明一下，這兩部分的考題形式。Part 3 基本上是一對男女雙方的對話，多數是四句話有些考題只有三句，聽完每組對話後，你要回答三個問題。Part 4 則是一人的獨白，最少六、七句話，可能更長。同樣的聽完每個題組的對話後，也要回答三個問題。

跟前面 Part 1 和 Part 2 不同的是，所有題目與答案都是先印在題本中，這也是考生可以先看題目和答案的原因。記住既然考題印了出來，就是要你先看，不去先看考題是你自己要放棄權利。I cannot emphasize more that 先看題目與答案絕對是 Part 3 和 Part 4 裡面最重要的關鍵！尤其是新多益考試裡，有一項和台灣一般英文不一樣也是最特別的規定（以下直接引用多一官方考試應試須知），『測驗時在試題本或其他物品上抄寫題目、答案、劃線或作任何記號』還有官方網站裡的多一常見問題中，『許多考生因為聽信補習班的答題技巧教授或是網路謠傳，容易誤觸這個規定，以為劃記後有擦拭乾淨就不算違規，但是要提醒大家的是，只要有劃記的動作即為違規，而不是大家誤傳的擦掉就沒關係喔』，嚴重的話可以取消應試資格。因為你不能在題本上寫下任何剛剛聽到的訊息，先看題目和答案就更加重要了。

Part 3 和 Part 4 的準備其實和前面的 Part 1、Part 2 相差不大，主要的差別在考試技巧。在應考 Part 3、Part 4 時會先撥放一段 direction，在這個時候，不要去聽 direction，而是要先看第一組考題的三個題目和答案。

一開始的 direction 基本上有三十秒左右，只要你稍微有點英文基礎，絕對可以在這三十秒內看完三題題目和答案，我實際上跟許多學生測試過，只要你英文有國中程度，都可以在三十秒內把三題題目和答案看過至少一到兩遍。可是千萬記得一點，看題的同時，要注意一下是否聽到："questions 41 through 43" 或是 "questions 71 through 73"，聽到後，立刻要把注意力放到聽對話，同時看著你已經看過的三題題目和答案，只要你一聽到相關的答案，立刻作答。在最佳狀況下，你可以在對話結束前就把三題寫完，如果如此恭喜你！記得不要再聽接下來的對話，立刻去看下一組的三題題目和答案。

以下我先用幾個例子讓你熟悉一下這兩部分的考題：
首先先播放 Part 3 的 direction，趁著這個時間先看前三題的題目和答案。在對話即將開始時，轉而邊看題目邊聽對話，記得邊聽對話邊選聽到的答案，如果對話聽完，還有一兩個題目沒聽出來，看個順眼的答案，不要猶豫的選下去，趁著在撥放這三題題目時，去看下三題的題目和答案。

1. Where most likely is the place?

   (A) An office

   (B) A restaurant

   (C) A grocery store

   (D) A hotel

2. How much is the breakfast?

   (A) There is no charge at all.

   (B) 6 dollars

   (C) 10 dollars

   (D) 15 dollars

3. How many ice machines on each floor?

   (A) 1

   (B) 2

   (C) 3

   (D) 4

4. When most likely is the time?

   (A) 10 AM

   (B) Noon

   (C) 2 PM

   (D) 4 PM

5. What are they going to have?

    (A) Chinese food

    (B) Pizza

    (C) Hamburgers

    (D) Milk

6. How are they going to go there?

    (A) On foot

    (B) Drive a car

    (C) Take a bus

    (D) Ride a train

聽力腳本

Part 3

Directions: In this section of the test, you will hear some conversations between two persons. You will need to answer three questions according to what they talk about in each conversation. Select the best response to each question and fill up the space corresponding to answer (A), (B), (C) or (D) on your answer sheet. The conversation will be spoken only once and it is not printed in your test book.

Questions 1 to 3 refer to the following conversation.

W: Your room is 505 and here are the key cards and the free breakfast coupons. It's served between 6 and 10 in the restaurant to your left.

M: Thanks. Where can I get some ice and how much does it cost?

W: On each floor, there is one ice machine on each end of the hallway. You can use the ice bucket which is provided in the room to get the ice free of charge. Is there any other thing that I can help?

M: No. Thanks.

Question number 1: Where most likely is the place?

Question number 2: How much is the breakfast?

Question number 3: How many ice machines on each floor?

Questions 4 to 6 refer to the following conversation.

M: Time for lunch, do you want to try some Chinese food today?

W: I had Chinese last night. How about hamburgers? I heard Shake Shack opened a new restaurant right around the corner of Wellborn Road and Pizza Drive. It's only a three-minute walk so driving is not required.

M: Shake Shack, the fast food restaurant that's popping up everywhere? I'd like to try their milkshake, too.

W: What are you waiting for? Let's go.

Question number 4: When most likely is the time?
Question number 5: What are they going to have?
Question number 6: How are they going to go there?

解析 ○

先對一下答案：D A B B C A。再來解釋一下這題目

1. Where most likely is the place?

    既然說到 room number, key cards 還有 breakfast 當然是 (D) A hote。

2. How much is the breakfast?

    有提到 Free breakfast coupons，也就是 (A) There is no charge at all.。

3. How many ice machines on each floor?

    有聽到 One on each end of the hall way，hallway 的兩端，所以選 (B) 2。

4. When most likely is the time?

    既然是 time for lunch，所以選 (B) Noon。

5. What are they going to have?

有提到 I had Chinese last night. How about hamburgers? 答案是 (C) Hamburgers，這段裡的 Pizza Drive 是路的名字。

---

6. How are they going to go there?

提到了 a three-minute walk，所以選 (A) On foot。

考完後覺得如何？是不是在第二題或是第三題卡了一下？注意到沒？就算給妳再多十秒鐘甚至是一分鐘，只要你沒聽出任何一題的答案，給你再多的時間都不會有任何差別！既然如此，如同我一直強調的，沒聽到的答案，看個順眼的立刻選下去，不要猶豫，絕對不要浪費了看下三題的寶貴時間。

鍛鍊英語耳 ○

接下來要告訴你如何練習聽懂 part 3 的聽力考試。

請先念一下這句：

W: Your room is 505 and here are the key cards and the free breakfast coupons. It's served between 6 and 10 in the restaurant to your left.

（這裡的 coupon 就是所謂的折價券，記得不要硬背，多念幾次 the free breakfast coupons，就會對 coupon 這個字有 FU，也就容易記了。）

接下來聽一下 Track 24

是不是聽懂了？如果你沒法一口氣聽懂，把這兩句話分開一句、一句的聽，就可以聽懂了。

請你念下一句：

Thanks. Where can I get some ice and how much does it cost?

聽一下 Track 25

聽懂了，對吧！

再念下一句：

On each floor, there is one ice machine on each end of the hallway. You can use the bucket provided in the room to get the ice free of charge. Is there any other thing that I can help?

聽一下 Track 26

同樣的，如果你沒法一口氣聽懂，把這幾句話分開一句、一句的聽，就可以聽懂了。

最後念一下：

No. Thanks.

聽一下 Track 27

把對話分段聽懂後，一定要再次把全部對話完整聽一次，才能應付正式的考試。

完整對話試試看 Track 28

同樣的，試試第二組試題：

先念

Time for lunch, do you want to try some Chinese food today?

聽一下 Track 29

念一下

I had Chinese last night. How about hamburgers? I heard Shake Shack opened a new restaurant right around the corner of Wellborn Road and Pizza Drive. It's only a three-minute walk so driving is not required.

這裡的 Shake Shack 反正就是一家餐廳，而且應該是賣漢堡的餐廳。後面的 Wellborn Road 和 Pizza Drive，反正就是兩條路，既然是 Pizza Drive，這裡的 pizza 當然就不是披薩了。

聽一下 Track 30

沒法一口氣聽懂就先一句、一句的聽，然後一口氣聽完這女士的話。

再念下一句

Shake Shack, the fast food restaurant that's popping up everywhere? I'd like to try their fries and milkshake too.

這裡的 that is popping up everywhere 就是到處 popping up 冒出來，簡單吧！milkshake 把 milk shake 以後，milkshake 當然就是奶昔了。

聽一下 🎧 Track 31

再念最後面的

What are you waiting for? Let's go.

聽一下 🎧 Track 32

當然，總要把完整對話一口氣聽懂： 🎧 Track 33

題目中譯 ○

其實到這裡 part 3 應該就可以結束了，只是我還是不能免俗的附上中文翻譯，如果你已經看懂了，跳過這段翻譯，直接看下一段。如果還有問題，以下的中文翻譯是給你參考用的，千萬記住，不要用中文而聽懂英文，英聽要一聽就懂，腦子裡不能有中文。

問題 1-3 對話內容

W: Your room is 505 and here are the key cards and the free breakfast coupons. It's served between 6 and 10 in the restaurant to your left.

你的房間號碼是 505，房卡和免費早餐券在這裡。早餐在六到十點在你左手邊的餐廳裡供應。

M: Thanks. Where can I get some ice and how much does it cost?

謝謝，哪裡有冰塊，多少錢？

W: On each floor, there is one ice machine on each end of the hallway. You can use the ice bucket which is provided in the room to get the ice free of charge. Is there any other thing that I can help?

各層樓的通道的兩邊都有製冰器，你可以用房間裡提供的桶子來裝冰塊，完全免費。還有其他事需要我幫忙嗎？

M: No. Thanks.

沒了，謝謝。

問題 4-6 對話內容

M: Time for lunch, do you want to try some Chinese food today?

該吃午飯了，今天要試試中式午餐嗎？

W: I had Chinese last night. How about hamburgers? I heard Shake Shack opened a new restaurant right around the corner of Wellborn Road and Pizza Drive. It's only a three-minute walk so driving is not required.

我昨晚吃過了，漢堡如何？我聽說在 Wellborn Road 和 Pizza Drive 路口，有家新的 Shake Shack 剛開張。走路只需要三分鐘就不需要開車了。

M: Shake Shack, the fast food restaurant that's popping up everywhere? I'd like to try their milkshake too.

Shake Shack 那家到處開張（冒出來）的速食餐廳？我也想試試他們的奶昔。

W: What are you waiting for? Let's go.
那還等什麼，走吧！

接下來試試 Part 4，記得趁著在播放 Part 4 的 direction 時，先看前三題的題目和答案。在對話即將開始時，轉而邊看題目邊聽對話，記得邊聽對話邊選聽到的答案，如果對話聽完，還有一兩個題目沒聽出來，看個順眼的答案，不要猶豫的選下去，趁著在播放這三題題目時，去看下三題的題目和答案。

| 小練習 | Track 34 |

7. Who most likely is the speaker?

    (A) A bus driver

    (B) A park ranger

    (C) A tourist

    (D) A tour guide

8. What is prohibited on the bus?

    (A) Taking pictures.

    (B) Ringing the bell.

    (C) Smoking.

    (D) Asking questions.

9. What do you do to ask for help?

(A) Push a button.

(B) Call for help.

(C) Yell to the driver.

(D) Raise your hand.

10. What kind of service does the company provide?

(A) Screening service.

(B) Shipping service.

(C) On line shopping

(D) Packaging service.

11. What do you need to provide to the US shopping web site when you want to buy goods through this service?

(A) The company's US address

(B) Your phone number

(C) The company's phone number

(D) The company's name

12. How much is the annual membership?

(A) 260 dollars

(B) 160 dollars

(C) 60 dollars

(D) 6 dollars

Part 4

Directions: In this section of the test, you will hear some talks given by a single speaker. You will need to answer three questions according to what the person mentions in the talk. Select the best response to each question and fill up the space corresponding to answer (A), (B), (C), or (D) on your answer sheet. The talk will be spoken only once and it is not printed in your test book.

Questions 7 to 9 refer to the following talk.

Welcome to Red Rock National Park, I will be the guide leading your tour today. Here are a few rules that I would like you to follow for your own safety. First, there is no smoking on the bus, please extinguish all smoking material and put them away immediately in the trash bag provided. Second, all children who are five years old and under should avoid sitting near the window and must be accompanied by an adult at all times. Third, please do not stand up when the bus is in motion. Finally, if you need help during the tour, please press the button above your head to ring the bell.

Question number 7

Who most likely is the speaker?

Question number 8

What is prohibited on the bus?

Question number 9

What do you do to ask for help?

Questions 10 to 12 refer to the following talk.

For a Taiwan resident like you, it's really tough to buy any goods from those US shopping web sites that do not ship merchandize overseas. This is where we step in. Simply click and buy what you want, fill in our US address on the web site, provide your international address to us and we will send it to you. Save up to 70% on international shipping and get your product within four days by becoming our member! Our service also includes free repackaging to minimize weight, free consolidation of multiple-store orders, and pre-shipment screening for broken or prohibited items. You can enjoy all the above services for as little as $60 a year.

Question number 10

What kind of service does the company provide?

Question number 11

What do you need to provide to the US shopping web site when you want to buy goods through this service?

Question number 12

How much is the annual membership?

解析

先對一下答案：D C A B A C。再來解釋一下這六題：

7. Who most likely is the speaker?

獨白中提到I will be leading your today.，所以是 (D) A tour guide。

8. What is prohibited on the bus?

"no smoking on the bus" (C) Smoking. 如果不認識 prohibit 這個字，多念幾次：Smoking is prohibited. 就會有 FU 了。

9. What do you do to ask for help?

"if you need help during the tour, please press the button"，答案是 (A) Push a button.。

10. What kind of service does the company provide?

"we will send it to you" 還有 "Save up to 70% on international shipping"，所以是 (B) Shipping service.；(C) On line shopping 是在美國網站，不是在這家公司。

11. What do you need to provide to the US shopping web site when you want to buy goods through this service?
"Simply click and buy what you want, fill in our US address on the web site"，所以是 (A) The company's US address 貨品先送到他那裡，然後他才幫你送到你家裡。

---

12. How much is the annual membership?
"$60 a year"，故答案選 (C) 60 dollars

鍛鍊英語耳 〇

試過這六題後感覺如何？會不會覺得 Part 4 稍稍難了一點？不論你的感覺如何，還是先來練一下聽懂 Part 4 的聽力測驗。

同樣的，**先念一下**
Welcome to Red Rock National Park, I will be the guide leading your tour today.
再聽 Track 35

這就聽懂了，對吧。**接下來念**
Here are a few rules that I would like you to follow for your own safety.

然後聽 Track 36

再念下一句

First, there is no smoking on the bus, please extinguish all smoking material and put them away immediately in the trash bag provided. 既然是no smoking當然要extinguish（熄滅）all smoking material，extinguish這個字不要硬背，把extinguish all smoking material多念幾次就OK了。

聽下一句 Track 37

念下一個規定

Second, all children who are five years old and under should avoid sitting near the window and must be accompanied by an adult at all times.

這裡的accompanied by an adult，小孩當然需要accompanied by an adult對吧！

聽一下 Track 38

念最後一個規定

Third, please do not stand up when the bus is in motion.

接下來聽 Track 39

念最後一句

Finally, if you need help during the tour, please press the button above your head to ring the bell.

聽最後一句 Track 40

不可避免的，**再次把整篇試著一次聽懂** 🎧 Track 41

再來試試下一篇：

念一下

For a Taiwan resident like you, it's really tough to buy any goods from those US shopping web sites that do not ship merchandize overseas. 你就是個 Taiwan resident（居民），Taiwan resident 有 FU 吧！

聽一下 🎧 Track 42

再念

This is where we step in. step in 直翻是走進來，這裡就可以當作加入、參與甚至幫忙，重點是：This is where we step in. 要一念就懂！

聽 🎧 Track 43

下一句

Simply click and buy what you want, fill in our US address on the web site, provide your international address to us and we will send it to you.

聽 🎧 Track 44

再念一句

Save up to 70% on international shipping and get your product within four days by becoming our member!

聽一句 🎧 Track 45

再來念

Our service also includes free repackaging to minimize weight, free consolidation of multiple-store orders, and pre-shipment screening for broken or prohibited items. 這裡的 consolidation of multi-store orders，既然是 multi-store orders 當然要先 consolidate （合併、整合）一下，再念一下：consolidation of multi-store orders，對 consolidation 這個字，就會有 FU 了。

接下來聽 Track 46

最後念

You can enjoy all the above services for as little as $60 a year.

聽一下 Track 47

完整的再聽一次 Track 48

最後還是要翻譯一下，同樣的，如果你已經看懂了，跳過這段翻譯，直接看下一段。如果還有問題，以下的中文翻譯是給你參考用的，千萬記住，不要用中文而聽懂英文，英聽要一聽就懂，腦子裡不能有中文。

Question 7 to 9

Welcome to Red Rock National Park, I will be the guide leading your tour today.
歡迎來到 Red Rock 紅岩國家公園，我是您們今天的嚮導。

Here are a few rules that I would like you to follow for your own safety.
以下是一些我希望你能遵守，攸關安全的規定。

First, there is no smoking on the bus, please extinguish all smoking material and put them away immediately in the trash bag provided.
首先，在巴士上不能抽菸，請熄滅所有香菸，並把菸蒂放到我們提供的垃圾袋裡。

Second, all children who are five years old and under should avoid sitting near the window and must be accompanied by an adult at all times.

第二點，所有五歲以下的小孩都不能靠窗坐，而且一定要有大人陪同。

Third, please do not stand up when the bus is in motion.

第三點，車子開動時，請勿站立。

Finally, if you need help during the tour, please press the button above your head to ring the bell.

最後，如果你需要幫忙，請按你頭上方的鈴聲按鈕。

Questions 10 to 12

For a Taiwan resident like you, it's really tough to buy any goods from those US shopping web sites that do not ship merchandize overseas.

居住在台灣的你，很難到那些不送貨到海外的美國購物網站去買東西。

This is where we step in.

這就是我們能幫你的時候了。

Simply click and buy what you want, fill in our US address on the web site, provide your international address to us and we will send it to you.

簡單的點選、買下你要的東西，在美國網站裡填上我們的美國地址，再提供你的地址給我們，我們就會把貨品運送給你了。

Save up to 70% on international shipping and get your product within four days by becoming our member!

成為我們的會員，可省下七成的國際運費而且運送只需四天。

Our service also includes free repackaging to minimize weight, free consolidation of multiple-store orders, and pre-shipment screening for broken or prohibited items.

我們並提供免費重新包裝來節省重量、免費整合多個網站的訂單以及運送前的貨物檢視以確保貨物的完整以及沒有違禁品。

You can enjoy all the above services for as little as $60 a year.

一年只需要 60 美金就可以享有以上所有的服務。

是不是覺得新多益 Part 3 和 Part 4 的聽力，沒那麼難了？就算是你認為最難的 Part 4，都變得比較簡單了！其實聽力的練習真的很簡單、很容易，最重要的一點就是：自己念，然後不看稿子的聽！一開始先一句、一句的來練習，聽懂以後就試著一整篇的聽，如果一時之間整篇無法完全聽懂，把它分成上下兩部份先分開聽。同樣的最後還是要讓自己能夠一整篇一口氣聽懂。說來好像有點難，只要是這麼試過，就可以發現，其實聽力真的不難，重要的是找對練習方法，也就是我一直強調的：自己先念、唸完後聽，就可以很輕易地聽懂。有沒有發覺一件很神奇的事：雖然你念的是美國腔，念完之後卻能幫助你聽懂英、澳腔！沒錯，只要練習的方法對了，英國腔、澳洲腔根本不是問題。

我相信有些讀者會覺得 Part 4 又臭又長，比起 Part 3 難多了，但是也會有些讀者認為，Part 4 好像比較簡單。如果你是少數的後者，恭喜你，你的程度高了一級。以一般台灣學生而言，多數都認為 Part 2 最簡單，Part 3 次之，Part 4 最難，當然大家都不會反對 Part 1 最簡單，也最容易拿分。在我的學生裡面，一開始沒有例外都認為如此。但是在加強你的聽力能力之後，你會發現，Part 4 雖然長，給的 information 卻也多，更有機會判斷出正確答案。Part 3 只是兩人間的簡短對話，可能一不注意就漏掉重點，Part 2 只有簡短的問題與三個答案，只要一恍神，很可能就沒法挑出答案。在此希望讀者都能把聽力，尤其是 Part 4 練到感覺起來比較簡單的地步。

閱讀測驗準備

前言

新多益的閱讀測驗中，分為三個大題，其中的 Part 5 句子填空和 Part 6 段落填空可以被歸類成是單字及文法題型，而 Part 7 的閱讀測驗中則有單篇及雙篇文章兩種不同的題型。

在談新多益閱讀測驗題型及其相關的文法、單字之前，我想先給一個英文閱讀的正確方法。如同我在先前所講的：考聽力時，『腦子裡不能出現中文！』。同樣的在考新多益閱讀單元時，『腦子裡一樣的不能出現中文！』，不管你寫的是單字題目、文法問題還是閱讀測驗，千萬不要習慣性的以中文思考！或許你會說，怎麼可能？！

別忘了，在看前面『聽力測驗準備』重點時，你可能已經有類似的想法，可是經過我在這本書所教的聽力練習方法後，你是不是覺得在考聽力時，真的中文都不見了！同義的，其實只要你找對方法練習，閱讀也是可以只要把句子念完，就可以了解，真的不需要中文翻譯來擋路。

2.1 新多益 Part 5 句子填空和 Part 6 段落填空

單字

先談談單字，台灣向來強調背『單字』的重要性，背『單字』、背『單字』『單字』還真的是一個字、一個字的背。還記得老師說每天背二十個單字，十天就可以背兩百個，五十天就一千個單字了。結果卻是只記住前幾天的單字，實際上效果如何，大家都很清楚。還有就像前面『為什麼新多益成績會撞牆』所講的，更糟糕的是，就算你將單字死背下來了，在考試時還是會出問題！除了先前所講的例子，我在這裡再給個例子。

Example

The data collected from our experiments - - - - - - the theory proposed by researchers from National Sun, Yat-Sen University.

(A) certified   (B) confirmed   (C) obligated   (D) entitled

按照字典的解釋，我們查到的結果如下：

(A) certify：證明、證實

(B) confirm：證實、確定、確認

(C) obligate：使負義務、強使

(D) entitle：給……權力（或資格）

說實話單單看中文意思，答案會好挑嗎？很不幸的，面對單字考題，台灣一般的參考書就是把題目翻譯出來，然後告訴你四個答案的中文意思，就算解釋過了。以這題而言，乍看之下，單看中文意思，四個答案不是那麼好挑吧！

就算你花些時間判斷出 (C) obligate：使負義務的、強使 和 (D) entitle：給……權力（或資格）不對，那怎麼從 (A) certify：證明、證實，和 (B) confirm：證實、確定、確認，這兩個答案裡選出正確的呢？可憐的是，新多益的單字考題裡面，尤其是比較難的高分單字考題裡，大多是這樣的類型，中文意思相近，英文用法上卻有差異的考題。這類的考題，用以往硬背單字方式來應試，以上面的這個例子而言，只是死路一條！

回到這題 certify 這個字，其實有兩個名詞：certificate 是證書的意思，還有 certification 也是檢定、保證的意思。所以當你被其他人或是機構 certified，通常都會給個 certificate。舉例來說，新多益考試超過 860，申請之後新多益官方機構就給你一份金色證照，證明你超過 860 分。如果你英檢中高級過關，GEPT 也會給你一份證書。基本上就是有個人或機構驗證你的能力或是資格，所以在這題裡不合適。

而 confirm 就是更好的答案了。如果你只是死背 certify：證明、證實，還有 confirm：證實、確定、確認，你真的可以選出答案嗎？這就是我在前面特別強調單字千萬不能死背、硬背，尤其是一個英文、一個中文的硬背，不只是費時、費勁而且效率差，更慘的是你會失去了原本英文裡隱含的意思。我在前面的聽力單元裡特別強調要多念、唸到有 FU，這個原則對記住單字也是一樣。前面提到了 fluency in English，你只要多念幾次，就會對 fluency 這個字有 FU，也容易記牢。好處不只如此，如果你只是硬背這個字流暢、流利、順暢，可能會有個問題，在中文裡的交通順暢，也是順暢啊，那可不可以用這個字 fluent 來形容順暢的交通。中文上面當然可以，只是英文裡面會用 smooth traffic，不會用 fluent。

台灣許多考生在新多益考試裡總是卡在某些關卡，有的人卡在 5、600 左右，有些怎麼補習怎麼認真準備就是考不到 7、800，在單字上面就只是硬背，沒能深入了解英文上面的用法，當然考不了高分。在本書裡蒐集了一些這類的考題，但是我不可能網羅所有考題，我的建議是多唸英文文章，培養自己對英文單字的 FU 才是正途。不過說實話如果你能把本書所蒐集的這類單字念熟，新多益的單字考題應該不會是你拿金色證書的障礙。以下是我所蒐集的一些單字資料：

afford

先講一個不難的單字：afford 如果你不認識，先不要急著查字典，看一下例句：

This car is so expensive that I cannot afford it.

就算你不認識這個字，唸完這句，這車很貴，所以我沒法 afford it 以後，是不是對這個字就有些感覺有點 FU 了？接下來才去查字典知道 afford 的意思是：買得起、有足夠的錢，先想想這樣的中文解釋，容易背嗎？接下來再把這個例句 "This car is so expensive that I cannot afford it." 多念個兩遍，是不是就容易記了？更棒的是，連這個字的用法都學會了！

再看以下的例子：

I cannot afford losing you.

I cannot afford to lose you.

"I cannot afford losing you." 跟 "I cannot afford to lose you." 都是正確用法，多念兩遍，自然而然就能將 afford 後面可以加名詞 / 代名詞、動詞＋ing 或是 to+ 動詞的簡單文法給記住，不管文法或是單字類的考題都沒問題。

spend vs cost

再來看看簡單的 spend 和 cost，如果你只是硬背，兩個字都是花錢，花費，中文解釋的差異不大，但是請看看英文例句：

I spent 500 dollars. (我花了 500 元。)

It cost me 500 dollars. (這個花了我 500 元。)

從這兩個例句中來看，是不是有發現 spend 和 cost 其實有很大的差異？差別是在於主詞的部分，spend 對的是人，而 cost 對的是物，而這個差異是你無法從硬背單字裡面學到的。我教過的學生中，都是跟他們講只要將 "I spend, It cost" 念個三、五遍就能記住之間的差異了，你說簡不簡單？

拼法相似

接下來談談許多台灣學生在背英文單字上的夢靨，那就是許多類似拼法的字都會搞混，而且越背越混亂、越搞不清楚，例如：

proper, prosper, (prosperity, prosperous), propose, (proposal), property

這幾個字是不是已經把你搞昏頭了？同樣的請先念以下的例句：

You need to get proper training before taking on more challenging assignments.

感受一下 proper training：適當的訓練，然後把 proper training 念個兩遍。

With the improving economy, companies are prospering.

感受一下 prospering 繁榮、興盛的 FU，有需要的話把 companies are prospering 多念兩遍。

You need to first propose a proposal for your project.

感覺一下提個議案 propose a proposal，再把 propose a proposal 念個兩遍。

You need to stay out of the private property.

體會一下 private property 私人財產，再把 private property 念個兩遍。

把以上的所有例句多念幾次，這些原先讓你混淆的字就很容易地搞清楚了，對吧！

contact, contract, content

首先注意一下發音，尤其是前兩個字 contact 裡面的 tact，以及 contract 裡的 tract。先把這兩個字的發音念對，然後念一下以下的例句：

You can contact me anytime.

Contact me 多念幾次。

You need to sign the contract first.

Sign the contract 多念幾次。

You need to read the content of the contract carefully.

Read the content of the contract 多念幾次。

是不是就把這幾個字弄懂了？不會再混淆了？如果你有類似的單字組合混淆的問題，先去找一些例句，多念幾遍問題就小多了。

雙義字

再來就給一些比較難的單字例句了，這些是所謂的雙義字，也就是同字不同義。

outstanding & address

There are two outstanding problems that need to be addressed immediately.

這裡的 outstanding 千萬不要當傑出的、顯著的來解釋，因為 problems 不可能傑出。這裡的 outstanding 是還沒完成、還沒解決的意思，還有後面的 address 可不要當地址！ problems 需要被 addressed 你覺得呢？當然是解決、面對。

其實 address 還有另一個意思，請看例句：

The president is addressing the media.

這裡的 addressing the media 是致詞、演説、演講都可以。接下來不要硬背，請將這兩個例句多念兩遍，唸到有 FU 才重要。

There are two outstanding problems that need to be addressed immediately.

The president is addressing the media.

sanction

再來是 sanction 這個字，在新聞裡面，sanction 這個字多半是制裁的意思，舉例來説：

US introduced various sanctions against Russia for backing separatists in eastern Ukraine (烏克蘭). 如果不認得 separatist 這個字，先想一下跟哪個字很像？是不是 separate 分開，而後面的 ist 就是人而已，所以 separatist 就會了對吧！

制裁懂了之後，很不幸地，sanction 另一個意思是認可、批准、支持的意思，先看例句：

To start the project, we need official sanction from the top management.

是不是可以感受到批准的意思？可怕的是，這幾乎跟上面制裁的意思完全相反，這種情形下只能多念例句，把兩種幾乎相反的意思感覺出來，多念一下：US introduced various sanctions against Russia for backing separatists in 烏克蘭.

直接念中文的烏克蘭也沒關係。

To start the project, we need official sanction from the top management.

這樣才能同時對這兩個完全相反的意思有 FU，才容易記住。

ordinary vs common

再來是 ordinary 和 common，這兩個字中文意思基本上都是普通的、平常的，要搞懂其實很簡單念一下：ordinary people, ordinary books, common sense, common ground 就可以了。

forecast vs predict/prediction

還有 forecast, predict/prediction，要感覺出 forecast 很簡單，只要記住 "weather forecast" 就可以了。所謂的 weather forecast，就是利用一些氣象資料來 forecast 天氣。

而 predict/prediction 有點憑感覺、靠 guts 的意思來做 prediction，有點 fortune teller 的味道。

distinguish

distinguish 這個字不能只是背「區別、識別」，應該是念一下：
It's really tough to distinguish Jerry from his twin brother.
We need to distinguish between right and wrong.
Jeremy Lin can be easily distinguished by his height.
甚至是
Yo-Yo Ma（馬友友）is a distinguished musician.
不只是記住了不同的意思，也同時把這個字的用法學了起來。

attribute

接下來是 attribute 這個字，字典裡說了，「把……歸因於、把……歸咎於」，你說這會好背嗎？先念一下例句：

The coach attributes our success to the rigorous training we went through previously.

先來個簡化版本：

The coach attributes our success to the training we went through.

也就是：教練 attributes 我們的成功 to 我們受過的訓練，是不是對 attribute 有感覺了？還需要去硬背「把……歸因於、把……歸咎於」嗎？重要的還要把 attribute the success to the training 裡的 to 也順便記住了。

再來看看 rigorous training 能夠讓你成功的 training，當然是 rigorous（嚴厲的、嚴格的）training 對吧！

最後再把整句念一遍：

The coach attributes our success to the rigorous training we went through previously.

後面的 previously 是不是就直接唸出來了，根本不需要去考慮要用副詞還是形容詞。例句念個幾遍，不只是單字記住了，一些好的例句，還能同時讓你對文法也有了語感！這裡先順便提一下被動的用法：

Our success can be attributed to the rigorous training we went through previously.

comprise

許多學生在看到 comprise 這個字之後會立刻説「妥協」，請先看看以下的例句：

Under any circumstance, we cannot compromise our spotless/flawless reputation.

你覺得這裡的 compromise 會是妥協的意思嗎？應該更像犧牲或是放棄吧！但是你需要再去硬背 compromise 有犧牲、放棄的意思嗎？把上面的例句多念兩次不是更有效率！而且順便把 spotless 和 flawless 都感受出來了對吧！

再來念一下：

Under any circumstance, our spotless/flawless reputation cannot be comprised.

這時文法大師會出來説了：第一句 "We cannot compromise our reputation." 是主動，而第二句 "Our reputation cannot be comprised." 是被動！説實話，我倒覺得把這兩句多念幾遍，就會對這兩句直接有 FU，考文法的時候，根本不需要去 identify 哪句是主動，哪句是被動，直接把正確答案唸出來、選出來。（在此先預告一下，等會兒會專章講解，台灣學生最害怕、最搞不懂的主動、被動）

再來是：

Smoking will compromise your health.

這裡的 compromise 看來不是妥協也不能翻成犧牲、放棄，感覺上更像影響、危害對吧！對於 compromise 這個不難的單字，你真的需要去硬背這些不同的中文意思嗎？還是把上面的例句多念幾次，不只是記牢了 compromise 同時也對 circumstance, spotless, flawless 還有 reputation 都有 FU 了。更棒的是，連台灣學生一直搞不清楚的文法，主動、被動都學到了！What a **novel** idea. 先想一下這裡的 novel 絕不會是小說對吧！如果沒感覺，你先猜猜這裡的 novel idea 是好的 idea，還是壞的 idea？然後才去查字典，知道是新奇的、很棒的以後，再回來念幾次：What a novel idea. 是不是就記住了？

weather

先念一下例句：

Smaller animals may **weather** climate change better than bigger ones.

如果把 weather 當天氣解讀，首先天氣是名詞，而這裡的 weather 很明顯是動詞，絕對不對！整句話的意思是，小動物比起大動物更能 weather 氣候變遷（climate change）。先感覺一下這句話裡 weather 的意思，然後查字典，知道是忍受、度過的意思以後，再來把 "Smaller animals may weather climate change better than bigger ones." 多念兩次，還需要硬背 weather 這個當動詞時的意思嗎？説實話想想天氣這個名詞當動詞的意思會是？是不是熬過各種天氣的感覺？再把 weather climate change 多念幾次，FU 就有了！

再來幾個類似的例句練習：

Top managers need to exercise sound judgments in making critical decisions.

就會對這句裡的 exercise sound judgments, critical decisions 有 FU 了。

After the expansion is completed, the convention center can **accommodate** 500 persons.

就懂得 accommodate 這個字了。

A task **force** is formed for next year's business strategies.

這裡的 task force 就是所謂的專案小組。

As a Starbucks employee, you are entitled to free coffee. The full time staff is eligible for paid sick leave.

這兩句裡的 entitled to 和 eligible for 基本的用法和意思都一樣。

同義片語

再來介紹在中文裡同義的詞。

abide by / conform to / adhere to / comply with / obey, follow

這幾組片語的中文意義為「遵守、遵循」，記得多念幾次，以後不需要特別去管哪個是及物動詞，哪個不及物？也不需要特別去管要用 by, to 還是 with。

subject to

接下來念一下：

The price is **subject to** an additional 10% service charge.

意思就是價錢 is subject to10% 的服務費，這樣 "subject to" 就記得了。

persist in / persist with

The boss **persists in/with** keeping the money.

The boss **insists that we (should)** keep the money.

請將例句多念幾次及 "persist in"、"persist with" 還有 "insist that we (should)" 也多念幾次，在記單字的同時，順便可以記用法和句型，很棒吧！

舉了這麼多例子，目的就是希望你能擺脫以往，沒有效率硬背單字的習性，改成用文章、用例句輕鬆地記住單字和用法。記得在看文章或句子裡面，有單字不認識的時候，不要急著去查字典，先把句子多念幾次感覺一下這單字的意義，然後才去查字典，更重要的是查完字典後，不要硬背，把原來的句子多念幾遍，直接感受一下單字的意義，來瞭解進而記牢單字。最後，我想提醒你一下，在你念我在上面所給的單字例句時，在你在試著培養對單字的 FU 的時候，你的腦子有出現中文嗎？

在此我再把前面的一些例句寫出來：

- The car is so expensive I cannot afford it.
- You need to get proper training before taking on more challenging assignments.
- With the improving economy, companies are prospering.
- You need to first propose a proposal for your project.
- You need to stay out of the private property.
- There are two outstanding problems that need to be addressed immediately.
- The coach attributes our success to the rigorous training we went through previously.

- Under any circumstance, our spotless/flawless reputation cannot be comprised.
- What a novel idea.

是不是在你念句子的時候,腦子都沒中文!如果長一點的句子還是有中文,試著把句子按句意切成幾段,例如:

The coach attributes our success to the rigorous training we went through previously.

就可以切成:

The coach attributes our success / to the rigorous training / we went through previously.

是不是就可以一念就懂?這對你的閱讀速度真的很重要,只要你可以一念就懂,閱讀速度就會變快,後面我會繼續解釋這點。

文法

在這裡我先講一個很簡單的文法,所謂的反身代名詞,也就是以下這幾個字myself, ourselves, yourself, yourselves, himself, herself, themselves。我很討厭這些文法字眼,其實這些字眼對學生沒什麼幫助,只是讓學生覺得英文難而已,我用幾句簡單的例句說明:

John is talking to Jerry. John is talking to him.
John is talking to John.

很明顯地,前面的John跟後面的Jerry, him還有John,不是同一個人沒錯吧!問題是John可不可以跟他自己講話,也就是John自言自語嗎？當然可以！問題是怎麼說，後面那個人都不是 John ！於是英文只好出現 himself 這個字，"John is talking to himself." 來表示 John 跟自己說話，John 在自言自語。這個例子是不是讓你很清楚 myself, ourselves... 這些字的用法？根本不用去管那些無聊的文法專有名詞，甚至是國中學的，反身代名詞用在主詞跟受詞是同樣的人的時候。不要管那些專有名詞，那些中文解釋，直接把下面句子多念幾次就對了：

Mary calls herself a big sister.

We need to help ourselves.

She is looking at herself in the mirror.

They are blaming themselves for the mistakes.

是不是這樣就學會了！

接下來再講一個簡單的例子：

He finished the project himself.

其實只要說 He finished the project. 意思就到了，那為什麼要加上個 himself 變成 He finished the project himself. 說實話多念幾次，是不是就可以感覺到 He finished the project himself 只是用來強調他自己？這就是我常說的語感，文法規則從來就不應該是重點，多念幾次唸到有 FU，唸到有語感才是最重要的。

文法考題我很強調語感，尤其是所謂的詞性考題。先用一下前面的單字例句：

You need to get adequate/proper training before taking on more challenging assignments.

(adequate 比 proper 難一點順便記一下)

和另一個類似的例句：

You need to be adequately/properly trained before taking on more challenging assignment.

We provide various tour packages.

We provide a variety of tour packages.

裡面的 various 和 a variety of 就可以直接唸出來、選出來，不必去管哪個要用的是形容詞？哪個需要名詞？

再來是：

We highly value your sales and marketing experience.

If you experience any problem, please contact us.

你需要去記前一個 experience 是名詞，所以要用所有格 your，而後面的 experience 是動詞，所以要用主格 you 嗎？還是簡單的念一下：We value your experience 還有 If you experience any problem, please contact us. 就 OK 了。

再來一個：

Bad management is the major reason of the company's failure.

The company is badly managed.

把 bad management 和 badly managed 多念幾次，還需要去辨別哪個是名詞所以要用形容詞？哪個是動詞所以要用副詞？

再來一組例句：

This is a remarkable/dramatic improvement.

Touch screen technology improved remarkably/dramatically.

這兩句中的 remarkable improvement=improved remarkably
dramatic improvement=improved dramatically

還需要例子嗎？ rapid growth, growing rapidly 這種方式來解題是不是
又快又準？比起你去判斷是動詞還是名詞？該要用形容詞還是副詞？來得
簡單明瞭多了！而這些就是我強調的「反覆地念」所培養出來的語感。

小練習

接下來我舉幾個考生常會有疑問的題目來說明：

1. Visitors are required to register at the front desk ------
   entering the building. (A) in order to
   (B) upon
   (C) about
   (D) during

解答

(A) in order to 應該是接 in order to **enter** the building 而題目是
entering the building 所以錯
(C) about 句意就像 about something 也是錯
(D) during 一邊進辦公室一邊註冊，當然錯
答案是 (B) upon

如果你覺得是運氣好選對了，先把答案帶進原句唸個一、兩遍：

Guests are required to register at the front desk upon entering the building.

如果你選錯了，先把答案帶進原句唸個三、四遍：

Guests are required to register at the front desk upon entering the building.

這裡的 upon 有種一進去就要註冊的感覺，對吧！

或許你會覺得奇怪，為什麼有原句唸個一、兩遍和原句唸個三、四遍？其實很簡單，當你是運氣好選對了，多多少少意味著，你有些正確的語感，只是語感不夠強烈而已，所以把原句唸個一兩遍來加強你的語感。

如果你選錯了，表示你對這題的語感根本就是錯的，為了把錯誤的語感改回來，勢必要多唸個好幾遍才行。只有多唸才能去除你原先錯誤的感覺，進而培養你的正確語感。還有請注意一點，這不是交作業，匆匆忙忙地唸五遍不如慢慢地唸兩遍，慢慢唸一邊唸、一邊體會一下這個句子，就像你享受美食，細嚼慢嚥才能體會的到食物裡的芳香。

再來一題：

2. - - - - - - the committee approves the renovation project for the historical building located in downtown area will depend on the final voting result of its members.

(A) If
(B) Whether
(C) Although
(D) Until

解答

選出來了嗎？這題的答案是 (B) Whether。先把這句話的句型解釋一下，可以簡化成

It will depend on the final voting results.

也 就 是 説 "Whether the committee approves the renovation project for the historical building located in downtown area" 這麼一整串的字，其實可以用 It 取代！還有前面這一整串：Whether the committee approves the renovation project for the historical building located in downtown area 其 實 只 是：Whether the committee approves the renovation project ~~for the historical building located in downtown area~~ 後面被我刪掉的部分只是 project 的細節。所以整句只是：（橘色字請加框）

Whether the committee approves the renovation project (or not) for the historical building located in downtown area will depend on the final voting result of its members.

句子裡面的（or not）是我加上去的，因為 whether.... or not 是台灣一般所教的句型，到這裡你應該可以看懂這句話，也知道為什麼答案是 (B) Whether 了。

但是接下來的可能還更重要，因為我要解釋為什麼其他答案是錯的，而且要告訴你什麼情況下，這些答案才會對。先解釋一下 if，if 這個字所帶的句型其實很簡單，就是 if A is true, B is ture. 也就是説 if A 成立, B 也成立。如果答案要變成 (A) 題目就要改成

If the committee approves the renovation project for the

historical building located in downtown area , the construction will begin next month.

再來說到語感，當你念到 If the committee approves the renovation project, 是不是就感到如果條件成立，那當然這句話只講了一半還沒講完，後面才是重點的感覺對吧！把整句：

If the committee approves the renovation project for the historical building located in downtown area , the construction will begin next month.

唸完語意才完整了。如果你對這句話還不是那麼有 FU，慢慢的把這句話念個兩遍應該就 OK 了。

接下來講講 although，這個字用法上其實跟 if 相差不大，也是 Although A, B. 就是 although A 發生了，B 還是要完成。

舉個例子：although 馬上要下雨，我們還是要去露營。
Although it is going to rain, we will still go camping.
這樣就懂了對吧！

最後是最簡單的 until，不過我說簡單，其實不見得，先講講大家都學過的 not... until，網路上查查看，多半是把 not... until 解釋成：直到……才。說實話就是這個解釋讓大家英文學的亂七八糟！不相信嗎？聽聽我的說法。

先用個簡單的例句：

He didn't come home until 9.

按照上面的說法（直到……才），這句的意思是：他直到九點才回家。看到問題了嗎？首先你得從句子後面開始 until 9 調到前面變成直到九點，這不打緊，接下來要把前面的 he didn't come 否定變肯定，改成他才來，先前後對調，然後否定變肯定，歷經萬難的才把這句很簡單的 "He didn't come until 9."，變成「直到九點他才來」，好大的工程啊！

其實這句話真的很簡單，先念 "He didn't come"，一念就懂沒問題吧！再來念 "until 9"，再合起來念一次，是不是 he didn't come 一直都是 didn't come，until 9（他才 come），也就一下就感覺到 He didn't come until 9 就是：他九點到！

你覺得是一念就直接懂，還是要前後顛倒，然後再否定變肯定的先翻成中文才懂比較好？好了，到這裡懂了 until 的意思和用法，回到原題目，如果答案是 until 那題目應該改成：

Until the committee approves the renovation project for the historical building located in downtown area , we will not start the project.

簡單地說原句應該是：We will not start the project until it is approved by the committee. 為了強調 until 這部分，把它調到句子最前面而已。

接下來看看 receive 和 arrive 的用法差別，請念以下的例句：

The application form must be received by the end of the week.

The application form must arrive by the end of the week.
記得要一念就懂，你可沒時間去管什麼主動還是被動。

不管是文法或是閱讀考題，最重要的技巧就是：把句子簡化。只要你能把句子簡化，許多考題立刻變得很簡單。

3. The cost of repairing the damage caused by the severe thunderstorm last week ------- to be more than 100,000 dollars.

(A) is expecting

(B) expected

(C) is expected

(D) expects

解答

這句的架構其實很簡單，只是：The cost ~~of repairing the damage caused by the severe thunderstorm last week~~ ------- to be more than 100,000 dollars. 看出這點加上正確的語感，立刻可以選出 (C) is expected 才是正確答案。或許有人會問了，為什麼？簡單的說，不管是 is expecting, expected 或是 expects 基本上都是 someone is expecting something, someone expected something 還有 someone expects something（也就是所謂的主動形式），跟空格後面的 to be more than 根本不符合，你可以先把答案帶進去先念個幾遍：The cost is expected to be more than 100,000 dollars. 看出來了嗎？正是標準的被動！如果你對主動、被動觀念不是很清楚，別急，再強調一次等一下我會專題解釋，在此先念一下：

The cost is expected to be more than 100,000 dollars.

The government expects the cost to be more than 100,000 dollars.

"The government expects the cost" 基本上就是我前面說的 someone expects something。

時態

1. The letter we received last week - - - - - - from the travel agent.
   (A) is coming (B) came
   (C) comes (D) will come

解答

這句其實只是 The letter - - - - - - from the travel agent. 被去掉的 we received last week 只是用來描述這封 letter，既然這封 letter 是 last week 收到的。當然答案是 came。

2. Mary - - - - - - - four years working for AAA Inc., where she worked as Technical Writer.
   (A) spent (B) spends
   (C) cost (D) costs

解答

首先既然是 Mary 就可以把 (C) 和 (D) 跟 cost 有關的答案先刪掉，（還記得我說的 I spend, it costs 嗎？），再來後面的 where she **worked** as Technical Writer，所以答案是 (A) spent，簡單吧！

3. By the time the report about the internet marketing trend ------- up on the newspaper, the information was already outdated.

(A) shows   (B) showed

(C) is showing   (D) will show

解答

如果對 by the time 沒什麼 FU，我先給個中文例句：By the time 你到電影院，電影早開演了。這樣就有 FU 了吧！既然後面的 the information **was** outdated 當然前面要是 (B) showed，接下來先把答案帶進去原句，然後念個一兩遍：

By the time the report │about the internet marketing trend│ **showed** up on the newspaper, the information **was** already outdated.

注意到沒？中間的 about the internet marketing trend 是可以完全省略而不影響句子的架構。

單字的文法、用法

1. ------- objections coming from the local residents, the mayor pushes on with his economically ambitious but environmentally troublesome construction project.

(A) Despite   (B) With

(C) Although   (D) Because

解答

這題一樣是語感最重要，還記得最前面所講的：despite low income growth, 中國是贏家。所以這題是 (A) Despite objections coming from the local residents, the mayor pushes on with his economically ambitious but environmentally troublesome construction project.

這題也可以作為一個用來強調硬背單字不是辦法，例句才是王道的例子。假設你硬背單字，先查一下字典 despite 的意思是：儘管、任憑，although 的意思是：雖然、儘管，這兩個意思有任何不同嗎？當然這時文法大師又出來說了：despite 是介系詞而 although 是連接詞，好有道理喔！不過問題來了，難道我在背單字的時候，除了中文意思以外還要背詞性？背中文意思都搞死學生了還得背詞性！或許有人說，反正把中文意思和詞性硬背下來就可以了，其實這下問題更大了，我舉個例子，那 however 呢？既可以當副詞還可以當連接詞，那我要怎麼背！回到我一直強調的觀點，「例句的重要性」，將 "despite low income growth, despite the high temperature, despite the objections" 念個幾遍你就知道 despite 要直接名詞，不可以接一句話。是不是簡單多了？

在這裡我順便講一下 (B) With 這個答案，這個答案意思不對，如果題目改成：**With** objections coming from the local residents, the mayor temporarily **halts** his economically ambitious but environmentally troublesome construction project. 有人反對，當然 mayor 就得 temporarily halts his project. 不是嗎？

主動與被動

主動與被動永遠是台灣人的致命傷，在解釋為什麼台灣人老是學不好主動、被動之前，我先解釋一下英文裡所謂的被動文法。其實英文的被動文法真的很簡單，只有兩個簡單的規則，你不信嗎？耐著心看下去。

首先當然要先講一下主動：也就是大家應該看過的 S + V + O，所謂的主詞加動詞加受詞，講了半天不如用一個例句解釋：

The story touches me.

（這裡我要強調一下，在你唸這個例句時，記得一定要把 touches 後面要加的尾音：es 輕輕地唸出來，因為這是大家在國一就學到的：現在式主詞第三人稱單數，動詞要加 s，這裡是變成要加 es，把 The story touch**es** me. 多念幾次，語感出來以後，下次唸到第三人稱現在式，你的腦子就會自然而然的加 s 了）順便提一下，可不要把 touch 解釋成接觸喔！這裡的 touch 就算真的是 touch 接觸，説的也是 touch 到我的心，既然 touch 到心坎裡了，當然就是感動了，所以整句的架構就是：the story 主詞，touch 動詞，而 me 當然就是受詞了。到這裡沒問題吧！

再來要講主題也就是被動了，既然是被動當然就是把後面的受詞 me 調到前面去當主詞，當然後面就要接動詞，以英文來説，這就有個小問題了，如果這個動詞形式上不做任何變更，哪怎麼會知道前面的主詞其實是受詞呢？所以被動的文法規則就來了，

被動的文法規則一：先把原來的動詞改用過去分詞，然後在它的前面加上個 be 動詞，所以句子就變成：S + be 動詞 + Vpp（過去分詞）。

也就是說當你看到 be 動詞加過去分詞的時候，前面的主詞就是受詞，也就是所謂的被動！看到這裡懂了嗎？

如果有些不清楚，我不怪你，用一堆中文來解釋英文文法，不如看以下的例句。先把前面的例句再看一下：

The story touches me.

先把 me 掉到前面當主詞，也就變成 I 了，接下來 touch 變成 touched 有就是加 ed 變過去分詞，前面的 be 動詞因為是 I，當然就是 am，所以句子就成為：

I am touched (by the story).

看完例句後是不是就清楚了？再看一次兩個句子間的不同：The story touches me. I am touched (by the story). 這就是被動的第一個文法規則：動詞形式是 be 動詞 + 過去分詞，就這麼簡單！

接下來應該有人會問了，那時態呢？英文句子有時態，被動當然也有。讓我們先看看被動的基本句型：主詞 + be 動詞 + 過去分詞，如果在時態上要有所變動，過去分詞是不可能改的，所以要表現出時態，只有一個地方了，沒錯！就是 be 動詞。所以

被動的文法規則二就是：所有時態用 be 動詞表示！

說了這麼多，你或許還不是很清楚，接下來請看例句，就可以輕鬆的明白了。

先看：

I am touched by the story.

如果要改成過去式，**touched** 不能改，只能改 be 動詞，在這裡就是

am，改成 was 就可以了，所以就是：I was touched by the story. 要改成未來式，同樣的 touched 不能動，所以就在 am 前面先加 will 再把 am 改成原形，就變成：

You will be touched by the story.

（我把 I 改成 you 只是因為這樣句意比較合理，You will be touched. 比 I will be touched 更合理一點。）

接下來講一些複雜一點的，先來個現在完成式好了，同樣的保留 touched 然後把這句裡的 be 動詞 am 前面先加 have 或是 has，既然是 I 當然就是 have，在來把 am 變成過去分詞也就是 been 所以句子就變成了：I have been touched by the story. 再看現在進行式，規則很簡單：動詞前面加個 be 動詞然後動詞本身加 ing。同樣的保留 touched，從 am 著手，am 前面先加 be 動詞，既然是 I 也就要加 am，然後原先的動詞 am 加 ing 變成 being，所以句子就變成：

I am being touched by the story.

如果是 you 當然句子就是：

You are being touched by the story.

簡單吧！其實說句真的，把以下的例句多念幾遍，什麼時態都會了。

I am touched by the story.

I was touched by the story.

You will be touched by the story.

I have been touched by the story.

I am being touched by the story.

最後，我再把英文裡被動文法的兩個基本規則重述一遍：

1. 把原句的動詞改成過去分詞，然後在前面加個 be 動詞。

2. 句子的所有時態，用 be 動詞表示。

如果覺得這樣還是麻煩，我簡單的用一句話把被動文法講完：英文的被動就是把動詞改成過去分詞，然後在前面加上 be 動詞，而英文裡的時態就以 be 動詞來表達。就這麼一句話沒錯！如果你還有任何疑問，請把上面的五個例句多念幾遍，應該就懂了。

好了，英文的被動文法講完了，也教過了，沒問題了吧！這下或許會有人說了：不可能！被動文法如果這麼簡單，為什麼大家會搞不懂、學不好？其實被動學不會，問題不在英文，在中文！如果你不相信，請看我的解釋。我先舉個最簡單的例子：你車停哪？我車停在停車場。這個回答：我車停在停車場。簡單吧！問題是當你要把這句話寫成英文的時候，老師就說了：車不會自己停，車一定是被停下來的，所以英文要寫成：

My car was parked in the parking lot.

如果這個例子還不更清楚請看下一句：

His success was expected.

這句話應該一看就懂吧！接下來請你回答一個問題：把這句話翻成中文，沒問題吧。試試看，要怎麼用中文表達這句很簡單的英文。卡住了吧，怎麼寫都不對是不是？請看看我的幾個翻譯：『他的成功早在預料之中。』、『我們早就料到他會成功。』、『他會成功早就看的出來。』注意到沒？怎麼翻都是主動，重點是只要你按句意翻成被動，整句中文念起來都怪怪的。

舉例來說，他的成功早就被（我們）預料到了。你覺得跟：他的成功早在（我們的）預料之中。哪句唸起來比較像中文？其實在中文裡，預料、預期、猜到基本上都是用主動形式表達，不管你怎麼講，就是很少用被動。以前面停車的例子來看，你還可以感覺出來，車不會自己停，一定是被停。以這幾個預料、預期、猜到來說，你會感覺出來是，誰預期誰、還是誰被誰預期？再舉個例子：朋友生病了，（他）需要照顧。朋友住院了，我需要照顧他。第一句按文法而言應該是他需要被照顧吧，可是中文只要說他需要照顧就可以了，而第二句的我需要照顧他，這個受詞『他』可不能省啊！有了受詞

『他』，這句就是主動，沒有受詞『他』，這句就成了被動。主動、被動的分別竟然是看有沒有受詞！有受詞就是主動，沒受詞就是被動。

還要更極端的例子嗎？請告訴我，太陽曬屁股和屁股曬太陽，一樣不一樣？一時之間沒有idea？每次在上課中我都會問這個問題，多數人會直覺地說不一樣！但是請你看以下的句子：太陽都曬屁股了，還不起床！屁股都曬太陽了，還不起床！能不能告訴我，為什麼太陽曬屁股等於屁股曬太陽？？明明把主詞和受詞對調了，結果句意卻完全一樣！！為什麼狗咬人不等於人咬狗，而太陽曬屁股卻等於屁股曬太陽！在教文法的時候，我時常開玩笑的說，全世界的語文裡面，大概只有中文會有這種，主詞（太陽）和受詞（屁股）對調以後，竟然意思會完全一樣的文法！這下你應該了解，大家在學英文被動文法上面會出問題，竟然是因為我們的母語中文！只要你在學英文的時候，用中文去想，我保證你在學英文被動文法時，就會出問題！

再回到原先的例子 "His success was expected.",這句話其實很簡單,你可能一看就懂,問題就出在你要把它翻成中文的時候,一定會卡住!我常跟學生講,既然看懂了,幹嘛翻中文!翻成中文只是找自己麻煩而已!這正是我在前面會說『同樣的在考新多益閱讀單元時,「腦子裡一樣的不能出現中文!」,不管你寫的是單字題目、文法問題還是閱讀測驗,腦子裡不能出現中文!』

尤其是閱讀測驗,念文章的時候腦子出現中文,只會把你的閱讀速度打慢下來,新多益閱讀原本時間就不夠,腦子出現中文,只會讓你看文章和回答題目時更慢、更浪費時間。

接下來我再舉幾個主動、被動的例句來做文法說明。先看一下例句:
It's amazing. / I am amazed. / To my amazement.
It's boring. / I am bored.
It's embarrassing. / I am embarrassed. / To my embarrassment.

不要小看上面的例句,在新多益考試甚至在日常生活這樣的句型其實很常見。但是也常有人弄錯。先讓你感覺一下:既然是 It's amazing. You are amazing. 沒問題吧!如果我說:I am amazing. 你覺得可不可以?有些學生說不可以,其實這是文化的關係,東方人講究謙虛,重群體,所以有些人會覺得 I am amazing. 太過臭屁,感覺不好,而西方人比較強調個人,I am amazing. 有何不可?到這裡應該沒問題吧!

接下來的 It's boring. 所以 You are boring. 沒問題吧,但是,"I am boring." 呢? It's boring. You are boring. 你真的很無聊、你是個無

聊人，看到這裡，你說你會不會這麼講自己 I am boring. ？應該不會這麼説吧！但是現實生活裡，卻偶而會聽到有人講 "I am boring." 對吧。接下來我再講回中文。先想一下，You are boring. 翻成中文是：你很無聊，而 I am bored. 翻成中文是：我很無聊。注意到沒？你很無聊裡的『很無聊』，跟我很無聊裡的『很無聊』意思差很多，甚至完全相反！你應該從來沒想過在中文裡面，同樣的字詞卻會因為主詞是你還是我，而有完全不同的意思！其實這也是有人會把我很無聊講成 I am boring. 就是因為英文沒學好再加上愛現英文。回到主題，同樣的句子絕對符合文法的 I am amazing. 和 I am boring. 卻有這麼大的差別！這就是語感的重要性，當你有語感了你最多只會說：I am amazing. 絕不會説：I am boring. 講到這裡我又想説一下文法。看看："It's frightening. I am frightened." 是不是一念就懂？你需不需要先去分辨哪一個是主動哪一個是被動？

有些人説了英文要搞懂文法以後才能了解句意，如果真是這樣的話，那大家聽力根本不用考了，題目是一句接一句的講出來，考生哪有時間先去分辨時態？哪句是主動哪句是被動？聽力沒有什麼祕訣，直接聽懂就對了。從這個簡單的例子就可以知道，不管聽力還是閱讀，語感才是最重要的，有了語感，考試才會輕鬆愉快。新多益閱讀原先時間就不太夠，閱讀測驗之時，大家卻還都用中文去試著了解英文句子，時間會夠才怪！

我再舉個例子説明，以下的例句每句都值得你多念幾次把語感培養起來。先講講很多學生都搞不清楚的兩個字 rise 和 raise，先看看字典是怎麼説的。

rise：上升、上漲、升高

raise：舉起、抬起、提升

從中文意思來看，相差不大，這也是很多學生搞不清楚這兩個字之間的差異的最大原因，因為多數學生都是硬背單字，因為中文的意思相差不大，自然搞不清楚了。我喜歡用例句解釋，這兩個字也不例外，請先看例句：

The prices are rising.

The prices are raised.

乍看之下，這兩個字差別還真的有限。這時文法大師又來了，說第一句是主動，而第二句是被動，但是這兩個字的差異是什麼？單只是主動或是被動，還是沒有太大的感覺吧！

接下來請看我的解釋：先說 rise，簡單的講：sunrise, sunset：日出和日落，這兩個字沒問題吧！也就是說黎明時刻一到 the Sun 自然的就 rises，黃昏時間一來 the Sun 自然就 sets，沒問題吧？

再來是 raise，我最常用這個例句：raise the white flag 意思是？沒錯就是舉白旗，隱含的意思就是一定有人舉。這麼解釋下來，你應該對這兩個字有 FU 了吧！回到原先的兩個例句："The prices are rising. The prices are raised." 先看第一句，是不是感覺到這句話只是在強調價格上漲了，至於為什麼會漲？是誰讓價格漲的？I really don't care.

至於第二句就隱含了價格會漲是有原因的，所以 "The prices are raised."，對吧！如果以寫文章來說，當作者一開始寫了 The prices are rising. 你覺得作者接下來會寫什麼？當然是這些 rising prices 會有什麼影響？舉例來說，Inflation is coming. 沒錯吧！如果作者一開始寫的是：The prices are raised. 是不是感覺上接下來會寫為什麼 The prices are raised. 是供需失調？還是原物料上漲？在來把這兩句念一下：The prices are rising. The prices are raised. 是不是就有 FU 了？更棒的是，腦子裡根本不用去辨別哪句是主動？哪句是被動？

再講一個許多新多益考生會有疑問的句型，同樣的先看例句（例句裡面的三個字 commit, devote 還有 dedicate 在這句型之下，不只是用法相同，連意思都相近，我的建議是每次用其中一個字來念例句，分三次把這三個字念完）：

I commit/devote/dedicate myself to the project.
I am committed/devoted/dedicated to the project.

這時文法大師又來了，解釋說：看到沒？第一句是主動，而第二句是被動。你看第一句裡的受詞 myself 在第二句變成了主詞 I，所以後面的動詞要加 ed 而且前面要加 be 動詞 am，這麼一解釋，讓這簡單的兩句話變得好有學問，讓學生聽的點頭如搗蒜，霎時覺得這老師太厲害了，不過問題是，就算搞懂了哪個是主動，哪個是被動？（更何況，兩句的主詞都是 I），真的對學生有幫助嗎？

說實話，句子解釋的有沒有學問根本不要緊，重點還是：你念完這兩句後有 FU 嗎？先念第一句，在此我簡單的用 commit 做例子：

I commit myself to the project.

這句很容易了解，因為句子的架構跟中文用法很像，就是我把我自己奉獻給了這個計畫，很簡單。念個一次，最多兩次應該就會有 FU 了。順道提一下，如果不認識 commit 這個字，念個兩次，對這個字就有感覺了，就像認識了剛搬進來的隔壁鄰居一樣，就這麼記住了，沒錯吧！

接下來念第二句：

I am committed to the project.

多念個兩遍，也就了解這句話了。再來，請你把這句話翻譯成中文，又卡住了吧！我全心全意地做這個計畫，我- - - - -這個計畫，底線裡的內容不管你用什麼中文字去填，基本上都是被主動形式，因為只要是被動語氣，就不像中文。這再次證明，英文句子念過以後懂了就好，千萬不要做翻譯，把句子翻譯成中文只會卡死自己。既然念過後懂了，請你把這兩句再念個幾遍：

I commit myself to the project.

I am committed to the project.

我會叫你再多念幾遍是有原因的，這幾次唸下來以後，念念這句："I am committing..." 是不是就感覺後面要接個 something 這句話才完全，舉例來説：

I am committing my time.

I am committing most of my energy.

I am committing myself.

不只如此，你還會覺得接下來要接個 to some other thing，也就是：

I am committing my time to charity work.

I am committing most of my energy to the final exam.

I am committing myself to you.

再看第二個例句，當你念到：I am committed 的時候，自然而然的就感覺立刻要接 to something 對吧！舉例而言：

I am committed to our relationship.

I am committed to charity work.

I am committed to working out the solution.

注意到最後一句了嗎？因為你的語感是 I am committed to something 自然而然的就會接上 I am committed to working out the solution. 根本不用去想 committed to 裡面的 "to"，其實是介系詞所以 work 要加 ing 變成 I am committed to working out the solution. 這下你應該了解把例句念到有 FU 的重要性了吧！

最後我再用另外兩句來做這部分的總結：

I have something embarrassing to admit.

I am embarrassed to admit that...

其實這兩句話是前面 It's embarrassing, I am embarrassed, to my embarrassment, 的延伸，你也可以簡單的只念：something embarrassing 還有 I am embarrassed. 如果新多益考試出現了這類的考題，你會需要去判斷哪個主動哪個被動？所以哪個要用 ing 哪個要加 ed 嗎？是不是直接把答案念一念，把最順口的選出來就對了。再給個例子，把以下兩句多念幾遍：

improve customer satisfaction

keep customers satisfied。

關係代名詞

關係代名詞其實很簡單，只是一種用關係代名詞，把兩個句子合起來變成一個句子的方法。請看以下的例子：

The boy is wearing a hat.

The boy is my brother.

變成：The boy **who** is wearing a hat is my brother. 是不是很簡單？

注意一下上面兩句都有 the boy，而下面的一句只是用 who 代替了第一句裡的 the boy 就把兩句話合起來變一句了。由此可見，所謂的關係代名詞只是用一個代名詞（舉例來說：who, which）取代了那個共同的名詞，然後用這個關係代名詞把兩句變成一句話。請看前面的例句，兩句裡面都有個 boy，把第二句裡的 the boy 用 who 取代再加到第一句裡的 boy 後面，就變成：

The boy who is wearing a hat is my brother.

再看一個例子：

This is my neighbor's dog.

The dog barks all night.

兩句裡面都有 dog，把第二句裡的 dog 用 which 取代再接到第一句裡的 dog 後面，就變成：This is my neighbor's dog which barks all night.

接下來，先講一個新多益會考的基本文法，也是要看到關代的時候，第一個要知道的關鍵，認出這個關代取代的是哪個名詞，這點其實很簡單，超過一半以上就是前面的那個名詞。舉例來說：

We need a secretary who speaks fluent English.

We need engineers who have marketing knowledge.

第一個的 who 代替的就是前面的 secretary，而第二個的 who 代替的正是前面的 engineers。

接下來就是新多益測驗中會考的重點了，關代後面的動詞就根據它所取代的名詞來決定。以第一個例子來說，who 取代的是 a secretary 所以就是：who (the secretary) speaks English，而第二個句子 who 取代的是 engineers 所以就是：who (engineers) have marketing knowledge。

說實話，你會不會覺得看了半天的中文文法解釋，不如看例句！我把這兩句例句再寫一次：

We need a secretary **who (the secretary)** speaks fluent English.

We need engineers **who (engineers)** have marketing knowledge.

接下來講一些有點變化的例子，請先看一組例句：

We need an engineer.

The engineer's expertise is web design.

前面一句是 an engineer 而後面的是 engineer's expertise，跟前面的例子有些不同，不過也很簡單，有 I/you/he/she 以及 my/your/his/her，所以 who 就成了 whose，這兩句也就變成：

We need an engineer **whose** expertise is web design.

簡單吧！

再來一組例句：

He is the new student. I met him yesterday.

這個更簡單了，有 I/you/he/she 以及 me/you/him/her 所以 who 就變成 whom，把這兩句話合起來就變成：

He is the new student **whom** I met yesterday.

再來，講一個很多人覺得很難搞懂，考試也常選錯的關代文法，更是許多文法書列出一堆規則，學生卻還是有問題的考題：什麼時候只能用 who/which 不能用 that，什麼時候只能用 that 卻不能用 who/which？碰到這種考題，記得兩個要點就可以了。第一句子看上去該用 who 或是 which，而答案卻同時有 who/which 和 that 優先選 who/which，除非有以下的狀況：

● the only person that,

● the second thing that,

● the most important job that,

● every employee that,

● the same person that

在這類的情形下選 that，我的建議是把上列 5 項多念幾次就對了，只要考題不是這類的形式，就優先選 who/which。至於其他文法書裡會特別講到的限定和非限定用法，以把文章看懂的觀點而言，跟懂不懂限定／非限定，沒什麼太大的關係，就算文法真考了限定／非限定用法，用我剛剛說的來挑答案就不會錯了。

再來就要講一下 what 和 where 了。先看一些關於 what 的例句：

This is not the toy which I ordered. = This is not what I ordered.

Money would tempt/seduce us to do things which we shouldn't do. = Money would tempt/seduce us to do what we shouldn't do.

再來念幾個 what 的例句：

What you know is not the truth.

He forgot what I said previously.

This is exactly what we need.

Can you understand what he is talking about?

這樣對 what 就會有 FU 了。

再來講 where，其實 where 很簡單，用來代替一個地方而已。請看例句：

This is the park where we first met. This is the book where you can find the data.

多念幾次就可以了。

最後講一個更多人沒搞懂，帶有介系詞的關係代名詞。這只在兩種強況下會發生，我先舉幾個第一種情況的例句：

The position **for** which you applied is already filled. John is the person **on** whom we can really depend.

The is the house **in** which we lived.

注意一下，這裡的介系詞其實是：applied for, depend on, live in, 説實話跟關代沒什麼太大關係。

所以第一類其實是跟著動詞來的。（這類跟著動詞的關代，新多益考的機會稍稍大一點。）同樣的，另一種情形也請你先看例句：

I need a paper **on** which I can draw a sketch.

This is the book **in** which you can find the data.

（還記得前面的：This is the book where you can find the data. 嗎？）這種情形比先前的例子要稍微難一點，不過只要搞懂關代的基本用法就簡單了，那就是本節最前面所講的『關係代名詞只是用一個代名詞取代了那個共同的名詞，然後用這個關係代名詞把兩句變成一句話。』倒推回來，將一句話，拆回成原先的兩句就可以看懂了。以第一句為例，可以拆成：

I need a paper.

I can draw a sketch **on the paper**.

而第二句可以拆成：

This is the book.

You can find the data **in the book**.

所以句子裡面的 on 和 in 其實是跟原先的句子架構有關。如果題目裡要你選介系詞，把題目拆成兩句話就可以輕鬆地選出正確答案了。不過這類選介系詞的題目，新多益不常考，反而是英檢出的機會比較大。

最後，如果你對 where 和 which 還有疑問，請再把以下兩個例句多念兩遍。

This is the book **where** you can find the data.

This is the book **in which** you can find the data.

假設語氣

在講許多學生都搞不清楚的假設語氣之前，先請大家看一句中文：『如果你認真一點，期末考英文就會過了。』看過以後，我想先問大家一個問題，期末考到底考了沒？我在課堂中問了幾位學生，有人說考過了，有人說還沒，其實很簡單加幾個字就知道了。「如果你認真一點， 上學期的 期末考英文就會過了。」；「如果你認真一點， 下禮拜的 期末考英文就會過了。」所以正確的答案是：不知道。這是中文，需要加上個時間點，你才會知道期末考考過了沒有。以英文而言，就沒這個問題了。

這也就談到了這個主題，所謂的假設語氣。先看個簡單的例句：

If you had worked harder, you would have passed the English test.

一看就知道，沒認真念書，當掉了，這就是假設語氣！前面講過，if 這個連接詞其實很簡單，它只是把一整句話切成兩段，有 if 的一段和沒有 if 的另一段，在這裡我就先解釋有 if 的這一段。If you had worked harder 基本結構就是 "if someone had done something,"，所以重點在 had done，好玩的是，多念個幾遍：if you had done something, if you had done something, if you had done something，自然而然，你就會感覺到字裡行間那個該念書沒念書、該努力沒努力、該寫沒寫、該做沒做的 FU。

而沒有 if 的那一段呢，基本上就是：would have/ should have/ could have，偶而加上 might have，所以上面例句的後半段也可以寫成：you could have passed the test，you should have passed the test 或是 you might have passed the test，通通可以，接下來多念幾次：

would have / should have / could have / might have

是不是就感覺到那個該過沒過、該贏沒贏、該得沒得的 FU，如果 FU 還不夠強，請你再念一下：

We would have won the game.（該贏沒贏）

He could have passed the test.（該過沒過）

You should have learned the lesson.（該學沒學）

有人或許會問那 would have/ should have/ could have/ might have 這幾個字之間有什麼不同？其實很簡單，你自己多念幾次，自然能感覺出這幾個字之間的不同，自然地對這幾個字會有 FU，不信的話，再念個幾遍，感覺一下，抓一下那個 FU。而第一個所謂的與過去事實相反的假設，也就在這個簡單的例句：

If you had worked harder, you would have passed the English test.

接下來講一個新多益實際會考的變化句型，其實不難，先看例句：

Had you worked harder, you would have passed the test.

其實只是把 had 調到句首去掉 if 而已，感覺上這還比較常出現，所以值得把這句多念幾次。

講解完了最常見的與過去事實相反的假設後該講剩下的一個所謂的與現在事實相反。同樣的先看例句：

If I were you, I would help them.

中文很簡單：「如果我是你，我就會幫他們。」英文可不太一樣，因為我永遠不會是你，所以就是不可能的假設，所以一定要用 were 不可以用

was，而這個 were 就是這裡最重要也是必須要知道的地方，不管什麼主詞，就是一定要用 were。

再舉個例子：

If dad were here, he would help us solve the problem.

看了這兩個例句，剩下的就簡單了。例如：

If I knew her, I would talk to her.

（是不是可以感覺到句意裡隱含著：I don't know her.）

If I had enough money, I would buy the house.

（感覺就是 I don't have enough money.）

把上面幾個例句多念幾次，就會對所謂的與現在事實相反的情況有 FU 了。

簡單的說，假設語氣用以下兩個例句就可以解釋清楚了。

If you **had worked** harder, you **should/would/could have** passed the English test. 還有 If I **were** you, I **would** help them. 至於其他的，在我看來，只是簡單的 if 句子而已。舉例來說：

If it rains tomorrow, we will cancel the picnic.

前面只是說個假如的狀況，假如前者（it rains）發生了，後者（cancel the picnic）就發生了。

在這裡我要特別提出一個新多益會考的題目，請先看例句：

If it should rain, I'll stay home and watch TV.

意思一樣：如果下雨，我就待在家裡看電視。同樣的 should 也可以調到句首變成：

Should it rain, I'll stay home.

而且後面的 should it rain 反而比較常考出來。

 ## 介系詞

介系詞可說是英文裡最難的文法，因為沒什麼道理可言，不過這裡有個好消息給你，新多益不會去考刁鑽艱澀的介系詞，要考也是常見常用到的介系詞，如果你對介系詞的考題有任何疑惑，我只有一句話給你：把答案帶到題目裡面，念個三、五遍，念到有 FU 就對了！如果對以下表格中所列出的不是很熟悉，就多念幾遍吧。

on the first floor	at all cost
on sale	at all times
on purpose	in 10 minutes
on schedule	over an hour
at the door	by means of
at the beginning	through the summer
at one's (your) disposal	across the river
at one's (your) expense	along the street
in July	in good shape
in the morning	in a rush
at noon	in short supply
in the evening	in charge of
at night	according to
on Monday	famous for

at the moment	angry at (with)
by himself	afraid of
on his own	believe in
at one's (your) convenience	capable of
on behalf of	familiar with
on the waiting list	interested in
under the new policy	worry about
beyond our control	tired of
on his way to Taiwan	apologize for
in a timely manner	belong to
think about	

念幾句完整的句子：

Send the report by Friday.

I'll be back in 30 minutes.

Finish the project within a week.

Choose two candidates among those applicants.

話說回來，老話一句，把你寫錯的題目，把正確答案帶回去原題，念個三、五遍就對了。

最後，我加上一些比較零散但卻重要的文法題目給大家。

It is important/essential/imperative/vital that we (MUST/ SHOULD) do something.

先簡單地把以下兩句念個幾遍：

It's important that we (must) finish the project on time.

It's essential that you (must) arrive the airport by 10.

記得要把括號裡的 must 一起念出來，因為只有把 must 念出來才知道原先有個 must 被省略掉了，所以後面要用原形！我對學生都會建議把這幾句多念幾遍：

It's important that we must...

It's essential that you must...

It's imperative that we must...

It's vital that we must...

以後看到考題自然而然的腦海裡就會帶出個 must 也就知道要接動詞原形了。同樣的句型還有：

The manager suggested/insisted/demanded/recommended that we (MUST/SHOULD) do something.

同樣的把以下的句型多念幾遍。

suggest that we must

insist that you must

demand that we must

recommend that you must

如果你覺得 should 比較順口當然可以用 should 來念。這兩類的題目，新多益偶而會考，要記得加原形動詞唯一的方法，就是前面多念個 must 或是 should，只有念多了、念順了這種題目才有辦法答對。

接下來請讀者先做以下的題目,然後對答案,如果你答對了恭喜你,答錯了,記得先把答案帶進去題目,多念幾遍,有任何疑問看我後面的解釋。如果覺得題目太少,還不夠過癮,放心本書後面有份完整的模考試題給你練習。

1. Visitors are ------- allowed to enter the R&D building for security reasons.
   (A) ever
   (B) never
   (C) rare
   (D) often

2. Lenovo has ------ in talks with IBM to purchase its personal computer division.
   (A) involved
   (B) fabricated
   (C) engaged
   (D) arranged

3. The research study focusing on the causes of climate change ------- that the coal burning power plants are the major contributors to the greenhouse gas emissions.
   (A) indicate
   (B) indicates
   (C) indicating
   (D) indicated

4. If she leaves at 2:30, she ------ at the airport on time.
   (A) would have arrived
   (B) arrived
   (C) is arriving
   (D) will arrive

5. If you ------- any problems after purchasing our product, please contact one of our customer service representatives.

(A) encounter (B) suffer

(C) reach (D) drop

這五題程度上都是超過五百分的題目，所以如果你覺得有些困難，其實是正常的。以下是這五題的答案：(B)、(C)、(B)、(D)、(A)。接下來是我對這五題的解釋。

解析

1. 某些讀者或許覺得 (C) rare 也可以，事實是要改成 rarely 才可以，如果你還覺得有問題，請把這句話多念幾次：Visitors are rarely allowed to enter the R&D building for security reasons.

2. 答案是 (C) engaged，有疑問的答案應該是 (A) involved 和 (D) arranged。先解釋一下 (A) involved 這個字的用法基本上是："I am involved with the big project."、"He is involved in this case." 要不然就是 "His job involves some business trips." 所以只要是人，這個字的用法就是：Someone is involved with/in something. 這裡的 Lenovo 是家公司，用法也就跟人一樣了。正確的寫法應為 Lenovo has been involved in talks with IBM to purchase its personal computer division.

再來是 (D) arranged，這個字也要多念培養出語感，看看例句：
John arranged a birthday party for his daughter.
Mary arranged with the teacher to have a weekly piano lesson.

Kevin arranged for his son to have a birthday party.

Arrange 這個字可以用在 arrange a party / arrange a meeting / arrange an interview，基本上就是 arrange something，另外就是 arrange for/with someone (to do something)，還有一個就是 arrange about something，這下有人會問了 arrange something 跟 arrange about something 有什麼不同？其實很簡單，念一下：You need to arrange the meeting. 還有 You need to arranged about the meeting. 是不是感覺上 arrange about the meeting 事情多多了，arrange the meeting 相較之下就簡單、輕鬆一點。如果 FU 還是不夠強，念一下：arrange the meeting / arrange (everything) about the meeting，就感覺出來了吧！

以這題而言，Lenovo has arranged the talks with IBM. 就可以了，如果加上後面的部分，嚴格來說要改成 "Lenovo has arranged talks with IBM for the purchase of its PC division." 或者是 "Lenovo has arrange meetings with IBM to talk about purchasing its PC division."

另外加一個重點，念一下：purchasing the PC division 還有 the purchase of the PC division，如果有疑問，我另外給一組例子：maintaining the system 還有 maintenance of the system。

3. 先把答案帶進去念個一遍：

The research study focusing on the causes of climate change indicates that the coal burning power plants are the major contributors to the greenhouse gas emissions.

這句話其實只是 The research study focusing on the causes of climate change indicates that something happens. 我只是把 something happens 寫得特別長，來擾亂你們而已。而 focusing on the causes of climate change 只是用來說明這個 study 的特性而已所以先可以先刪掉不看，如此一來這題目只剩下：The research study ------ that something happens. 很容易就能看出來答案是 (B) indicates。

當然如果題目改成 The research stud**ies** focusing on the causes of climate change ------ that.... 答案就是 (A) indicate，在這裡我要再提一下，題目可不是隨便寫長了就好，其實到處都可以是題目，以這題而言，我就可以把 focusing 當作另一個題目把 focus, focused, focuses 當作其他答案。這部分還有另一個寫法 The research study which focuses on the causes of climate change indicates that the coal burning power plants are the major contributors to the greenhouse gas emissions.

同樣的我也可以把這裡的 focuses 當作題目來出，而且如果題目是 the research studies 同樣的後面就該接 which focus on the causes...，這也正是我強調的，就算這題選對了，還是要把原題目多念幾遍，只要你多念，感覺自然而然地就會出來，就會有 FU。一個題目，整個句子到處都是題目，多念就對了。

4. 這題很簡單，培養出語感後，發現只有 (D) will arrive 最順，如果你這題選錯了先把題目多念幾次：

If she leaves at 2:30, she will arrive at the airport on time.

接下來我解釋一下其他答案。

(A) would have arrived 還 記 得 should have / could have / would have 嗎？沒錯就是所謂的假設語氣：if you had done something, she should have / could have / would have。如果這是正確答案，前面就應該是 if she had leaved at 2:30。

(B) arrived 前面是 if she leaves 後面就不可能是 arrived。

(C) is arriving, she is arriving 都看到 she is arriving 語氣都完整了，幹嘛在前面加 if，這不是很奇怪！如果改成 If she leaves at 2:30, she will be arriving at the airport on time. 就沒問題了。

5. 應該會有不少讀者問為什麼 suffer 不對，有些人可能也覺得 reach 應該也可以，對於這些讀者，我的説法是：你真的是硬背單字！先看一些 suffer 的 例 句：I cannot suffer this kind of humiliation. John has suffered from diabetes and high blood pressure for many years. 注意到沒？都是壞事！這句話很明顯是由廠商講出來的，所以根本不會希望 customers suffer 吧！同樣的先看一下 reach 的例句：

She is reaching for the books on the shelf.

（是不是感覺 she 把手伸的長長的去拿書？）

When will us reach Taichung?

reach for the stars / reach for the sky

是不是有想要伸手探星、伸手觸天的感覺？如果你的 FU 還不是很強，這麼説好了，你會希望 customers 不要有 problems 還是希望他們 reach problems, reach for problems？這裡的正確答案，除了 encounter 以外還有 experience 也是個不錯的選擇。

Part 6 題型解析

講到 Part 6，最重要的是這部分題目的出題方式，我通常會問學生，Part 5 每一句出一題，到 Part 6 卻要設計出六、七句話，有時甚至超過十句卻只有三題，出題老師為什麼要這麼麻煩？特別另外來個 Part 6？乾脆 Part 5 就可以了啊！這就是 Part 6 題目的重點了，有些文法和單字的答案，沒法從這句題目的話語裡看出來，需要看前後文才可以正確地選出答案。如果在這部分，看到題目後，一時之間選不出答案，千萬不要浪費時間，繼續看下去，再接下來的內容就可以幫助你選出正確答案了，請看以下的例子。

小練習　中標（選項請對在空格下方）

On Sunday, June 10, we - - - - - - the annual Job Fair for the newly

        (A) hosted

        (B) will be hosting

        (C) are hosting

        (D) would have hosted

graduating college senior students. This will be a whole day event, starting from 9:30 AM to 5:00 PM and more than 300 companies will be - - - - - - hand to actively recruit the best and

        (A) on

        (B) in

        (C) off

        (D) at

the brightest candidates. No registration is needed, but we do hope you prepare copies of your résumé and transcript and get properly dressed. Admission will be free if you show your ID at the reception desk. Please come and get the best chance of getting a job offer before your graduation. ------- the official web site

(A) Visit

(B) Go

(C) Stay

(D) Arrive at

at http://nsysu.edu/jobfair2015 for more details.

解析

1. 看到第一題，只是給個日期，根本不知道該用什麼時態，所以繼續看下去。第二句裡的 this will be 還有後面的 300 companies will be 知道第一題答案是 (B) will be hosting。

2. 第二題如果有疑問，請把以下的句子念個兩遍：
   More than 300 companies will be on hand for this event.
   Over 200 companies will be on hand for the Job Fair.
   We need to keep certain amount of money on hand for the possible emergency.

3. 第三題很簡單，Visit the web site 或是 Go to the web site. 就對了。其實 part 5 和 part 6 的最大差別，就在某些題目，你必須要看前後文才可以準確地選出正確答案，只要注意到這點，這兩部份其實沒什麼其他差別，如果你還想試試其他 part 6 的題目，還請你寫寫本書後面的模擬試題。

文章中譯

在 6 月 10 日星期天，我們為大四即將畢業的學生舉辦了一個就業博覽會。這將會是一整天的活動，從早上 9 點 30 到下午 5 點，會有超過 300 家的公司在現場徵選出最棒及最聰明的應試者。不需要註冊，我們希望您能準備好履歷、成績單及著正式的服裝。只需在接待台出示您的學生證，將能免費入場。請踴躍參加，好好把握住在畢業前就得到一份好工作的絕佳機會。詳情請洽活動官方網站 http://nsysu.edu/jobfair2015。

因為這本書的篇幅有限，單字和文法的題目就先說到這裡。不過有個重要觀念希望能再次的跟讀者強調一下，這本書不可能提供所有可能的考題或句型給你，畢竟篇幅有限，我能做的是提供給你觀念，該如何準備新多益甚至其他英文考試的正確方式。記得把不會的題目多念幾遍，培養你對句子裡面單字和文法的 FU。尤其是文法題目，如果你用傳統的文法概念解題，不只是浪費時間也容易弄錯，平時培養語感，考試的時候，直接選念起來順的答案既快又準，這才是正確的新多益考試方式。我在強調一下，這本書只是說明並解釋觀念，用我強調的方法來念你手邊的其他新多益書籍，用正確的方式來學習文法才能真正增加你的實力，進而在新多益考試上面拿到高分。

2.2 新多益 Part 7 閱讀測驗

在這裡我想先做個簡單的數學計算，新多益閱讀單元包含單字、文法和閱讀測驗，總共一百題，其中有 52 題單字和文法考題，48 題閱讀測驗，而閱讀測驗有分單篇文章和雙篇文章，單篇文章平均有九大題，每大題考兩到五題，共計 28 題，也就是有九篇文章要看，而雙篇文章共計四大題，每個大題有兩篇文章五題題目共 20 題，也就是閱讀測驗總共有 17 篇文章要看。這 100 題的考試時間是 75 分鐘，簡單的算術就可以知道平均答題速度是每三分鐘要寫四題，其中將近一半是總共有 17 篇文章的閱讀測驗！你覺得時間會夠嗎？這也是我在前面強調單字和文法必須要靠語感來解題的重要性。如果文法題目要去判斷哪個字是什麼詞性，又是哪個詞性修飾什麼詞，就算你能夠判斷出來，寶貴的時間也沒了。更不用說花時間判斷以後，答案還經常是錯的。記得文法靠語感，直接選念的順的就對了。當然你需要在準備新多益考試時就開始注重文法語感的培養，把所有不會、做錯的題目，將正確答案帶進去，把題目念個三遍、五遍。自然而然地就可以培養出你的語感。相信你在念完前面的文法單字章節後，應該已經知道這個訣竅和重點。只有這樣你才能省下足夠的時間來應付閱讀測驗。

另外我要特別強調一點，在考新多益的時候，其應試須知第 12 點有載明在題目卷上**不能有任何畫記**！請參照官方網站裡的新多益常見問題中，『許多考生因為聽信補習班的答題技巧教授或是網路謠傳，容易誤觸這個規定，以為劃記後有擦拭乾淨就不算違規，但是要提醒大家的是，只要有劃記的動作即為違規，而不是大家誤傳的擦掉就沒關係喔』所以在做新多益模擬考試的時候，讀者要特別針對這點多加練習。

在我參考了許多新多益書籍後，發現幾乎每本都把單篇文章分成好幾類，例如廣告、表單與表格文件、備忘錄、通知、電子郵件與信件、報導文章、報告書、訊息。其實在我看來這樣的分類對於答題的幫助不大，所以只需要分出兩類：表單、表格與圖表以及其他。至於為什麼我會特別把表單、表格與圖表分出來，是有我的原因，且稍待我等一下再解釋。

幾乎在所有的新多益閱讀測驗書籍，都要考生先看題目才回到文章找答案。這點我要特別強調是 **絕對的錯誤**，新多益閱讀測驗一定要先看文章，看完文章以後才來解題。你又問了為什麼？我相信只要考過新多益的考生，你先自問一下，是不是經常在看完題目以後，卻在文章裡找不到答案，於是又試著更快的掃描一次文章，結果還是找不到！這下傻眼了，明知道閱讀的時間不夠，卻在看了兩遍之後，連一題也解不出來。心裡就在，回去再找一次與先猜了再說之間，作痛苦的掙扎！更過分的是，新多益還很喜歡考：**以下哪個答案是錯的？以下哪個在文章裡沒提到？**這下可好了，要把文章裡的三個正確答案都找出來才能答對。結果第一次找到一個，再看一次又找到一個，這下又糾結了，是要再找一次還是在兩個之間猜一個？不需要多，只要來一兩個這樣的經驗，就會讓你考試當時心情大受影響。還有，只要聽老師檢討過英文閱讀測驗的人，應該都有以下的經驗：有些時候就算老師跟你說了這題的答案，就在這句裡面，你卻還是因為單字或其他關係看不懂這句話。都有人跟你講了魔鬼就藏在這句話的細節裡，卻往往因為幾個關鍵字不懂，找不出這個可惡的魔鬼！想想看如果都跟你講了答案就在這題裡，都還看不出來，你覺得考試的時候先看題目再回文章找答案時，你連答案就在這句裡都不知道對吧！你就算文章瞄了無數遍，唯一的感受就是此題沒答案，只是浪費了為了找這題答案的所有時間，而最後還是四個答案裡隨便猜一個，唯一花掉的，正是原先就不夠的寶貴時間。剛剛解釋過了，先看題目然後才回文章找答案，只會更浪費時間，何況新多益閱讀所考的文章基本上都不難，稍微有一點閱讀能力就可以看懂，在這 17 篇文章裡面，真正難的文章，其實只有單篇文章的最後一篇，還有雙篇文章的最後兩大題比較難而已，總共只有五篇比較難，其餘的文章程度都不高，先把文章看完，然後才來回答問題絕對比較省時間。

接著我解釋一下先看文章，看完文章以後，才來解題的好處。說實話哪次英文考試你所有單字都會的？再退一步來說，多數的閱讀測驗文章，你都會有些單字不懂對吧！而這就是先看文章的好處了。假設文章裡有幾句話因為有單字，你看不懂。正因為你看了全篇文章，自然會稍稍了解這邊文章講了什麼、說了那些東西。就算有幾個單字、幾句話看不懂，因為你對整篇文章的概略了解，還是可以感覺出這篇文章的大意。然後在答題時，因為掌握了大意，你往往可以先挑出一些不合理的答案，而且在你需要回去文章找答案時，因為對整篇文章的概略了解，你也會知道到哪一段去找答案。如果在那段裡找不到，你就知道是該猜答案了。就算如此，你已經去掉一些不合理的答案，猜對的機率自然比較高了。說到那些新多益常出現的**以下哪個答案是錯的？以下哪個在文章裡沒提到？**你很可能從題目所給的答案裡面，挑出兩個對的，也就是說就算你要回去文章找，也只需要找兩個答案而不是四個答案。至於最後一種，答案就在那句完全看不懂的情形，因為你對文章內容的概略了解，很可能還沒回去找，就知道藏在那個看不懂的句子裡。既然一開始就知道看不懂，那不用花時間找了直接猜。更棒的是在猜答案前，因為你對文章的概略了解，至少可以刪掉一兩個答案，不用花時間亂找，還可以增加猜對的機率。

接下來我從閱讀測驗題目的設計，來討論一下先看文章和先看題目的優缺點。順便讓大家瞭解一下，為什麼在前面我會說，先把文章看完，就算是猜答案前，也可以在猜之前先刪掉一些不合理的答案。我把一般閱讀測驗錯誤的題目分成以下幾類：最簡單的錯誤答案：信口胡謅、無稽之談。也就是文章完全沒提到，根本就是天外飛來一筆的答案。稍微難一點的答案：南轅北轍。也就是文章說南，答案卻道北，說高變成低之類的。再難一點的答案則是：含混不清、移花接木，故意把文章裡的說法岔開，或是提出文章裡有提到，卻跟題目不相關的小枝節來混淆考生的答案。最後最難的就是：斷章取義、以偏概全、倒因為果。就是故意渲染或把題目有關的小枝節拿來大做文章，或者是故意把因果關係搞混搞亂的答案。你可以把你任何的閱讀測驗題目拿來看看，是不是答案就在這幾類裡面？就像我說的簡單的閱讀測驗題目就以前兩種信口胡謅、無稽之談和南轅北轍為主，就算一時之間看不出正確答案，只要考生把三個這類的答案挑出來就可以輕鬆答對的題目。而難一點的閱讀測驗則是兩個前兩種答案配上一個移花接木、以偏概全、斷章取義的答案。最難最難的閱讀測驗，就是在正確答案裡加上一個簡單的配上兩個難的，如此而已。說實話這類最難的閱讀測驗題目，真的很少見，在新多益考試裡更是稀有。以上說的是錯誤答案的設計，以正確答案而言，如果是難的題目，在文章和正確答案裡，一定會用不同的單字、片語或是不同的說法來描述同一件事情，來增加考生解題的困擾。如果你先看完全篇文章就可以輕鬆的把信口胡謅、無稽之談的答案挑出來，只要程度不是非常差，選出南轅北轍的答案絕對不是難事。也就是說，除了少數異常艱難，新多益稀有的題目外，你絕對可以去掉兩個到三個答案，也就是我先前所講的：先把文章看完，就算是猜答案前，也可以在猜之前先刪掉一些不合理的答案。如果你還是沒辦法被我說服，請你看接下來的閱讀練習以及本書最後面的閱讀模考和詳解，你親自試過後就知道，先看文章的絕大好處了。

單篇文章小練習

在此我用兩個閱讀測驗的例子來說明，為什麼要先看文章比較好。你可以先看以下這篇文章，然後試著回答後面的題目。當然你更可以先看題目，然後才回到文章找答案，試試看會不會省時間。

There are many tasks in finding a job, including writing the résumé, getting references and preparing for the interviews. You can easily find many books talking about how to construct a résumé, what to wear for an interview and how to behave during one. Nevertheless, we are different and we are going to concentrate on the most important step in getting a job. Teach you how to answer questions during the interview.

First of all, you have to know the history and lots of information about the company you are interviewing with. It will help you tremendously to answer the related questions correctly and creatively. You have to remember the boring answer is the worst answer. Also, don't give a short answer, but don't get too long-winded, either.

The discussion above lists only some of the many tips illustrated in our recently published "Q&A Boxes". Want to learn more about answering interview questions? This is the book you have to buy. Please call us at 1-800-000-000 to order the book or get it on line at: www.interestingcareer.com.

1. What is the purpose of this ad?

  (A) To announce a contest.

  (B) To sell a mansion.

  (C) To hire an editor.

  (D) To promote a new book.

---

2. According to the passage, what is the most critical step to get a job?

  (A) Draft your résumé.

  (B) Get proper references.

  (C) Know more about the company.

  (D) Reply with the right answers during the interview.

---

3. What is "Q&A Boxes"?

  (A) A book.

  (B) A website.

  (C) A publishing house.

  (D) A magazine.

看過文章答完題目後，來看看我對這篇文章的解釋。第一句很簡單，Finding a job 會有 many tasks, including, writing A, getting B and preparing for C. 如果不認識 task 很簡單，（句子都寫了 including 三件事）也就是後面的三個 writing A, getting B 以及 preparing for C。

第二句：You can easily find many books talking about『三件事』，包括 how to construct, what to wear 還有 how to behave。這裡的 construct a résumé 可不要把 construct 當建築的意思喔！其實只要你把 construct a résumé 多念幾次就可以感覺出 construct 在這裡的意思了。英文裡有許多的語助副詞，偶而新多益考試裡也會出現，接下來的 nevertheless 正是其中之一。要搞懂選對這類的副詞，最重要的還是念到有 FU，就以這裡的 nevertheless 為例子，最好的方式就是將整句念一下，念過後，應該可以感受到 nevertheless 有種轉折的語氣，再接上後面的 we are different，就可以知道這裡的 we 是與其他的書相比較。在 and 後的句子，我們可以看出來這本書只專注在一件事上面，那就是 Teach you how to answer questions during the interview.

第二段的第一句很簡單，就是 you have to know the history and lots of information 如此而已。接下來講為什麼需要 know the history and information。因為可以幫助你在 interview 的時候回答問題。最後兩句則指出「回答不能 boring，及回答長度要洽當」。

第三段的第一句開始了真正的廣告，說明在最近才 published 的 "Q&A Boxes" 裡，上面所講的只是小小一部份而已。第二句為「想學更多，快去買書吧！」最後一句只是告訴你怎麼買？哪裡買？

1. What is the purpose of this ad?（這一篇廣告的目的是？）

   (A) To announce a contest.（公布比賽。）

   (B) To sell a mansion.（販售豪宅。）

   (C) To hire an editor.（雇用編輯。）

   (D) To promote a new book.（推銷一本書。）

   答案為 (D)，如果你先看題目然後才回去找答案，這題幾乎要整篇看完才會答，對吧！

2. According to the passage, what is the most critical step to get a job?（根據這一篇文章，要得到工作最重要的一個步驟是？）

   (A) Draft your résumé.

   (B) Get proper references.

   (C) Know more about the company.

   (D) Reply with the right answers during the interview.

   這題也簡單，應該選 (D)。

3. What is "Q&A Boxes"?（什麼是 Q&A Boxes？）

   (A) A book.

   (B) A website.

   (C) A publishing house.

   (D) A magazine.

   看過文章後，應該可以很容易地知道答案是 (A) A book。

找工作時有很多事要做，包括寫履歷、找推薦人和準備面試。你可以輕易地找到許多講解如何撰寫履歷，面試的時候該穿什麼、該怎麼回應的書。儘管如此，我們可不同，只專注在找工作時的最重要步驟：教你如何在面試時回答問題。

首先，你需要知道這家要面試你的公司的歷史和許多相關資訊。這會幫助你正確的回答、有創造力的回答問題。你需要記得無聊的答案是最壞的答案，同時記得，答案太短不好、太長也不對。

上面的討論只是我們最近出版的 "Q&A Boxes" 裡內容的一小部分．想知道如何回答面試問題？這就是你需要買的書，請打免付費電話：1-800-000-000 或是上網：www.interestingcareer.com 訂購。

想想看，先看題目然後回去找答案，以這篇測驗而言，可能要看超過兩遍才能找出三題答案。如果緊張的話，很有可能找了三遍還是沒法選出答案！還是聽我的勸，老老實實地先把文章看完吧！

接下來，我想跟大家講一下，一般補習班會怎麼教這篇閱讀測驗。這位老師會說，先看第一題題目，main purpose of this ad，請看最後一段，倒數第二句：This is the book you have to buy。再看第二題：the most critical step，的一段最後兩句：Nevertheless, we are different and we are going to concentrate on the most important step in getting a job. Teach you how to answer questions during the interview.。再看第三題：先在第三段第一句找到 Q&A Boxes 繼續看下去，This is the book you have to buy. 我敢保證甚至有些老師會說第一題都會了，第三題還是同一句，答案就出來了。然後說你看全篇文章只要找到三四句就答對了，然後誇口說他多厲害，只要跟他學會看題目找答案的技巧，閱讀測驗實在是太簡單了！更可怕的是，台下的學生還真的被唬得一愣一愣的全信了！你仔細想一下，這些名師不知道把這份講義教了多少遍，上千遍、上萬遍都有可能，閉著眼睛都會背了，當然知道哪一頁、哪一句。你呢？頭一次看到文章，找的到才怪！拜託拜託，以後千萬記得，一定是先看文章然後才答題。

或許你會覺得這篇文章是我特地挑的，以下是我從 102 學測英文閱讀測驗裡所挑的一篇來驗證我的說法。在此我要強調一下，學測閱讀測驗的文章和題目都比一般的新多益閱讀測驗還要難，我在前面也說了新多益單篇文章的最後一篇還有雙篇文章的最後兩大題都才是最難的，而學測閱讀測驗的難度就跟這三大題的題目相差不遠，如果你能看懂下面這篇文章，以新多益的閱讀測驗程度而言，已經足夠拿金牌證照（超過 860）了。

The Swiss army knife is a popular device that is recognized all over the world. In Switzerland, there is a saying that every good Swiss citizen has one in his or her pocket. But the knife had humble beginnings.

In the late nineteenth century, the Swiss army issued its soldiers a gun that required a special screwdriver to dismantle and clean it. At the same time, canned food was becoming common in the army. Swiss generals decided to issue each soldier a standard knife to serve both as a screwdriver and a can opener.

It was a lifesaver for Swiss knife makers, who were struggling to compete with cheaper German imports. In 1884, Carl Elsener, head of the Swiss knife manufacturer Victorinox, seized that opportunity with both hands, and designed a soldier's knife that the army loved. It was a simple knife with one big blade, a can opener, and a screwdriver.

A few years after the soldier's knife was issued, the "Schweizer Offizier Messer," or Swiss Officer's Knife, came on the market. Interestingly, the Officer's Knife was never given to those serving in the army.

The Swiss military purchasers considered the new model with a corkscrew for opening wine not "essential for survival," so officers had to buy this new model by themselves. But its special multi-functional design later launched the knife as a global brand. After the Second World War, a great number of American soldiers were stationed in Europe. And as they could buy the Swiss army knife at shops on military bases, they bought huge quantities of them. However, it seems that "Schweizer Offizier Messer" was too difficult for them to say, so they just called it the Swiss army knife, and that is the name it is now known by all over the world.

1. What is the main purpose of the passage?

   (A) To explain the origin of the Swiss army knife.

   (B) To introduce the functions of the Swiss army knife.

   (C) To emphasize the importance of the Swiss army knife.

   (D) To tell a story about the designer of the Swiss army knife.

2. What does "**It**" in the third paragraph refer to?

   (A) The Swiss army needed a knife for every soldier.

   (B) Every good Swiss citizen had a knife in his pocket.

   (C) Swiss knives were competing with imported knives.

   (D) Canned food was becoming popular in the Swiss army.

3. Why didn't the Swiss army purchase the Swiss Officer's Knife?

    (A) The design of the knife was too simple.

    (B) The knife was sold out to American soldiers.

    (C) The army had no budget to make the purchase.

    (D) The new design was not considered necessary for officers to own.

---

4. Who gave the name "the Swiss army knife" to the knife discussed in the passage?

    (A) Carl Elsener.   (B) Swiss generals.

    (C) American soldiers.   (D) German businessmen.

文章看懂了嗎？題目答得如何？以下是我對這篇文章的解說：

"The Swiss army knife is a popular device that is recognized all over the world." 看到這句我要把一個大家絕對都聽過的文法：關係代名詞，在這裡把它講清楚。這句裡的 that 就是所謂的關係代名詞，看到關係代名詞只要遵照以下我所說的三個重點，就變得很簡單了。

1. 先把這個關係代名詞所代替的名詞找出來

    其實這是最簡單的，超過八成就是關係代名詞前面的那個名詞，在這裡就是前面的 device

2. 把關係代名詞所帶的整句話找出來（這句話就是文法裡所說的關係子句）在這裡就是 that is recognized all over the world

3. 這也是最重要的一點，先把這**整句話刪掉不看**

所以這句就變成了：The Swiss army knife is a popular device that is recognized all over the world.。這裡的 Swiss 大寫所以是專有名詞，什麼刀最 popular（最有名）？當然是瑞士刀嘍！所以可以猜測 Swiss 是瑞士。將簡化的句子看懂後，就要把刪去的加回來了，很明顯的，that is recognized all over the world 只是用來加強說明是個什麼樣的 device 而已。這裡的 recognize，先感覺一下這句裡說的一個全世界都 recognized 的東西，你覺得 recognize 會是？就算到這裡還是沒有 FU，查過字典以後知道是認出、識別的意思後，將句子再念一次，這樣是不是對 recognize 這個字就有 FU 了？記得千萬不要 recognize：認出、識別，recognize：認出、識別，這麼硬背！把例句多念幾次唸到有 FU，絕對會比硬背更容易記住這個字。第二句中的 Switzerland, Swiss 看來就是系出同源對吧！這裡的 citizen 明顯的是人，Swiss citizen 的 citizen 你說呢？在 pocket 裡面一定會有的東西，你說 pocket 會是？前面都是好話，但在第 3 句的開頭接了一個 but，你說 humble 是好是壞？那 humble 會是？可不要說是謙遜的或是謙恭的因為這可是好的意思，明顯的跟句意不合！把 But the knife has humble beginnings. 多念幾次，感受一下這個不太好的意思，也就是一開始不怎麼樣，就可以了。

第二段開始指出在 19 世紀末，Swiss 陸軍 issued 他的軍人一把槍，你說 issue 會是？接下來的 screwdriver 和 dismantle 不懂，但是 clean 清潔總知道吧！在清潔槍枝前一定要？你猜 dismantle 會是？要一個 special screwdriver 才能 dismantle and clean it 就算不知道 screwdriver 是什麼東西總知道是個用來 dismantle and clean 槍枝的工具吧！如果你還是覺得不放心，我勸你查字典不如 Google 一下 screwdriver 的圖片，看過圖片後想忘記都難！第二句中指出軍隊裡最 common 的食物，會是什麼樣的食物？所以 canned food 會是？ Swiss generals decided to issue each soldier a standard knife to serve both as a screwdriver and a can opener. 看到這句就可以感覺出 general 這個官不會小。一把 knife 可以作為 screwdriver 和 can opener 的用途，這樣對軍人而言是不是就很實用！

在第三段的第一句中又來了個關係代名詞，這個比較簡單前面加了個逗號所以直接把 who 後面的先刪掉。前面才說了官很大的 general 決定 issued 每位 soldier 一把 standard knife，你說這個 It 指的會是？ lifesaver 就是 life 加上 saver 夠簡單吧！ Swiss knife maker 當然是作 Swiss knife 的人嘍。當然最後還是得把剛剛刪掉的句子放回去，這裡的 who 當然就是 Swiss knife makers，所以也就是這些 Swiss knife makers 要跟比較便宜的 German imports compete 當然會 struggling，還有 German 的東西要到 Switzerland 賣，當然要先 import 到 Switzerland 不是嗎？第二句看起來比較長，其實架構很簡單。首先 head of the Swiss knife manufacturer Victorinox 很明顯的是用來說明 Carl Elsener 而已，還有後面的 that the army loved 也是關係子句，所以這兩部分當然就是面對相同的命運：先刪掉再說！將句子簡化成 "In 1884, Carl Elsener seized that opportunity with both hands, and designed a soldier's knife."。架構看懂了以後再來講細節，用兩隻手 seized that opportunity，你說 seize 除了抓住還會是什麼？最後一句就簡單了，一把刀有三個東西：one big blade, a can opener, and a screwdriver。Blade 不知道，查過字典後知道是刀身、刀鋒後，再把句子多念幾次是不是就有 FU 了？

第四段的第一句中，issue 這個字又來了，念了這麼多次總該有 FU 了吧！ "Schweizer Offizier Messer," or Swiss Officer's Knife 其實

就是 A or B，看懂 B 就可以了，而且說實話 A 的 "Schweizer Offizier Messer," 我還真看不懂。第二句裡的 those serving in the army 可以看成 those who serving in the army 也就是那些 those serving in the army 的人，意思就是有趣的是，那些刀從來沒給 those (who) serving in the army。第三句就要解釋一下了，這句其實只是 A so B 也就是說，有了 A，so B 這個結果就發生了，也就可以把這句從 so 切斷分開來看。裡面的 with a corkscrew for opening wine 的作用，其實跟關係子句一模一樣都是用來說明 the new model，所以可以先刪掉變成：The Swiss military purchasers considered the new model not "essential for survival," Swiss military purchaser 前面一直用 army，這裡改用 military。這個 purchaser 就是買東西的人，也就是所謂的採購，其實就算你不知道 purchaser 是採購，從後面的 er 字尾也可以知道是某種人，也就是軍方的某種人，認為這個 new model not "essential for survival," 如果看不出『非生存所必須』，總可以感覺出不怎麼重要對吧！而刪掉的部分 the new model with a corkscrew for opening wine 只是說這個 new model，有個 corkscrew 用來 opening wine，就算 corkscrew 不懂，總可以知道它是個用來開酒瓶的工具對吧。既然前面都說了不怎麼重要，so 只好自己買沒錯吧！第四句以 But 開始，指出這個 knife 是 multi-function design，依文章前面所說可以推測是有很多種工具的設計。要注意，這裡的 launch 可不要翻成發射，將句子多念個幾次，感受一下「它的多功能設計，launched 這把刀成為一個全球品牌（global brand）」。你會感覺不出來 launch 的意思嗎？第五句：二次大戰後很多美國大兵 stationed 在歐洲。第六句中指出他們在 military bases 可以買到，還有買一大堆（bought huge quantities of them）。最後一句指出 "Schweizer Offizier Messer" 對他們而言，不太會念，所以被改稱為 "Swiss army knife"。

題目解析 ○

1. 這篇文章的主旨為何？

    (A) To explain the origin of the Swiss army knife.

    （解釋瑞士刀的由來）

    (B) To introduce the functions of the Swiss army knife.

    （介紹瑞士刀的功能。）

    (C) To emphasize the importance of the Swiss army knife.

    （強調瑞士刀的重要性。）

    (D) To tell a story about the designer of the Swiss army knife.

    （述説瑞士刀設計者的故事。）

    有提到 (B) 中所述的，但是只有兩三句，所以這個答案以偏概全，錯！
    (C) 連以偏概全的資格都稱不上；(D) 跟 (B) 一樣聊聊兩句，也是以偏概全，錯！答案是 (A)，整篇文章介紹瑞士刀的歷史緣由。

在這裡我順道提一下，一般補習班在看到這類的 main purpose，major idea of the passage，往往就會説先看 topic sentence 也就是文章的第一句，最多就是看完第一段就可以回答了。再回到的一段，就算你仔細看完，只知道跟 Swiss army knife 有關，還是沒法回答第一題對吧！如果你草草的把文章看下去，一不小心就會選到哪些以偏概全的答案了，只有老老實實地先把整篇文章看完，這題才會有絕對的把握。

2. What does "**It**" in the third paragraph refer to?

    （第三段中的 It 指的是什麼？）

    (A) The Swiss army needed a knife for every soldier.

（瑞士軍隊需要給每個士兵的刀。）

(B) Every good Swiss citizen had a knife in his pocket.

（每一位優良的瑞士市民在她的口袋中都有一把刀。）

(C) Swiss knives were competing with imported knives.

（瑞士刀在跟進口的刀競爭。）

(D) Canned food was becoming popular in the Swiss army.

（罐頭食物在瑞士軍隊中變的流行。）

以文章裡解釋，選 (A)。

---

3. Why didn't the Swiss army purchase the Swiss Officer's Knife?

（為什麼瑞士軍隊不再購買瑞士刀？）

(A) The design of the knife was too simple.

（刀的設計太過簡單。）

(B) The knife was sold out to American soldiers.

（刀都賣給了美國士兵。）

(C) The army had no budget to make the purchase.

（軍隊沒有預算購買。）

(D) The new design was not considered necessary for officers to own.

看過文章以後可以輕易的判斷出來 (A) 與文章敘述不符，(B)：美國人在二次大戰後才開始買，比停止採購的時間晚，錯。(C)：從頭到尾沒提到瑞士軍方沒錢，也是錯！所以選 (D)。

4. Who gave the name "the Swiss army knife" to the knife discussed in the passage?

(A) Carl Elsener.
(B) Swiss generals.
(C) American soldiers.
(D) German businessmen.

這題夠簡單吧 (C) 老美不會念 "Schweizer Offizier Messer" 就乾脆給個 "the Swiss army knife" 的名字。

從以上這篇學測英文而來的閱讀測驗，也可以證明，閱讀測驗確實需要先看文章然後才來解題，這才是省時省事的正確方法，更何況一般新多益閱讀測驗的文章都不難，更該先把文章看完才對！

再來是文章的翻譯：

瑞士刀是個全世界都認得，很受歡迎的裝備。瑞士有個俗語，每個好公民的口袋裡，都該有把瑞士刀，可是這瑞士刀一開始，卻不是那麼的受歡迎。

十九世紀末期，瑞士陸軍配發一把，需要特殊螺絲起子才能拆解、清潔的槍給他的軍人。同時，陸軍裡罐頭食物也越來越普遍。瑞士將軍決定配發一個是個螺絲起子，也是個開罐器的標準刀具給每個軍人。

對於當時跟比較便宜的德國進口品競爭激烈競爭下，掙扎求生存的瑞士刀具製造商，這可是救命仙丹。在 1884 年，瑞士刀具製造商 Victorinox 的老闆，Carl Elsener 以雙手緊抓著這個機會而設計了一把刀子，深獲陸軍好評。它是把有著很大刀刃、開罐器和螺絲起子的刀子。

軍人用刀配發後幾年，"Schweizer Offizier Messer" 或稱為瑞士陸軍刀正式上市。有趣的是，這軍刀從來沒有給過那些服役中的軍人，瑞士軍方採購人員認為這附上用來開酒瓶軟木塞螺絲錐的最新瑞士刀，並不是生存的必需品，因為開酒瓶並非 " 攸關生死 "，所以需要的軍人只能自己購買。但是這個特殊的多功能設計卻讓瑞士刀成為全球性的品牌。二次大戰後，許多美國軍人駐紮在歐洲。因為他們在基地的商品店裡就可以購買瑞士刀，就買很多把。然而 許多美國軍人駐紮在歐洲。因為他們在基地的商品店裡就可以買到，而 "Schweizer Offizier Messer" 對這些美國軍人真的很難發音，他們就直接稱之為瑞士刀，也因此讓這個名字風行全球。

雙篇文章小練習

前面我曾經提到坊間許多新多益書籍都把閱讀文章分成好幾類,在此我解釋一下為什麼我說只需要分出兩類:表單、表格、圖表、會議議程、行程表以及其他種類會這麼分。我一直強調,閱讀測驗,尤其是新多益的閱讀測驗,一定要先把文章看完,然後才解題。我也用兩篇閱讀測驗來說明這樣做的好處,就算文章有一些部分或單字沒能完全看懂,從前後文多少可以推敲出這些不懂部分和單字的意思,畢竟文章是前後連貫的,所以不管是備忘錄、通知、電子郵件,還是信件、報導文章、報告書、訊息,不要去分類這類的文章,一律先看文章才回答題目。但是表單、表格、圖表、會議議程、行程表就不同了,這類的文章內容基本都是條列式,也就是根據日期、時間或是個別的項目,一開始就分好了。所以你只需要看一下大小標題,瞄一下附註,實際內容不需細看就可以開始答題,這類的文章是例外,你不需要仔細看文章內容,就可以直接答題。以下我給個例子:

Enjoy your Mekong River tour with My Tours

We design two fantastic packages; choose the one that best fits you and your family.

Package 1

- Full two-hour River vessel tour
- 2-day, 1-night accommodations at Mekong Hotel with complimentary breakfast
- 25% discount at the Mekong souvenir shop

Adults 18-60	$100	Seniors 60+	$70
Teens 13-17	$80	Kids 4-12	$50

Package 2
Everything from package 1 and

- 30% discount at the Mekong River Grand Restaurant
- Free admission to the river front fireworks show ($50 value)

Adults 18-60	$130	Seniors 60+	$100
Teens 13-17	$110	Kids 4-12	$80

For more information, please call +856 71 345 678 or visit us at www.mytours.com

1. How much is it for a family of four, age 46, 42, 15 and 10, if they like to enjoy the fireworks with the river tour?
   (A) $330
   (B) $450
   (C) $200
   (D) $480

2. How long is the river tour?
   (A) one hour
   (B) 90 minutes
   (C) two hours
   (D) three hours

題目解析

看到這篇文章的標題就知道是旅行社的廣告，下面又有 Package 1 和 Package 2，顯然是兩種套裝行程，很快的瞄一下，注意到 package 2 裡面的 everything from package 1 and 知道只是加了一些東西到 package 1 而已，不須細看，直接答題。

第一題，fireworks with the river tour 顯然是 Package 2，剩下的只是數學計算而已，在此我先表明，新多益考試裡我還沒看到像這題這麼複雜的數學計算，以後的新多益也不會出這類的計算。在這裡我只是覺得好玩而出個數學題。2*130 + 110 + 80 = 450。

第二題，更簡單了，Full two-hour River vessel tour，這裡的只是強調整整兩小時或是足足兩小時。從上面的例子就可以看出這類的表單、表格、圖表、會議議程、行程表，不需要細看內容，把大小標題，附註看過以後就可以直接答題了，除此之外的文章，還是老老實實的先把文章看完再答題吧。我保證絕對會比先看題目然後回文章找答案還要省時間！

中譯 ○

跟「我的旅行」一起享受湄公河之旅

我們設計兩種很棒的行程，請選擇一個最適合你和你家人的行程。

一號行程

- 足足兩小時遊船
- 兩天一夜湄公河旅店住宿，並附早餐
- 湄公河禮品店 75 折優惠

成人 18-60	$100	長者 60+	$70
青少年 13-17	$80	小孩 4-12	$50

二號行程
包含所有的一號行程以及

- 湄公河黃金餐廳 7 折優惠
- 免費湄公河畔煙火秀（價值：$50）

成人 18-60	$130	長者 60+	$100
青少年 13-17	$110	小孩 4-12	$80

如需更多資訊，請打：+856 71 345 678 或是到以下網址查詢：

www.mytours.com

最後我想提一下許多學生都問過我的問題，要如何提高閱讀能力與閱讀速度？其實我只有一句話：多讀就對了！不過在此我也有個但書，要讀稍微超過自己程度的文章！如果書籍或是文章，你可以一念就知道個八、九成，換更高程度的書籍來念。如果你不知道自己程度如何，先去書局找個高一的英文參考書或教科書來念裡面的文章，然後視情況看就看高一文章或是往下國二、國三或是往上到高二甚至高三。如果高三的課文都可以看懂，程度就足以考新多益了。還有你也可以考慮到我的 FB 粉絲專頁「跟TC 學英文」，去看我分享的文章和影音檔案，找你自己有興趣的文章來看。記得『多聽、多讀，聽懂、讀懂』就是增進英文程度的不二法門。

Part

新多益模
擬試題及詳解

3

Unit 1 新多益模擬試題 一聽力篇

前言

在你準備回答這份模擬試題前,我想先提醒一點:這份試題的目的是用來提升你的新多益程度,所以題目程度會比較難,尤其是比起正式的新多益考題。請不要以這份考題所答對的題目來預測你的新多益成績,如果如此,很可能會大大的打擊你的信心。如果你對答案後發現,考得還不錯,也不要太高興,因為在正式考試時,你的應試心情一定會比寫模考試題還要緊張多了,也因此你的正式考試成績會打一點折扣。我要再次提醒一下聽力的考試技巧,在 Part 1 和 Part 2,聽到每個答案時,要立刻判斷是對?是錯?還是沒把握?如果你沒有八、九成以上的把握,就把答案列為不知道,然後把筆點在那個答案上面,接下來判斷其他答案,如果有其他更好屬於對的答案,立刻就選,如果沒有繼續點在那個沒把握的答案,在聽完所有答案後,如果沒有更好的答案,就把被點上的答案填起來。至於 Part 3 和 Part 4,記得趁播放 direction 的時候先把前三題的題目和答案看過,只要有時間就多看幾遍,在聽 Part 3 的對話或是 Part 4 的獨白時,只要有答案,立刻圈選起來,聽完後,如果還有任何題目沒聽出來,立刻看個順眼的答案選起來,絕對不要浪費時間在考慮答題上面,三、五秒內把剩下的題目答完,然後立刻看下三題,再說一次,絕對不要把時間花在考慮答案上,用那寶貴的時間看下三題的題目!

LISTENING TEST

In the listening test, you will be asked to demonstrated how well you understand spoken English. The entire Listening test will last approximately 45 minutes. There are four parts and directions are given for each part. You must mark your answers on the separate answer sheet. Do not write your answers in your test book.

PART 1

Directions: For each question in this part, you will hear four statements about a picture in your test book. When you hear the statement, you must select the one statement that best describes what you see in the picture. Then find the number of the question on your answer sheet and mark your answer. The statements will not be printed in your test book and will be spoken only one time.

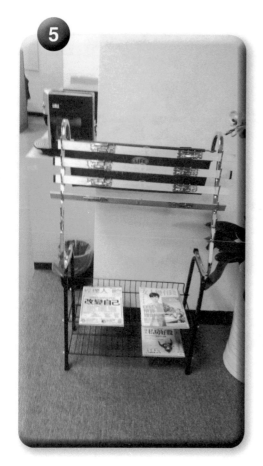

Track 50

 ▶ Track 50

PART 2

Directions: You will hear a question or statement and three responses spoken in English. They will not be printed in your test book and will be spoken only one time. Selected the best response to the question or statement and mark the letter (A), (B), or (C) on your answer sheet.

11. Mark your answer on your answer sheet.
12. Mark your answer on your answer sheet.
13. Mark your answer on your answer sheet.
14. Mark your answer on your answer sheet.
15. Mark your answer on your answer sheet.
16. Mark your answer on your answer sheet.
17. Mark your answer on your answer sheet.
18. Mark your answer on your answer sheet.
19. Mark your answer on your answer sheet.
20. Mark your answer on your answer sheet.
21. Mark your answer on your answer sheet.
22. Mark your answer on your answer sheet.
23. Mark your answer on your answer sheet.
24. Mark your answer on your answer sheet.
25. Mark your answer on your answer sheet.
26. Mark your answer on your answer sheet.
27. Mark your answer on your answer sheet.

28. Mark your answer on your answer sheet.
29. Mark your answer on your answer sheet.
30. Mark your answer on your answer sheet.
31. Mark your answer on your answer sheet.
32. Mark your answer on your answer sheet.
33. Mark your answer on your answer sheet.
34. Mark your answer on your answer sheet.
35. Mark your answer on your answer sheet.
36. Mark your answer on your answer sheet.
37. Mark your answer on your answer sheet.
38. Mark your answer on your answer sheet.
39. Mark your answer on your answer sheet.
40. Mark your answer on your answer sheet.

PART 3

Directions: You will hear some conversations between two people. You will be asked to answer questions about what the speakers say in each conversation. Select the best response to each question and mark the letter (A), (B), (C), or (D) on your answer sheet. The conversation will not be printed in your test book and will be spoken only one time.

41. Who most likely are the speakers?

    (A) They are tourists.

    (B) They work for the sales and marketing team.

    (C) They are colleagues.

    (D) They are reporters.

42. Who is Sam Walters?

    (A) A new employee for the company.

    (B) A retailer.

    (C) The new Marketing VP.

    (D) The president of the company.

43. What does the woman think of Mr. Walters?

    (A) He will be able to do a good job.

    (B) She needs some detail information about him first.

    (C) He isn't really qualified for the job.

    (D) Only time can tell.

44. What are they talking about?

    (A) Some overseas clients.

    (B) A new restaurant.

    (C) A new employee.

    (D) A good meeting place.

45. What will happen next Monday?

    (A) Clients will visit the company.

    (B) Grand opening for the restaurant.

    (C) The president will be coming from overseas.

    (D) A event celebration will be held.

46. What does the man suggest?

    (A) Take the business card.

    (B) Take the clients to a better place.

    (C) Check and make sure the address is correct.

    (D) Call and reserve first.

47. Who do the speakers work for?

    (A) A motor manufacturer.

    (B) A newspaper company.

    (C) A publisher.

    (D) An advertising agency.

48. When will the man be able to finish his work?

    (A) Tuesday.

    (B) Wednesday.

    (C) Thursday.

    (D) Friday.

49. Why did their client pay the magazines?

    (A) To put an advertisement.

    (B) To get a good review.

    (C) To put the artwork on display.

    (D) To subscribe the magazines.

50. Why did the man call the woman?

    (A) To say hello.

    (B) To check the order status.

    (C) To cancel his order.

    (D) To arrange for a delivery.

51. What did the man buy?

    (A) A computer software.

    (B) A desk.

    (C) A monitor.

    (D) A computer.

52. What does the woman ask for?

   (A) The man's name.

   (B) The man's telephone number.

   (C) The date when the order was placed.

   (D) The reference number of the order.

53. What does the proposal suggest?

   (A) Participating a marathon.

   (B) Marketing new line of running shoes.

   (C) Helping city mayor.

   (D) Sponsoring a public event.

54. Why do they need a booth?

   (A) To send out gifts.

   (B) To set up a shop for new products.

   (C) To help the city.

   (D) To promote the event.

55. What can be implied about Mr. Thompson?

   (A) He is a talented runner.

   (B) He has the authority of approving the proposal.

   (C) He is an expert in running shoe design.

   (D) He will not come to the regional meeting.

56. What is the man trying to do?

    (A) Purchase two plane tickets.

    (B) Exchange the seating.

    (C) Attend a ball game.

    (D) Cancel a reservation.

57. What does the woman say about the rest of the tickets?

    (A) Seating cannot be assigned.

    (B) They are cheaper.

    (C) They are exchangeable.

    (D) They are not refundable.

58. What suggestion does the woman make?

    (A) Arrive earlier.

    (B) Buy the tickets on the internet.

    (C) Purchase through a convenience store.

    (D) Order the reserved seats.

59. Where most likely are the speakers?

    (A) At an airport.

    (B) At a restaurant.

    (C) In a taxi.

    (D) In a hotel.

60. What kind of transportation did the woman take?

    (A) Airplane.

    (B) Bus.

    (C) Taxi

    (D) Train.

61. What will the woman probably do next?

    (A) Take a rest.

    (B) Have a meal.

    (C) Watch TV.

    (D) Go online.

62. What are they discussing?

    (A) A trip itinerary.

    (B) A computer software.

    (C) A new employee

    (D) A company brochure

63. Who most likely is the man?

    (A) A manager

    (B) A customer

    (C) A sales clerk

    (D) A new employee

64. What does Melissa actually do?

(A) Helps fill out the timesheet.

(B) Collects the report and send it in.

(C) Indicates the correct button.

(D) Demonstrates the machine.

65. What are they discussing?

(A) A company benefit.

(B) College education.

(C) Marketing strategy.

(D) A university professor.

66. How would an employee do to get compensated?

(A) By registering a class.

(B) By attending all lectures.

(C) By getting a good enough grade.

(D) By calling Personnel Department.

67. When is the application deadline?

(A) July 3.

(B) July 13.

(C) July 20.

(D) July 30.

68. Where most likely are the speakers?

    (A) At a clothing store.

    (B) At a dry cleaner.

    (C) At a grocery store.

    (D) At a park.

69. Who most likely is the woman?

    (A) A bank teller.

    (B) An accountant.

    (C) A store clerk.

    (D) A nurse.

70. What does the man think about the woman's suggestion?

    (A) It's time consuming.

    (B) It's too rough.

    (C) It's great.

    (D) It looks fine.

> **PART 4**
>
> **Directions:** You will hear some talks given by a single speaker. You will be asked to answer three questions about what the speaker says in each talk. Select the best response to each question and mark the letter (A), (B), (C), or (D) on your answer sheet. The talks will not be printed in your test book and will be spoken only one time.

71. What is the purpose of the announcement?
    (A) To talk about app design
    (B) To introduce a lecturer
    (C) To talk about college education
    (D) To introduce a training session

72. What is the topic of the session?
    (A) App design
    (B) Bachelor party
    (C) Web marketing
    (D) Internet advertising effectiveness

73. Where most likely is the event taking place?
    (A) At a university
    (B) At a convention center
    (C) At a restaurant
    (D) At an airport.

74. What kind of company is this?

    (A) A customer service company

    (B) A credit card company

    (C) A telephone manufacturer

    (D) A bank

75. What number should the listener press to talk to a customer service representative?

    (A) 4

    (B) 5

    (C) 6

    (D) 9

76. According to the talk, what should a listener do to listen to the message again?

    (A) Press 0

    (B) Press 1

    (C) Hang up and dial again

    (D) Stay on the line

77. What kind of job is it advertising?

    (A) Computer programmers

    (B) Computer technicians

    (C) Language instructors

    (D) Design managers

78. How long is the course?

(A) One month

(B) Two months

(C) Three months

(D) Four months

79. How can someone get the class schedules?

(A) Visit the office

(B) Go online

(C) Call the center

(D) Write a letter

80. Who is the intended audience?

(A) Tourists

(B) Job candidates

(C) Cafeteria staff

(D) New employees

81. Where is the talk being given?

(A) A tourist stop

(B) A restaurant

(C) A hotel

(D) An office

82. What is true about the meal card?

    (A) It's free for every employee

    (B) The maximum amount on it is 10 dollars.

    (C) It can be used only one time.

    (D) It can be used to pay for food.

83. What season is it?

    (A) Spring.

    (B) Summer.

    (C) Fall

    (D) Winter.

84. Who is the speaker?

    (A) A bus driver.

    (B) A tour guide.

    (C) A park ranger

    (D) A tourist

85. Which animal is being warned about?

    (A) Wolves.

    (B) Moose.

    (C) Bears

    (D) Foxes

86. Who is the intended audience?

(A) Regular customers.

(B) New product presenters.

(C) Company executives.

(D) Car owners.

87. What does the speaker say about the red sports car?

(A) It is properly parked.

(B) It is damaged.

(C) It could be ticketed.

(D) It's condition is fine.

88. What is going to happen next?

(A) Presentation practice.

(B) Formal demonstration.

(C) Kitchen appliance introduction.

(D) Opening of the Consumer Electronic Fair.

89. Who is the speaker?

(A) A contestant

(B) A reporter

(C) A weatherman

(D) A contest judge

90. How many years has the contest been held in the place?
    (A) Two.
    (B) Four
    (C) Six
    (D) Ten

91. What is going to happen next?
    (A) An interview.
    (B) A food eating contest.
    (C) A weather report.
    (D) A test.

92. Who is going to talk about the importance of the event?
    (A) Chief Executive Officer
    (B) Chief Operating Officer
    (C) Head of Human Resources
    (D) Computer Chief

93. Which department does Mr. Huang work for?
    (A) Human Resources.
    (B) Computer.
    (C) Sales and Marketing.
    (D) Research and Development.

94. Who is going to host the last session?

    (A) Head of Human Resources.

    (B) COO.

    (C) Computer Chief.

    (D) Head of Sales and Marketing

95. What is the main topic of the talk?

    (A) How to improve your social skills.

    (B) How to do a trick.

    (C) How to give a great presentation.

    (D) How to give a thought-provoking question.

96. What is a suggested technique?

    (A) Answer a thought-provoking question.

    (B) Show an extraordinary statistic.

    (C) Don't tell Jokes.

    (D) Ask a complex question.

97. When is the best time to catch the audience's attention?

    (A) Five to ten minutes after the speech.

    (B) As soon as possible.

    (C) it's not necessary.

    (D) Not mentioned in the talk.

98. Where most likely is the announcement taking place?

    (A) In an airport

    (B) In a hotel

    (C) On an airplane

    (D) On a cruise ship

99. What will happen shortly after the announcement?

    (A) Drink will be served.

    (B) Passengers can leave their seat.

    (C) Flight attendants will walk around.

    (D) Dinner can be taken.

100. How much is a glass of soda?

    (A) Free.

    (B) Five dollars.

    (C) Ten dollars.

    (D) Fifteen dollars.

2 Unit 新多益模擬聽力試題解析

前言

如果你對題目有任何疑問，我會希望你先看我的解釋，只要能聽懂每題的答案就可以輕易選出正確答案。如同本書裡一直強調的，腦子裡出現中文其實對聽力只有阻礙，不可能會有任何幫助。如果你需要中文翻譯才能搞懂答案，那你的聽力永遠考不好。我其實不想在聽力部分附上翻譯，在出版社勸說之下，我還是附上翻譯，但是要記得，在聽力考試時，你絕對不需要翻譯，腦子裡不應該有中文！為了避免大家看翻譯，我把翻譯放到最後面了。在你考過模考以後，如果你沒注意到，Part 1 和 Part 2 的一個答題關鍵，我再次的提醒你：聽到每個答案時，你立刻判斷，是對？是錯？還是沒把握？你要有八、九成以上的把握，才判斷對、錯只要沒有八、九成以上的把握就當作不知道，靠剩下的答案來選出正確答案。

Part 1 詳解（這份詳解裡的中文是給你參考用的，要練聽力最重要的是自己先念過確認念過就懂，然後閉著眼睛聽。如果你需要中文才能了解，聽力考試一定完蛋！）

腳本 & 解析

1. Look at the picture marked number 1 in your test book.

   (A) The room is full of boxes.

   (B) One of the men is carrying a backpack.

   (C) All of them are packing their stuff.

   (D) The lights are turned off.

   解析

   (A) full of boxes，沒錯！

   (B) 圖片裡根本沒有 backpack，更不用說 carrying a backpack，順便提一下 backpacker 就是所謂的背包客，那你應該知道 backpack 是什麼了。

   (C) 只有一個人有點 packing 的動作。

   (D) 整個房間都亮著。

   所以答案是 (A)。

2. Look at the picture marked number 2 in your test book.

   (A) She is talking to her colleague.

   (B) She is using a computer.

   (C) She is trying to reach for a folder on the shelf.

   (D) She is taking a rest.

   解析

   (A) 沒看到任何 colleague，注意一下 college 和 colleague 這兩個字，colleague 就是 co-worker 也就是同事。如果不認識這個字，千萬不要硬背，想像一下你的同事就在你身邊，然後對著他 /

她多說幾次 colleague，就可以記住了！

(B) 右邊好像是個 computer 不很確定，但是 using 錯了。

(C) 看她手伸得長長的，當然是 reaching 嘍。

(D) 生龍活虎的，不可能是 taking a rest。

3. Look at the picture marked number 3 in your test book.

    (A) She is wiping the monitor.

    (B) She is talking on the phone.

    (C) She is typing on the keyboard.

    (D) She is listening to music with an earphone.

解析

(A) 沒有 wiper 怎麼去 wiping。

(B) 既沒 talking，也沒看到 phone。

(C) 完全正確！

(D) 旁邊有個 earphone 但是沒戴上，更不可能 listening。

4. Look at the picture marked number 4 in your test book.

    (A) They are talking to each other.

    (B) There is a teapot on the table.

    (C) She is raising her hand.

    (D) He is taking a nap.

解析

(A) 就算右邊的男士有 talking，也不是 to each other。

(B) 看到桌上種中間的東西沒？沒錯那個東西就是個 teapot，如果真不知道，盯著那個 teapot，多念幾次 teapot。

(C) 兩個人的手都在桌上，不可能是 raising a hand。

(D) 生龍活虎的，哪來的小睡（nap/napping）？

5. Look at the picture marked number 5 in your test book.

(A) Newspapers on the rack are being removed.

(B) Magazines are displayed on a newspaper rack.

(C) One man is reading a magazine.

(D) The trash can is full.

解析

(A) 確實沒看到 newspapers，但是沒看到人，當然不可能 **being** removed。（我相信很多書裡面會特別把這句話解釋為現在進行式還是被動，然後說這個答案是錯的。問題是在聽這句話的時候，你會有時間去判斷這句話是現在進行式，還是個被動？根本不可能！如同我解釋的：沒看到人，當然不可能 **being** removed。）

(B) 沒錯！如果不知道，圖片裡的報架就是 newspaper rack，magazine rack 也可以算對。對於多益考試，其實還有其他幾個字需要認識一下，請你到 google 圖片搜尋裡 https://www.google.com.tw/imghp?hl=zh-TW&tab=wi，去找一下這幾個字 和 詞，shelves, racks, cabinet, office cabinet 和 kitchen cabinet，邊看著那幾個圖，邊念相關的字、詞，就可以輕鬆地記起來了。

(C) 沒看到 man 當然更不可能 reading。

(D) 圖片裡的 trash can 空空的，不可能 full。

6. Look at the picture marked number 6 in your test book.

    (A) He is holding a basket.

    (B) He is waving his hand.

    (C) He has his helmet on.

    (D) He is dressed for hot weather.

解析

    (A) holding a basket 錯，holding a helmet 才對！如果不認識 helmet 這個字，他手上拿的就是個 helmet。

    (B) 確實是 waving his left hand。

    (C) helmet 在手上，並沒戴上。

    (D) 穿了件大外套，不可能是為了 hot weather。

7. Look at the picture marked number 7 in your test book.

    (A) They are working on the railing.

    (B) They are walking up stairs.

    (C) One of the people is wearing a scarf.

    (D) They are cleaning the stairs.

解析

    (A) railing 指的是最前面那位女士邊上樓邊握著的欄杆，working on the railing 就是修理 railing，如果是 walking on the railing，那就是特技表演。

    (B) 確實是 walking up the stairs。

    (C) 前面的章節就提過 scarf 了，錯！

    (D) cleaning 錯！

8. Look at the picture marked number 8 in your test book.

(A) He is peeking through a microscope in a laboratory.

(B) He is wearing protective goggles.

(C) He is reading a document.

(D) He is busy typing.

解析

(A) 確實是 peeking through a microscope，在 laboratory 裡也沒錯。這裡要注意英、澳腔裡的 laboratory 這個字。

(B) protective goggles 去 Google 圖片搜尋裡找一下就知道這句錯了。

(C) 沒看到任何 document，

(D) 也沒有 typing。

9. Look at the picture marked number 9 in your test book.

(A) Cars are parked on both sides of the street.

(B) There is severe traffic congestion on the road.

(C) Trees are planted along both sides of the road.

(D) The parking lot is full of cars.

解析

(A) 這是塞車（traffic jam, traffic congestion），不是停車。

(B) 這樣的 traffic congestion 還真的是 severe。

(C) 沒看到 plants，更沒有在 both sides of the road。

(D) 這根本不是 parking lot。

10. Look at the picture marked number 10 in your test book.

(A) They are sitting in a parking lot.

(B) The man is climbing a tree.

(C) They are resting on a bench in a park.

(D) They are standing up from the chair.

解析

(A) sitting 沒錯，但不是在 parking lot。

(B) climbing a tree? You must be kidding.

(C) resting on a bench 對，in a park 地點也沒錯！

(D) 他們是 sitting 沒看到要 standing from the chair。

Part 1 中譯

再強調一次，翻譯是給你參考的，而且說實話，如果需要翻譯來參考，你的聽力就有很大的進步空間

1. 請看試題本上標號 1 的照片。

(A) 房子裡到處是箱子。

(B) 其中一個人拿著個背包。

(C) 所有人都在打包。

(D) 燈關掉了。

2. 請看試題本上標號 2 的照片。

(A) 她正跟同事說話。

(B) 她在用電腦。

(C) 她手伸長的要拿架上的文件夾。

(D) 她正在休息

3. 請看試題本上標號 3 的照片。

(A) 她在擦拭電腦螢幕。

(B) 她在講電話。

(C) 她在鍵盤上打字。

(D) 她用個耳機聽音樂。

4. 請看試題本上標號 4 的照片。

(A) 他們在互相交談。

(B) 桌上有個茶壺。

(C) 女士正舉著手。

(D) 男士在休息。

5. 請看試題本上標號 5 的照片。

(A) 架上的報紙正被移開。

(B) 報架上有雜誌。

(C) 有個人在看雜誌。

(D) 垃圾桶滿了。

6. 請看試題本上標號 6 的照片。

(A) 他拿著個籃子。

(B) 他正在揮手。

(C) 他帶著個安全帽。

(D) 他穿著熱天的衣服。

7. 請看試題本上標號 7 的照片。

(A) 他們正在修欄杆。

(B) 他們正往樓上走。

(C) 其中一個人帶著圍巾。

(D) 他們正在清理樓梯。

8. 請看試題本上標號 8 的照片。

(A) 他在實驗室裡透過顯微鏡看東西。

(B) 他帶著個護目鏡。

(C) 他在看文件。

(D) 他忙著打字。

9. 請看試題本上標號 9 的照片。

(A) 車停在馬路兩邊。

(B) 路上塞車很嚴重。

(C) 馬路兩邊都種樹了。

(D) 車停滿了停車場。

10. 請看試題本上標號 10 的照片。

(A) 他們坐在停車場。

(B) 男士在爬樹。

(C) 他們在公園長椅上休息。

(D) 他們正從椅子上站起來。

11. Are you nervous about your presentation next Monday?

(A) I've been preparing for it for several months. I am ready for it.

(B) I am not nervous at all, since it is the only chance for me to get the promotion.

(C) You will be working on the presentation material.

解析

你會對下星期一的報告感到緊張嗎？

其實這個問題簡化就只是Are you nervous? (about the presentation)

(A) 我已經準備了好幾個月了。I am ready for it. 都已經 preparing for it 幾個月了，I am ready，完全正確。

(B) 因為這是我唯一能獲得晉升的機會，所以我一點都不緊張。如果是 the only change to get the promotion，不緊張才怪！

(C) 你將要做報告的題材。問的是 are you 回答怎麼可能是 you will be！怎麼樣也該是 I 或是 we。

12. Rumor has it; CEO is resigning from his position.

(A) I am not going to resign. I am staying.

(B) Where did you hear it? We'd better stop it from spreading.

(C) Yes, our CEO just re-signed a big customer.

解析

有傳言說執行長辭職了。

(A) 我沒有要辭職，我要留下來。問的是 CEO，跟你、我都沒關係。

(B) 哪聽來的？不要四處亂說。正確答案！

(C) 對，我們的 CEO 才再簽了一位大客戶。題目是 resign，這個答案故意用 re-sign 來混淆你。就算這題的 rumor has it 聽不懂，還是可以答題對吧！所以記得，考試時如果有聽不懂的部分，不要去想專注在你聽懂的就對了！這絕對是聽力應考的關鍵：專注在你聽懂的。Rumor has it 謠傳、聽說，CEO is resigning 辭職。

13. Should I wait here or should I come back a bit later?

(A) Yes, you need to sit down.

(B) This wouldn't take long.

(C) Wait a minute, something is wrong here.

解析

在這等一下還是待會再來？（二選一）

(A) 是的，你必須坐下。二選一不可能是 yes/no，還有 sit down 也不對。

(B) 不會太久（等一下好了）。轉了個彎的答案。

(C) 等一下，有些不對勁。

14. Do I have to personally pick up the package?

(A) We can deliver it for you.

(B) One package per person, please.

(C) You can drive a pickup truck.

解析

我需要親自拿包裹嗎？

(A) 我們可以幫你送貨。正確答案。

(B) 一人一件行李。

(C) 可以開卡車。

15. Do you need any assistance in setting up the conference room?

    (A) The conference room is right over there.

    (B) The meeting ended already.

    (C) Yes. I can use all the help I can get.

解析

需要幫忙布置會議室嗎？

(A) 會議室就在那邊。

(B) 會議已經結束了。

(C) 當然，越多人幫忙越好。正確答案

16. Will you be here for the seminar tomorrow?

    (A) I don't need a seminar.

    (B) I can do it for you.

    (C) You can count on it.

解析

你會去明天的會議嗎？

(A) 我不需要研討會。

(B) 我可以幫你。

(C) 你儘管放心吧。意思就是我一定會去，正確答案，順便把 You can count on it 多念幾次。

17. We passed the first hurdle, but we are not out of the woods yet.

(A) More hurdles are needed.

(B) Just keep working hard and we are going to be fine.

(C) The woods just arrived.

解析

我們過了第一關，但是我們還沒脫離危險。

過了第一關，但是還沒脫離危險、還不算安全。(還沒走出森林)

(A) 需要更多柵欄。錯！

(B) 繼續努力就不會有問題。沒錯！

(C) 木頭剛到。錯！

對於這題我想多解釋一下，基本上新多益在聽力上面，像這類 out of the woods 片語出現在考題裡的機會其實不是很大，那你應該會問了，為什麼出這題？其實有個含意。多益聽力還有其他任何的聽力測驗，你把每個字、每個片語都聽懂的機會應該是趨近於 0 吧！所以在聽力考試時，如何藉由聽懂的部分來判斷答案也是個很重要的技巧，而這個重點，在這本書裡我也提了好幾次！以這題而言，如果不知道 out of the woods，其實你還是有很好的機會來選出正確答案！先看一下這句話的前半部：We passed the first hurdle，我在做個假設好了，你不知道 hurdle 這個字(別緊張，hurdle 這個字還有點程度，不懂的人絕不在少數)，所以這裡會變成 We passed the first something，感覺上應該是好的，對吧！但是接下來的 but we are not out of the woods yet 也不知道 out of the woods 但是從 but 就知道後面不是好事，是不是就像聽到 We are OK for now but⋯ 整句話聽起來就不是好事，把題目的 FU 感受到後，看看三個答案，首先 (A) 和 (C) 的答案聽起來都有點像題目，關於 part 2，我一直強調聽起來很像的就是錯！從這裡多多少少可以挑出錯的答案，但是消去法真的不保險。再講回題目，We passed the first hurdle but we are not out of the woods yet 聽起來就不是好事，答案 (B)，是不是感覺還蠻激勵的？感覺對了，就可以考慮選為正確答案，其實在聽力考試，尤其是 Part 2 的問題，把題目和答案的口氣感覺出來，對你答題其實有很大的幫助，我會出這題，甚至本書裡 Part 2 其他的題目，你都可以試試看感覺一下題目和答案的口氣，如果真有些字、詞沒聽懂，就用你所感覺出來的口氣來答題！記得專注在你聽懂的，然後注意講話的口氣，和你聽到的感覺，這都是重點！

18. Our latest product will give our competitors a run for their money.

(A) Everyone will be short of the money.

(B) The production is going to be a problem for us.

(C) I know. It should sell well with its low price and high performance.

解析

我們最新的產品會讓對手很頭痛。

先把後面的 give our competitors a run for their money 念個兩次，是不是可以感覺到這會是個很炫的 product ？

(A) 每個人都會缺錢。

(B) 生產會是個問題。

(C) 我知道，低價以及高性能，會賣得很好。正確答案。

19. What do you prefer? Go to a movie or stay home and watch TV?

(A) Either one is OK with me.

(B) Yes, I enjoyed the movie.

(C) No, I'll take a look at the TVs.

解析

喜歡哪個，看電影還是待在家裡看電視？（二選一的題型）

(A) 兩個都 OK。正確答案。

(B) 對，我很喜歡這部電影。二選一 yes/no 就錯了，我喜歡那部電影也不對。

(C) 不，我會去看（比較）一下電視。take a look at the TV 其實是在電器行比較各個電視，也是錯。

20. How do you get to the train station?

(A) I usually go by bus.

(B) An airplane will do.

(C) By the end of the week.

解析

你怎麼去車站？

(A) 我通常搭巴士。正確答案。

(B) 飛機也可以。

(C) 這禮拜之前。

21. Why isn't Ms. Nagasaki in her cubicle?

(A) Every other week.

(B) I thought she is on the left.

(C) She called in sick.

解析

為什麼 Ms. Nagasaki 不在她的位置上？

(A) 每兩個禮拜。

(B) 我以為她在左邊。She left 才對。

(C) 她請了病假。正確。

22. I have a reservation for four people.

(A) Your reservation is the best.

(B) Your name, please.

(C) The forth one.

解析

我訂了位，四個人。

(A) 你訂的位子最棒。

(B) 請問你的名字。正確。

(C) 第四個。

23. Didn't you have a college degree?

(A) Yes, from the State University of New York.

(B) No, I don't agree.

(C) Please send it to the Personnel Department.

(解析)

你不是有大學學位？

(A) 是的，紐約州立大學。正確答案。

(B) 不，我不同意。

(C) 請送到人資部門。

24. Where should I put the recliner?

(A) Please send it by air.

(B) Right over there.

(C) Please put it off.

(解析)

我該把這活動躺椅放哪？

注意，就算你不知道 recliner(可以躺下來的沙發)，還是可以聽出 where should I put it/the thing? 根本對答題不會有影響。再說一次：專注在你聽懂的部分。

(A) 請用空運。

(B) 就在那裏。正確答案。

(C) 請延後。

25. Where did you put the annual report?

   (A) The manager has it.

   (B) The reporter is right over there.

   (C) Once a week will do.

   解析

   你把年度報告放哪裡呢？

   (A) 在經理手上。正確答案。

   (B) 記者就在那。

   (C) 一個禮拜一次就 OK。

26. How about Chinese food for lunch?

   (A) I like Chinese New Year.

   (B) That's a great idea.

   (C) I'd like to have dinner.

   解析

   中午吃中餐如何？（提議）

   (A) 我喜歡過年。

   (B) 這主意很棒。正確答案。

   (C) 我想吃晚餐。

27. Why did you take the bus?

   (A) My car broke down this morning.

   (B) I can take you to the bus station.

   (C) I just want to ride my bike.

你為什麼搭車？

(A) 今早車壞了。正確答案。

(B) 我可以載你到車站。

(C) 我只想騎腳踏車。

28. Do you want to go to a movie tonight or are you too busy?

(A) I'll move in today.

(B) Jennifer likes the show.

(C) I'll let you know later today.

去看電影好嗎？還是你在忙？

(A) 我今天會搬進去。movie 改成 move in。

(B) 珍妮佛喜歡那個秀。

(C) 今天晚點再跟你說。正確答案。

29. Thanks for helping us move into the new house.

(A) It's the least I can do.

(B) Your help is greatly appreciated.

(C) I'd like to move in, too.

謝謝你幫忙搬新家。

(A) 小事一件。直翻：我所能做的最簡單、最小的事，正確答案。不用去管它的中文意思，多念幾次：It's the least I can do. 就對了。

(B) 感謝你的幫忙。問題裡對你說，怎麼可能用你來回答！
(C) 我也想搬進來。題目裡是 move into，這裡改成 move in, too，
想要混淆你！

30. How much business traveling is needed for the job?
   (A) The job is in Jakarta.
   (B) Roughly every other month.
   (C) I have no problem with it.

   解析

   這工作出差的機會多大？
   (A) 工作地點在雅加達。
   (B) 大概每兩個月一次。every other hour 每兩小時一次，把 every
       other month 和 every other hour 多念兩次，就會有 FU 了。
   (C) 我沒問題。

31. Did you have a chance to see the financial report?
   (A) Yes, and it is fabulous.
   (B) I didn't get the weather report.
   (C) We have a chance for sure.

   解析

   你有機會看到財務報告嗎？
   (A) 看到了，很棒。正確答案。
   (B) 我沒拿到氣象報告。
   (C) 我們當然有機會。

32. There aren't enough chairs for all the participants.

(A) The chairman will come and join us.

(B) I'll get some extra ones.

(C) Help me move more tables.

解析

椅子不夠坐。

(A) 主席會來參加。

(B) 我去多搬一些來。正確答案。

(C) 幫我多搬些桌子。

33. Haven't we received the renovation plan?

(A) The plane arrived in New York.

(B) I'll check with the receptionist.

(C) Office remodeling is done.

解析

還沒收到整修計畫嗎？

(A) 飛機已經到紐約。plan 改成 plane，錯。

(B) 我去櫃檯確認一下。完全正確。

(C) 辦公室整修已經完成。

34. It is hot today.

(A) We need some hot water.

(B) We need more new equipment.

(C) I'll open the window and let some cool air in.

今天可真熱！

這種肯定句的問題最難，因為你根本無法預測答案！所以需要把題目和答案都聽懂才行。

(A) 我們需要熱水。太像了，錯！

(B) 我們需要新儀器。

(C) 我來開窗，讓涼風吹進來。完全正確！

35. Do you know where the headquarters is?

(A) It's on Broadway Street.

(B) I have a quarter.

(C) Yes, please tell me.

你知道總部在哪嗎？

(A) 在 Broadway Street。正確。

(B) 我有個夸特。兩毛五的硬幣。

(C) 是的，請告訴我。既然知道，怎麼會要別人告訴你。

36. Why don't we take a rest?

(A) I'd like to finish this section first.

(B) We don't need to do it.

(C) The reason cannot be told.

休息一下好嗎？（提議）

(A) 我想把這部分先做完。（然後才休息），正確。

(B) 我們不需要做。

(C) 原因不能說。

37. Where should we hold the employee meeting?

(A) Three-thirty.

(B) We'll need one of the larger rooms.

(C) Refreshments would be needed.

解析

員工會議應該在哪兒舉行？

(A) 三點半。

(B) 需要個大一點的房間。（說出個必需的條件）轉了兩個彎的答案。

(C) 需要點心。

38. The new secretary is doing a great job, isn't she?

(A) Much better than I expected.

(B) I don't recognize her at all.

(C) She likes to go shopping.

解析

新來的秘書做的很棒，對吧！

(A) 比我預期的好多了。正確。

(B) 我完全認不出她。

(C) 她喜歡購物。

39. What would you recommend from the menu?

(A) I'll bring you the menu.

(B) The fish is really tasty today.

(C) It's the chef's specialty.

解析

菜單裡你會建議哪些菜？

(A) 我去拿菜單給你。

(B) 今天的魚很可口。正確。

(C) 這可是廚師的拿手菜。

40. Do you know the fastest way to get to the airport?

(A) The express shuttle would be your best bet.

(B) It's ten miles away.

(C) At least two months.

解析

你知道去機場最快的方法嗎？

Highway 高速公路，express way 快速道路，shuttle bus 接駁車，再來是 express shuttle 快速接駁車，千萬不要硬背，把這幾個字、詞：highway, express way, shuttle bus, express shuttle 多念幾遍就對了。

(A) 快速接駁車會是你最好的選擇。

(B) 十英里以外。

(C) 至少兩個月。

在看解答前,我再強調一次,Part 3 和 Part 4 的練習要一句一句的念,然後閉著眼睛一句一句的聽,先確認每一句分開後都可以聽懂,然後整篇一起聽,畢竟考試的時候不會一句一句的分開放,目標永遠是整篇一次可以聽懂。

Questions 41-43 ▶ refer to the following conversation.

M: Did you hear that our company just named the new VP of Marketing?

聽說了公司剛宣布新的行銷副總嗎?

W: No, I haven't. Please fill me in with the details.

沒聽說,請告訴我細節。

M: We first tried to hire someone from outside, but Sam Walters, previously the Internet Marketing Director, was promoted as the VP of Marketing.

原先想從外面找,後來內升,原本的 Internet Marketing Director 網路行銷協理 Sam Walters 升為行銷副總。

W: From what I know, he is capable of the new job and will be able to lead the marketing team successfully. He may need a little bit of time, though.

就我所知,他可以勝任也可以成功領導行銷團隊。

41. Who most likely are the speakers?

他們可能是什麼樣的人、什麼職業?

(A) They are tourists.

他們是觀光客。

(B) They work for the sales and marketing team.

他們在業務行銷團隊工作。（只有談論行銷副總，沒有説到他們的部門）

(C) They are colleagues.

他們是同事。

(D) They are reporters.

他們是記者。

42. Who is Sam Walters?

Sam Walters 是誰？

(A) A new employee for the company.

公司新員工。

(B) A retailer.

零售商。

(C) The new Marketing VP.

新的行銷副總。

(D) The president of the company.

公司總經理。

43. What does the woman think of Mr. Walters?

這位女士對 Walters 先生的看法是？

(A) He will be able to do a good job.

他可以勝任。（最後一段提出）

(B) She needs some detail information about him first.

她需要先知道些有關他的詳情。

(C) He isn't really qualified for the job.

他不夠格。

(D) Only time can tell.

過段時間才能知道

Questions 44 - 46 refer to the following conversation.

W: Have you heard that there is a new restaurant opening on Main Street.

有沒有聽説 Main Street 上開了家新餐廳？

M: It's Red Dragon Dining. I went there last Friday for the grand opening, great atmosphere, terrific food, courteous service.

是 Red Gragon Dining。我上週五才去，氣氛佳、食物棒、服務又有禮。

W: I have some clients coming from overseas next Monday. Do you think it's a good place for a meal?

我下週一有國外客戶來訪，去那兒吃飯 OK 嗎？

M: Yes, but you'd better make a reservation first. Here is the business card with their address and phone number. Please take it.

可以啊，但最好先預訂。這是他們的名片上面有地址和電話。

44. What are they talking about?

他們談些什麼呢？

(A) Some overseas clients.

國外客戶。

(B) A new restaurant.

一家新餐廳。

(C) A new employee.

新的員工。

(D) A good meeting place.

開會的好地方。

45. What will happen next Monday?

下週一有什麼事？

(A) Clients will visit the company.

客戶會拜訪公司

(B) Grand opening for the restaurant.

餐廳開幕。

(C) The president will be coming from overseas.

總經理由國外來訪。

(D) An event celebration will be held.

有個慶祝活動。

46. What does the man suggest?

男士的建議是？

(A) Take the business card.

收下名片。

(B) Take the clients to a better place.

帶客戶到更好的地方。

(C) Check and make sure the address is correct.

確認地址正確。

(D) Call and reserve first.

先打電話預訂。

Questions 47 - 49 refer to the following conversation.

W: Matthew, would you be able to finish the artwork by Friday? We need it for the advertising campaign for the new car models starting next week.

Matthew，你禮拜五可以完成那個藝術品（或是畫作）嗎？我們在下星期開始的新車廣告中要用。

M: I'll be putting the final touch to it on Thursday so it should not be a problem at all. 我禮拜四時會做最後的收工，所以應該沒問題。

W: Good. Our client has bought spaces in magazines and newspapers with some on the front page.

客戶已經買下雜誌和報紙的頁面，有些還是在封面。

M: I am sure it will be a success.

我相信會很成功

47. Who do the speakers work for?

說話的人是為誰工作？

(A) A motor manufacturer.

汽車製造商。

(B) A newspaper company.

報社。

(C) A publisher.

出版社。

(D) An advertising agency.

廣告商。

48. When will the man be able to finish his work?

男士會什麼時候完成工作？

(A) Tuesday.

週二。

(B) Wednesday.

週三。

(C) Thursday.

週四。

(D) Friday.

週五。

49. Why did their client pay the magazines?

客戶為什麼會付錢給雜誌

(A) To put an advertisement.

放廣告。

(B) To get a good review.

得到好評價。

(C) To put the artwork on display.

展示藝術品。

(D) To subscribe the magazines.

訂閱雜誌。

Questions 50 - 52 ▷ refer to the following conversation.

M: Hello, I purchased a computer desk from your website at the end of last month, but I haven't received it yet. Could you check it for me, please?

Hello，上個月月底我在網路上買了你們的電腦桌但是到現在還沒收到，可以幫忙查一下嗎？

W: Certainly, sir. Do you, by any chance, have the order number?

當然可以，請問有訂單號碼嗎？

M: Yes, it's 326 8652.

有的，是 326 8652。

W: Mr. Ramirez, right? According to the computer record, it left our warehouse on Wednesday, May 2, so it should arrive tomorrow. Please give us a call again if you didn't receive it by that day.

Ramirez 先生對吧！根據紀錄，貨物週三 5/2 出倉庫應該明天會到。如果還沒到，請再打電話給我們。

50. Why did the man call the woman?

這位男士為什麼打電話？

(A) To say hello.

打招呼。

(B) To check the order status.

查一下訂貨狀況。

(C) To cancel his order.

取消訂單。

(D) To arrange for a delivery.

安排送貨。

51. What did the man buy?

這位男士買了什麼？

(A) A computer software.

電腦軟體。

(B) A desk.

一張桌子。

(C) A monitor.

一個螢幕。

(D) A computer.

一台電腦。

52. What does the woman ask for?

女士要求了什麼？

(A) The man's name.

男士的名字。

(B) The man's telephone number.

男士的電話號碼。

(C) The date when the order was placed.

何時訂貨的。

(D) The reference number of the order.

訂單資訊。（訂單號碼）

Questions 53~55 refer to the following conversation.

W: Freddy, did you have a chance to review my proposal for sponsoring the city marathon? I put it on your desk.

Freddy有時間看看我那份贊助城市馬拉松的提案嗎？我放在你桌上。

M: Yes, Fiona, I did and I love your idea. With our new line of running shoes launching next month, this would be a great way to increase the market awareness.

有啊，Fiona，我看過後很喜歡。對下個月要上市的新系列跑鞋，這會是很棒的機會來增加市場知名度。

W: I thought so, too. We could also set up a booth to hand out souvenirs with our company logo.

我也這麼認為，可以設立個攤位來送附有公司標誌的紀念品。

M: Hey, why don't you join me to the regional meeting this Friday and present your ideas to the marketing director, Christopher Thompson?

乾脆跟我一起去週五的區域會議把你的主意講給行銷協理Christopher Thompson聽聽，怎樣？

53. What does the proposal suggest?

提案建議了什麼？

(A) Participating a marathon.

參加馬拉松。（贊助，不是參加）

(B) Marketing new line of running shoes.

行銷新的系列跑鞋。

(C) Helping city mayor.

幫助市長。

(D) Sponsoring a public event.

贊助個活動。

54. Why do they need a booth?

為什麼需要個攤位？

(A) To send out gifts.

送禮物。（對話中是 souvenirs，選項中是 gifts。）

(B) To set up a shop for new products.

設置商店來賣新產品。

(C) To help the city.

幫助這城市。

(D) To promote the event.

宣傳個活動。

55. What can be implied about Mr. Thompson?

可以推測出 Thompson 先生是什麼？

(A) He is a talented runner.

他很會跑步。

(B) He has the authority of approving the proposal.

他有權利核准這個提案。

（順便念一下 authority, authorize, authorization）

(C) He is an expert in running shoe design.

他是設計慢跑鞋的專家。

(D) He will not come to the regional meeting.

他不會參加會議。

Questions 56-58 ◀ refer to the following conversation.

M: I'd like two tickets to tonight's ball game, sitting as close to the court as possible.

我要兩張今晚球賽的票，越靠近球場越好。

W: Sorry, all reserved seats are sold out and we only have general admission tickets. The seating is available on a first-come first-served basis.

抱歉，所有可以劃位的票都賣完了，只剩先到先坐的一般門票。

M: Well, that would be fine. So, next time, I would need to come here even earlier for the reserved seats.

好吧，還是要買，所以下次我要更早來了。

W: Actually, you can order tickets on the team's official website. It's more convenient.

你可以在官方網站直接買票更方便。

56. What is the man trying to do?

男士要做什麼？

(A) Purchase two plane tickets.

買兩張飛機票。

（可不要聽到 tickets 而且在答案上看到 tickets 就選了這個答案）

(B) Exchange the seating.

換位子。

(C) Attend a ball game.

　看球賽。

(D) Cancel a reservation.

　取消預定。

57. What does the woman say about the rest of the tickets?

女士說剩下的票是？

(A) Seating cannot be assigned.

　不能指定座位。(沒有劃位的位子，只剩先到先坐的)

(B) They are cheaper.

　比較便宜。

(C) They are exchangeable.

　可以交換。

(D) They are not refundable.

　不能退錢。

58. What suggestion does the woman make?

女士建議了什麼？

(A) Arrive earlier.

　早點來。

(B) Buy the tickets on the internet.

　上網路買。

(C) Purchase through a convenience store.

　透過便利商店買。

(D) Order the reserved seats.

　買可以預訂位子的票。

W: I have a reservation for a single room for two nights under the name of Barbara Sandiego.

我預訂了兩晚的單人房，名字是 Barbara Sandiego。

M: Just give me a minute, Ms. Sandiego. Room 1205, here is the keycard, and the elevator is on your left.

請稍等，Sandiego 小姐，您的房號是 1205，這是鑰匙卡，電梯在左邊。

W: Is there any place around here for a quick bite? I am starving and tired after a long flight.

附近有地方吃便餐嗎？搭了長途飛機後，我可是又餓又累。

M: Exit the front door and go left. There is a sandwich shop one block away and a restaurant across the street from it.

走出門後左轉，過條街後有間三明治店，對面有家餐廳。

59. Where most likely are the speakers?

這兩人在哪裡？

(A) At an airport.

機場。

(B) At a restaurant.

餐廳。

(C) In a taxi.

計程車內。

(D) In a hotel.

旅館。

60. What kind of transportation did the woman take?

這女是用了什麼交通工具？

(A) Airplane.

飛機。

(B) Bus.

巴士。

(C) Taxi.

計程車。

(D) Train.

火車。

61. What will the woman probably do next?

女士接下來會做什麼？

(A) Take a rest.

休息

(B) Have a meal.

吃飯

(C) Watch TV.

看電視

(D) Go online.

上網

M: Excuse me, Melissa. Do you have time? I am having trouble with the timesheet reporting system.

不好意思，Melissa 有時間嗎？工時報告系統我有些問題。

W: I am not surprised. Almost all new employees have problems with the software. It's confusing, especially for new users like you.

習慣了，幾乎所有新員工都不太會用，尤其像你這樣的新手。

M: I did go through the online tutorial yesterday, but I just don't know how to submit the report after filling it out.

我看了線上介紹，但是就是不知道怎麼在填好後把報告送出去。

W: Oh, the submit button is on the lower left hand corner of the screen; the one that says send. Just click it and you are done. Let me know if you have any further questions.

在螢幕左下角有個按鈕上面寫著 send 就對了。有任何其他問題再問我。

62. What are they discussing?

他們在討論什麼？

(A) A trip itinerary.

旅遊行程表。

(B) A computer software.

電腦軟體。（有提到 system 和 screen）

(C) A new employee.

新員工。

(D) A company brochure.

公司簡介手冊。

63. Who most likely is the man?

這男士可能是？

(A) A manager.

經理。

(B) A customer.

客戶。

(C) A sales clerk.

銷售店員。

(D) A new employee.

新員工。

64. What does Melissa actually do?

Melissa 做了什麼？

(A) Helps fill out the timesheet.

幫忙填工時表。

(B) Collects the report and send it in.

收集報告並送出去。

(C) Indicates the correct button.

指出正確的按鈕。

(D) Demonstrates the machine.

示範操作機器。

Questions 65 - 67 refer to the following conversation.

M: Did you read the email that our company is going to pay for the tuition for the evening classes at City College?

你看到那封說公司會付城市大學夜校學費的 email 了嗎？

W: That's a really nice benefit. I'd like to learn more about marketing strategy. But I don't know how to sign up.

這可是好福利，我想學行銷策略，但是不知道如何報名。

M: Just contact the Personnel Department, and they will tell you all the details you need. You need to apply by July 30th. Oh, one more thing, you need to score a grade of C or better to get reimbursed.

跟人資部門聯絡就會把詳細資料給你。7/30 前要申請，還有成績要 C 以上才會補助。

W: That's not a problem. I'll call them and get registered by July 20th.

那不是問題。我會打電話並在 7/20 前申請。

65. What are they discussing?

他們在討論什麼？

(A) A company benefit.

公司福利。

(B) College education.

大學教育。(只講了上課，沒談到更深的，故 (A) 較恰當。)

(C) Marketing strategy.

行銷策略。

(D) A university professor.

大學教授。

66. How would an employee do to get compensated?

員工要怎麼做才能拿到補助？

(A) By registering a class.

註冊個課程。

(B) By attending all lectures.

每堂課都出席。

(C) By getting a good enough grade.

拿到夠好的成績。（要拿到 C 以上才有補助。）

(D) By calling Personnel Department.

跟人資部門聯絡。

67. When is the application deadline?

申請期限是？

(A) July 3.

7 月 3 日。

(B) July 13.

7 月 13 日。

(C) July 20.

7 月 20 日。（是女士自訂的時間。）

(D) July 30.

7 月 30 日。（公司公告的期限）

W: The shirt looks good on you.

這襯衫穿在你身上很好看。

M: OK, I'll take it and here is my credit card. By the way, how do I clean it? Can I use a washing machine?

我要買，這是信用卡，還有這要怎麼洗？可以用洗衣機嗎？

W: Washing machine could be too rough for it. Hand wash is a better option.

洗衣機對這襯衫會有些粗暴。手洗比較好。

M: That would be too much trouble. I'll send it to the dry cleaner.

這太麻煩了，我還是送乾洗好了。

68. Where most likely are the speakers?

談話地點在哪裡？

(A) At a clothing store.

服飾店。

(B) At a dry cleaner.

乾洗店。

(C) At a grocery store.

蔬果雜貨店。

(D) At a park.

公園。

69. Who most likely is the woman?

這女士是？

(A) A bank teller.

銀行櫃檯人員。

(B) An accountant.

會計。

(C) A store clerk.

店員。

(D) A nurse.

護士。

70. What does the man think about the woman's suggestion?

男士對女士建議的看法是？

(A) It's time consuming.

花太多時間。

(B) It's too rough.

太粗暴了。

(C) It's great.

很棒。

(D) It looks fine.

看來不錯。

同樣的，Part 4 的練習要一句一句的念，然後閉著眼睛一句一句的聽，先確認每一句分開後都可以聽懂，然後整篇一起聽，目標永遠是整篇一次可以聽懂。

Questions 71-73 refer to the following announcement.

Good afternoon, everyone. I'd like to introduce Floyd Pichardo who is going to lead the Internet Marketing training session. After graduating from Texas A&M University with a bachelor degree in Computer Engineering, Mr. Pichardo joined Facebook as a product engineer. Five years later, he started his own company, App Store, focusing on App design. After producing some of the most well received Apps, the company was bought by Twitter. With Mr. Pichardo's humorous personality and expertise on web marketing, I am sure the session will be fun and informative. After this session, there will be a break and refreshments will be served right outside of the conference room. Now, let's give a hand to Mr. Floyd Pichardo.

大家午安。我要介紹一下待會兒要引領網路行銷課程的 Floyd Pichardo， 在 Texas A&M University 主 修 Computer Engineering 畢業後，Pichardo 先生加入了 FB 成為產品工程師。

五年後成立自己的公司 App Store，專精 App 的設計。在做出些很受好評的 App 後，公司被 Twitter 買下。Pichardo 先生個性幽默，還有網路行銷方面的專長，我保證這階段會很有趣也很有幫助。這階段結束後，請稍做休息，會議室外有點心。現在，請掌聲歡迎 Mr. Floyd Pichardo。

71. What is the purpose of the announcement?

這段宣布的目的是什麼？

(A) To talk about app design.

說明 App design。

(B) To introduce a lecturer.

介紹主講人。

(C) To talk about college education.

說明大學教育。

(D) To introduce a training session.

介紹一個訓練課程。（介紹人而不是介紹這個 session。）

72. What is the topic of the session?

課程主題是？

(A) App design.

App 設計。

(B) Bachelor party.

單身派對。（結婚前給男方的單身 party）

(C) Web marketing.

網路行銷。

(D) Internet advertising effectiveness.

網路廣告的有效性。

73. Where most likely is the event taking place?

地點最可能在哪裡？

(A) At a university.

大學裡。

(B) At a convention center.

會議中心內。（在新多益考試裡可以把這四個字都當會議來看：
conference, convention, seminar, workshop，雖然這四個
會議的範圍、形式和目的都不同，不過新多益不會考這麼細。）

(C) At a restaurant.

餐廳。

(D) At an airport.

機場。

Questions 74 - 76 refer to the following telephone message

You've reached the automatic customer response system. If you know your party's extension, please dial it now. To open a new account, please press 1. To transfer funds between your accounts, press 2 now. To pay your credit card balance, please press 3. To report a lost or stolen credit card, press 4. To request a new check book, press 5 now. To speak to a customer service representative, press 9. This message will automatically repeat itself.

這是客戶自動回應系統,請撥分機號碼。開新帳戶請按一;帳戶間轉帳請按二;付信用卡請按三;通報遺失信用卡請按四;申請新支票請按五;找客服人員請按九。這訊息會自動重複。

74. What kind of company is this?

這是什麼公司?

(A) A customer service company.

客服公司。

(B) A credit card company.

信用卡公司。

(C) A telephone manufacturer.

電話製造商。

(D) A bank.

銀行。(有提到開戶、信用卡及支票的業務,所以選銀行)

75. What should the listener press to talk to a customer service representative?

要找客服人員要按幾號?

(A) 4

(B) 5

(C) 6

(D) 9

76. According to the talk, what should a listener do to listen to the message again?

根據留言，要怎麼做才能再聽一次？

(A) Press 0.

按 0。

(B) Press 1.

按 1。

(C) Hang up and dial again.

掛掉重播。

(D) Stay on the line.

留在線上。（會重複播放）

Questions 77 - 79 ◯ refer to the following advertisement

Looking for a way out of the boring, minimum waged job you are having right now?

Dreaming of the most exciting, well compensated jobs? Computer Technology Training Center is your answer. We will prepare you to work as a computer programmer, the most rewarding job in the US as well as the world. Learn to write the hottest computer languages, Java, C, C++, Python, Perl and more. Our evening and weekend courses are designed for people who have to work weekdays just to make ends meet. Yes, they are designed for you and in four months, you will start a whole new chapter of your life. New classes start every two months. Visit our website www.trainingcenter.com for class schedules and cost. You will be glad you did.

想為你現在的無聊低薪工作找個出路嗎？夢想著一個令人興奮又高薪的工作嗎？Computer Technology Training Center 就是你的答案，我們會讓你成為一個電腦程式工程師，在美國以及世界各地最有前途的工作。學會寫最紅的電腦語言，Java, C, C++, Python, Perl 還有更多。我們有夜間和週末的課程，專門為白天要上班的人而設計。是的，專為你所設計的，而且四個月後你的人生就會有一個新的旅程。

每兩個月就有新課程。請至我們的網站查看課程和費用，日後你會為你所做的感到高興。

77. What kind of job is it advertising?

廣告中提到的工作是什麼？

(A) Computer programmers.

電腦程式設計師。

(B) Computer technicians.

電腦技師。

(C) Language instructors.

語言講師。

(D) Design managers.

設計經理。

78. How long is the course?

課程多長？

(A) One month.

1 個月。

(B) Two months.

　　2 個月。

(C) Three months.

　　3 個月。

(D) Four months.

　　4 個月。

79. How can someone get the class schedules?

　　怎麼得知課程時間？

(A) Visit the office.

　　拜訪辦公室。

(B) Go online.

　　上網。

(C) Call the center.

　　打電話。

(D) Write a letter.

　　寫信。

Questions 80 - 82 refer to the following talk

This is the last stop of our tour today, the cafeteria. It is open from 7 to 10 in the morning and 12 to 2 for lunch. Hot food is stationed on your left hand side, and salad bar is on your right with sandwiches and snacks at the far end. There is a meal card in your employee orientation pack with 10 dollar credit on it. When you finish selecting your food, just go to the checkout counter. After the cashier adds up your purchase, just swipe the card to pay for the meal. You can recharge the card with the machine right at the entrance of the restaurant. Let's now have a 10 minute Q&A session and we'll wrap up the tour right after that.

這是今天行程的最後一站，餐廳。從早上七點開到十點，中餐時間是中午十二點到兩點。熱食在左邊，沙拉吧在右邊，三明治和點心在後面。在你的新進員工講習袋裡有張裡面已經有十元儲值的餐廳卡。選完食物後直接到收銀櫃台，在收銀員算好帳後，直接刷餐卡付錢。你可以使用餐廳入口的機器來儲值。現在開始十分鐘提問，然後就結束今天的行程。

80. Who is the intended audience?

觀眾是？

(A) Tourists.

觀光客。

(B) Job candidates.

職缺候選人。

(C) Cafeteria staff.

餐廳員工。

(D) New employees.

新進職員。（有提到 employee orientation，是新員工參加的，故選 D）

81. Where is the talk being given?

地點在哪裡？

(A) A tourist stop.

觀光景點。

(B) A restaurant.

餐廳。（cafeteria 可稱是員工餐廳）

(C) A hotel.

旅館。

(D) An office.

辦公室。

82. What is true about the meal card?

哪項關於餐卡的敘述是正確的？

(A) It's free for every employee.

不用交錢。

(B) The maximum amount on it is 10 dollars.

最多十塊。（10 元是已經儲值的金額）

(C) It can be used only one time.

只能用一次。

(D) It can be used to pay for food.

可以用來付餐點。

Questions 83 - 85 refer to the following talk

Good morning everyone. Welcome to Denali National Park and Preserve. I am Victor Quasimodo, and I'll be leading your tour today. Right now, we are driving along the Denali Park Road. If we are lucky enough, we could spot some grizzly bears wandering around the park. Just coming out of winter hibernation, they are hungry and extremely dangerous in the current spring season. Even with patches of snow still existing, wolves, moose, Dall's sheep, foxes, and squirrels are already active this time of the year. Morning and evening hours are the best time of the day to see the wildlife. Since the bus trip takes more than 8 hours, I can assure you that you would have the chance of seeing wild animals in action. It would take half an hour to our next stop, so please sit back and enjoy the beautiful scenery of the park.

早安各位，歡迎來到 Denali National Park 保護區。我是 Victor Quasimodo，你們今天的嚮導。現在我們正在 Denali Park 路上。運氣好的話，可以看到灰熊在園區閒逛。剛從冬眠醒來，在這春季，牠們可是既餓又危險。就算地上還有積雪，狼、麋鹿、白大角羊、狐狸和松鼠在每年的此時已經很活躍。早上和傍晚是最好的觀賞野生動物的時間。因為這整個旅程耗時八小時，你絕對有機會看到些活動中的野生動物。接下來還要半小時才會到下個景點，請放輕鬆欣賞一下這園區的美麗風光。

83. What season is it?

現在什麼季節？

(A) Spring.

春。

(B) Summer.

夏。

(C) Fall.

秋。

(D) Winter.

冬。

84. Who is the speaker?

講話的人是誰？

(A) A bus driver.

巴士司機。

(B) A tour guide.

導遊。

(C) A park ranger.

公園警察。

(D) A tourist.

觀光客。

85. Which animal is being warned about?

有對哪種動物提出警告？

(A) Wolves.

狼。

(B) Moose.

麋鹿。

(C) Bears.

熊。（有提到剛結束冬眠的熊，又餓且危險）

(D) Foxes.

狐狸。

Questions 86 - 88 ○▷ refer to the following talk

Welcome to the Consumer Electronic Fair. For the participants here, today's rehearsal is the final chance for you to fine tune your presentation and make your live demonstration later on even more successful. Please give me a minute here. I just got a note indicating a red sports car with a license plate of DSC-445 is illegally parked right at the back entrance of the kitchen. Please promptly move your car before it is towed with a hefty fine. Thanks for your cooperation. Now let's get back to the originally planned schedule and welcome the first demonstration from Media Electronics.

歡迎來到 Consumer Electronic Fair。對於現場的參加者，這將是你們最後一個排練你們簡報，並讓你們稍後的現場展示更加成功的機會。請先給我一分鐘，剛收到訊息，有部紅色跑車車牌是 DSC-445 違規停在廚房後門。請在被拖吊罰款前趕快移開車子，感謝你的合作。現在回到原先的時程並歡迎第一個由 Media Electronic 所帶來的展示。

86. Who is the intended audience?

針對的觀眾是？

(A) Regular customers.

一般消費者。

(B) New product presenters.

新產品展示員。(有提到是最後一個排練的機會)

(C) Company executives.

公司高層管理人員。

(D) Car owners.

汽車擁有人。

87. What does the speaker say about the red sports car?

關於那部紅色跑車，講話者說了什麼？

(A) It is properly parked.

正確的停放。

(B) It is damaged.

受損了。

(C) It could be ticketed.

可能會被開單。

(D) It's condition is fine.

狀況還好。

88. What is going to happen next?

接下來是什麼？

(A) Presentation practice.

展示演練。

(B) Formal demonstration.

　　正式的展銷。

(C) Kitchen appliance introduction.

　　介紹廚房用具。

(D) Opening of the Consumer Electronic Fair.

　　正式開始 Consumer Electronic Fair。

Questions 89 - 91 ▶ refer to the following report

This is Sandy Bradley of KBTX, reporting live from this year's Hot Dog Eating Contest.

This is the tenth time for the city to hold the annual speed eating challenge. I'll be interviewing one of the contestants, Jeff "The Beast Man" Butler.

A relatively new comer, he instantly became a rising star at his 2013 debut at Nathan's Famous Hot Dog Eating Contest. In the following year, he participated in six more competitions, winning two of them and getting top five finishes in the other four. This event is really important to Mr. Butler, because it is the first time for him to join this traditional contest held in Texas. With the fast rising reputation, we believe this won't be his last. In a little while we'll have a talk with him, but first, Bob will take a look at the weather for the following days and see if it will affect the contest.

我是 KBTX 的記者 Sandy Bradley，在今年的 Hot Dog Eating Contest 現場報導。這是本市鎮第十次舉辦的年度大胃王比賽。稍後我會採訪其中之一的參賽者，Jeff " 野獸人 " Butler。對一個新人而言，他在 2013 首次出賽就在 Nathan's Famous Hot Dog Eating Contest 裡成為明日之星。接下來的一年，他參加了六次比賽，贏了兩次並在其他四次裡都拿到前五名。這次比賽對 Butler 先生很重要，因為這是他首次來德州參加這個比賽。以他急速上升的名聲，我們相信這不會是最後一次。

稍後我會跟他聊聊不過先請 Bob 幫我們看一下接下來幾天的氣象，並看看是否會影響這項比賽。

89. Who is the speaker?

報導者是誰？

(A) A contestant.

參賽者。

(B) A reporter.

記者。

(C) A weatherman.

氣象主播。

(D) A contest judge.

裁判。

90. How many years has the contest been held in the place?

比賽已經在這地方辦了幾年？

(A) Two.

2 年。

(B) Four.

    4 年。

(C) Six.

    6 年。

(D) Ten.

    10 年。（每年 1 次，已有 10 次）

91. What is going to happen next?

    接下來是？

    (A) An interview.

        訪談。

    (B) A food eating contest.

        大胃王比賽。

    (C) A weather report.

        氣象報告。

    (D) A test.

        測試。

Welcome to the new employees training center. Later on, on behalf of the Chief Executive Officer, our Chief Operating Officer, Antonio Chen, will give a short talk about the meaning and the importance of this training. Then, Ms. Sandy Huang from Personnel Department will give an overview of the company's employee benefits, as well as rules and regulations. We'll have a lunch at noon in the cafeteria for one hour. At one o'clock, Mr. James Fujita, the Computer Chief, will introduce the computer system and the security measures. Then, our head of Sales and Marketing, Ms. Maria Bernard, will let us know what the future holds for our company. Mr. Babu Gala, head of Personnel Department, will wrap today's event. We hope you will enjoy today's arrangement and now, let us welcome our COO, Mr. Chen.

歡迎來到新員工訓練中心。等會兒，我們的營運長 Antonio Chen 會代表執行總裁，簡短的説一下關於這項訓練的意義和重要性。接下來，會由人資部門而來的 Sandy Huang 會介紹員工福利還有相關的規定和規範。中午在餐廳有一小時的午飯，一點電腦主管 James Fujita 會介紹電腦系統和安全規定。然後業務及行銷主管 Maria Bernard 會講解公司的未來展望。人資主管 Babu Gala 會總結今天的訓練。希望你們會喜歡今天的安排，接下來讓我們歡迎 COO 陳先生。

92. Who is going to talk about the importance of the event?

誰會來談這個活動的重要性？

(A) Chief Executive Officer.

執行總裁。

(B) Chief Operating Officer.

營運長。

(C) Head of Human Resources.

人資主管。

(D) Computer Chief.

電腦主管。

93. Which department does Ms. Huang work for?

黃小姐屬於哪個部門？

(A) Human Resources.

人資。

(B) Computer.

電腦。

(C) Sales and Marketing.

業務及行銷。

(D) Research and Development.

研發。

94. Who is going to host the last session?

最後一部分是由誰主持？

(A) Head of Human Resources.

人資主管。

(B) COO.

營運長。

(C) Computer Chief.

電腦主管。

(D) Head of Sales and Marketing.

業務暨行銷主管。

Questions 95-97 ○ refer to the following talk

During our seminar today, we will practice a few essential presentation skills you can use. It is crucial to grab your audience's attention right after the presentation starts. Don't wait for another 5 to 10 minutes. There are a number of techniques that might do the trick. For example, give your audience a thought-provoking question. Please don't take any complicated question that will probably drag on forever. Keep it simple and interesting and yet gets them into the topic you are going to talk about. You can also try giving them an amazing statistic that will get their attention. An unusual or remarkable visual aid is a good way to go as well. Of course, suitable humor never hurts. An enjoyable presentation is much easier to pay attention to than a dull one.

在今天的 seminar 裡，我們會練習你日後會需要的一些重要的 presentation 技巧。在一開始就要能抓住觀眾的注意力，這一點非常重要。不必等什麼五分鐘、十分鐘。有些技巧可以達到這個目的。例如給個讓觀眾可以想想的問題，不要太複雜那會耗上太多時間。簡單又有趣，能夠帶到你所要講的主題。你也可以給個令人驚訝的統計數字。不尋常或是引人矚目的圖片影像也是個好方法。當然適當的幽默感也有幫助，一個有趣的簡報比起無聊的會更讓人注目。

95. What is the main topic of the talk?

主題是？

(A) How to improve your social skills.

如何增進社交技巧。

(B) How to do a trick.

如何弄個小把戲。

(C) How to give a great presentation.

怎麼給個很棒的簡報。

(D) How to give a thought-provoking question.

怎麼給個讓人深思的問題。

96. What is a suggested technique?

建議的技巧是什麼？

(A) Answer a thought-provoking question.

回答一個讓人深思的問題。（不要想太久的問題）

(B) Show an extraordinary statistic.

展現一個不尋常的統計數字。

(C) Don't tell Jokes.

不要講笑話。（沒有提到）

(D) Ask a complex question.

問個複雜的問題。（要不複雜的問題）

97. When is the best time to catch the audience's attention?

抓住觀眾最好的時機是？

(A) Five to ten minutes after the speech.

演講開始五到十分鐘後。

(B) As soon as possible.

越快越好。（一開始就要，故選 B 最恰當）

(C) It's not necessary.

不需要。

(D) Not mentioned in the talk.

沒有提到。

Ladies and gentlemen, the Captain just turned off the Fasten Seat Belts sign, and you may now move around in the cabin. However, we always recommend that you keep your seat belt fastened while seated. In a few minutes, our flight attendants will start serving dinner, and the choices are chicken or beef. Beverages and a complimentary glass of red wine or white wine are also available. Whisky and other alcoholic beverage will be five dollars a glass. Now, you can just sit back, relax, and enjoy the flight. Thank you.

各位先生女士，機長剛剛把繫上安全帶的燈熄掉了，現在可以在客艙裡行動。然而，我們建議您在座位上時還是要繫安全帶。幾分鐘後空服員會開始送晚餐您可以選雞肉或是牛肉。飲料還有一杯紅酒或白酒都是免費的。威士忌和其他酒精飲品則是一杯五塊。現在請您坐好休息享受一下旅程，謝謝！

98. Where most likely is the announcement taking place?

這個宣布最可能在哪裡？

(A) In an airport.

機場。

(B) In a hotel.

旅館。

(C) On an airplane.

飛機上。

(D) On a cruise ship.

遊輪上。

99. What will happen shortly after the announcement?

宣布完後會有什麼事發生？

(A) Alcoholic beverage will be served.

會送上酒精飲料。

(B) Passengers can leave their seat.

乘客可以離開座位。

(C) Flight attendants will walk around.

空服人員會四處走動。

(D) Dinner will be served.

會送上晚餐。

100. How much is a glass of soda?

一杯汽水多少錢

(A) Free.

免費。

(B) Five dollars.

5元。

(C) Ten dollars.

10元。

(D) Fifteen dollars.

15元。

新多益模擬試題
—閱讀篇

前言

在你嘗試這份模考閱讀試題前,我想再強調一些事情。在你嘗試過本書的模考聽力考題後,應該知道它確實比一般的新多益聽力題難。以下的閱讀考題比起新多益考題只會更難,這份新多益聽力與閱讀考題不是用來做新多益程度或實力的測試,而是要用來培養你的新多益實力,所以基本上這份閱讀考題不會有基本題,幾乎所有題目都在中等、中上或是更高的難度。

以下的單字和文法考題,是我在新多益教學裡面,發現台灣一般中等和中上程度考生也不會或是容易做錯的題目。我想藉由這些題目進一步提升讀者的程度。閱讀測驗也一樣,基本上不會有簡單的考題。如果你模考題目錯的比預期的多,這是正常的現象。更重要的是看一下我所提供的詳解,確認自己在真正的新多益考試時,碰到類似的題目可以正確地回答出來,這才是這份模考題目的意義!

LISTENING TEST

In the reading test, you will read a variety of texts and answer several different types of reading comprehension questions. The entire Reading test will last 75 minutes. There are three parts, and directions are given for each part. You are encouraged to answer as many questions as possible within the time allowed.

You must mark your answers on the separate answer sheet. Do not write your answers in your test book.

PART 5

Directions: A word or phrase is missing in each of the sentences below. Four answer choices are given below each sentence. Select the best answer to complete the sentence. Then mark the letter (A), (B), (C), or (D) on your answer sheet.

101. The merchandise has arrived at the warehouse and is ready to be - - - - - - to retailers.

(A) transacted

(B) distributed

(C) published

(D) disposed

102. The - - - - - - is extremely important to the project, and you have to handle it carefully.

(A) function

(B) profession

(C) task

(D) role

103. - - - - - - - hard David tries, his manager never seems satisfied.

(A) However

(B) What

(C) Which

(D) How

104. Please take a look at the new employee brochure and - - - - - - - any questions to Mr. Bradley, bradley@activeinc.com.

(A) ask

(B) answer

(C) direct

(D) prepare

105. We need to - - - - - - - the issue to the top management before it causes more serious problems.

(A) inform

(B) flag

(C) observe

(D) obtain

106. Affordable computer graphics technology has ------ improved the visual effects in movies.

(A) sincerely   (B) famously

(C) remarkably   (D) fruitlessly

107. The development is still very ------ at this point, and plans could still change.

(A) concrete   (B) fluid

(C) ambitious   (D) flowing

108. Because the company profit is rising, our salary is ------.

(A) raise   (B) raising

(C) raises   (D) raised

109. Make yourself interesting by being ------ in others.

(A) interesting   (B) interest

(C) interested   (D) interests

110. We are ------ for anything that might happen.

(A) preparing   (B) prepare

(C) preparation   (D) prepared

111. There are five thousand students and many of - - - - - - are from Tokyo.
    (A) who   (B) whom
    (C) them   (D) that

112. Of the two applicants, John is the - - - - - - qualified for the job.
    (A) best   (B) better
    (C) most   (D) well

113. You need to read the manual - - - - - - so we don't miss out on any details.
    (A) completion   (B) completely
    (C) complete   (D) completed

114. Facebook has been the world's - - - - - - social networking site for the last 10 years.
    (A) leader   (B) lead
    (C) leads   (D) leading

115. - - - - - - - yesterday was Jasmine birthday, her colleagues took her to lunch.
    (A) Because   (B) During
    (C) Although   (D) That

116. - - - - - - you choose to take the challenge, we will have the proper training set up for you.
(A) Would
(B) Should
(C) Might
(D) May

117. With more and more overseas clients, we need a secretary who - - - - - - fluent English.
(A) speak
(B) speaks
(C) speaking
(D) spoke

118. It's important that he - - - - - - the project on time.
(A) finish
(B) finishes
(C) finished
(D) finishing

119. To - - - - - - the problems of digital divide, proactive efforts must be taken to ensure all residents have access to the internet.
(A) interpret
(B) address
(C) possess
(D) grasp

120. In a presentation, you need to efficiently and effectively - - - - - - your idea to the audience.
(A) convert
(B) diversify
(C) neglect
(D) convey

121. As a Star Café's employee, you are - - - - - - for free coffee while working.

(A) eligible

(B) entitled

(C) obligated

(D) responsible

122. Bill Gates has been - - - - - - - to the Bill & Melinda Gates Foundation after stepping down as CEO of Microsoft.

(A) devoting

(B) devoted

(C) devote

(D) devotes

123. The president of the company is expected to - - - - - - - a statement regarding the tragic accident happened on the construction site.

(A) speak

(B) expose

(C) issue

(D) reply

124. You need to close the window as - - - - - - - as possible to prevent any cold air from coming in.

(A) tightly

(B) tight

(C) tightness

(D) tighten

125. Great care must be taken to avoid - - - - - - - the main structure while we are renovating the building.

(A) damage

(B) damaged

(C) to damage

(D) damaging

126. The government will provide - - - - - - shuttle bus service to accommodate extra visitors for the exhibition to be held next week.

(A) various

(B) frequent

(C) numerous

(D) routine

127. After Ms. Chan was promoted to sales director, she - - - - - - the responsibility for company's marketing strategy.

(A) assumed

(B) considered

(C) delivered

(D) attributed

128. - - - - - - - John wasn't officially trained, he became an accomplished singer and composer.

(A) Despite

(B) Although

(C) Because

(D) If

129. An early and accurate - - - - - - of SARS is vitally important in the survival of the patients.

(A) diagnose

(B) diagnostic

(C) diagnostically

(D) diagnosis

130. We really enjoyed the spectacular and - - - - - - - view after reaching the top of mountain.

(A) fascinating

(B) fascinated

(C) fascinate

(D) fascination

131. ------- of personal income tax would stimulate the economy by getting more disposable money into citizens' hands.

(A) Reducing
(B) Reduction
(C) Reduced
(D) Reducible

132. Yesterday, dad made John ------ the car.

(A) washed
(B) washing
(C) to wash
(D) wash

133. ------ structural problems caused by earthquake need to be reported immediately.

(A) There are
(B) Every
(C) Any
(D) A

134. Despite the long meeting, we did not ------- any final decision.

(A) reach
(B) arrive
(C) address
(D) communicate

135. We need to do our job ------ than previously planned to finish the project on time.

(A) quicker
(B) quick
(C) more quickly
(D) quickly

136. Finance manager discovered that the accountant had not been ------- the checks into the adequate banking account.
(A) deposit
(B) depositing
(C) deposited
(D) deposits

137. Had the operator known how to reach Mr. Jackson, she ------ him.
(A) would have called
(B) called
(C) calls
(D) would call

138. If you are concerned about the ------ rate increases, an option of prepaying three-month bill at existing rate will be provided.
(A) possible
(B) considerable
(C) current
(D) destructive

139. Great company leaders usually ------ sound judgement before making critical decisions.
(A) refuse
(B) promote
(C) ignore
(D) practice

140. Although we spend a lot of time on social media, they are anything ------ social.
(A) but
(B) apart from
(C) nevertheless
(D) besides

Directions: Read the text that follow. A word or phrase is missing in some of the sentences. Four answer choices are given below each of the sentences. Select the best answer to complete the text. Then mark the letter (A), (B), (C), or (D) on your answer sheet.

Questions 141-143 refer to the following article.

An invoice is a - - - - - - - document issued by the seller to the

141. (A) commercial
     (B) technical
     (C) popular
     (D) public

buyer, and it would list information like products, quantities, and mutually agreed prices for products and/or services which the seller has to provide. Technically, payment - - - - - - negotiated by

142. (A) records
     (B) terms
     (C) documents
     (D) settlement

both parties are independent of the invoice. Part of the total cost could have already been paid as the - - - - - - payment.

143. (A) before
     (B) received
     (C) down
     (D) earlier

In this case, the maximum number of days allowed for the buyer to pay for the rest of the payment would also be listed.

Questions 144 - 146 ○▷ refer to the following announcement.

City Community Center - - - - - - an internet marketing seminar on

               144. (A) holds

                    (B) held

                    (C) has held

                    (D) will be holding

Sunday, Aug. 14. Several renowned internet marketing experts will be on hand to talk about the latest website marketing trends and advise you on - - - - - - to be successful in the internet age.

               145. (A) whether

                    (B) how

                    (C) if

                    (D) what

The cost is $60 for a single participant. For a group of over five people, the cost is $50 per person. If you are interested, please call toll-free at 1-800-123-4567 or go to our website at www. citycommunitycenter.org to register. There is a - - - - - - number of

                         146. (A) limited

                              (B) defined

                              (C) constraint

                              (D) random

seats, so please act soon before it's too late.

Under the enormous pressure coming from the public as well as the government, Charter Bus and its labor union reached a/an ------- settlement on salary increase, ending the one-month

147. (A) convenient
    (B) brief
    (C) substitute
    (D) tentative

strike. Both sides would keep ------ for a final salary agreement.

148. (A) negotiating
    (B) negotiates
    (C) negotiated
    (D) negotiate

Upon hearing the news, the mayor said "We are glad to hear that the residents can finally get the public transportation they ------ need."

149. (A) desperate
    (B) desperately
    (C) desperation
    (D) desperateness

Questions 150-152 ○ refer to the following advertisement.

Feeling exhausted? Want to get away from the summer heat?
It is time for you to take a break from your busy work and go on a
vacation.

Just make a call to **Ultimate Alaska Travel**, and you will enjoy
an incredible summer vacation. Our tour ------- to Alaska's

150. (A) guide
　　 (B) equipment
　　 (C) package
　　 (D) position

beautiful Glacier Bay National Park and Preserve is only **$895** per
person, which includes ------ in a five-star hotel, flight tickets,

151. (A) admission
　　 (B) entrance
　　 (C) access
　　 (D) accommodation

and ------ breakfasts. If you are planning to go with a friend, it's

152. (A) complimentary
　　 (B) reimbursed
　　 (C) refundable
　　 (D) payable

only **$1,595** for the both of you. What are you waiting for? For
more information, please call toll free **800-111-2233**, or visit our
website at www.ultimate-alaska-travel.com.

Directions: In this part you will read a selection of texts, such as magazine and newspaper articles, letters, and advertisements. Each text is followed by several questions. Select the best answer for each question and mark the letter (A), (B), (C), or (D) on your answer sheet.

Question 153-154 ○▶ refer to the following notice.

The annual employee " **Summer Fun Day**" will be held on Friday, June 12, in the courtyard right outside the main entrance. Refreshments will be provided by our cafeteria staff. Please contact David Ng at ext. 456 by June 5, to let him know if you'll be joining. Also, Jennifer Banister is in charge of entertainment activity. Please call ext. 469 by June 1, if you have any idea that can help her. Be sure to come and enjoy a fun day with your colleagues.

153. What is the purpose of this notice?
(A) To tell employee about a company ceremony.
(B) To announce an upcoming company party.
(C) To let the company staff know that there is refreshment for the activity.
(D) To introduce cafeteria staff.

154. Why would employees call Jennifer?
(A) To let her know if they are joining the activity or not.

(B) To inform her that they are interested in showing their singing talent.

(C) To help her arrange the refreshments.

(D) To give her their ideas for the decoration.

Questions 155 ~ 157 refer to the following schedule.

Summer Camp for Young Journalists, Sports Journalist Association

Tour of Sporting News Publishing House, July 17th

9:30 - 10:00 A.M.	Gathering at the entrance of Community Center
10:00 A.M.	Departing for Sporting News Publishing House
11:00 – 11:50 A.M.	Lecture, Keith Patrick, "How to be a News Anchor?"
12:00 – 12:50 P.M.	Lunch at the cafeteria (Ham and cheese sandwich or hamburger) *
01:00 – 01:50 P.M.	Touring the satellite news receiving station
02:00 – 02:50 P.M.	Visiting the new editing room
03:00 – 03:50 P.M.	Q&A with sporting news reporters
04:00 P.M.	Returning to Community Center

* If you have any special meal requirement, please contact Michelle Anderson at 409-512-1212.

155. Who arranged this event?

(A) Sports Journalist Association

(B) Sporting News Publishing House

(C) Community Center

(D) Keith Patrick

156. What is the activity right after lunch?

(A) Hearing a talk

(B) A visit to the satellite news receiving station

(C) A tour of the news editing room

(D) A meeting with reporters

157. What should Emmy Donahue, a vegetarian, do for her lunch?

(A) Choose between sandwich and hamburger.

(B) Bring her own food

(C) Notify Community Center

(D) Call Michelle for her special need.

Clear Lake College Summer Lectures

Clear Lake College is proud to announce its summer line up of guest lectures. These popular and creative talks aim to inspire the imagination of the audiences and create greater interest in science. All lectures are free and open to students, faculty and local residents and no advance reservation is required. Because seating is limited, it will be strictly allocated on a first come first served basis. Please call Cathy at 415-543-2468 if you need further information.

Monday, August 4th

"Black Holes: the history and the latest finding"

Dr. John Lepont, Professor of Astronomy

Dr. Lepont will talk about black holes. What have we learnt about them from space telescopes in the past decade? Is there really a giant black hole at the center of our galaxy? Do they hold the key to our galaxy's future?

Wednesday, August 6th

"Was Einstein right?"

Mrs. Judith Syths, Director of research at Rockwell Labs

And Dr. Paul Owens, Professor of Physics

As modern physics probes ever deeper into the mystery of the atoms, more answers are being found, but, at the same time, more and more questions have emerged. Join the debate as two of the rising stars on modern physics discuss about "Was Einstein right?"

Friday, August 8th

"DNA: the origins of life"

Dr. Richard Hawkins, Geneticist,

The origins of life. Where did we all come from? And where are we going? From Darwin to DNA, what does the future hold for mankind?

All lectures are going to be hosted by the Professor Vincent Lee, Dean of Studies, and concluded with the Q&A session.

158. What is the purpose of the lectures?

    (A) To get a clear image of the lecturers.

    (B) To intrigue the audience into science.

    (C) To get more students for the college.

    (D) To recruit new professors to the college.

159. What do you need to do to attend one of the lectures?

    (A) Call Cathy.

    (B) Arrive early.

    (C) Become a student of the college.

    (D) Make a reservation.

160. James Edwards really enjoys hearing different perspectives from the same topic. Which lecture would he be interested in joining?

(A) "Black Holes: the history and the latest finding"

(B) "Was Einstein right?"

(C) "DNA: the origins of life"

(D) None of them.

161. Who is the moderator for the lecture "Was Einstein right?"

(A) Dr. John Lepont.

(B) Dr. Paul Owens.

(C) Dr. Richard Hawkins.

(D) Professor Vincent Lee.

Questions 162-165 ○ refer to the following article.

After Japan was hit by a devastating 8.9 magnitude earthquake that demolished most of its phone system, some employees of NHN Japan, a subsidiary of South Korean internet company Naver, are determined to find a better communication solution without using phone lines. Three months later, in June, 2011, the app, LINE was born.

Released in June, 2011, Line gained 50 million users in less than a year. Within 18 months, it reached 100 million users. In April 2014, Line was claimed to have 400 million worldwide users. Unsurprisingly, it's the number one messaging app in

Japan. In February 2013, NHN Japan announced it would spin off Line and form Line Corporation, which would, however, stay as a subsidiary of Naver.

It's always interesting to compare the user numbers of some of the most popular messaging apps. According to Wikipedia, in March 2015, Line has 560 million registered users, comparing to over 1 billion with WeChat, the most prominent messaging app in China. Also, WhatsApp, which switched from a free to paid service just to avoid growing too fast, has 800 million in April, 2015.

In order to get into China, Line suppresses content to abide by government censorship requirement, which is confirmed publicly by Line as quoted in the following. "LINE had to conform to local regulations during its expansion into mainland China, and as a result the Chinese version of LINE, LIANWO, was developed. The details of the system are kept private, and there are no plans to release them to the public." There is no other limitation to Line, except that you can only access your Line account by one mobile device and one personal computer. Different mobile numbers or e-mail addresses are needed to install the app for additional mobile devices.

With the ever-evolving characteristic of the internet age, Line will need to continue it's development and adaptation to stay relevant in the intensely competitive messaging apps' war.

162. What is the most suitable title for this article?

(A) What are the Massaging Apps?

(B) The reason Line was developed

(C) Introduction to Line

(D) Line's history and its challenges

163. According to the article, which of the following statement is **FALSE**?

(A) WhatsApp is free.

(B) Comparing to Line and WhatsApp, WeChat has more registered users.

(C) WeChat is the most popular messaging app in China.

(D) Line was born because of an earthquake.

164. According to the article, which of the following statement is true?

(A) Line is owned by a Korean company.

(B) Line is the fastest growing messaging app.

(C) Line gets into China market without any major changes.

(D) Line is the most popular messaging app in Asia.

165. What is the limitation of Line?

(A) The same Line account cannot be accessed from multiple mobile devices.

(B) Line can only be used when there is an earthquake.

(C) You have to know Japanese to use Line.

(D) Line has to remain mostly unchanged to keep the current users.

Booking your vacation is easy with Fun World.
We do all the work, and you'll have all the fun.
For only $199, you get to enjoy one amusing and
spectacular day in New York.

Start your day with a yummy continental breakfast in Condor Hotel. After that, you will hop on a tour bus for a lively day of sightseeing with a professional and entertaining tour guide. The morning itinerary includes Central Park and the Cathedral of Saint John the Divine, a truly stunning church.

An appetizing, luxurious lunch will follow at Happy Restaurant. In the afternoon, we will visit the world famous Times Square and Metropolitan Museum of Art. And don't think we've forgotten the most well-known icon of America, the Statue of Liberty. We will cruise out and visit the great lady in the late afternoon to conclude our tour.

Our package includes:
*Continental breakfast
*Gourmet lunch
*Metropolitan Museum ticket
*Afternoon tea
*Admission to the Statue of Liberty
We will give you a day of precious life time experience in New York City.

166. What is Fun World?

    (A) An amusement park.

    (B) A travel agency.

    (C) A shopping mall.

    (D) A hotel.

167. Which following item is included in the package but wasn't mentioned in the description?

    (A) A visit to Metropolitan Museum.

    (B) A delicious lunch.

    (C) An afternoon tea.

    (D) A breakfast.

168. What is the last stop of the tour?

    (A) A visit to one of the New York's great ladies.

    (B) The Cathedral of Saint John the Divine.

    (C) Happy Restaurant.

    (D) Statue of Liberty.

Ms. Sandra Bullock

Director, Department of Sales and Marketing

1055 Stevens Creek Blvd.

Cupertino, CA 95014

Dear Ms. Sandra Bullock,

Thank you for taking your valuable time to interview me on Friday, June 12 regarding the Marketing Manager opening. I am grateful for the opportunity to discuss my qualification for the position with you.

After talking to you, I am even more convinced that I am one of the best candidates for the position. With good communication skills, five years of proven marketing experience and fluency in Chinese and Spanish, I know I can contribute to the success of the company after joining the existing strong sales and marketing team. Should you have any further question about my qualification, please contact me. I am looking forward to hearing from you soon.

Sincerely yours,

James Wang

169. What is the purpose of this letter?

    (A) To show that he is grateful of getting interviewed.

    (B) To demonstrate his interest in the job.

    (C) To inform Ms. Sandra Bullock that she can contact him for any question.

    (D) To try to get an interview.

170. Who is Ms. Sandra Bullock?

    (A) A recruiting officer.

    (B) A job applicant.

    (C) A director.

    (D) A human resources manager.

171. Which of the following is **not** the reason that James thinks he is the best candidate?

    (A) He can communicate with colleagues and clients effectively.

    (B) He has the expertise in multiple languages.

    (C) He has experience in the managerial job.

    (D) He is capable of marketing.

172. What will James most likely do next?

    (A) Call Sandra to confirm she gets the letter.

    (B) Visit the company.

    (C) Try to get Sandra to call him.

    (D) Wait for Sandra to call him.

▢ To:	Catherine<catherinem@foreveryoung.com
From:	Sandy<sandyt@foreveryoung.com>
Date:	Fri., 6/19, 2015
Subject:	Thank you!

Dear Catherine,

I wanted to let you know that I am leaving my position at Forever Young Cosmetics. I'll be starting a new position as a special assistant to the president at Charming Fragrance next Monday.

Having worked with you for more than two years, I truly appreciate having you as my mentor and helping me get familiar with my work. I am sure I'll miss you, and I feel terrible that I cannot work with you anymore.

Let's keep in touch.

My personal email is sandy1234@yahoomail.com and my cell phone number is (408)725-1305.

Thank you from the bottom of my heart.

Sandy

173. What type of email is this?

(A) A welcome email.

(B) A farewell email.

(C) A thank you email.

(D) A congratulation email.

174. When will Sandy start working at her new job?

(A) 6/20.

(B) 6/21.

(C) 6/22.

(D) 6/23.

Question 175 - 177 ○▶ refer to the following letter.

Mr. Owen Wilson

Human Resources Manager

Village Hotel, 64 Angel St.

Palm Springs, CA 92263

Dear Mr. Wilson,

I am writing to apply for the Village Hotel front desk job opening advertised in Leisure Travel Monthly.

I have worked at Grand Hotel since graduating from Hospitality and Tourism University with a major in Hotel Management three years ago. I enjoy working with colleagues and providing the best service to the guests. I have also worked briefly as a waitress in the hotel restaurant. My patience in handling customer complaints has won me "Employee of the Year" at Grand Hotel last year. My fluency in Chinese and Taiwanese is another important skill in helping increasingly important Chinese tourists.

Although I enjoy my work at Grand Hotel, unfortunately, it is closing down next month, as you have probably known. Regretting not being able to work there, I know I am well prepared for the new challenge of working for the best hotel in the area.

Enclosed please find my résumé and references. I am looking forward to hearing from you soon.

Sincerely yours,

Tiffany Hung

175. What kind of job is Tiffany applying for?
    (A) A receptionist.
    (B) A teacher.
    (C) A waitress.
    (D) A supervisor.

176. Why is Tiffany trying to get a new job?

    (A) She majored in Hotel Management.

    (B) She is going to lose her job in a month.

    (C) Her language skill is not helpful in the old job.

    (D) She doesn't enjoy working with her colleagues.

177. What is not stated as her strength for the new job?

    (A) She is a good team player.

    (B) Her experience in dealing with unsatisfied customers.

    (C) She is good at multiple languages.

    (D) She is ready for new challenges.

Questions 178-181 ○ refer to the following news report.

THE BRISTOL INTERNATIONAL BALLOON FIESTA

The Bristol International Balloon Fiesta is held annually just outside the city of Bristol in the south west of England. It has become one of the region's most popular and spectacular tourist attractions. Held in August on a large country estate on the edge of Bristol, it is now Europe's biggest balloon festival. Regular crowds of over 100,000 attend daily for four days of activities.

Mass launches are held every morning and evening where hundreds of balloons can be seen taking off almost at the same time. You will have to be up early, however, to see the morning launch as it's held at 6 am. The evening launches are at 6 pm.

One of the most popular events is the night glow. Usually on two consecutive evenings during the festival, dozens of tethered balloons are lit and inflated in the early evening. They then glow in the dark timed to music. This is followed by a spectacular fireworks display. Many people say that the night glow is the highlight of the whole festival.

The fiesta, which began in 1979, used to be held in September, but due to poor weather leading to muddy grounds and canceled flights, the fiesta was moved to its present August dates after 1988.

Over the years the fiesta has become well-known for its strangely shaped balloons. At first, locally manufactured balloons in the shapes of bottles, cartoon characters and even supermarket trolleys were regularly seen. Now international teams, from all over the world, participate in the festival with their own specially designed balloons. Recently, there have been UFOs from the US and Kiwis from New Zealand.

The entertainment is not just limited to the balloons. With fairground rides, air displays, and plenty of stalls to keep children happy during the day.

And possibly the best part of the fiesta is that it is totally free. There is no charge to enter the event. With around half a million visitors expected through the gates this year, if you do make the trip, you certainly won't be alone.

178. Why was the festival moved from September to August?

(A) The weather is hotter and more suitable for balloons.

(B) It rains less in August.

(C) The nights are darker.

(D) It's summer vacation time for children.

179. What is the most popular event at the festival?

(A) The night glow.

(B) The mass launches.

(C) The air shows.

(D) The fairground rides.

180. What has the balloon festival become famous for?

(A) Spectacular air shows.

(B) Food stalls for children.

(C) Fireworks displays.

(D) Balloons that look like other things.

181. What's the reason that might discourage someone from visiting?

(A) The cost.

(B) The night glow.

(C) The crowds.

(D) The UFOs.

Computer programmer wanted

Tech Solutions Ltd. is looking for a full time computer programmer. Experience in programming graphics and familiarity with the latest video game consoles are a must. A degree in computer science is preferable, but any applicant with proper programing skills will be considered. An understanding of the latest game designing platforms like GameMaker, Construct 2, Stencyl, Fleixel or Unity is definitely a plus.

Send resume and supporting documents by August 28th to Anna Wong, Tech Solutions, 29 Ark Street, Edinburgh, Scotland or email techsolutions@game.co.uk

📖To:	Anna Wong
From:	Alexey Pajitnov

I am writing to you regarding to the advertisement at the local job center for a computer programmer. I am currently working as a computer trainer for a major bank, but my passion is programming, especially for game apps.

Enclosed please find my full resume. I am also sending you some links to my app designs because, as you will see from my resume, I didn't study computer science while at university. I am sure that these apps which were built on Unity platform will give you a good idea of the level of my skill as a programmer.

Please do not hesitate to contact me if you need any further information regarding my qualification to the job.

Sincerely
Alexey Pajitnov

182. What is Tech Solutions Ltd.?
     (A) A software developer.
     (B) A maker of game consoles.
     (C) A computer manufacturer.
     (D) A graphics design company.

183. What does Alexey Pajitnov say that demonstrates his qualifications for the job?
     (A) His capability of building something based on a platform.
     (B) His job as a computer trainer.
     (C) The apps he designed.
     (D) His resume.

184. What does the advertisement say is NOT necessary required for applying the job?
     (A) Knowledge of game consoles.
     (B) A resume.
     (C) Skills as a programmer.
     (D) A computer science degree.

185. What products does Tech Solutions Ltd. want to develop?

(A) Games for personal computers.

(B) Software for game consoles.

(C) Software for bank training.

(D) Game design platform.

Questions 186-190 refer to the following article and email.

The Red House in Wanhua District, Taipei City, is proud to present Shamlet from Ping Fong Acting Troupe. A theatrical play inspired by Hamlet, a world renowned tragedy written by William Shakespeare, Shamlet, on the surface, is an ironic comedy. However, after watching the entertaining plays, you can feel the tiny bitterness in life shown in various scenes. Hugh K. S. Lee, the director, presents the play by showing the struggling troupe trying their best to perform Shamlet on stage. Changing roles, handling affairs, and showing the inside stories of the actors and the actresses are the most important factors that cause the failing performance of Shamlet. Facing the inevitable catastrophe with the numerous accidents and mistakes, all actors and actresses stick together and insist on one believe, "We Shall Return". The last scene doesn't really present the official ending of the show, but it gives the audience the chance of searching the message hidden in the performance. One more thing for those who are planning to enjoy the show, get to know a little bit more about Hamlet. It will help you tremendously in understanding the hidden meaning of Shamlet.

For ticket information, please refer to the following table.

Date	Time	Membership		Regular person	Student
		Gold	Silver		
Friday, 7/21	7:30 PM	700	750	1000	500
Saturday, 7/22	7:00 PM	700	750	1000	500
Sunday, 7/23	7:00 PM	700	750	1000	500

To reserve your seats, please email reservation@redhouse.org.tw

To:	reservation@redhouse.org.tw
From:	Lawrence Lo <lawrence.lo@mediatech.com.tw>
Subject:	ticket reservation for Shamlet
Date:	7/3

I'd like to reserve two tickets for Shamlet on Saturday, 7/22. The following is my order information.

Name: Lawrence Lo

Membership number: MJ2345

Number of tickets: 2 (700 each) with the total cost of 1400

Payment: Master card, number: 4321 5678 9012 8765, expiration date: 09/17

Address: No. 5, Lane 146, Sec. 1, Tingzhou Rd., Taipei City 100

Besides order confirmation, please also reply us with the ticket exchange and cancellation policy.

Sincerely,

Lawrence Lo

186. What mostly likely is Shamlet?

    (A) A movie to be shown in a theater.

    (B) A tragedy based on Hamlet.

    (C) A comedy stage show.

    (D) A show for kids from Ping Fong Acting Troupe.

187. Who is the director of Shamlet?

 (A) Ping Fong Acting Troupe.

 (B) The Red House.

 (C) William Shakespeare.

 (D) Hugh Lee.

188. Based on the two passages, what kind of member is Lawrence Lo?

 (A) A gold member.

 (B) A silver member.

 (C) A student member.

 (D) Not commented.

189. How does Lawrence pay for the show?

 (A) Cash.

 (B) Check.

 (C) Credit card.

 (D) Money order.

190. What additional information does Lawrence ask?

 (A) What to do if the show is cancelled.

 (B) What will happen if he cannot go to the show?

 (C) Where to call for the show's detail information.

 (D) Direction to the Red House.

HTC is partnering with Valve to make virtual reality dream come true

Taipei, Oct 5, 2015 – After years of collaboration with Valve, HTC is finally ready to unveil their virtual reality (VR) offering, the HTC Vive.

On Nov. 19, exactly one week before Thanksgiving, which is the busiest shopping season in the US, HTC and Valve will be hosting a conference in Las Vegas to officially introduce Vive to the general publics. Previously announced at Mobile World Congress, Vive has been regarded as one of the strongest VR competitors to the FB's Oculus Rift. Most of the users who have tried on Vive give rave review and thoroughly enjoy the experience.

The laser base station that comes with the system can track your location in the room and project it into the VR world, and it will even warn you if you are getting too close to a wall. The other real achievements for Vive are the motion-tracking wands and controllers which will allow you to walk around, confidently pick up random objects, check it and keep it or throw it away.

Coming from the gaming industry, Valve has an **impeccable** reputation in PC and mobile games and obviously, gaming will be the first and the most important application for the system. We hope you can join us on Nov. 19, in Las Vegas to experience the world's first VR system for consumers.

To:	allison@htc.com.tw
From:	bin@htc.com.tw
Subject:	Let's talk about the Vive launching conference
Date:	10/19

Let me first congratulate you on the fine job you did for the press release of Vive launching conference. It was well written, concise, and most importantly to the point and interesting.

As your supervisor probably has informed you, you will be helping with the preparation of the launching conference. I'd like to talk to you in more detail, but I will be on business trips to Southeast Asia and Europe and will not be coming back to Taiwan until early Nov. During this time, email would be the best way to reach me.

I'd like to meet with you exactly two weeks before the event in our HQ. I know you are probably really nervous about this new assignment but with your past job performance and your capability that has been shown during the last few years, we are confident that you will be doing a great job for the conference preparation.

BR,

Bin

191. Oculus Rift is a

(A) Gaming system.

(B) VR platform.

(C) FB's tool.

(D) Mobile game.

192. According to the press release, what did not come with the Vive?

(A) A laser system.

(B) A game.

(C) A system that can follow your move.

(D) Some controllers.

193. The word **impeccable** in paragraph 4, line 1, is closest in meaning to

(A) awful

(B) clean

(C) exact

(D) wonderful

194. From the email, what can be inferred about Allison?
    (A) She is experienced in preparing and setting up a conference.
    (B) She is really good at writing stories.
    (C) She is a Valve employee.
    (D) It's probably the first time she helps preparing for a conference.

195. When will Bin meeting with Allison?
    (A) 10/19
    (B) 11/5
    (C) 11/12
    (D) 11/19

Reba McEntire

38 Ford St.

San Marcos, Tx 78666

EasyJet Claim Office

EasyJet Airline

1 EasyJet Plaza,

Orlando, FL 32801

Dear Sir/Madam,

I am writing with regard to my badly damaged luggage during my trip from San Jose to Austin. I was traveling from Mineta San Jose Airport to Austin-Bergstrom Airport on EasyJet flight EJ2857 on April 3. Upon picking up my luggage from the baggage claim area, I noticed that two wheels were missing and the top handle was detached from it. I immediately reported it to the EasyJet office at the Bergstrom Airport and properly filled out the damaged baggage claim form.

I already had my baggage checked at a local luggage retailer, Howard Limited, to see if it's repairable. They feel that only the two missing wheels could be fully repaired, but the I already had my baggage checked at a local luggage retailer, Howard Limited, to see if it's repairable. They feel that only the two missing wheels could be fully repaired, but the handle would be tough to fix and thus they would suggest a replacement. Please see the enclosed copy of estimate for more detail. I would like to request that EasyJet reimburse me for the cost of a new luggage as shown in the estimate. Also, on that date, because of the damaged luggage, I wasn't able to take any public transportation from the airport and had to take a taxi. I would also ask EasyJet to reimburse me for the $50 taxi fare.

Yours sincerely,

Reba McEntire

Howard Limited: Authorized Delsey Retailer
43 Oran St. Austin, Tx 78745

Estimate of Repair Date: April 6

Item to be repaired: Delsey Helium Aero 29 luggage

Repairs to be done: Replace two wheels and reattach handle

Estimated cost: $ 30 (please see notes below)

Notes: The two wheels can be fully repaired, but it would not be possible to securely reattach the handle because the handle attachment pad was too severely damaged. The cost to replace it with the same model is $ 140.

196. What is the purpose of the letter?

    (A) To report a damaged item.

    (B) To complain about the baggage service.

    (C) To request a refund.

    (D) To claim some expenses.

197. Why did Ms. McEntire visit Howard Limited?

    (A) To check for a new suitcase.

    (B) To complain about the damaged luggage.

    (C) To inquire about an estimation for repair work.

    (D) To pay a bill.

198. What company made the damaged luggage?

    (A) Delsey

    (B) Howard Limited

    (C) EasyJet

    (D) San Marcos

199. Why did Ms. McEntire enclosed a document?

    (A) To provide a physical evidence of the damaged luggage.

    (B) To prove that the luggage had been repaired.

    (C) To support her claim for the reimbursement.

    (D) To suggest EasyJet a better way of handling luggage.

200. How much is the total amount of reimbursement asked by Ms. McEntire?
    (A) $ 30
    (B) $ 140
    (C) $ 170
    (D) $ 190

新多益模擬閱讀試題解析

做完考題後，是不是覺得真的比較難？其實更重要的是，如何把題目看懂、學會，確保自己在日後的考試碰到類似的題目時能夠答對，才是這份考題最大的目的。以下就是我的解說，用來幫助你了解題目，進而選出正確答案。再來我要再強調一次，如非必要不要看題目的中文翻譯，我根本不想把題目翻譯成為中文，如果你要靠中文翻譯才能了解題目，多益絕對考不了高分，對於這些考題，我只是不能免俗地加上中文翻譯，有些閱讀測驗的文章，如果我覺得已經講解得很清楚，文章就不會翻譯了，再強調一次，讀者如非必要，不要去看翻譯。

PART 5

101. The merchandise has arrived at the warehouse and is ready to be - - - - - - to retailers.

(A) transacted
(B) distributed
(C) published
(D) disposed

解析

題目提的是 merchandise 貨物、商品，當然就是 to be distributed to the retailers。書、雜誌 (books, magazines) 之類的出版品才會用到 to be published。而 transact 這個字比較常見的是名詞：transaction，你到 ATM 去存錢、領錢或是轉帳，每一次都是一個 transaction，簡單

的說把你的存摺拿出來，裡面每一行的紀錄就是一個 transaction。最後的 dispose，如果你查字典八成是：處置、布置、處理之類的意思，不過我常講背單字切記不要把單字背死了，最終極的 dispose 當然就是丟棄，還有念一下以下的例句：The money is at your disposal. 簡單的講就是任你處置。

中譯

貨物已經抵達倉庫，可以 - - - - - - 到零售商了。

(A) 處理、交易　　(B) 配送　　(C) 出版　　(D) 處置、處理

---

102. The - - - - - - is extremely important to the project, and you have to handle it carefully.

(A) function

(B) profession

(C) task

(D) role

解析

先解釋一下比較不合適的兩個答案：profession 在這裡意思算是職業，還有在一個 project 應該不會有 role 角色之類的答案。role 這個字用在 movie 電影和 play 戲劇、舞台劇上比較合適。再來是 function，這個字我會希望你先想到 multifunction printer 也就是所謂的 all-in-one printer，至於 task 這個字簡單的講比較難的 job 就是 task！如果你對這題的答案還有些疑問，請注意一下這題的後半部：you have to handle it carefully 很明顯地這裡的 it 指的就是答案，當然 handle the task carefully 好多了，如果是 function 應該是：you have to design the function carefully。

這個 ------ 對這計畫很重要，你必須小心處理。

(A) 功能　　(B) 職業　　(C) 工作　　(D) 角色

---

103. ------- hard David tries, his manager never seems satisfied.

(A) However　　　　　(B) What

(C) Which　　　　　　(D) How

解析

這題其實有點 tricky，however 一般都認為是副詞，其實在一種狀況下它是個連接詞，當 however 當作是 no matter how 的時候，就是連接詞。這裡就是個最好的例子：No matter how hard David tries, his manager never seems satisfied. 所以答案是 However。

中譯

------ David 怎麼努力，他的經理永遠不滿意。

(A) 不論　　(B) 什麼　　(C) 哪個　　(D) 如何

---

104. Please take a look at the new employee brochure and ------ any questions to Mr. Bradley, bradley@activeinc.com.

(A) ask　　　　　　(B) answer

(C) direct　　　　　(D) prepare

解析

如果是ask應該是ask the teacher a question，而answer句意不對，如果是prepare questions應該是prepare questions for interview或是prepare questions to ask（someone），答案是direct。這裡的direct意思上有把問題指給、指向Mr. Bradley，不過如同我一直強調的，把整句話不去想中文，多念幾次就對了。

中譯

請看一下新的員工手冊，並將任何問題 - - - - - - Mr. Bradley，bradley@activeinc.com。

(A) 問　　(B) 回答　　(C) 轉給　　(D) 準備

---

105. We need to ------- the issue to the top management before it causes more serious problems.

(A) inform (B) flag
(C) observe (D) obtain

解析

這題其實還蠻有程度的，先看兩個比較不合適的答案，observe如果都已經observe到問題了就該report給top management，而obtain基本上獲得、取得，issue基本上不太會是好事，obtain總會希望obtain好事，沒有人會希望obtain an issue。我猜應該會有不少人選inform，這個字是我常用來解釋為什麼背單字不可以一個英文、一個中文的硬背的例子。如果你只是背了inform通知，按照中文翻譯，絕對是正確答案，可惜的是新多益考的是英文！inform這個字的基本用法是：inform someone of something，如果答案是 inform 題目就應該是：inform the top management of the issue！這題的正確答案是 flag，flag 這個字大家一般背的意思是旗子，不過細心一點的讀者應該會注意到這裡的 flag 當作動詞用！名詞當動詞用在英文裡是很常見的事，flag 旗子當動詞用，當然就是插旗子了，你說人們插旗子的目的是？當然是用來吸引大家的注意，所以這題是 flag the issue to the top management。新多益考題裡，尤其是高分的考題，有許多是這類的題目，不過這類的新多益高分題，其實還是很有人性的，一般在四個答案裡都會有兩個比較簡單的答案，也就是說程度不錯的學生，稍稍注意一下往往就可以把其中的兩個答案先刪掉，如同這題裡的 observe 和 obtain，考生在剩下的兩個答案裡面再自行挑出比較好或是比較不好的答案，如果你對 inform someone of something 的用法不熟，就很容易挑錯了，再說回來，如果你知道 inform 這個字的感覺不太對，那就該挑比較不熟的 flag！如果你對 flag 沒感覺，那不要考慮 flag 這個答案，針對剩下的 inform 感覺一下，看你覺得 inform 比較好？還是比較不好？如果你對剩下的答案感覺不到七十分以上，就選剩下的那個沒感覺的答案！

中譯

我們必須把這些爭議在變成更大問題前，------ 高層。

(A) 通知　　(B) 讓（高層）明白　　(C) 觀察　　(D) 獲得

---

106. Affordable computer graphics technology has ------ improved the visual effects in movies.

　　(A) sincerely　　　　　　(B) famously

　　(C) remarkably　　　　　(D) fruitlessly

解析

這題應該不難，寫信寫到最後往往都會寫上 Sincerely yours（誠摯的、誠懇的），憑這點就該感覺不合適吧！ famous 句意不合，fruitless 直翻沒有水果，當然就是沒有收穫、無效，答案是 remarkably。

中譯

成本合宜的電腦動畫科技已經 − − − − − − 增進了電影的視覺特效。

(A) 誠懇地　　　(B) 著名地　　　(C) 明顯地　　　(D) 無效地

107. The development is still very − − − − − − at this point, and plans could still change.

    (A) concrete   (B) fluid

    (C) ambitious   (D) flowing

解析

重點在後面的 plans could still change，既然 could still change 就可以先把 concrete 和 ambitious 去掉，這裡的 flowing 你應該可以感覺不合適吧！ development 又不是 water 或 air，不是流體 development 不可能 flowing，所以選你沒感覺的 fluid。這裡的 fluid 原本是液體，變成形容詞，引申為很可能會改變。concrete 原本是（鋼筋）混凝土，當形容詞當然就成了實在的、具體的。ambitious 是野心的，例句：After finishing his first novel of 50,000 words, he is aiming a far more ambitious one, a novel of 200,000 words. flowing 是流動，例句是：After the heavy rain, the water is flowing rapidly.

目前而言整個發展還是 ------，計畫可能還會改變。

(A) 具體的　　(B) 不確定　　(C) 野心的　　(D) 流動的。

---

108. Because the company profit is rising, our salary is ------.

(A) raise
(B) raising
(C) raises
(D) raised

解析

在講解這題前，我想先解釋一下 rise 和 raise 這兩個字的差別，先看兩個例句：The prices are rising. 和 The prices are raised. 先把這兩句唸個幾遍再說。兩句都是價格增加了，只是單純的以文法而言，前一句是主動而後一句是被動，不過就算這麼說了，你應該還是感覺不出很大的差異吧！前一句簡單的說價格上漲了，後一句說的則是（被動地）價格被提高了，在這裡我要強調一下：把 The prices are raised. 多念幾次，尤其是 are raised 再念幾次，感覺出句意裡 are raised 被提高的感受，不需要去想文法上面是主動還是被動，反正就是 The prices are raised. 直接跟 The prices are rising. 在英文句意上面做比較！把兩句裡的差別感覺出來！所以前一句 The prices are rising. 簡單的敘述價格上漲，而第二句：The prices are raised. 就可以感受到價格會漲上來是有原因的！因為 The prices are raised. 當然有原因！回到這題，salary 不會無緣無故的 rising，salary 當然是 raised 才對！因為 profit is rising，salary 當然 is raised。

中譯

因為公司利潤增加了，我們的薪水也 - - - - - - 。

(A) 提高（動詞原型）　　(B) 提高中（加 ing）

(C) 提高（加 s）　　　　(D) 被提高

---

109. Make yourself interesting by being - - - - - - in others.

(A) interesting　　　　　(B) interest

(C) interested　　　　　(D) interests

解析

在講解這題前，我還要先舉幾個例句：it's amazing, I am amazed, to my amazement 和 it's surprising, I am surprised，與 it's boring, I am bored 同樣的以文法而言，第一句的說法都是主動 it's amazing, it's surprising 和 it's boring，而第二句 I am amazed, I am surprised 和 I am bored 都是被動。但是，聽到或看到每個句子時你有時間去想是主動還是被動嗎？其實還是要跟前一題一樣，唸到有直接的感覺，每句話一念出來就感受到語句間的意思，這才是對的方法！現在看一下第一組：it's amazing, I am amazed 基本上可以看成 your performance is amazing（所以當然是 amazing performance），或是 I am amazed by your performance。是不是一念就懂這兩句的意思了，再把它們多念幾次，下次有類似的考題就可以直接選念比較順的答案，就是正確答案了，也就是我一直強調的把語感唸出來，用語感來解題，絕對比較快，也比較準！因為 it's surprising, I am surprised 基本上跟 it's amazing, I am amazed 很類似，我就不另外說明了。再來是 it's boring, I am bored。it's boring, he is boring, you are boring，這三句沒問題吧！

注意到沒？後兩句的意思其實是 He is a boring person. You are a boring person. 跟 I am bored 的意思真是天差地遠！再強調一次：把 it's boring, he is boring, you are boring 和 I am bored 多念幾次，感覺真的不一樣對吧！直接把感覺唸出來，就不用去想哪句是主動，哪句是被動了！這題 by being interested in others 就是正確答案，把答案帶進去原題目多念幾次就對了！

(中譯)

先對旁人 ------ 才會讓你變得有趣。

(A) 有趣的（加 ing）　　(B) 使有興趣（原型）

(C) 感興趣的（加 ed）　　(D) 有興趣（加 s）

---

110. We are ------ for anything that might happen.
    (A) preparing　　　　　(B) prepare
    (C) preparation　　　　(D) prepared

(解析)

如果讀者對於主動、被動的考題有任何疑慮時，我都會建議把主動和被動的句型同時寫出來，然後多念幾遍就對了。以這題而言出了原本的題目：We are prepared for anything that might happen. 以外，我會再增加一句：We are preparing everything we can in advance. 然後叫學生把這兩句多念幾遍。第一句其實只是 We are prepared. 意思就完整了，而第二句則是 We are preparing everything，多念幾次你就會感覺到 we are preparing everything 的 preparing 後面就是要接個東西（something 或是 everything）句意才會完整，把這感覺唸出來後，根

本不用想句型是主動還是被動,直接把念的順的答案選出來就對了!這題
答案當然是 (D) We are prepared for anything that might happen.

中譯

對任何可能發生的事情,我們都已經 - - - - - - 了。

(A) 準備(加 ing)　　(B) 準備(原型)

(C) 準備(名詞)　　(D) 準備(加 ed)

---

111. There are five thousand students and many of - - - - - - are
　　　from Tokyo.
　　　(A) who　　　　　　　　(B) whom
　　　(C) them　　　　　　　　(D) that

解析

這題要特別注意一下題目裡的 and,既然已經有連接詞 and 這裡就要選
them。如果去掉題目裡的 and,把題目改成 There are five thousand
students, many of - - - - - - are from Tokyo. 就要選關係代名詞
whom(當作連接詞)。同樣的把以下兩句唸個幾遍:There are five
thousand students **and** many of them are from Tokyo. 還有 There
are five thousand students, many of whom are from Tokyo.

中譯

這有五千個學生,而且 - - - - - - 多數是從東京來的。

(A) 誰　　(B) 誰(受格)　　(C) 他們　　(D) 那個

112. Of the two applicants, John is the - - - - - - qualified for the job.

(A) best

(B) better

(C) most

(D) well

解析

這題要特別注意把以下的例句多念幾次，the more experienced of the two (candidates), the taller of the two, the better qualified of the two. 記得有了 of the two（兩者間）當然就是 the taller of the two, the better qualified of the two, the more beautiful of the two 記得把這些例子多念幾次就對了。

中譯

這兩位申請者裡面，John 是那個 - - - - - - 勝任的那一個。

(A) 最好　　(B) 比較好　　(C) 最　　(D) 好

---

113. You need to read the manual - - - - - - so we don't miss out on any details.

(A) completion

(B) completely

(C) complete

(D) completed

解析

後面既然有了 don't miss out on any details 前面當然要 read the manual completely，許多補教名師會說 completely 是副詞用來修飾動詞 read。我會說把以下兩句話多念幾次：read the complete manual, read the manual completely，根本不需要管什麼形容詞修飾名詞或

是副詞修飾動詞,再念幾次:read the complete manual, read the manual completely 就 OK 了。

Part1

中譯

你需要把手冊讀 - - - - - - 我們才不會漏失任何細節。

(A) 完整（名詞）　　(B) 完整地

(C) 完整（原型）　　(D) 完整（加 ed）

Part2

114. Facebook has been the world's - - - - - - social networking site for the last 10 years.

(A) leader

(B) lead

(C) leads

(D) leading

解析

Facebook has been the world's leading social networking site for the last 10 years. 簡單吧！如果答案一定要是 leader,那題目就要改成 Facebook has been **the world's leader in social networking** for the last 10 years. 如果還有疑問,再念幾次:Facebook has been the world's leading social networking site. 還　有 Facebook has been the world's leader in social networking. 唸到有 FU 就對了！

中譯

在十年內,臉書已經變成世界領先的社群網站。

(A) 領先者　　(B) 領先（原型）　　(C) 領先（加 s）　　(D) 領先（加 ing）

（直接唸英文容易多了！）

Part3

115. - - - - - - yesterday was Jasmine's birthday, her colleagues took her to lunch.

(A) Because
(B) During
(C) Although
(D) That

解析

這題前後顯然有因果關係，當然選 (A) Because。答案裡的 although 在後面的題目會另外講解，這題就在這裡打住。

中譯

- - - - - - 昨天是 Jasmine 的生日，她同事請她吃午餐。

(A) 因為 　　(B) 在……其中 　　(C) 雖然、儘管 　　(D) 那個

---

116. - - - - - - you choose to take the challenge, we will have the proper training set up for you.

(A) Would
(B) Should
(C) Might
(D) May

解析

這題就很簡單是 (B) Should，整句話是：Should you choose to take the challenge, we will have the proper training set up for you. 這題我需要另外講一下假設語氣。先看一下兩個例句：If I **were** you, I **would buy** the car. If I **had** money, I **would** lend it to you. 第一句很明顯我當然不是你，先再念一次：If I **were** you, I **would** buy the car. 記得一定是用 were！第二句：If I **had** money, I **would** lend it to you. 很明顯的我沒錢，這兩句就是大家常聽說的，與現在事實相反。不過重點永遠是例句，再把這兩句多念幾次：If I **were** you, I **would** buy the car. If I **had** money, I **would** lend it to you. 再來另一個例句：If you **had studied** harder, you **would have** passed the test.

其實基本句型在 if 的部分是：if someone had done something，而後面的部分很簡單，就是：should have/ would have/could have/ might have，只要聽到 should have/ would have/could have/ might have 就是基本的（與過去事實相反的）假設語氣。if 部分的 if someone **had done** something 加上後面的 should have/ would have/could have/ might have 就是完整的假設語氣。再看個例句：If you **had studied** harder, you **would have** passed the test. 簡單吧！這裡還可以有個小小的變化，同樣的用例句說明：**Had** you **studied** harder, you **would have** passed the test. 只是 had 調到前面取代了 if 而已。假設語氣基本上就講完了，但是以多益而言，還有另一個相關的句型會考，同樣的先看例句：If it should rain, we will not go outside.

Should it rain, we will not go outside. 這樣的句型多益基本只會考後面的例句，也就是把 should 調到前面取代了 if，再把例句念一遍：**Should** it rain, we will not go outside. 如同這題原先的題目，考的只是 should 這個字，再把原本的題目念一次以後就不會有問題了。

(中譯)

如果你選擇接受挑戰，我們會提供給你適當的訓練。

（這題的四個答案我就不翻了。）

117. With more and more overseas clients, we need a secretary who - - - - - - fluent English.

(A) speak

(B) speaks

(C) speaking

(D) spoke

解析

這題關鍵就在認出關係代名詞 who 取代了哪個名詞。在這裡代替的正是前面的 a secretary，也就是所謂的第三人稱單數，所以答案是(B) speaks。記得看到關係代名詞最重要的一件事：它代替了哪個名詞？這樣就簡單了！

中譯

因為有越來越多的海外客戶，我們需要一位能說流利英文的秘書。

(A) 說（原型）　(B) 說（加 s）　(C) 說（加 ing）　(D) 說（過去式）

---

118. It's important that he - - - - - - the project on time.

(A) finish

(B) finishes

(C) finished

(D) finishing

解析

這題很難，讓我好好的說明一下。同樣的先看例句：It's important/vital/imperative/essential that we **MUST**... 注意一下我特別強調的是 MUST，既然是 must 當然就接動詞原型，所以這題的答案是(A) finish，整句話是：It's important that he (MUST) finish the project on time. 其實在早期的英文裡面確實有 must 或是 should，問題是後

來在習慣上把 must, should 省略了，這下可讓大家出問題了，沒了 must, should 感覺上好像突然蹦出個動詞原型，我對大家的建議就是把 It's important that we must; It's vital that we must; It's imperative that we must; It's essential that we must 多念幾次，把 must 這個字很自然的加進來，才會選出後面的動詞原型，注意一下這幾個字：important, vital, imperative, essetial 基本上都是重要的意思，既然是很重要當然就要 that we MUST 了。選出原型動詞後 must 就可以功成身退的被去掉。另一個類似的句型是：suggest/demand/ask/request/insist/recommend that we MUST… 這幾個字都有建議、要求、堅持之類的意思，同樣的把例句多念幾次，尤其是 that we MUST，把 must 這個字念到習慣，才有辦法記得後面要加原型動詞。

中譯

他（必須）準時完成計畫真的很重要。

(A) 完成（原型）　　(B) 完成（加 es）

(C) 完成（過去式）　(D) 完成（加 ing）

---

119. To - - - - - - the problems of digital divide, proactive efforts must be taken to ensure all residents have access to the internet.

　　(A) interpret　　　　　(B) address

　　(C) possess　　　　　(D) grasp

解析

我先把兩個比較不可能的答案指出來，對於不認識這兩個字的讀者我提供例句給你，The interpretation of the Bible has changed throughout the years.（只是把 interpret 改成名詞 interpretation 而已），如果對 interpretation 還是沒感覺，查一下字典發現是解釋、闡明、詮釋的意思後，再回來把這例句念幾遍。利用例句來加深你對 interpretation 這個字的印象，就容易記住這個字了！看看另一個字和例句：Some people have youth, but not energy, while others possess energy, but not youth. 如果你不認識 possess 把這句唸個兩遍，尤其是前面的 have youth, but not energy 對比上後面的 possess energy, but not youth 對於 possess 這個字是不是就有 FU 了？我常講單字不要硬背，例句會比單字本身還要重要，而且好的例句更能加深印象，幫助你記住單字。再來看看 grasp，After taking a computer course, John finally had a good grasp of computer programming. 還有 He has difficulty grasping some of the concepts we are studying in our computer class and he really needs some help. 這兩句念過後，是不是對 grasp 這個字就有 FU 了！如果還沒有查一下字典，知道 grasp 是抓緊、抱住、理解的意思，再回來念這兩句就容易了對吧！最後該講正確答案 (B) address 這個字了。這個字除了大家所熟知的的住址以外，還有其他的意思，先看例句：The president is addressing the media. 這裡的 address 是演說、演講之類的意思，請看另一個例句：The text of the speech will be available to the press at the end of his address. 而 address 還可以用成面對、解決（問題）的意思，如同這個題目，以下是另一個例句：If the government fails to address the pollution problem, our future generation will face the terrible consequence. 把這幾個例句多念幾遍，address 這個字的幾個用法就沒問題了。其實這個題目裡還隱藏了個重要的單字，沒錯就是 proactive

這個字！ proactive 這個字基本上就是：往前看，所以就是前瞻性的、主動的、先一步的之類的意思，說實話這個字的中文意思還不是那麼容易背對吧！我的建議就是那幹嘛背中文意思！直接念：proactive efforts, proactive actions 容易多了。

中譯

要 - - - - - - 數位鴻溝的問題，必須採取前瞻性的行為來確保所有市民都能上網。(A) 解釋、詮釋　(B) 面對、解決　(C) 擁有　(D) 抓住、理解（你說這四個單字是要背中文意思，還是念例句比較容易？）

---

120. In a presentation, you need to efficiently and effectively - - - - - - your idea to the audience.

(A) convert
(B) diversify
(C) neglect
(D) convey

解析

先給個例句來解釋一下 convert：We just finished converting one of the bedrooms in our house into a playroom for the kids. 簡單的講就是 convert a bedroom into a playroom 是不是就對 convert 有 FU 了！再來個 diversify 的例句：It is necessary for our business to diversify our product line if we want to attract a greater range of customers. 既然要 attract a greater range of customers 當然需要 diversify（多角化、多樣化）our product line。接下來是 neglect，同樣的請看例句：He was so busy that he neglected his health. 忙到 neglected his health，是不是就有忽視、忽略的感覺了！最後是這題

的正確答案，而題目本身就是個好例句：在一個 presentation 裡，你當然需要 effectively convey 你的 idea to the audience！其實 convey 這個字還蠻有意思的，We need to convey the passengers by bus to the airport. It's hard to convey my feelings into words. 前面是 convey the passengers，後面是 convey my feelings（或是 ideas）在英文上面就是 convey 這個字可以用在實體的東西如：passengers，也可以用在不是實體的東西如：feelings, ideas，是不是這個字就簡單的記住了！你真的需要去分別記住運送、搬運還有傳達、表達這兩種不太一樣的中文意思嗎？反正就是 convey some real things 還有 convey feelings, ideas 就 OK 了！

中譯

在這個報告裡，你需要有效的把你的點子 - - - - - - 給觀眾。
(A) 轉換　　(B) 多角化 (C) 忽略、忽視　(D) 傳達

---

121. As a Star Café's employee, you are - - - - - - for free coffee while working.
(A) eligible　　　　　　(B) entitled
(C) obligated　　　　　 (D) responsible

解析

這題其實很簡單，you are eligible for free coffee 還有 you are entitled to free coffee 念個幾次就對了！剩下的兩個答案就請你看例句了：You are obligated to go to work by 9 o'clock. You are obligated 每天九點以前上班，是不是有 FU 了！You are responsible for your young children's action. 是不是就可以輕鬆的了解 responsible for ！

中譯

身為星咖啡的員工，工作時 - - - - - - 喝免費的咖啡。

(A) 有資格的　　(B) 給予權利　　(C) 有義務的　　(D) 有責任的

---

122. Bill Gates has been - - - - - - - to the Bill & Melinda Gates Foundation after stepping down as CEO of Microsoft.
　　(A) devoting　　　　　　　　(B) devoted
　　(C) devote　　　　　　　　　(D) devotes

解析

這題其實還有另外兩個非常類似的字，我在這兒一起介紹。先看個例句：I commit/devote/dedicate myself to the project. 這句話你要把三個字 commit, devote, dedicate 分開來把這句念三次。先簡單的解釋一下這句話：我 commit （devote, dedicate) 我自己在這個 project 裡了。是不是這三個字都有貢獻、奉獻之類的意思？接下來講個簡單的文法：主動和被動。I commit / devote / dedicate myself，三個字的受詞都是 myself，把 myself 搬到前面當主詞，結果還是I，接下來把 commit/devote/dedicate 加上 ed，然後前面加個 be 動詞，在這裡就是 am，再來把 to the project 加進來，所以被動句型就變成：I am committed/devoted/dedicated to the project. 簡單吧！同樣的把這三個字 committed/devoted/dedicated 分開來把這句子個念一遍！再用這三個字做例子，把以下共六句話再念一遍：I commit myself to the project. I am committed to the project. I devote myself to the project. I am devoted to the project. I dedicate myself to the project. I am dedicated to the project. 有沒有一念就懂？更重要的是在你念句子當中，你有時間去分辨哪句是主動、哪句是被動嗎？還是多念幾次，考試的時候，把那個念起來最順的答案選出來就 OK 了！

(中譯)

自從由微軟總裁位置退下來後，比爾 · 蓋茲就把自己奉獻給比爾與梅琳達 · 蓋茲基金會了。

(A) 奉獻（加 ing)   (B) 奉獻（加 ed)

(C) 奉獻（原型）   (D) 奉獻（加 s)

---

123. The president of the company is expected to ------- a statement regarding the tragic accident happened on the construction site.

    (A) speak   (B) expose

    (C) issue   (D) reply

(解析)

先看答案 (A) speak 如果要當演說、說明的話，應該是 speak to someone。舉例來說：The president is expected to speak to the media. (B) expose 是暴露、揭發的意思，例如：If you are exposed to sunlight for too long, you might get skin cancer. 而 (D) reply 基本上是回覆、回應的意思，例如：I sent an email to my manager asking for a day off, but I have not received any reply yet. 這題的答案是：(C) issue 其實這個題目就是個 issue 的好例句。

中譯

公司總經理預計要對建築工地所發生的意外事件發表聲明。

(A) 說　　(B) 暴露　　(C) 發表、發布　　(D) 回答

---

124. You need to close the window as ------ as possible to prevent any cold air from coming in.

(A) tightly

(B) tight

(C) tightness

(D) tighten

解析

對於這類 as ------ as 的題目我通常會建議只把空格留下來，而把其中的 as… as possible 先全部去掉，以這題為例，先把題目看成：You need to close the window as ------ as possible to prevent any cold air from coming in. 這題就變得很簡單了，只是 close the window tightly 而已。另外舉個類似的例子：The job market is as ------ as last year's. 同樣的四個答案，這也是先把空格以外的東西先去掉 The job market is as ------ as last year's. 題目就變成 The job market is ------ 當然是 The job market is tight. 簡單吧！記得看到 as ------ as something 的題目時，把空格以外的部分都先刪掉，不看題目就會變的很簡單了。

中譯

你必須將窗戶盡可能地關緊，避免讓任何冷空氣進來。

(A) 緊緊地　　(B) 緊的　　(C) 緊密　　(D) 使變緊

125. Great care must be taken to avoid ------- the main structure while we are renovating the building.

(A) damage
(B) damaged
(C) to damage
(D) damaging

解析

這題其實很簡單，把以下的例子多念幾遍：finish reading, avoid damaging, keep going, consider taking (a bus), stop smoking, quit doing, resist fighting, delay paying, postpone sending, suggest cooperating, recommend choosing 念多了、念順了就直接把念起來比較順的，加了 ing 的答案選出來了。注意一下這裡的 suggest cooperating, recommend interviewing 跟前面的 suggest / demand / ask / request / insist / recommend that we MUST 的句型可是有很大的不同，不要搞混了，我的建議還是多念幾次就對了。

中譯

修復建築物時，我們必須非常小心以避免破壞了建築物。

(A) 破壞（原型）
(B) 破壞（加 ed）
(C) 破壞（前面加 to）
(D) 破壞（加 ing）

126. The government will provide ------ shuttle bus service to accommodate extra visitors for the exhibition to be held next week.

(A) various
(B) frequent
(C) numerous
(D) routine

解析

這題有點小 tricky，先看看後面的 to accommodate extra visitors 既然是 accommodate extra visitors 答案就不可能是 routine 例行的、日常的。如果你不太認識 routine 這個字，念一下：a routine job, routine work, 還有 I routinely drink coffee in the morning. 接下來的 various 各種各樣的，還有 numerous 許多的、數不清的，這兩個字都是用在可以數的東西，例如：various tour packages（還有另一個 a variety of tour packages）和 numerous ideas 接下來看一下題目裡的 shuttle bus service，既然 service 沒有 s，答案就不可能是 various 和 numerous 因 為 various packages, various colors, numerous ideas, numerous project， 這 題 的 答 案 是 frequent shuttle bus service。

中譯

政府會提供頻繁的接駁車服務給下週來參觀特展的額外訪客。

(A) 多樣的　　(B) 頻繁的　　(C) 許多的　　(D) 例行的、日常的

---

127. After Ms. Chan was promoted to sales director, she - - - - - - the responsibility for company's marketing strategy.

(A) assumed
(B) considered
(C) delivered
(D) attributed

解析

先看兩個不可能的答案，既然被 promoted，當然不可能 considered 還 有 delivered responsibility。 先 看 attribute 的 例 句：The coach attributes our success to the rigorous training we went through. 教練 attributes 我們的成功 to the rigorous training。是不是可以感覺出 attribute 的意思？查過字典後發現是把…歸因於、認為是…的屬性或品質，其他的先不說，你覺得這個中文意思會好記嗎？知道意思後回來再念一次例句，念完後是不是覺得 attribute 這個字好記多了？可能又有人會說了 attribute 還可以當名詞，這很簡單，同樣的先看個例句：John's greatest attribute is his ability to work under tremendous pressure. 和 Kindness is one of Mary's best attributes. 是不是也有 FU 了！最後是這題的答案 (A) assumed 先把原題目當例句念一遍，一般都會把 assume 當成假定、認為、以為之類的意思，其實在這裡你應該可以感覺出是取得、承擔之類的意思。新多益考試裡的高分題目就常常出現這類的單字，說實話碰到了就把句子多念幾遍，這類的字和意思真的不容易硬背，多念例句，念到對這些字有 FU 才是王道。

中譯

自從陳小姐升任為業務主任後，她就承擔了公司行銷策略的責任。
(A) 取得、承擔　　(B) 認為　　(C) 傳遞　　(D) 把……歸因於

---

128. ------- John wasn't officially trained, he became an accomplished singer and composer.
    (A) Despite
    (B) Although
    (C) Because
    (D) If

解析

這裡我要針對 although 和 despite 特別講一下，這兩個字你要是當單

字用硬背的，我敢保證你會出問題！查一下字典你就會發現這兩個字在字典的解釋上面幾乎沒什麼不同，都是雖然、儘管之類的意思，但在英文上面這兩個字卻又很大的不同。先把這題的答案 (B) Although 帶到原題念一次。接下來看 despite 的例句：Despite his illness, he still went to work. 注意到沒 although 接一整句話（Although John wasn't officially trained），而 despite 卻是 despite his illness，這就是兩字間的差別了！很簡單再念兩個 despite 的例子：despite the high temperature, despite the bad weather，多念幾次就知道 despite 直接接個名詞，以後就不會有問題了。其實這題目的後半部也有個很不錯的單字，你猜 accomplished 這個字是好是壞？一定是好事對吧！所以就是很棒的、很厲害的之類的意思不是嗎？不要小看了 accomplished 也有可能出現在考題裡。

中譯

雖然 John 未曾接受過正式的訓練，他還是成為了著名的歌手和作曲家。

(A) 儘管（後接名詞）　　(B) 儘管（後接句子）　　(C) 因為　　(D) 如果

---

129. An early and accurate - - - - - - of SARS is vitally important in the survival of the patients.

    (A) diagnose　　　　　　(B) diagnostic

    (C) diagnostically　　　　(D) diagnosis

解析

這題其實可以用來證明只要你正確的語感有了，有些題目就算你答案完全不認識還是可以選出正確答案。(C) diagnostically 顯然是副詞，(B) diagnostic 基本上只是把 (C) 的 ly 去掉而已（tic 和 tical 的字尾基本上可以認為一樣），所以是形容詞，看到這裡如果你不知道形容詞加 ly 變副詞，其實關係不大，只要你把我這本書裡的所有句子都能念過幾遍，自然就會知道了，根本不需要去記！剩下的 diagnose 如果不認識沒關係，英文字念多了 compose, expose, dispose 念多了就知道 diagnose / di AG nose/（注意重音）是個動詞，剩下的 (D) diagnosis 自然就是名詞，答案是 (D) diagnosis /di ag NO sis/（注意重音），再來就是把題目多念個幾遍，是不是就可以感覺出 diagnose 診斷、偵測的意思了，真的很容易背對吧！

中譯

早期、準確的診斷出 SARS 對患者的存活率非常重要。

(A) 診斷（動詞）　　(B) 診斷的　　(C) 在診斷方面　　(D) 診斷（名詞）

---

130. We really enjoyed the spectacular and ------- view after reaching the top of mountain.

(A) fascinating　　　　　(B) fascinated

(C) fascinate　　　　　(D) fascination

解析

這題其實很簡單，前面也講過了，先念一下：It's fascinating, I am fascinated，所以就是 the view is fascinating, the fascinating view，不需要考慮就選 fascinating view 了。後面的 after reaching the top of the mountain 也可以寫成 after arriving at the top of the mountain。

中譯

我們在抵達山頂後，真的很享受那壯觀且迷人的景色。

(A) 迷人的　　(B) 著迷的　　(C) 迷住　　(D) 魅力

---

131. ------- of personal income tax would stimulate the economy by getting more disposable money into citizens' hand.

(A) Reducing

(B) Reduction

(C) Reduced

(D) Reducible

解析

這題基本上也很簡單，把 reducing personal income tax 和 reduction of personal income tax 多念幾次就對了。再給個例子：introducing new products 和 introduction of new products，OK 了吧！這題裡面還有兩個字要特別提一下，先念一下這題的前半部：Reduction of personal income tax would stimulate the economy. 降低個人所得稅會 stimulation the economy 你猜 stimulate 是好是壞？是不是有刺激、激勵的意思！接下來 by getting more disposable money into citizens' hand 只是說明為什麼會 stimulate the economy 而已。看看 disposable 這個字，還記得前面說過 The money is at your disposal. 嗎？這裡只是把 disposal 改成 disposable money 變了詞性而已，意思基本上還是一樣：money at your disposal, disposable money 如此而已，簡單吧。

降低個人所得稅會讓市民手裡有更多可支配的金錢，就可以刺激經濟了。

(A) 減少（加 ing）   (B) 減少（名詞）

(C) 減少（加 ed）   (D) 可減少的

---

132. Yesterday, dad made John - - - - - - the car.

    (A) washed   (B) washing

    (C) to wash   (D) wash

解析

125 題講了些後面要加 ing 的動詞，如果沒印象再給幾個例子：finish reading, avoid damaging, keep going, consider taking (a bus), stop smoking, quit doing, resist fighting, delay paying, postpone sending, suggest cooperating, recommend choosing。這題講的是不一樣的動詞，所謂的使役動詞，首先我很討厭這個名字「使役」動詞，這個名稱只會害死學生，我就不去細說，先給你個例句：Let me have it made. 這句話裡有三個動詞：let, have, make，記住這句，就可以記住這三個動詞，不過我可以先講 let 這個字不會考，雖然如此 let 還是可以幫你記住這三個字的用法，例句：Disney 電影 Frozen（冰雪奇緣）的主題曲 Let it go，還有 Let me do it. Let the kids play. 因為這個字 let 太常見了，考的機會真的不大。不過熟悉了 Let it go. Let me do it. 和 Let the kids play. 對於 have 和 make 就容易了，看例句：Have the kids clean the room. Make John wash the car. Have Mary work with Tom. Make Ken sit in the room. 基本上跟 let 一樣 let/have/make someone do something 這裡的 do（還有其他的 clean,

wash, work, sit）都是原型，把這些例子多念幾次就對了。當然事情沒有這麼簡單，同樣的給例子：Make the room cleaned. Have the car washed. 所謂的過去分詞表示被動，如同我在前面一直強調的多念就對了，不必去管什麼主動、被動！ Have the kids clean the room. Have the room cleaned. 還有 Make John wash the car. Make the car washed. Have the car parked. 是不是就有FU了！最後再回到我講過的例句：Let me have it made. 所以這題是：Yesterday, dad made John wash the car. 有些人會提出 help，念例句：The coach helps us practice playing basketball. 以及 The coach helps us to practice playing basketball. 也就是説 help 後面接原型或是加上 to 都可以，help us (to) practice playing basketball。當然還有更多的動詞後面要加 to 舉例來説：ask him to play, want me to work, tell her to come，説實話這類的動詞是最多的，因為這類後面接 to 的動詞實在太多了，我的建議就是把後面加 ing 的和後面接原型的念熟就對了。

中譯

昨天老爸要 John 洗車子。

(A) 洗（加 ed）　　(B) 洗（加 ing）

(C) 洗（前面加 to）　(D) 洗（原型）

---

133. - - - - - - structural problems caused by earthquake need to be reported immediately.

(A) There are　　　　(B) Every

(C) Any　　　　　　(D) A

先看 (A) There are 同樣地先給例句：There are students (in the classroom). There are flowers (in the garden). 是不是感覺到念完 There are students 和 There are flowers 句意就完整，就是一句話了！看看題目後面不只是 caused，還有 need to be reported 看到這裡就知道 (A) 不對。接下來的 every 和另一個字 each，我要你先看一下：everyone, each one，簡單的講就是 every 和 each 後面都要接 one，所以如果 every 和 each 要成為正確答案，題目一定要是 every structure problem, each structural problem，只能是 problem（因為 every 和 each 只能接 one），當然答案 (D) A 更只能是 A problem！所以答案是 (C) Any 整句就是 Any structural problems caused by earthquake need to be reported immediately.

解析

任何地震所造成的結構問題，都需要立刻被報導出來。

(A) 那裡有……　　(B) 每一個　　(C) 任何　　(D) 一個

---

134. Despite the long meeting, we did not ------- any final decision.

(A) reach
(B) arrive
(C) address
(D) communicate

解析

先看不對的答案，address 當然不是接 decision，address 應該是 problem, issue，同樣 communicate 不可能接 final decision，例句：

A great leader must be able to communicate effectively with the team members. (B) arrive 在這裡要 arrive at any final decision 答案是 (A) reach。

中譯

既使經過了漫長的會議，我們還是沒能取得任何最終的決定。

(A) 達成、取得 (B) 抵達 (C) 發表 (D) 溝通

---

135. We need to do our job ------ than previously planned to finish the project on time.

(A) quicker　　　　　　　(B) quick

(C) more quickly　　　　(D) quickly

解析

這題有一點點小 tricky，先看到後面的 than 自然前面要 more 才可以變成 more than 所以答案要是所謂的比較級。就可以先殺掉 (B) quick 和 (D) quickly。剩下的只是決定要 quicker 還是 more quickly，簡單先念一下 We need to do a quick job. We need to do the job quickly. 所以答案是 (C) more quickly 整句話就成為：We need to do our job more quickly than previously planned to finish the project on time.

中譯

我們需要做的比原先計畫的還要快，才能準時完成這計畫。

(A) 更快一點（形容詞比較級）　　(B) 快的

(C) 更快一點地（副詞比較級）　　(D) 快一點地

136. Finance manager discovered that the accountant had not been ------- the checks into the adequate banking account.

(A) deposit

(B) depositing

(C) deposited

(D) deposits

解析

這類的主動、被動題型只要你有任何問題,最簡單的就是把正確答案帶進去多念幾次,以這題而言基本上是主動題型,那我建議你把題目改成被動題型再念幾次,同時把主動和被動都念熟就對了。先把正確答案(B) depositing 帶到句子裡唸個幾遍。再來把 deposited 代入,也唸個幾遍。這兩句的重點是:The accountant had not been depositing the checks (into the adequate banking account). 和 The checks had not been deposited (into the adequate banking account). 如果不認識的話順便學學 adequate(適當的)這個字。多念幾次就可以感覺 depositing the checks 和 checks were not deposited(注意一下,我只是改了個簡單的時態而已)是不是就有 FU 了!以文法來說 deposit 當主動,後面就一定要接受詞所以一定是 depositing the checks,當 check 被調到前面當主詞,句子當然就成為:checks were not deposited 了。如果你對任何這類的主動、被動題目有問題,這裡就是個好例子,把兩種型態的例句都寫出來,然後多念幾遍就對了!

中譯

財務經理發現會計還沒把支票存入適當的銀行帳戶裡。

(A) 存放(原型)

(B) 存放(加 ing)

(C) 存放(加 ed)

(D) 存放(加 s)

137. Had the operator known how to reach Mr. Jackson, she
- - - - - - him.

(A) would have called   (B) called

(C) calls   (D) would call

解析

這題又是基本的假設語氣，只是把 had 掉到最前面取代了 if 而已，如果還是有問題回去念一下 16 題的解釋。

中譯

如果操作員知道該如何聯絡到傑克森先生的話，她早就打給他了。

(A) 打電話（前面加 would have，call 後面加 ed）

(B) 打電話（加 ed）

(C) 打電話（加 s）

(D) 打電話（前面加 would）

138. If you are concerned about the - - - - - - rate increases, an option of prepaying three-month bill at existing rate will be provided.

(A) possible   (B) considerable

(C) current   (D) destructive

解析

這題要先注意到後面的 prepaying three-month bill at existing rate 尤其是 existing rate 如果是 current rate increases 表示已經漲價了，怎

麼可能會有 prepaying existing rate 這樣的 option？ destructive 語意根本不對不需要考慮。再來是 considerable，先看個例子 considerable amount of money 你覺得是錢多還是錢少？ considerable 基本上就是多，如果 rate increases 確定很高、很多，那大家一定是先 prepay 了不是嗎？這個 option 大家都會 take，大家都會 take 的 option 基本上就不應該稱做 option，有些人要，有些人不要才會是 option。所以答案是 (A) possible 就是因為 possible rate increase 有可能而已，才會給個可以 prepay at existing rate 的 option，是不是就懂了！

（中譯）

如果你擔心費用可能會增加，我們會提供一個以現有價格先預付三個月的選項。

(A) 可能的　　(B) 相當多的　　(C) 當前的　　(D) 破壞的

---

139. Great company leaders usually ------ sound judgement before making critical decisions.

(A) refuse

(B) promote

(C) ignore

(D) practice

（解析）

這題首先要知道 sound judgement 到底是好是壞？我先給個例句好了：We had a nice and sound evening. 你說呢？ nice and sound 再念一次，所以 sound judgement 基本上就是 good judgement，知道了 sound judgement 後 (A) refuse 拒絕 (C) ignore 忽略就可以先去掉了，如果不認識這兩個字，看看例句吧，My decision is final and I refuse to discuss it any further. 再來 ignore 這個字，這個字跟先前介紹的 neglect 是同義字，所以前面 120 題的例句改一下就可以了，He was so busy that he neglected/ignored his health. 忙　到 neglected/ignored his health，是不是就有忽視、忽略的感覺了！再來解釋一下 promote 這個字，其實 promote 基本上就是兩個用法：promote someone 和 promote something，promote someone 就 是 升 官、晉升，例句：Jack was promoted to be the marketing director. 而 promote something 可以看作是 promote new products，宣傳新產品。最後解釋一下正確答案 (D) practice 在這裡是實行、實施之類的意思，其實這題還有一個更難一點的答案：exercise 這個字除了大家熟知的運動、鍛鍊、練習之外，還可以有運用、行使的意思，同樣的我的建議就是把 practice 和 exercise 帶進題目裡，當例句多念幾次：Great company leaders usually practice/exercise sound judgement before making critical decisions.

中譯

優秀的公司領導者通常在下重要的決策前，會做出好的判斷。

(A) 拒絕　　(B) 提升　　(C) 忽視　　(D) 實行、實施

---

140. Although we spend a lot of time on social media, they are anything - - - - - - social.

(A) but

(B) apart from

(C) nevertheless

(D) besides

這題其實只是個慣用語：anything but，先看個例句：The teacher's explanation is anything but clear. 字面上的意思是：除了 clear 以外的 anything，也就是完全不 clear。再給個例句：I enjoy drinking anything but soda. 除了 soda 以外的 drink 都愛喝。再來看個完全相反的用法和句型：He is nothing but a coward. 注意一下這句話基本上是：He is nothing. 他什麼都不是！所以 He is nothing but a coward. 在 nothing 後面加個 but 基本上就成為 He is a coward. 在把先前的 I enjoy drinking anything but soda. 看一下，這句其實只是：I enjoy drinking anything. 什麼都喝，所以 I enjoy drinking anything but soda. 變成什麼都喝就是不喝 soda。看看其他例句：The service is anything. 這個 service 什麼都是，The service is anything but good. 就是不夠好。將兩句再念一次，是不是有 FU 了！記得把這裡的例句多念幾遍，念到腦子對英文直接有 FU 就對了。

中譯

雖然我們花了很多時間在社交媒體上，但那根本不是社交。

(A) anything but 根本不是　　(B) 除了　　(C) 然而　　(D) 此外

PART 6

Question 141-143 ○ refer to the following article.

An invoice is a __141.__ document issued by the seller to the buyer, and it would list information like products, quantities, and mutually agreed prices for products and/or services which the seller has to provide. Technically, payment __142.__ negotiated by both parties are independent of the invoice. Part of the total cost could have already been paid as the _ __143.__ payment. In this case, the maximum number of days allowed for the buyer to pay for the rest of the payment is also listed.

141. (A) commercial（商業的、商務的）
　　　(B) technical（技術的）
　　　(C) popular（流行的）
　　　(D) public（公立的、大眾的）

解析

第一句中的 information 後面的 like 只是說明什麼樣的 information，like 後面所舉例的 information 有三個：products，quantities 和 (mutually agreed) prices，什麼樣的 (mutually agreed) prices？ prices for products and/or services 而這些 products and/or services 哪來的？ products and/or services which the seller has to provide 這樣是不是完全看懂了！(C) popular 和 (D) public 應該都懂吧！不過我還是給例句："阿妹（or 張惠妹）is one of the most popular singers in Taiwan." 還 有 "建 中 is a public high school, but 再興 is a private one."（public 和 private 一起念、一起記）。

再來看一下 (B) technical 技術的、科技的，先念一下例句：Edward possesses the technical knowledge required to deal with computer problems. 簡單一點的還可以是：You need to read the technical documents completely. You need to read the complete technical documents. 最後是正確答案 (A) commercial 商業的、商務的，把 commercial 帶進原題就是個好例句，這題的前半部其實只是：An invoice is a commercial document. 如此而已，後面只是解釋是什麼樣的 commercial document，a commercial document (which is) issued by the seller to the buyer 由 the seller issues 給 buyer 的 commercial document。

142. (A) records（紀錄）
　　 (B) terms（條件）
　　 (C) documents（文件）
　　 (D) settlement（協議）

解析

能夠被 negotiated 的不會是 record 紀錄，也不會是 document 文件，畢竟 record 和 document 都是雙方 negotiated 之後所同意的東西，再來是 (D) settlement，先看例句：The top management is trying to get a settlement with the union to end the strike. 如果不知道的話，這裡的 union 是工會、strike 是罷工，所以這句話的意思是：高層管理試著跟工會取得個 settlement 來停止罷工，settlement 在這裡有解決、協議的意思，再給個例句：The union was originally hoping to get a

5% pay raise, but had to settle for 3% at the end. Union 原先希望得到 5% 的加薪，最後 settle 在 3%，是不是對 settle 有 FU 了！最後是正確答案 (B) terms，在這裡要 payment terms（付款條件）一起念，在這裡我想直接解釋一下什麼是 payment terms。First payment at contract signed: 10%, second payment at the end of phase I: 30%, third payment at the end of phase II: 30 %, final payment at the end of the project: 30%，這就是個 payment terms。簡單一點的例子是：down payment（頭期款或首款）20%, final payment 80%，這也是個 payment terms。

143. (A) before
     (B) received
     (C) down
     (D) earlier

解析

題目裡面已經說了 have been paid 已經付錢過了，就可以把 before, received 和 earlier 去掉了。因為這三個答案基本上都是廢話，句子前面說了 have been paid 就不用再講 before, received, earlier 了，所以答案是 down payment 也就是所謂的訂金、頭期款，在這裡千萬不要只背 down payment：訂金、頭期款，看個例句：You need to pay 10% of the total amount of money as the down payment. 句子念過後再把 down payment 多念幾次，就會有 FU ！

Unit 4　新多益模擬閱讀試題解析　**389**

City Community Center __144.__ an internet marketing seminar on Sunday, Aug. 14. Several renowned internet marketing experts will be on hand to talk about the latest website marketing trends and advise you on __145.__ to be successful in the internet age. The cost is $60 for a single participant. For a group of over five people, the cost is $50 per person. If you are interested, please call toll-free at 1-800-123-4567 or go to our website at www.citycommunitycenter.org to register. There is a __146.__ number of seats, so please act soon before it's too late.

144. (A) holds
     (B) held
     (C) has held
     (D) will be holding

解析

這題看答案很明顯的是考時態不過題目裡只看到了 Sunday, Aug. 14，但是今天是哪一天完全沒有 idea。以這題來說，看不出答案就先往下看下去。第二句，基本上是 several experts will be on hand to talk about something. 所以很明顯的，這題答案是 (D) will be holding。這類的題目在新多益 Part 6 是很標準的題目，需要參考前後文的時態來挑答案，有時一些單字題單看一題會有幾個可能的答案，那就需要看前後文，根據前後文的語意來選出最合適的答案。

145. (A) whether
　　　(B) how
　　　(C) if
　　　(D) what

解析

接下來看 145 題，這四個答案裡，應該可以立刻看出 (C) if 一定錯！接下來應該會有些考生看出來 (D) what 也不對！先給兩個例句：I don't understand what you are talking about. What you are thinking is nonsense. 再來給個 whether 的例句：We need to look at all the different sides of this deal before we decide whether to accept it (or not). 原先 whether 一般在後面都會接 or not，但是現在省掉 or not 的越來越多了，所以基本上用了 whether 就有個二選一選項的感覺，所以這也不是答案。最後把答案 (B) how 帶進去題目念一遍，這句的基本架構是：Several renowned internet marketing experts will be on hand to talk about one thing (the latest website marketing trends) and advise you on another thing. 這樣就把這句話完全看懂了。

146. (A) limited
　　　(B) defined
　　　(C) constraint
　　　(D) random

解析

依題目就可以先把 (B) defined 和 (D) random 先刪掉，再來是刪 constraint，如果你只是背單字 constraint：約束、限制，或許你會認為為什麼 constraint：約束、限制不是正確答案，原因很簡單，新多益考的是英文用字，不是中文意義的解釋。看看 constraint 的幾個例句：The boss has turned down our request to expand the division due to financial constraints. The growth of our company has been seriously constrained by the poor economy. We have to shut down our website due to budget constraints. 是不是有感覺到 constraint 有那種被綁住，動彈不得的感覺！所以答案是 (A) limited，照例把答案帶到題目裡當例句念幾次。

Questions 147-149 refer to the following news report.

Under the enormous pressure coming from the public as well as the government, Charter Bus and its labor union reached a/an __147.__ settlement on salary increase, ending the one-month strike. Both sides would keep __148.__ for a final salary agreement. Upon hearing the news, the mayor said "We are glad to hear that the residents can finally get the public transportation they __149.__ need."

147. (A) convenient（方便的）

(B) brief（簡短的）

(C) substitute（代替的）

(D) tentative（暫時性的）

解析

如果你對這題暫時沒有答案，就先往下句看下去。第 2 句中提到 keep - - - - - - for a final…，顯然前面的 settlement 並不是 final 的 settlement。來解釋一下選項，(A) 算是最簡單的，念一下 convenience stores (7-11) 就可以記住 convenience 了，7-11 就是 convenience stores：便利商店，記住了 convenience 當然就認識了 convenient。(B) 的例句：We'll take a brief restroom break and then be back to continue the discussion. 既然是 restroom break 當然就是 brief 簡短的。這裡我還要提一下，brief 還可以當動詞用是簡報的意思，請看例句：The sales director is giving a briefing to our potential clients. 是不是就有 briefing 簡報的 FU！(C) 的例句：Jenny is substituting for Candy, who is at home with a flu. 既然 Candy is at home with a flu，Jenny 就需要 substitutes her 代替、取代。還有 a substitute teacher 就是個代課老師。再來一個：Thomas Edison once said that there is no substitute for hard work. 這裡的 no substitute for hard work 懂了吧！最後是正確答案 (D)，這裡我們可以多看一下 tentative 這個字的意思，先查一下字典，tentative：試驗性的、嘗試的、暫時的、暫定的、躊躇的、猶豫的，想一下既然是暫時的那就不是永久的，當然就可以是試驗性的，畢竟都是要試驗 OK 以後才能變成永久的。還有躊躇的、猶豫的。給個例句：The actor is tentative about singing in the show, unsure of whether he has the capability. 既然是個 actor 要他 singing in the show 當然會 tentative，在這裡 tentative 一定是躊躇的、猶豫的對吧！想想看，一般人對 tentative 的東西自然會有些 tentative，看到這裡你不覺得 tentative 在英文的用法就是一個，只是為了翻譯成中文，在中文裡變成了好幾個不同的意思！想一下如果你硬背

tentative 這個字，這幾個不太一樣的中文意思容易背嗎？記的住嗎？還是把英文例句多念幾次，念出對 tentative 的感覺就容易記了。

148. (A) negotiating
    (B) negotiates
    (C) negotiated
    (D) negotiate

解析

這題還記得前面講到的：finish reading, avoid damaging, keep going, consider taking (a bus), stop smoking, quit doing, resist fighting, delay paying, postpone sending, suggest cooperating, recommend choosing 嗎？既然是 keep going 當然這題就是 keep negotiating，簡單吧！

149. (A) desperate
    (B) desperately
    (C) desperation
    (D) desperateness

解析

這題需要個副詞來修飾動詞 need，所以應該可以直接選出 they desperately need。文法是一定要記的，但只有反覆的念例句，培養語感，才能迅速地選出正確答案。

Questions 150-152 ○ refer to the following advertisement

Feeling exhausted? Want to get away from the summer heat? It is time for you to take a break from your busy work and go on a vacation.

Just make a call to **Ultimate Alaska Travel**, and you will enjoy an incredible summer vacation. Our tour __150.__ to Alaska's beautiful Glacier Bay National Park and preserve is only **$895** per person, which includes __151.__ in a five-star hotel, flight tickets, and __152.__ breakfasts. If you are planning to go with a friend, it's only **$1,595** for the both of you. What are you waiting for? For more information, please call toll free **800-111-2233**, or visit our website at **www.ultimate-alaska-travel.com**.

150. (A) guide
     (B) equipment
     (C) package
     (D) position

解析

tour guide 是導遊、equipment 是儀器、設備，position 位置都不好。答案 (C)，tour package（套裝的旅遊行程）。在這裡我要多解釋一下 equipment 和另一個字 facility 的差別，equipment 比較簡單，基本上就是大家熟知的儀器、設備，facility 就難一點了，不過只要記住一句簡單的話『可大可小』就 OK 了，在這裡我稍稍解釋一下，台積電晶圓二廠和五廠都在同一個地點，facility 大的時候就可以把整個台積電晶圓二廠和五廠的廠區是為一個 facility，而裡面的二廠和五廠又可以分別看成不同的 facility，進到晶圓廠裡面的一些儀器設備，也可以看做是一些 facilities 這就是我說的 facility『可大可小』。另外還有一點我想提一下，那就是 some equipment, a few facilities，注意到兩者的差別了沒？equipment 沒加 s 而 facility 成為了複數，文法上的說法 equipment 不可數，而 facility 可數，如果你覺得這也太複雜了，跟你說個好消息，新多益不會直接考 equipment 不可以加 s！對於這類題目的新多益考法，我給兩個簡單的例子：a little water, a few drops of water 基本考法就是：a - - - - - - juice, a - - - - - - cups of juice 選項會有 little, few 和其他無關緊要的答案，或者是 - - - - - - trouble, - - - - - - troubles 選項會有 much, many，這類題目很簡單 juice 沒有 s 所以是 a <u>little</u> juice，cups 有 s 所以是 a few <u>cups</u> of juice。下一個一模一樣，前面的 trouble 沒有 s 所以是 much trouble 後面的 troubles 有 s 所以是 many troubles，很容易吧！另外我要講一下 a little 和 little 的差別先給例句：I have a little water. I have little water. 各是什麼意思？其實很簡單：I have a little water. 我有些水，而在 I have little water. 裡的 little 意思是很少、幾乎沒有，所以簡單的說 I have little water. 就是我沒有水。另外給個例子：I have a little money. 基本上就是我有（些）錢，而 I have little money. 意思就是我沒錢！理論上而言 a few 和 few 跟 a little 和 little 應該有類似的意思，不過只是用 few 的情形看到的不多，就算有也都是以 I have very few friends. 加個 very 來強調 few friends.

151. (A) admission（入場費）
　　 (B) entrance（入口）
　　 (C) access（通道）
　　 (D) accommodation（膳宿）

解析

admission 基本上用在 theme parks, amusement parks, concerts 之類的情況，entrance 更不用說了，對於 access 先給幾個例句：I cannot access the account with the password. With your badge, you cannot get access to the office building. It's important for all citizens to have access to affordable medical insurance. 基本上 access 可以是個 account 帳號，一個實體的東西 office buildings，也可以是個非實體的東西 medical insurance。好玩的是這幾種狀況用中文的翻譯卻是不一樣的詞語，這也是另一個單字不能硬背的例子。最後只剩下正確答案 (D) accommodation 了，在我解釋 accommodation 這個字之前，先講一個在新多益考試很重要的解題技巧。我先前已經提過在閱讀考試裡，往往你都可以先選出兩個不合適的答案，所以基本上每個題目裡，你都會面對在剩下的兩個答案裡選出正確答案的情況。以這題而言，如同我先前所說的，多數考生應該可以一眼看出 entrance 不對，再來應該也可以挑出 admission 不是好答案，這就只剩下 access 和 accommodation，根據新多益的出題特性，如果你認為這個答案不到 70 分就選剩下的那個，沒什麼把握甚至是不認識的答案。到這裡，有些讀者會說了，如果我認為 access 有 70 分呢？那我對你的建議就是：不要再硬背、死背單字了，多念例句、多念文章，把句子和裡面的單字念到有 FU 就對了。接下來解釋 accommodation 這個字，畢竟認得所有答案才是最保險的。首先最簡單的就是把 accommodation 帶進原題目當例句念個幾遍，當然你更可以把下一題的答案帶進來一起念。還有其他的例句：The government is building temporary accommodation for people whose homes were destroyed by the typhoon. 如果唸完這兩句之後，感覺上已經明白 accommodation 這個字但是卻説不出 accommodation 這例句裡的中文意思，我會先説把句子完全看懂就可以了，不要去管這字的中文意思了，再來會恭喜你把 accommodation 這個字真的學起來了，因為了解了這單字再例句裡的意思才是真正的學英文，如果你需要借助中文意思甚至中文翻譯才能明白英文句子的意思，你永遠學不好英文！這正是我根本不想在書裡提供翻譯的原因！假設你還是想知道 accommodation 在這裡的中文意思，先把句子再念一遍，然後才去查字典，根據句子的上下文你應該可以看出在這兩句裡 accommodation 的意思應該是：方便、方便設施和住處、膳宿的意思。接下來我想問你，你覺得 accommodation：方便、方便設施，住處、膳宿好背嗎？容易記住嗎？如果不好背、不好記，幹嘛硬去背、硬去記，把例句多念幾次不就 OK 了！

152. (A) complimentary（贈送的）
　　　(B) reimbursed（補償的）
　　　(C) refundable（可退費的）
　　　(D) payable（可支付的）

解析

complimentary breakfast 指的是含在住宿中的免付費早餐，其他 3 個選項依題意都不正確。

小叮嚀

再解釋接下來的閱讀測驗之前，我想先再次強調一下，要記單字和學文法最好的方法就是閱讀，我希望大家在對過答案後，要確認自己可以把這裡面的每篇文章裡的每個句子都看懂！我常跟學生講，從高中以後，有哪次英文考試，你可以說考試裡的每個單字我都認識？有許多老師用這點來強調「早就叫你背單字，你就不信！」我的看法反而是，既然一定會有單字不認識，如何讓你自己在有單字的狀況下還是能夠把句子看懂，把文章搞清楚，這才是最重要的技能不是嗎？在看完我文法單字的解析之後，你應該會發現，就算你有些單字不懂，事實上你還是可以把句子和文章看懂，而閱讀測驗的文章更是可以讓你加強練習這項技能。就算你這後面的閱讀測驗寫得還不錯，我相信以下的文章你一定有些單字不認識，有些句子看不懂，我希望你能學著把句子看懂，把單字念到有FU，藉由這些文章來記單字、學文法，學英文最重要的是：read to learn，用閱讀來學習英文，這才是學習英文的正途！

PART 7

Question 153-154 refer to the following notice.

1. The annual employee "Summer Fun Day" will be held on Friday, June 12, in the courtyard right outside the main entrance.

2. Refreshments will be provided by our cafeteria staff.

3. Please contact David Ng at ext. 456 by June 5, to let him know if you'll be joining.

4. Also, Jennifer Banister is in charge of entertainment activity. Please call ext. 469 by June 1, if you have any idea that can help her.

5. Be sure to come and enjoy a fun day with your colleagues.

文章解析

這篇文章很簡單,就算裡面有些單字,重點抓到了就可以看懂了。

1. The annual employee "Summer Fun Day" will be held on 這一天(Friday, June 12), in 這個地方(the courtyard right outside the main entrance)。假設你在考試,是不是這樣就把句子看懂了?至於裡面有什麼單字,不會影響到你看懂句子對吧!如果你不知道 courtyard,很簡單就是 main entrance 外面的 yard,至於 yard 這個字更簡單,念一下 front yard, backyard(前院、後院)。

2. 先講 cafeteria 這個字,在字典裡往往會解釋為自助餐館,其實不是很對,其實多數情況下是員工餐廳或是簡餐餐廳,簡單一點當餐廳就可以了。如果你不知道 refreshments,到 Google 圖片蒐尋找一下 refreshments,然後邊看著(有飲料有點心的)圖片,邊念

refreshments 就可以了。把這句再看一次，就可以清楚知道這裡的 cafeteria 正是員工餐廳。

3. 很清楚就是在幾號之前（by June 5）要打哪個分機（at ext. 456）給誰（David Ng）來報名參加，簡單吧！這裡的 ext. 其實是 extension 認識嗎？先給個例句：We need more time to finish the project, so please extend the deadline for us. 時間不夠當然就需要 extend the deadline，認識了 extend 自然就會知道名詞 extension，再給個詞，去 Google 圖片蒐尋找一下 extension cords，沒錯 extension cords 就是延長線，至於 extension 為什麼會是分機，稍稍想一下，分機就是從總機所 extend 出來的不是嗎？

4. Jennifer Banister 就 是 in charge of entertainment activity. Entertainment 不知道簡單念一下 entertainment industry（注意 industry 的念法是 /IN dus try/ 重音在最前面，entertainment industry 娛樂業所以 entertainment 就是娛樂。下一句只是說如果你有 idea 可以 help Jennifer Banister 就跟他聯絡。

5. 只是說希望大家都參加而已，裡面的 your colleagues 可不要跟 college 搞混了，colleagues 在新多益考試就當作 co-workers：同事。看懂了文章，該看看題目了。另外提一下，經過我的解釋看懂文章之後，你還需要看中文翻譯嗎？

153. What is the purpose of this notice?
    (A) To tell employee about a company ceremony.
    (B) To announce an upcoming company party.
    (C) To let the company staff know that there is refreshment for the activity.
    (D) To introduce cafeteria staff.

解析

這是典型的出題方式，這四個答案裡，可以清楚的先看出來 (D) 顯然是錯的，先殺掉。再來是 (C)，這句有沒有提到？Refreshments will be provided by our cafeteria staff. 連由誰來提供都說了，當然有提到！但這東西（refreshments）是最重要的重點嗎？當然不是，這答案是經典的以偏概全，錯！剩下兩個答案：(A) 和 (B)，如果你一時看不出這兩個答案的重點，我就會講，請你在答案裡面挑出一個字，只准挑出一個字，你會挑哪個字？或許有人會說 tell 和 announce，問題是這兩個字基本上意思一樣對挑答案沒幫助，所以請你再挑一次，同樣的只准挑一個字，這次應該可以選出 ceremony 和 party 了吧！認得這兩個字的人應該可以挑出正確答案了，在此我還是提供例句給大家。Olympics 大家都知道吧！每一屆的 Olympics 一開始一定會有 opening ceremony 和最後結束前也一定會有 closing ceremony，沒錯就是開幕典禮和閉幕典禮，懂了嗎？ ceremony 當然就是典禮，接下來把 opening ceremony 和 closing ceremony 多念幾遍，你說 ceremony 還需要硬背嗎？接下來是 party 有部分台灣學生硬背單字都把 party 當成舞會，其實不對，Party 多半是大家聚在一起的一個聚會。文章裡提到了 the annual employee "Summer Fun Day"，答案當然是 (B)。

154. Why would employees call Jennifer?

    (A) To let her know if they are joining the activity or not.

    (B) To inform her that they are interested in showing their singing talent.

    (C) To help her arrange the refreshment.

    (D) To give her their ideas for the decoration.

解析

先看 (C)，refreshments 由 cafeteria staff 負責，(C) 錯，再看 (D)，文章裡應該都沒提到 decoration 吧，錯！最後看一下剩下的 (A)，報名要找誰？如果忘記了回去文章看一下，顯然是 David Ng 所以 (A) 錯！既然四個答案有三個是錯的，那正確答案一定是剩下的 (B)，從第 4 句中可得到映證。

Questions 155-157 ○ refer to the following schedule.

1. Summer Camp for Young Journalists, Sports Journalist Association
2. Tour of Sporting News Publishing House, July 17th
3. (* for special meal needs)

9:30 - 10:00 A.M.	Gathering at the entrance of Community Center
10:00 A.M.	Departing for Sporting News Publishing House
11:00 – 11:50 A.M.	Lecture, Keith Patrick, "How to be a News Anchor?"
12:00 – 12:50 P.M.	Lunch at the cafeteria (Ham and cheese sandwich or hamburger) *
01:00 – 01:50 P.M.	Touring the satellite news receiving station
02:00 – 02:50 P.M.	Visiting the new editing room
03:00 – 03:50 P.M.	Q&A with sporting news reporters
04:00 P.M.	Returning to Community Center

4. * If you have any special meal requirement, please contact Michelle Anderson at 409-512-1212.

文章解析

我一直強調多益閱讀測驗要先看文章，但是這也有例外。如果你看到文章是 figure, table, survey results, meeting agenda, tour itinerary 這類的內容，這些 figure, table, survey results, meeting agenda, tour itinerary 內部的內容要先跳過不看，可是前後的大小標題和特別標記，如 * 之類的句子還是要先看。以這題為例：

1. 先看一下標題，很明顯是由 Sports Journalist Association 所辦的 Summer Camp for Young Journalists，如果你不認識 journalist 其實沒關係，反正 ist 結尾八成是某類人士就夠了。

2. 只是在 July, 17th 有個參觀 Sporting News Publishing House 的 tour 就對了。

3. 最後看到了個 *，這一定要看一下 (* for special meal needs) 顯然是給些對 meal 有 special request 的人。接下來的行程先忽略過不看，等看到題目時，再來找。

4. 這裡的 * 一定要看：反正是你對 meal 有 special requirement 的人請 contact Michelle Anderson 就對了。

155. Who arranged this event?
     (A) Sports Journalist Association
     (B) Sporting News Publishing House
     (C) Community Center
     (D) Keith Patrick

解析

這題簡單吧，顯然是 (A) Sports Journalist Association 你可不要去選 (B) Sporting News Publishing House 這可是他們要參觀的地方。

156. What is the activity right after lunch?
(A) Hearing a talk
(B) A visit to the satellite news receiving station
(C) A tour of the news editing room
(D) A meeting with reporters

解析

看到題目寫 after lunch 趕快去看一下行程，lunch 之後的行程是在 01:00 – 01:50 P.M.，安排 Touring the satellite news receiving station，所以答案是 (B)，這裡基本上只是把文章裡的 tour 改成答案裡的 visit 而已。

157. What should Emmy Donahue, a vegetarian, do for her lunch?
(A) Choose between sandwich and hamburger.
(B) Bring her own food
(C) Notify Community Center
(D) Call Michelle for her special need.

解析

這題重點來了，你要是認得 vegetarian 就很簡單，但是就算你完全不認識這個字，我敢保證你還是選的出正確答案。如果不認識 vegetarian

這個字，你也可以注意到前後各有個逗點，我常跟學生講，兩個逗點之間先拿掉，這句話就變成：What should Emmy Donahue do for her lunch?，很明顯的兩個逗點之間的話語只是用來形容、說明 Emmy Donahue 這個人而已。還記得那個 * 嗎？而且題目說了 for her lunch，很明顯答案是 (D)。最後把這篇文章裡的單字做個總整理。念過碩博士的應該知道 paper 分兩種：conference paper 和 journal paper，在這裡的 journal paper 就是所謂的期刊、雜誌之類的意思，而 journalist 就變成人了，所以簡單地把 journalist 當記者就 OK 了。再來是 depart/departure 這個字要跟另外一個字一起念一起記 arrive/arrival，先念一下 departure 和 arrival 也就是所謂的出發／抵達，再來想請你想像一下開車進到桃園機場，一開始你會看到以下的標誌：Terminal 1 和 Terminal 2 以及相關的航空公司，那應該可以猜到 Terminal 1 和 Terminal 2 就是一號航廈和二號航廈，接近 terminal 後你會看到 departure/arrive，想想看你開車到機場不是接機就是送機，那送機就要到 departure 而接機要到 arrival，所以在這裡的 departure 就是出境，而 arrival 當然就是入境了。講到這裡你需要硬背嗎？還是把 Terminal 1, Terminal 2 和 departure, arrival 多念幾次，唸到有 FU 就可以了！再來看一下 Lecture, Keith Patrick, "How to be a News Anchor?" 是不是可以感覺出 Keith Patrick 這個人會有個關於 "How to be a News Anchor?" 的 lecture，lecture 也就是演講。

Clear Lake College Summer Lectures

1. Clear Lake College is proud to announce its summer line up of guest lectures.

2. These popular and creative talks aim to inspire the imagination of the audiences and create greater interest in science.

3. All lectures are free and open to students, faculty and local residents and no advance reservation is required.

4. Because seating is limited, it will be strictly allocated on a first come first served basis.

5. Please call Cathy at 415-543-2468 if you need further information.

A. **Monday, August 4th**

"Black Holes: the history and the latest finding"

Dr. John Lepont, Professor of Astronomy

Dr. Lepont will talk about black holes. What have we learnt about them from space telescopes in the past decade? Is there really a giant black hole at the center of our galaxy? Do they hold the key to our galaxy's future?

B. **Wednesday, August 6th**

"Was Einstein right?"

Mrs. Judith Syths, Director of research at Rockwell Labs

And Dr. Paul Owens, Professor of Physics

As modern physics probes ever deeper into the mystery of the atoms, more answers are being found, but, at the same time, more and more questions have emerged. Join the debate as two of the rising stars on modern physics discuss about "Was Einstein right?"

C. Friday, August 8th

"DNA: the origins of life"

Dr. Richard Hawkins, Geneticist,

The origins of life. Where did we all come from? And where are we going? From Darwin to DNA, what does the future hold for mankind?

6. All lectures are going to be hosted by the Professor Vincent Lee, Dean of Studies, and concluded with with Q&A session.

1. 一個 (Clear Lake) college announce summer 會有個 lineup of guest lectures 簡單的講就是 summer 會有些 guest lectures 對吧！

2. 我們先看這是什麼樣的 talks？popular and creative talks。誰的 imagination？the audiences。什麼樣的 interest？interest in science，是不是架構就懂了！句中的 aim 和 inspire 認識嗎？如果不知道，也不必慌！其實很容易，這裡的 aim to inspire 你覺得是正面還

是反面？整句話再看一次，應該會感覺就是很正面不是嗎！接下來我就解釋一下這兩個字 aim 和 inspire，先給個 inspire 的例句：Jeremy Lin inspires a lot of Taiwanese basketball players. 先設想一下這句話的意思，Jeremy Lin inspires 很多台灣的 basketball players. 首先可以確定 inspire 絕對是正面的意思，再來想請你先猜猜 inspire 的意思，不管對錯先猜了再說。猜了之後才去查字典，原來 inspire 有鼓勵、激勵的意思，接下來再把這個例句多念幾遍，對 inspire 就有 FU 了！或許有人會說了，字典裡 inspire 還有很多其他的意思啊！回到字典看一下 inspire 其他的意思：驅使、賦予……靈感、給……以啟示、激起、喚起、引起、產生、煽動，說實話這些意思是不是就是 inspire！這些其實只是針對 inspire 在不同的句子裡、不一樣用法上所翻譯出來的各種中文意思！其他的不說，這麼多的解釋，這會容易背嗎？再看一下前面的例句，運動上是激發、激勵，文學和音樂上面不是就成了：賦予……靈感、給……以啟示，說到底了其實還是 inspire 對吧！再說一次，單字絕對不要硬背、硬記，語言是活的，硬背、硬記單字只會把活生生的英文給掐死了！接下來講一下 aim 這個字，同樣的先給例句：He hits the target without even aiming. 連 aiming 都不需要就能 hits the target 還有 The President was aiming his speech at the people in his own party who had been calling for his resignation. 先把 who had been calling for his resignation 去掉，意思很明顯就是總統 aiming 他的 speech 給他自己 party（同一個黨）的人，後面的 who had been calling for his resignation 只是說明什麼樣的人而已，calling for his resignation 的人，如果不認識 resign, resignation 查過字典後知道是辭職的意思回來再念幾次就容易記了。到這裡應該可以感覺出 aim 是瞄準、針對這類的意思了吧！就算你還是沒 FU 再把例句念個兩次就 OK 了

3. 所有的課程是免費及開放給後面的 students, faculty and local residents，就算 faculty 不認識，不會影響你看懂句子對吧！公司裡叫 staff，大學裡就叫 faculty，faculty 指的就是大學裡的教職員如此而已。local residents 當然就是當地居民。如果不認識 advance，先拿掉變成 no reservation is required 是不是就懂了！再回來想一下，預約都是事先的預約，不可能會有之後的吧，所以就可以猜出 advance 有事先的含意。

4. 就算你不知道 strictly allocated，但完全不會影響你看懂句子。查過字典後知道 strict 是嚴格的、嚴厲的而 allocate 是分配、分派。

5. 基本上只是 Call Cathy for more information.

接下來的幾個 lectures 基本上看一下標題和主講者就可以了，如果你看一下內容當然也 OK，只是這是本參考書，我當然要解釋一下。

A. Black Holes 直翻黑洞，這裡的 latest 可不要直接當作最後面的，既然是最後面當然也就是最新的。Dr. John Lepont, Professor of Astronomy 會研究黑洞的 professor 你猜會是哪個科系？Astronomy 當然是天文學。主題敘述這句很簡單只是我們從 space telescopes 學到了什麼？telescope 不認識的話，請 Google 圖片搜尋一下，而 in the past decade 只是講個時間段落。接下來是 galaxy 的中心真的有個巨大的黑洞嗎？這裡的 galaxy 就算不知道，只要看的出來是個地方就 OK 了。而會有黑洞的地方，galaxy 當然就是銀河系。最後的 key 你直接當鑰匙其實也還 OK，加上一點想像力，key to our galaxy's future 就可以看懂了，語文是活的，不要念死了。

B. 試著把 Einstein 念一下應該就會明白是愛因斯坦，不過就算你不認識 Einstein，知道他是個人也就夠了。跟著介紹兩個 lecturers 會談到 Einstein 的教授，physics 是物理。主題敘述中第一句的架構很簡單

As 一件事發生了，另一件事也發生了，but 同時另一件事也出現了。先看 as 的事 As modern physics probes ever deeper into the mystery of the atoms, probe 不認識其實沒關係更深入的 probes 到 the mystery of the atoms 就算 atoms 不知道也該可以猜出一個跟 physics 有關的東西吧！查過字典後知道 atom 是原子、mystery 是秘密，反正就是現代物理學更深入的 probes 到 the mystery of the atoms 到這裡先感覺一下 probe 再去查字典發現是探索、探查、探測的意思後再把原句念一次是不是就對這幾個單字有 FU 了。接下來 more answers are being found，簡單吧。再來 but, at the same time, more and more questions have emerged 如果 emerge 不知道再念一下 more and more questions have emerged 對照到前面的 more answers are being found 有沒有 FU？你說 emerge 除了出現還會是其他意思嗎？這裡順道提一下 emerging countries 就是新興國家，而 emerge 是浮出來、出現那 submerge 當然是沉下去、淹沒嘍！emerge、submerge 一起念、一起記。最後把原句唸個幾次是不是更幫助你對所有單字有 FU，也更容易記住這些單字。最後的 Join the debate as 後面這件事發生了，as two of the rising stars (on modern physics) discuss about "Was Einstein right?" as 兩個 rising stars discuss about「這個主題」回到原先的標題。如果 debate 不認識反正就是 as 兩個人 discuss about "Was Einstein right?"（大家來）join the debate 就對了，debate 這個字在接下來的解題裡會解釋。

C. 會研究 DNA 的人當然是個 geneticist，就算你不知道 geneticist 遺傳學家，知道這是個跟 DNA 有關的人也就夠了。主題敘述中的 Darwin 多念幾次就有機會念出達爾文。整句應該不難能看出是說 Darwin 及 DNA 與 mankind 未來之間的關連性。

6. 這句只是說 All lectures are going to be hosted by 這個人，Dean of Studies 講一下他的來歷，及最後都有個稱為 Q&A 的 session (question and answer)。

158. What is the purpose of the lectures?
    (A) To get a clear image of the lecturers.
    (B) To intrigue the audience into science.
    (C) To get more students for the college.
    (D) To recruit new professors to the college.

(解析)

題目是指 Lectures 演講的 purpose 目的？

一眼可以看出 (C) 和 (D) 都錯！如果 recruit 不認識，每個大學每年的新生訓練，都會有 clubs 社團在外面 recruit new members，招募新成員，懂了嗎？記得把 recruit new members 多念幾遍。再來看 (B) 顯然重點是 intrigue 這個字，這個字意思合理就對了，假設你不認識 intrigue 這個字，只好看一下 (A)，你覺得這一系列的 lectures 的目的會是 get a clear image of the 演講者嗎？怪怪的耶！所以答案是 (B)。先感覺一下 intrigue 在這裡的意思，然後查字典發現是陰謀、策畫 (顯然是壞事) 還有激起……好奇心、想像力 (顯然是好事)，好玩的是，英文裡面 intrigue 多半用在好事，偏偏字典都先寫成壞事，其實很簡單，知道 intrigue 可好可壞就 OK 了。再來把這個選項多念幾遍就對了。

159. What do you need to do to attend one of the lectures?

(A) Call Cathy.

(B) Arrive early.

(C) Become a student of the college.

(D) Make a reservation.

解析

這題應該沒問題吧！根據文章中可刪掉 (C)、(D)！至於 (A)，文章裡說需要更多資訊，才 call Cathy，並不是必須。而第 4 句提到 first come first served，答案當然是 (B)arrive early。

160. James Edwards really enjoys hearing different perspectives from the same topic. Which lecture would he be interested in joining?

(A) "Black Holes: the history and the latest finding"

(B) "Was Einstein right?"

(C) "DNA: the origins of life"

(D) None of them.

解析

先試一下了解這題意應為「James Edwards really enjoys 從同樣的 topic 裡去 hearing different perspectives。」，那應該選哪個 lecture ？選哪個 lecture 會有不同的 perspectives 就對了。

單看答案應該就可以感覺（當然更保險的是去原始章節裡去 check）(B) 才有機會在同一個 topic 裡面會有不同的 perspectives，說實話，既然有不同的 perspectives 是不是就應該不是一個主講人而已。好巧喔，答

案真的是 (B)，再來去查字典發現在這裡 perspective 是看法、觀點的意思後，老規矩，請把原句多念幾次。

161. Who is the moderator for the lecture "Was Einstein right?"
    (A) Dr. John Lepont.
    (B) Dr. Paul Owens.
    (C) Dr. Richard Hawkins.
    (D) Professor Vincent Lee.

解析

假設你不認識 moderator 這個字，應該也會有感覺不會是 lecturer 主講人吧。答案裡面都是主講人只有 (D) Professor Vincent Lee 不是主講人，當然就選 (D)，接下來當然要解釋一下 moderator 這個字，感覺一下後去查字典，知道是仲裁者後，回來想一下 "Was Einstein right?" 這個專題裡有什麼特色？有兩個演講者，還有 "Join the debate as..."，兩個人討論 "Was Einstein right?" 查一下 debate 討論、辯論，是不是忽然之間一切豁然開朗了！把 join the debate 多念幾次，debate 就可以輕鬆記住了。

1. After Japan was hit by a devastating 8.9 magnitude earthquake that demolished most of its phone system, some employees of NHN Japan, a subsidiary of South Korean internet company Naver, are determined to find a better communication solution without using phone lines.

2. Three months later, in June, 2011, the app, LINE was born.

3. Released in June, 2011, Line gained 50 million users in less than a year. Within 18 months, it reached 100 million users. In April 2014, Line was claimed to have 400 million worldwide users.

4. Unsurprisingly, it's the number one messaging app in Japan.

5. In February 2013, NHN Japan announced it would spin off Line and form Line Corporation, which would, however, stay as a subsidiary of Naver.

6. It's always interesting to compare the user numbers of some of the most popular messaging apps.

7. According to Wikipedia, in March 2015, Line has 560 million registered users, comparing to over 1 billion with WeChat, the most prominent messaging app in China.

8. Also, WhatsApp, which switched from a free to paid service just to avoid growing too fast, has 800 million in April, 2015.

9. In order to get into China, Line suppresses content to abide by government censorship requirement, which is confirmed publicly by Line as quoted in the following.

10. "LINE had to conform to local regulations during its expansion into mainland China, and as a result the Chinese version of LINE, LIANWO, was developed. The details of the system are kept private, and there are no plans to release them to the public."

11. There is no other limitation to Line, except that you can only access your Line account by one mobile device and one personal computer. Different mobile numbers or e-mail addresses are needed to install the app for additional mobile devices.

12. With the ever-evolving characteristic of the internet age, Line will need to continue its development and adaptation to stay relevant in the intensely competitive messaging apps' war.

文章解析

1. 這句很長，但很簡單。還記得 as 一件事發生，另一件事也發生了。這裡只是變成 after 一件事發生，另一件事也發生了。先看 after 的事，這裡的 that 帶了一整句話，只要知道 that 指的就是 earthquake 後再把這句話也刪掉，句子就變成：After Japan was hit by a devastating 8.9 magnitude earthquake. 這下可看懂了吧！如果不知道 devastating，念一下 a devastating earthquake，

devastating 是好是壞？不用查字典都會有些感覺吧！再來看 that demolished most of its phone system，前面講過了，只要先知道 that 就是 earthquake 就可以了，也就是說 earthquake demolished most of its phone system，就算你不知道 demolished 應該也猜得出不會是好事吧！查一下字典知道是破壞、毀壞後，再把這一句多念幾次，devastating 和 demolish 就一起記住了。接下來是後面的另一件事，在這另一件事裡又有兩個逗點，當然就先把兩個逗點之間的先全部刪掉，所以句子就變成：some employees of NHN Japan are determined to find a better communication solution without using phone lines 既然 phone lines 都已經被 demolished 當然要找 a better communication solution without using phone lines 簡單吧！再來看一下逗點間的部分 a subsidiary of South Korean internet company Naver 顯然只是說明逗點前面的 NHN Japan 而已，就算你不認識 subsidiary 分公司、子公司也沒關係。

2. Three months later, in June, 2011, the app, LINE was born. 這句沒問題吧。

3. 不到一年就 gained 50 個 million 的 users。18 個月內就達到 100 個 million 用戶。在 2014 的 4 月，Line 宣稱在世界各地有 400 個 million 的 users。（單純描述其快速成長。）

4. 不意外地，它是日本第一的 messaging app。

5. 這裡的 spin off 懂嗎？原先 Line 是 NHN Japan 的一部份現在被 spin off 出來，不過還是 Naver 的 subsidiary。"spin off"：分割、分裂出來，有 FU 吧。

6. 把一些最 popular 的 messaging apps 拿出來比較一下 user numbers 總是一件有趣的事。

7. 根據維奇百科，在 2015 年三月，Line 有 560million 的註冊 users，而在中國最 prominent 的 messaging app, WeChat 有 over 1 billion。就算你不知道 prominent 也可以猜到是好的意思吧！所以 prominent 當然是出名、顯著、重要之類的意思。

8. 還有擁有 800 million users 的 WhatsApp 由 free switched 到 paid service 反而是要 avoid growing too fast.（avoid growing 多念幾次）。

9. 為了進入 China, Line suppresses content 以 abide by 政府的 censorship requirement 而 which 後面只是提出證據而已。這裡的 suppress 是好是壞？用來 abide by 大陸政府的 censorship requirement，先把這幾個單字猜一下才去查字典。suppress 壓制、隱瞞（説實話只能説到七成左右的意思），abide by 應該可以猜出是遵循之類的意思吧！在這裡順便把另外幾個 abide by 的同義字講一下：abide by、comply with、conform to、obey。

10. 這句架構也很簡單：一件事發生，and as a result 另一件事發生。前一件事的 conform to local regulations 如果不懂 regulations 應該可以感覺出 regulations：規則、規範吧！句中指出，在中國拓展的期間，Line 必須 conform to local regulations，as a result, Chinese version of Line 就被 developed。下句中，如果你不知道 details, private 和 release，念過後查字典知道是 detail 細節，private 私下的、非公開的，release 發行、發表後，把這句話再唸個兩遍，在這裡我順便提一下 private school、public school 私立學校和公立學校，是不是更有 FU 了！

11. Line 有一個限制，就是只能在一部手機及個人電腦來 access your Line account。如果要 install Line for additional mobile devices 就需要 different mobile numbers or e-mail address 懂了嗎？

12. 最後這句話有些有程度的單字，evolving、adaptation 及 stay relevant。 先看上半句：internet age 的 characteristic 就是 evolving（ever-evolving 的 ever 只是用來強調持續、一直的意思而已），查過字典以後知道 characteristic 是特性和 evolving 是發展、演化、變化以後，是不是真的覺得 internet age 的 characteristic 就是 evolving？ 後面的 continue its development and adaptation 如果不知道 adaptation，其實認識 development 就可以看懂句子了。至於 adaptation 可以看一下 adapt 其實要學 adapt 這個字可以從達爾文的演化論來看，基本上就是 survival of the fittest：（最）適者生存。survival of the fittest 強調的就是物種需要 adapt to the environment 適應環境，讓自己成為 the fittest，自然就會 survive，但是要適應環境是不是就需要改變（自己），所以 adapt 也就會隱含有改變之類的意思了。再念一下 continue its development and adaptation 就有 FU 了。下半句為 continue its development and adaptation 才能 stay relevant 在這 intensely competitive messaging apps' war。首先你應該可以感覺出這個 apps' war 不只是 competitive 還是 intensely competitive， 那 stay relevant 應該是正面的意思對吧！考試實在不知道單字的狀況下，能夠理解到這樣已經足夠了。這裡的 relevant 其實是從 related, relative 而來的，基本上就是有關、相關之類的意思，查了一下字典發現 relevant 是相關的、恰當的甚至是關係重大的，把這些意思帶回原句裡的 relevant 還是沒能完全的貼切對吧！簡單念一下這一句，是不是比較有 FU 了！簡單地講就是在這個 war 裡面還能 stay relevant，就算中文意思沒能 100% 的貼切解釋出來 relevant，對 relevant 這個英文字直接有 FU 才是最重要的。

162. What is the most suitable title for this article?

(A) What are the Massaging Apps?

(B) The reason Line was developed.

(C) Introduction to Line.

(D) Line's history and its challenges.

解析

選出適當的標題。

(A) 可以直接先刪掉；(B) 有沒有提到？當然有，但是顯然不是重點，以偏概全錯！(C) 也不是文章重點；(D) 前面講 history 後面說 challenges 完全正確！

163. According to the article, which of the following statement is FALSE?

(A) WhatsApp is free.

(B) Comparing to Line and WhatsApp, WeChat has more registered users.

(C) WeChat is the most popular messaging app in China.

(D) Line was born because of an earthquake.

解析

選出錯誤的敘述。

因為你已經看過文章，就算你一時無法判斷出 (B) 跟 (C) 是對是錯，你知道哪裡去找 clues 線索，請看句 7、8，前面解釋過了 prominent，你可以看出來是好的意思，所以 WeChat, the most prominent messaging app in China，講的應該就是 (C)，而這兩句一看清楚數字後，也可以知道 (B) 對。至於 (D) 文章一開始就提到了，再看 (A) 因為文章已經看過，你也就知道前一個答案裡的 Also, WhatsApp, which switched from a free to paid service just to avoid growing too fast, has 800 million in April, 2015. 就可以看出來 (A) 是錯的。

164. According to the article, which of the following statement is true?

(A) Line is owned by a Korean company.

(B) Line is the fastest growing messaging app.

(C) Line gets into China market without any major changes.

(D) Line is the most popular messaging app in Asia.

解析

題意為要選出正確的敘述。

(B) 錯，因為在成長速度上，Line 根本比不上其他的 messaging apps。

(C) 錯，因為有改變（請看句 9）。(D)，句 7 中有提到中國的 WeChat 用戶超過 1 billion，所以錯。回去看 (A)，句中提到是 subsidiary of South Korean internet company，sub- 通常有往下的、下面的之意，所以不難猜出可能是附屬或是子公司之意，所以答案是 (A)。

165. What is the limitation of Line?

(A) The same Line account cannot be accessed from multiple mobile devices.

(B) Line can only be used when there is an earthquake.

(C) You have to know Japanese to use Line.

(D) Line has to remain mostly unchanged to keep the current users.

(B) 和 (C) 一看就知道錯的很離譜！先看 (D) 好了，看句 12 可以感覺出在 這 intensely competitive messaging apps' war 裡面一定要 continue its development 看到這裡就知道 (D) 錯！回去看 (A)，還記得那句 you can only access your Line account by one mobile device and one personal computer，答案當然是 (A)。

Question 166-168 refer to the following advertisement.

1. ***Booking your vacation is easy with Fun World.***
   We do all the work, and you'll have all the fun.
   For only $199, you get to enjoy one amusing and
   spectacular day in New York.

2. Start your day with a yummy continental breakfast in Condor Hotel.

3. After that, you will hop on a tour bus for a lively day of sightseeing with a professional and entertaining tour guide.

4. The morning itinerary includes Central Park and the Cathedral of Saint John the Divine, a truly stunning church.

5. An appetizing, luxurious lunch will follow at Happy Restaurant.

6. In the afternoon, we will visit the world famous Times Square and Metropolitan Museum of Art.

7. And don't think we've forgotten the most well-known icon of America, the Statue of Liberty.

8. We will cruise out and visit the great lady in the late afternoon to conclude our tour.

9. Our package includes:

*Continental breakfast

*Gourmet lunch

*Metropolitan Museum ticket

*Afternoon tea

*Admission to the Statue of Liberty

10. We will give you a day of precious life time experience in New York City.

文章解析

1. 第一句的 booking 是預定、預約、登記的意思。知道後把整句再念一次就有 FU 了。接下來只是解釋為什麼 it's easy. 因為第 2 句。第三句只是說出價錢 $199 而後面的 one amusing and spectacular day in New York。就算你不知道 amusing 和 spectacular 也可以感覺出這兩個字都是好的意思吧！查過字典後知道了 amusing 好玩的、有趣的，spectacular 驚人的、壯觀的以後再念一下 one amusing and spectacular day 就可以輕鬆地把這兩個字記住了。

2. 這裡的 yummy 就算不知道也可以猜出來就是好吃的，continental breakfast 反正就是一種叫做 continental 的 breakfast 就對了。簡單的講就是歐式早餐，說實話你把它當成西式的早餐也可以。

3. 可簡化成 Hop on a (tour) bus for a (lively) day of sightseeing with a (professional and entertaining) tour guide，這裡的 tour bus 就算不懂也就當 bus 就對了。後面的 sightseeing，在紐約搭 tour bus 做 sightseeing 不是觀光遊覽會是什麼？接下來的 lively, professional, entertaining 都是好事就對了。這裡的 professional

職業的、專業的和 entertain 娛樂、歡樂，可以參考以下的例子：

Jeremy Lin is a professional basketball player.

Minions（小小兵）is an entertaining movie, and we had a great time watching it.

4. 如果不知道 itinerary（旅遊行程表），反正就是 morning itinerary 包括兩個地方 Central Park 以及 Cathedral of Saint John，如果 Cathedral 不認識沒關係，反正這就是個 church，而且還是個 stunning church，反正 stunning（超讚的）絕對是好事。而 itinerary 還可以這麼記，只要你參加一個 tour，旅行社就醫定會給這個 tour 的 itinerary 好讓你知道每天的行程要去那些 tourist attractions（景點），還可以順便學一下 tourist attractions（景點）。

5. 在 Happy Restaurant 會有個 lunch 而且是個 appetizing, luxurious 的 lunch，就算不認識 appetizing（令人開胃，讓人有食慾）和 luxurious（奢侈豪華的）有關係嗎？反正都是好事就可以了，注意一下 appetizing 令人開胃，讓人有食慾會好背嗎？還是把 an appetizing, luxurious lunch 多念幾次，念到有 FU 才重要，而且連 luxurious 都一起記下來了。

6. 下午會去 Times Square 和 Metropolitan Museum of Art，Times Square（時代廣場）每年除夕夜在紐約倒數計時的地方當然是 world famous 而 Metropolitan Museum of Art 反正就是個 Museum of Art 藝術博物館。

7. 去紐約當然要去看一下 the Statue of Liberty 自由女神像，多念幾次 the Statue of Liberty 順便學一下 statue，the Statue of Liberty 是 the most well-known icon of America，美國最有名的 icon，另外來一句：Taipei 101 is the most iconic building in Taiwan. 念一下 icon /EYE con/, iconic /eye CO nic/ 有 FU 了吧！

8. 如果不知道 cruise out，基本上 Statue of Liberty 位置在 Liberty Island 上面，所以就需要 cruise out 才到的了。

9. 整個 package 包含的內容。我要給個 gourmet 的例子：Chinese gourmet, French gourmet 中、法美食，gourmet 是法文，發音是 [`gʊrme]。

10. 我們給您在紐約一整天的 precious life time。

166. What is Fun World?
    (A) An amusement park.
    (B) A travel agency.
    (C) A shopping mall.
    (D) A hotel.

解析

Fun World 是什麼？

依題意選 (B) 旅行社。(A) 是遊樂場、(C) 購物中心、(D) 是飯店。

167. Which following item is included in the package but wasn't mentioned in the description?
    (A) A visit to Metropolitan Museum.
    (B) A delicious lunch.
    (C) An afternoon tea.
    (D) A breakfast.

解析

哪一項在 package 裡面但是沒有在 description 裡？

看一下 package 裡面有什麼？將句9與以上8句比較後，可發現(C) Afternoon Tea 沒有在敘述中。

168. What is the last stop of the tour?
     (A) A visit to one of the New York's great ladies.
     (B) The Cathedral of Saint John the Divine.
     (C) Happy Restaurant.
     (D) Statue of Liberty.

解析

由句7、8可得知答案為 (D)。

Question 169-172 ○ refer to the following letter

1. Ms. Sandra Bullock

   Director, Department of Sales and Marketing

   1055 Stevens Creek Blvd.

   Cupertino, CA 95014

   Dear Ms. Sandra Bullock,

2. Thank you for taking your valuable time to interview me on Friday, June 12 regarding the Marketing Manager opening.

3. I am grateful for the opportunity to discuss my qualification for the position with you.

4. After talking to you, I am even more convinced that I am one of the best candidates for the position.

5. With good communication skills, five years of proven marketing experience and fluency in Chinese and Spanish, I know I can contribute to the success of the company after joining the existing strong sales and marketing team.

6. Should you have any further question about my qualification, please contact me.

7. I am looking forward to hearing from you soon.

Sincerely yours,

James Wang

文章解析

1. 看到信件之類的文章，收信人和寄信人的 information 可以不用看，如果題目有考到，回來再查都還來的及。

2. 感謝你 taking your (valuable) time to interview me on 這一天 regarding 這件事 (The Marketing Manager opening).

3. 這只是 I am grateful for the opportunity to discuss 後面這件事 with you。

4. 這句是在強力的推銷自己 I am more convinced that I 最適合。

5. 這句話很長，架構卻很簡單，只是 With A, B and C 三件事, I know I can contribute to the success (of the company) after joining the (existing strong sales and marketing) team. 而 A 就是 good (communication) skills, B 是 five years of proven marketing experience and C 就是 fluency in Chinese and Spanish 如此而已。

6. 可簡化成 Should you have any question, please contact me. 順道提一下，還記得新多益會考的假設語氣句型嗎？請回去再念個幾次。再來就是這裡的句子。當然還有最簡單，不算是假設語氣的 "If it rains tomorrow, we will cancel the picnic."。

7. 最後多念幾次 look forward to seeing you。再給你幾個 be used to it, be committed to it, come close to it。在這裡你可以多念這裡的 to it 因為既然是 to it 當然就是 be used to working with him, be committed to supporting our customers, come close to winning the game，如果你念 to it 覺得感覺不是那麼強當然可以念 be used to working with him, be committed to supporting our customers, come close to winning the game 你喜歡哪一組，就多念哪一組。最後就是信末常見的祝語及署名。

169. What is the purpose of this letter?
    (A) To show that he is grateful of getting interviewed.
    (B) To demonstrate his interest in the job.
    (C) To inform Ms. Sandra Bullock that she can contact him for any question.
    (D) To try to get an interview.

（解析）

這封 letter 的 purpose 為何？

這裡的 (A) 有沒有提到，當然有，但是重點很明顯的是強力的自我推銷，錯！看 (B)，自我推薦為正確答案，再來 (C) 跟 (A) 一樣想要混淆視聽，看一下 (D)：早就 interview 過了，所以錯。

170. Who is Ms. Sandra Bullock?

　　(A) A recruiting officer.

　　(B) A job applicant.

　　(C) A director.

　　(D) A human resources manager.

解析

如果忘記了 Sandra Bullock 沒關係，趕快回去看一下是收信人還是寄信人，再看一下她的 information：Director, Department of Sales and Marketing 所以答案是 (C) A director。

171. Which of the following is **not** the reason that James thinks he is the best candidate?

　　(A) He can communicate with colleagues and clients effectively.

　　(B) He has the expertise in multiple languages.

　　(C) He has experience in the managerial job.

　　(D) He is capable of marketing.

解析

還記得他推銷自己的強處是什麼嗎？如果忘記了，回去看一下句 5，答案是 (C)。

172. What will James most likely do next?

(A) Call Sandra to confirm she gets the letter.

(B) Visit the company.

(C) Try to get Sandra to call him.

(D) Wait for Sandra to call him.

解析

這題很簡單吧，look forward to hearing from you，就算不知道這個
答案 (B) 和 (C) 也可以先刪掉，看一下 (A) 會不會太過火了？這也可以挑
出 (D)。

Question 173-174 ○▶ refer to the following email

📖To:	1. Catherine<catherinem@foreveryoung.com
From:	Sandysandyt@foreveryoung.com
Date:	Fri., 6/19, 2015
Subject:	Thank you!

2. I wanted to let you know that I am leaving my position at Forever Young Cosmetics.

3. I'll be starting a new position as a special assistant to the president at Charming Fragrance next Monday.

4. Having worked with you for more than two years, I truly appreciate having you as my mentor and helping me get familiar with my work.

5. I am sure I'll miss you, and I feel terrible that I cannot work with you anymore.

6. Let's keep in touch.

   My personal email is sandy1234@yahoomail.com and my cell phone number is (408)725-1305.

7. Thank you from the bottom of my heart.

Sandy

文章解析

1. 同樣的 email 裡的收信人寄信人都不用看，考題考到時再回來 check 就可以了。

2. 要離開公司的開場白。

3. 下禮拜一到另一個公司擔任另一個位置。

4. 這句話是基本的分詞構句，不過只要能把句子看懂就好。簡單地說：跟你共事了兩年多，I truly appreciate having you and helping me 如此而已。

5. 然後來個離別前的感謝。

6. 希望保持聯絡，並留下個人的 contact information。

7. 最後的感謝及署名。

173. What type of email is this?

    (A) A welcome email.

    (B) A farewell email.

    (C) A thank you email.

    (D) A congratulation email.

解析

(A) 和 (D) 可以先刪掉 (B) 是 farewell 而 (C) 是 thank you，有沒有講到 thank you ？當然有，是不是重點，當然不是，答案是 (B) A farewell email.

174. When will Sandy start working at her new job?

    (A) 6/20.

    (B) 6/21.

    (C) 6/22.

    (D) 6/23.

解析

這題有點 tricky 信中只提了 next Monday 一開始或許會有疑惑，不過既然是封 email，自然會有寄 email 的日期，看一下是 Fri., 6/19 所以 next Monday 是 (C) 6/22。

1. Mr. Owen Wilson

   Human Resources Manager

   Village Hotel, 64 Angel St.

   Palm Springs, CA 92263

   Dear Mr. Wilson,

2. I am writing to apply for the Village Hotel front desk job opening advertised in Leisure Travel Monthly.

3. I have worked at Grand Hotel since graduating from Hospitality and Tourism University with a major in Hotel Management three years ago.

4. I enjoy working with colleagues and providing the best service to the guests.

5. I have also worked briefly as a waitress in the hotel restaurant.

6. My patience in handling customer complaints has won me "Employee of the Year" at Grand Hotel last year.

7. My fluency in Chinese and Taiwanese is another important skill in helping increasingly important Chinese tourists.

8. Although I enjoy my work at Grand Hotel, unfortunately, it is closing down next month, as you have probably known.

9. Regretting not being able to work there, I know I am well prepared for the new challenge of working for the best hotel in the area.

10. Enclosed please find my résumé and references. I am looking forward to hearing from you soon.

Sincerely yours,

Tiffany Hung

文章解析

1. 個人資料

2. 只是 apply for a job 而已，後面的 advertised in Leisure Travel Monthly 只是說明在哪裡看到的謀職廣告。

3. 三年前從 Hospitality and Tourism University 這個大學主修 Hotel Management 這個學系後就在 Grand Hotel 這個旅館工作了。

4. 當然要講一下自己喜歡這樣的工作。

5. 也曾 briefly（短暫地）做過 hotel restaurant 裡的 waitress。

6. 接下來要介紹自己的強項了。簡化後是 My patience has won me employee of year with Grand Hotel last year.

7. 說明國台語流利對公司的好處，先前講過了 fluent, fluency 應該記得了吧。強調一下國台語會很有幫助。

8. 說明離職原因，同行的應該知道另一家 hotel 要關門了。

9. 必須離職雖然遺憾，但強調自己已經 well prepared 並同時稱讚一下要去面試的公司。

10. 講一下隨信所 enclosed 的 résumé 和 references。加上祝語及署名。

175. What kind of job is Tiffany applying for?

　　(A) A receptionist.

　　(B) A teacher.

　　(C) A waitress.

　　(D) A supervisor.

解析

如果無法立刻判斷出答案也可以先刪掉(B)和(D)，接下來只是判斷答案是(A)還是(C)！就算忘記了，回去文章喵一下就知道是(A) A receptionist。

176. Why is Tiffany trying to get a new job?

　　(A) She majored in Hotel Management.

　　(B) She is going to lose her job in a month.

　　(C) Her language skill is not helpful in the old job.

　　(D) She doesn't enjoy working with her colleagues.

解析

如果沒辦法立刻看出來，至少可以直接先刪掉(D)和(A)，現在直接看剩下的兩個答案就可以判斷出來正確答案是(B)，因為現在的hotel馬上要關門大吉。在這裡我要強調一下，人腦其實是個很有意思的東西，當你要從四個答案裡選出最好的答案時，人腦會負荷不來，沒辦法判斷。但是人腦在二選一的情形下就很厲害。所以我一直都在強調如果一時看不出答案（四個答案選一個），那你就先針對每個答案來判斷是對還是錯，也就是讓大腦針對每個答案來看對或是錯，在對和錯之間二選一，這是大腦的強項，刪去兩個答案後就把題目變成二選一了，在此時又可以用哪個比較對還是哪個比較錯，來判斷正確答案，又是大腦最厲害的二選一，這樣下來，你就可以輕鬆的判斷出最好的答案了。尤其在新多益考試裡一定要先刪兩個答案再說。

177. What is not stated as her strength for the new job?
　　(A) She is a good team player.
　　(B) Her experience in dealing with unsatisfied customers.
　　(C) She is good at multiple languages.
　　(D) She is ready for new challenges.

解析

哪個不是她的強項呢？

這題應該可以先判斷出 (C) 和 (B) 是強項，接下來要在 (A) 和 (D) 之間挑出哪個比較對或是哪個比較錯。還記得 I enjoy working with colleagues in providing the best service to the guests. 嗎？至於 (D)，說實話憑什麼我可以說 ready for new challenges 才是重點吧！簡單的講 ready for new challenges 只是講一件事實，不能算是強項。答案是 (D) She is ready for new challenges.

THE BRISTOL INTERNATIONAL BALLOON FIESTA

1. The Bristol International Balloon Fiesta is held annually just outside the city of Bristol in the south west of England.

2. It has become one of the region's most popular and spectacular tourist attractions.

3. Held in August on a large country estate on the edge of Bristol, it is now Europe's biggest balloon festival.

4. Regular crowds of over 100,000 attend daily for four days of activities.

5. Mass launches are held every morning and evening where hundreds of balloons can be seen taking off almost at the same time.

6. You will have to be up early, however, to see the morning launch as it's held at 6 am. The evening launches are at 6 pm.

7. One of the most popular events is the night glow.

8. Usually on two consecutive evenings during the festival, dozens of tethered balloons are lit and inflated in the early evening.

9. They then glow in the dark timed to music.

10. This is followed by a spectacular fireworks display.

11. Many people say that the night glow is the highlight of the whole festival.

12. The fiesta, which began in 1979, used to be held in September, but due to poor weather leading to muddy grounds, and canceled flights the fiesta was moved to its present August dates after 1988.

13. Over the years the fiesta has become well-known for its strangely shaped balloons.

14. At first, locally manufactured balloons in the shapes of bottles, cartoon characters and even supermarket trolleys were regularly seen.

15. Now international teams, from all over the world, participate in the festival with their own specially designed balloons.

16. Recently, there have been UFOs from the US and Kiwis from New Zealand.

17. The entertainment is not just limited to the balloons. With fairground rides, air displays, and plenty of stalls to keep children happy during the day.

18. And possibly the best part of the fiesta is that it is totally free. There is no charge to enter the event.

19. With around half a million visitors expected through the gates this year, if you do make the trip, you certainly won't be alone.

文章解析

1. 反正就是個 balloon fiesta 每年在 Bristol 這個位於 England 西南方的城市舉行。如果不認識 balloon 查一下 Google 圖片搜尋，而 fiesta 其實是西班牙文就當作 festival 就可以了，不過就算你完全不知道 fiesta 也可以感覺出節日節慶這類的意思，尤其是在你繼續往下看了以後，就會清楚了。

2. "tourist attractions" 觀光景點還記得嗎？忘了的話，把 tourist attractions 多念幾次。

3. 就算你不知道 estate 地產、資產、遺產，也不會影響你看懂這句其實只是說八月在 Bristol 旁邊舉辦，現已成為歐洲最大的 balloon festival。這裡順便再提一下 real estate 就是房地產。

4. 四天的活動，每天超過 100,000 人參加。

5. 後面的 hundreds of balloons can be seen taking off almost at the same time 就可以讓你知道 mass launch 是發射、升空的意思了吧！

6. 只是說明 mass launch 的時間而已。

7. 這裡的 glow 認識嗎？如果不認識反正就是 night glow 晚上就對了。

8. 如果不認識 tether 這個字，反正就是 tethered balloons，也就是很多 balloons tethered 在一起，然後被 lit 和 inflated。如果不認識 inflation，順便學一下。在經濟上，inflation 就是通貨膨脹，而 deflation 就是通貨緊縮，所以 inflate 自然就是膨脹，而 deflate 當然就是緊縮、縮小。如果不知道 lit 其實是由 light 而來的也沒關係，繼續看下去。

9. 然後這些 tethered balloons 會 glow in the dark 而且是 timed to music，time 當動詞，所以是（時間上）跟著音樂而 glow in the dark，既然是 in the dark 你猜 glow 會是？就算不知道看了字典知道

glow 發光、發熱，tether 拴住、綁住，然後把這幾句多念幾次就會對裡面的單字就會有 FU 了。

10. 接下來就是 fireworks 煙火了。

11. 許多人認為 night flow 是整個 festival 的 highlight。

12. 這句話很長，架構很簡單，記得兩個逗點之間先刪掉就對了。剩下的只是 the fiesta used to be held in September but, due to 後面這個原因, the fiesta was moved to August。到底是什麼原因呢？是壞天氣 leading to muddy 的地面和 cancelled flights。這樣就知道了 mud 泥土、泥漿 muddy 泥濘的了吧！

13. 開始有奇形怪狀的 balloons 了。

14. 一開始是 locally manufactured 的 bottles 和 cartoon characters 的 balloons，cartoon 卡通裡面 character 角色後來甚至 supermarket trolleys 都出現了，就算不知道 trolley 反正就是 supermarket 的一個東西就是了，trolley 簡單的說就是車子，小手推車、飛機的餐車大到電車甚至 bus 都可以。

15. 現在來自世界各國團隊都以 specially designed balloons 來參與盛會。

16. 最近還有美國來的 UFOs 還有紐西蘭的 Kiwis 念了之後就知道是奇異果。

17. Entertainment 這個字又見到了，應該認識了吧，entertainment 可不只是 balloons 而已，有 fairground rides、air displays 和 stalls 來 keep 小孩 happy。這裡的 fairground 基本上就是舉辦 fair 的地點也可以稱作商展場以及露天遊樂場，而 fairground rides 當然就是一些展場的遊戲設施，而 stalls 則是展場的店鋪攤位。

18. 這場盛會最大的好處竟然是 free 免費的。

19. 今年預計 half a million 五十萬會來參觀,有這麼多人如果你去的話,當然絕不會覺得 alone。

178. Why was the festival moved from September to August?
    (A) The weather is hotter and more suitable for balloons.
    (B) It rains less in August.
    (C) The nights are darker.
    (D) It's summer vacation time for children.

解析

為什麼從九月移到八月?

其實 (A), (C), (D) 文章裡都沒提到。請參考句 11,可以看出答案是 (B) It rains less in August。

179. What is the most popular event at the festival?
    (A) The night glow.
    (B) The mass launches.
    (C) The air shows.
    (D) The fairground rides.

解析

最 popular 的 event 是什麼?

看上去 (D) 是專門給小孩的,錯!(C) 沒有特別提到,講到的類似主題是 air display 也是專門給小孩的,錯!剩下的兩個答案裡 (B),在文章沒有特別說到是否 popular 而 (A),在文章的句 7 及 11 有提到其受歡迎的事。所以答案是 (A) The night glow。

180. What has the balloon festival become famous for?

(A) Spectacular air shows.

(B) Food stalls for children.

(C) Fireworks displays.

(D) Balloons that look like other things.

解析

問有名的理由。

(B) 一開始就可以刪掉，再來 (A) 也只提到 air display，也是給小孩的也錯。剩下的 (C) Fireworks displays 文章裡說到是在 night glow 之後 This is followed by a spectacular fireworks display. 也就是整個 night glow 的一部分，不像是答案，而 (D) 在句 13 中有提到文章裡有 Over the years the fiesta has become well known for its strangely shaped balloons. 其實只是把文章裡的 well know 改成 famous 而已，答案是 (D)。

181. What's the reason that might discourage someone from visiting?

(A) The cost.

(B) The night glow.

(C) The crowds.

(D) The UFOs.

解析

有什麼原因會 discourage visitors ？

(A) 不可能，因為這可是 free，(B) 非常 popular 也不對，(D) the UFOs 文章裡只提到 UFO 形狀的 balloons，跟實際的 UFO 沒關係所以也錯。到這裡其實在考試裡已經可以選 (C) the crowds，可是這是參考書，還記得最後面的 With around half a million visitors expected through the gates this year, if you do make the trip, you certainly won't be alone. 只是把最後一句偏正面的敘述改成比較實際的觀點而已，答案是 (C)。

> **Questions 182-185** ○▷ refer to the following advertisement and email.

Computer programmer wanted

1. Tech Solutions Ltd. is looking for a full time computer programmer.
2. Experience in programming graphics and familiarity with the latest video game consoles are a must.
3. A degree in computer science is preferable, but any applicant with proper programing skills will be considered.
4. An understanding of the latest game designing platforms like GameMaker, Construct 2, Stencyl, Fleixel or Unity is definitely a plus.
5. Send résumé and supporting documents by August 28th to Anna Wong, Tech Solutions, 29 Ark Street, Edinburgh, Scotland or email techsolutions@game.co.uk

1. 某間公司在找全職 computer programmer。

2. 一定要有 programming graphics 的經驗而且要熟悉 latest video game consoles，如果不知道 console 反正就是個跟 video game 有關的東西，其實舉一些 video game consoles 的例子你就懂了，Game Boy, Play Station, Wii, Xbox 都是 video game consoles。

3. 學位只是 preferable，有 programming skills 就 OK。

4. 列出一堆 game designing platforms 做例子，希望有意應徵者要能了解 latest game designing platforms，platform 不懂，先知道一下就是火車站的月台，同時也可以當作平台來解釋。

5. 要在哪天之前把相關資料寄給誰，還有相關的資訊。

📖To:	Anna Wong
From:	Alexey Pajitnov

1. I am writing to you regarding to the advertisement at the local job center for a computer programmer.

2. I am currently working as a computer trainer for a major bank, but my passion is programming, especially for game apps.

3. Enclosed please find my full resume. I am also sending you some links to my app designs because, as you will see from my resume, I didn't study computer science while at university.

4. I am sure that these apps which were built on Unity platform will give you a good idea of the level of my skill as a programmer.

5. Please do not hesitate to contact me if you need any further information regarding my qualification to the job.

Sincerely

Alexey Pajitnov

文章解析

1. 因為看到 local job center 的工作廣告而寫信。

2. 目前在一家 bank 裡當 computer training 但是 passion 是 programming 尤其是 programming for apps，如果不知道 passion 先感覺一下 passion 在這句話裡的意思，才去查字典，passion 熱情、激情，再回來把 but my passion is programming, especially for game apps 念個幾次。

3. 因為大學不是主修 computer science 自然另外寄了一些自己的 app design 連結來當作 reference。

4. 而且這些 apps 是在 Unity platform 上所 built 自然能給對方一些 ideas about 他的 programming skills。

5. 最後總要寫一句 please contact me if you need more information，原句裡的 please do not hesitate to contact me 還記得 hesitate 嗎？如果沒印象，先猜一下 do not hesitate to contact me 也就是要 contact me 絕對不要 hesitate，感覺一下以後查字典知道是猶豫、遲疑的意思，再唸個幾次 do not hesitate to contact me，hesitate 就容易記了。

182. What is Tech Solutions Ltd.?

(A) A software developer.

(B) A maker of games consoles.

(C) A computer manufacturer.

(D) A graphics design company.

解析

(C) 是製造電腦的，可以先刪掉。(B) 選項，因為徵人廣告中強調的，很明顯不是做 game console。(D) A graphics design company，文章裡雖然講到 programming graphics 但是很明顯設計出來的 graphics，是拿來用在 video games 上，所以 (D) 錯！在這裡千萬不要看到 developer 就當作是個人，這家公司很明顯是寫用在 video games 的 program 也就是 software 軟體，所以答案是 (A)。

183. What does Alexey Pajitnov say that demonstrates his qualifications for the job?

(A) His capability of building something based on a platform.

(B) His job as a computer trainer.

(C) The apps he designed.

(D) His resume.

解析

(B) 和 (D) 可以先殺掉，剩下 (A) 和 (C)，再看看第 2 篇中的句 4，可以簡化成：these apps will give you a good idea of the level of my skill as a programmer 刪掉的 which were built on Unity platform 只是

解釋這些 app 是從哪個 platform 所 built 起來的，所以答案是 (C)。別忘了，他大學不是主修 computer science 所以附上這些他所設計的 apps，來強調他的 programming skills。

184. What does the advertisement say is NOT necessary required for applying the job?
(A) Knowledge of games consoles.
(B) A resume.
(C) Skills as a programmer.
(D) A computer science degree.

解析

familiarity with the latest video game consoles a must 所以 (A) 當然是 must。徵才廣告裡講了 Send résuméresume and supporting documents，所以 (B) 也是必須，剩下兩個答案。any applicant with proper programing skills will be considered，所以 (C) 看來也是必須，A degree in computer science is preferable 也就是 computer science degree 只是 preferrable 而已，所以答案是 (D)。

185. What products does Tech Solutions Ltd. want to develop?
(A) Games for personal computers.
(B) Software for game consoles.
(C) Software for bank training.
(D) Game design platform.

Tech Solutions Ltd. 要 develop 什麼樣的 products？
你應該可以看出 (A) 以及 (C) 都不對，文章裡有講到 games，但是不是給 PC 的 games 剩下 (B) 和 (D)，還記得題目嗎？如果沒印象再回去看一次 What products does Tech Solutions Ltd. want to develop? 很明顯 (D) Game design platform 不對，答案是 (B) Software for game consoles 給 game console 的軟體。

Questions 186-190 refer to the following article and email.

1. The Red House in Wanhua District, Taipei City, is proud to present Shamlet from Ping Fong Acting Troupe.

2. A theatrical play inspired by Hamlet, a world renowned tragedy written by William Shakespeare, Shamlet, on the surface, is an ironic comedy.

3. However, after watching the entertaining plays, you can feel the tiny bitterness in life shown in various scenes.

4. Hugh K. S. Lee, the director, presents the play by showing the struggling troupe trying their best to perform Shamlet on stage.

5. Changing roles, handling affairs, and showing the inside stories of the actors and the actresses are the most important factors that cause the failing performance of Shamlet.

6. Facing the inevitable catastrophe with the numerous accidents and mistakes, all actors and actresses stick together and insist on one believe, "We Shall Return".

7. The last scene doesn't really present the official ending of the show, but it gives the audience the chance of searching the message hidden in the performance.

8. One more thing for those who are planning to enjoy the show, get to know a little bit more about Hamlet. It will help you tremendously in understanding the hidden meaning of Shamlet.

9. For ticket information, please refer to the following table.

Date	Time	Membership		Regular person	Student
		Gold	Silver		
Friday, 7/21	7:30 PM	700	750	1000	500
Saturday, 7/22	7:00 PM	700	750	1000	500
Sunday, 7/23	7:00 PM	700	750	1000	500

To reserve your seats, please email reservation@redhouse.org.tw

文章解析

1. 台北市 Wanhua District 的 Red House is proud to present 由 Ping Fong Acting Troupe 帶來的 Shamlet。就算你明知這篇跟台北有關卻很可能因為一些字詞看不懂而無法全盤了解，但是這完全不會讓你看不懂句子！很明顯 Red House 就是個地方而 Ping Fong Acting Troupe 應該就是個團體，Shamlet 就是齣戲。

2. 先把 a world renowned tragedy written by William Shakespeare 和 on the surface（表面上）先去掉，句子就變成：A theatrical play inspired by Hamlet, Shamlet is an ironic comedy. 還記得

前面講過的 inspire 嗎？基本上這裡說的是 Shamlet 是被 Hamlet 所 inspired，而且 Shamlet 是個 ironic comedy，是齣 comedy 還是個 ironic comedy。如果忘記了 inspire 再把這句話念個幾次 These talks aim to inspire the imagination of the audiences. 還有 ironic 諷刺的，一樣給個例句：It's ironic that those students who dislike discussion activities are often those who need the oral skills the most. 不喜歡 discussion activities 的學生，卻往往是那些最需要 oral skills 的人，這就是 ironic。先前去掉的 a world renowned tragedy written by William Shakespeare 只是說明 Hamlet 而已。

3. 在欣賞過後，你可以感到在 various scenes 裡面所顯現的 tiny bitterness in life。這裡的 scene 可以是風景、景色當然也可以是場景、劇景。

4. Hugh K. S. Lee 也就是導演，以 showing the struggling troupe trying their best to perform Shamlet on stage 來 present the play。你覺得 struggling 是好是壞？就算你查過字典知道 struggle 是掙扎、奮鬥的意思，還是把 the struggling troupe trying their best to perform Shamlet on stage 念幾次比較有 FU 吧！

5. 這句其實只是 A, B, and C are the most important facotrs 而已，changing roles (A), handling affairs (B), and showing the inside stories (of the actors and actresses) (C) 這三個是最重要 factor 後面的 that cause the failing performance of Shamlet 這些 factors 產生了什麼後果 the falling performance，這樣看來 affairs 不會是好事，其實這裡的 affair 是婚外情的意思，而且查字典都不見得會查的到。還有這些 inside stories 顯然也不會是好 stories。

6. 既 然 是 with numerous accidents and mistakes 顯 然 facing the inevitable actastrophe 絕 不 會 是 好 事，inevitable 不 可 避 免 的，catastrophe 大 災 難，with the numerous accidents and mistakes 當然就會 facing the inevitable catastrophe。再念一次 the inevitable catastrophe，有 FU 了吧！Facing the inevitable catastrophe 之時，所有演員 stick together and insist on 一個 believe "We Shall Return"。這裡的 stick together 感覺得出是黏在一起也就是團結在一起吧，insist on 堅持，這整句就懂了吧。

7. 最後一個 scene 並沒有 present 這個 show 的 official ending，卻給了 audience 來 search performance 裡面的 hidden message (the message hidden in the performance) 的 chance。

8. 跟想要去看的人提一件事，多了解一下 Hamlet，會對你了解 the hidden meaning of Shamlet 有幫助，你覺得 tremendous 會是大還是小？

9. 訂票資訊請看下表。

因為這篇文章確實牽涉很多大家不見得知道的訊息，我也就把它翻譯出來，給大家參考。

文章中譯

位於台北市萬華區的西門紅樓，很高興帶來屏風表演班的莎姆雷特。由莎士比亞所寫的悲劇哈姆雷特而啟發的劇場戲劇莎姆雷特，表面上看來，是個諷刺喜劇。然而在看過整部戲劇後，你可以感受到許多場景裡所顯現出來生活中的些許苦楚。導演李國修以一個掙扎中的劇團，嘗試著在舞台上表現最佳的演出來演示整齣戲劇。角色更換、處理婚外情和顯現演員們的內心故事，這三點是造成莎姆雷特演出失敗的最重要因素。 在數不清的意外和錯誤之下，面對著無可避免地演出失敗災難，演員們團結一致並堅持著個理念『我們還會再回來』。最後一個場景並沒不是戲劇正式的結束，但是也給觀眾一個機會，來體會一下表演中所隱含的訊息。有件事要跟計畫要去觀賞的人提醒一下，了解一下哈姆雷特，這會讓幫助你體會出莎姆雷特隱含的意義。

📖To:	reservation@redhouse.org.tw
From:	Lawrence Lo <lawrence.lo@mediatech.com.tw>
Subject:	ticket reservation for Shamlet
Date:	7/3

1. I'd like to reserve two tickets for Shamlet on Saturday, 7/22. The following is my order information.

   Name: Lawrence Lo

   Membership number: MJ2345

   Number of tickets: 2 (700 each) with the total cost of 1400

   Payment: Master card, number: 4321 5678 9012 8765, expiration date: 09/17

   Address: No. 5, Lane 146, Sec. 1, Tingzhou Rd., Taipei City 100

2. Besides order confirmation, please also reply us with the ticket exchange and cancellation policy.

Sincerely,

Lawrence Lo

文章解析

1. 我想要 reserve two tickets for Shamlet on 7/22 這一天，以下是 my order information。包含有姓名、會員號碼、幾張票和價錢、信用卡付款、地址。

2. 除了 oder confirmation 以外，請 reply 給我 ticket exchange 以及 cancellation 的 policy。既然 order 了當然需要對方給個 order confirmation 確認。

186. What mostly likely is Shamlet?

    (A) A movie to be shown in a theater.

    (B) A tragedy based on Hamlet.

    (C) A comedy stage show.

    (D) A show for kids from Ping Fong Acting Troupe.

解析

Shamlet 最可能是？

(A)：講了一堆 on stage 不可能是 movie，(D)：從頭到尾沒講過 kids show，所以可以先刪掉。剩下 (B) 和 (C)，注意到沒？文章裡說了 Hamlet 是 tragedy 而 Shamlet 卻是個 ironic comedy，答案是 (C) A comedy stage show

187. Who is the director of Shamlet?

    (A) Ping Fong Acting Troupe.

    (B) The Red House.

    (C) William Shakespeare.

    (D) Hugh Lee.

導演是誰？

請看第一篇的句 4，正確答案為 (D)。

188. Based on the two passages, what kind of member is Lawrence Lo?
(A) A gold member.
(B) A silver member.
(C) A student member.
(D) Not commented.

根據這兩篇文章，Lawrence Lo 是什麼樣的 member？

這類的題目是多數新多益書籍還有許多新多益老師沒有特別強調的，而這類題目也是新多益考試所獨有的特色。你需要同時把兩篇文章看完看懂才有辦法回答。以這題而言，他買了兩張各 700 的票，回到第一篇，700 是 gold member，所以答案是 (A)。要回答這類的題目，你需要到第一篇或是第二篇先去找線索，然後根據這個線索去第二篇或是回到第一篇，去找出正確答案。這類題目其實不難只要你有準備，就很容易回答，但是如果沒注意到，看幾遍都沒太大作用。

189. How does Lawrence pay for the show?
(A) Cash.
(B) Check.
(C) Credit card.
(D) Money order.

解析

Lawrence 是怎麼付錢的？

請看第 2 篇句 1 的付款資訊，答案為 (C)。

190. What additional information does Lawrence ask?
　　　(A) What to do if the show is cancelled.
　　　(B) What will happen if he cannot go to the show?
　　　(C) Where to call for the show's detail information.
　　　(D) Direction to the Red House.

解析

Lawrence 問了什麼 additional information ？

答案裡的 (C) 和 (D) 一看就知道錯，剩下 (A) 和 (B)，看一下 email 最後面　的 Besides order confirmation, please also reply us with the ticket exchange and cancellation policy. 也就是 ticket exchange 的 policy 和 cancellation policy 先看一下 (B)：如果沒法去的話會如何？這講的不是 ticket exchange 換票吧！而 cancellation poilicy 當然就是 What to do if the show is cancelled，所以答案是 (A)。

1. HTC is partnering with Valve to make virtual reality dream come true

2. Taipei, Oct 5, 2015 – After years of collaboration with Valve, HTC is finally ready to unveil their virtual reality (VR) offering, the HTC Vive.

3. On Nov. 19, exactly one week before Thanksgiving, which is the busiest shopping season in the US, HTC and Valve will be hosting a conference in Las Vegas to officially introduce Vive to the general publics.

4. Previously announced at Mobile World Congress, Vive has been regarded as one of the strongest VR competitors to the FB's Oculus Rift.

5. Most of the users who have tried on Vive give rave review and thoroughly enjoy the experience.

6. The laser base station that comes with the system can track your location in the room and project it into the VR world, and it will even warn you if you are getting too close to a wall.

7. The other real achievements for Vive are the motion-tracking wands and controllers which will allow you to walk around, confidently pick up random objects, check it and keep it or throw it away.

8. Coming from the gaming industry, Valve has an impeccable reputation in PC and mobile games and obviously, gaming will be the first and the most important application for the system.

9. We hope you can join us on Nov. 19, in Las Vegas to experience the world's first VR system for consumers.

文章解析

1. HTC 與 Valve 合作讓虛擬實境 (virtual reality) 美夢成真

2. 在跟 Valve 合作數年後，HTC 終於可以 unveil 他們的虛擬實境 offering, 也就是 HTC Vive。這裡的 unveil 是由 veil 而來的，就是所謂的面紗，unveil 也就是拿掉 veil 面紗，所以 unveil 當然是揭幕、揭露、展現的意思，offering 當然是由 offer 來的。再把這句念一次。

3. 將兩個逗點之間先拿掉，所以這句就變成 On Nov. 19, HTC and Valve will be hosting a conference in Las Vegas to officially introduce Vive to the general publics. 兩家公司即將 officially 的在 Las Vegas introduce Vive 給一般大眾。逗點裡的 exactly one week before Thanksgiving 只是說明 11/19 正好是感恩節前一禮拜，而 which is the busiest shopping season in the US，只是說明感恩節是美國最大的購物季節。

4. 說明先前在 Mobile World Congress 裡 Vive 已經被 announced 了，也被視為 FB Oculus Rift（也是個虛擬實境系統）最強的挑戰者。

5. 還記得關係代名詞的處理方法嗎？認出這裡的 who 代替了哪個名詞，就是前面的 user，再來把 who 所帶的整句話認出來，在這裡就是：who have tried on Vive，接下來把這 who have tried on Vive 這句話刪掉句子就變成：Most of the users give rave review and thoroughly enjoy the experience. 這裡的 throughly 完全地、徹底地可不要跟 through 搞混了，還有既然是 enjoy the experienc 那 rave 是好是壞？ rave review 當然是很讚的 review。剛剛去掉的 who have tried on Vive 只是用來說明前面的 users，也就是 who have tried on Vive：試過 Vive 的 users。

6. 同樣的先針對關係代名詞 that 用同樣的方法認出 that comes with the system 整句殺掉，句子就變成 "The laser base station can track your location in the room and project it into the VR world, and it will even warn you if you get to close to a wall."。這句話很簡單，只是這個 laser base station 能夠 track 你的 location，project 你的 location 到 VR world（虛擬世界），還能夠（在 if you get to close to a wall 的時候）警告你。簡單的講這個 laswer base station 可以做三件事：track your location, project your location, and warn you。你可不要搞錯這裡 project 的意思喔！首先這裡 project 的發音應該是 pro-JECT，重音在後面，而 project it (your position) into the VR world 說的就是把你的位置投影（投射）到虛擬實境世界裡。

7. 這句也很長，不過把 which 後面的部分全部刪掉就變成：The other real achievements for Vive are the motion-tracking wands and controllers. 另一個成就是 motion-tracking wands 和 controllers，wand 不認識，沒關係反正就是個能夠 tracking motion 的東西，如果你喜歡看 Harry Potter 系列的電影，wands 就是魔法師人手一支的東西。再來看一下先前被刪掉的 which will allow you to walk around, confidently pick up random objects, check it and

keep it or throw it away 這裡的 which 很明顯說的就是 wand 和 controller 而這組的 wand 和 controller 可以讓你做到四件事：walk around, pick up, check it and keep it or throw it 是不是很簡單！這裡的 random 不懂沒關係，當作 pick up objects 就可以了，random 當數學術語就是隨機的，一般語言就是任意的。

8. 這裡只是把兩句話用 and 接在一起而已。先看前一句是說 Valve 這家公司是由遊戲市場而來，在 PC 和行動遊戲市場有個 impeccable 的 reputation，impeccable 不懂，也應該知道是好的 reputation。這個字意思是完美無缺、無懈可擊的意思，先給個例句：She deserves the gold medal with her impeccable performance. 感覺出來了嗎？再把句子念一次就可以了。

9. 希望大家能在 11/19 到 Las Vegas 來 experience 一下全球第一個給 consumers 的 VR system。

To:	allison@htc.com.tw
From:	bin@htc.com.tw
Subject:	let's talk about the Vive launching conference
Date:	10/19

1. Let me first congratulate you on the fine job you did for the press release of Vive launching conference.
2. It was well written, concise, and most importantly to the point and interesting.
3. As your supervisor probably has informed you, you will be helping with the preparation of the launching conference.

4. I'd like to talk to you in more detail, but I will be on business trips to Southeast Asia and Europe and will not be coming back to Taiwan until early Nov.

5. During this time, email would be the best way to reach me.

6. I'd like to meet with you exactly two weeks before the event in our HQ.

7. I know you are probably really nervous about this new assignment but with your past job performance and your capability that has been shown during the last few years, we are confident that you will be doing a great job for the conference preparation.

BR,

Bin

文章解析

1. 先獎勵一下她把 Vive launching conference 的 press release 做的很棒，前面另一篇閱讀文章講的 launch 是 mass balloon launch，這裡的 launch 則是 product launch，英文裡都是用 launch 這個字，可是翻成中文意思就不同了，前面說的是發射氣球、氣球升空，而這裡則是產品發表或發布，但是只要了解了英文上的用法，其實真的不需要硬背中文意思。

2. 如果 concise 不懂，應能感覺到是好事，concise 簡明的、簡潔的、簡短有力的，看個例句：Your presentation needs to be more concise and to the point to really grab the attention of the

audience. 說實話任何演講都應該 concise and to the point 對吧。

3. 先前已經通知過，你會幫忙準備這個 launching conference。

4. 想談一下細節，但是要持續出差到十一月初才會回台灣。

5. 最好還是用 email 來 reach me。

6. 希望在這個 event (launch conference) 兩週前在公司 HQ, headquarter 總部，見面談一下。

7. 這句很長其實不難，同樣的先把 that has been shown during the last few years 先刪掉，架構上就成為：I know you are nervous but with your performance and your capability, we are confident that 後面這件事。細節上是 you are (probably really) nervous (about this new assignment)，而刪掉的 that 指的就是 your performance and your capability，所以 that has been shown during the last few years 就是最近幾年所展現出來的 performance 和 capability。最後只是講一下，對 you will be doing a great job for the conference preparation 這件事有信心。

191. Oculus Rift is a
    (A) Gaming system.
    (B) VR platform.
    (C) FB's tool.
    (D) Mobile game.

解析

一看就知道 (C) 和 (D) 可以立刻刪掉，而 (A)，請看第一篇文章裡的句 8，就知道也是錯，答案是 (B) VR platform。

192. According to the press release, what did not come with the Vive?
(A) A laser system.
(B) A game.
(C) A system that can follow your move.
(D) Some controllers.

解析

印象深的應該可以挑出三個 come with Vive 的答案，就算你一時選不出來，回去文章瞄一下也會知道 (A)、(C)、(D) 都有提到，答案是 (B) A game。

193. The word impeccable in paragraph 4, line 1, is closest in meaning to
(A) awful
(B) clean
(C) exact
(D) wonderful

解析

從文章裡可以感覺出 impeccable 一定是好事，所以 (A) 和 (C) 可以先刪掉，把剩下的答案帶回原句就可以知道 (D) 才是正確答案。

194. From the email, what can be inferred about Allison?

(A) She is experienced in preparing and setting up a conference.

(B) She is really good at writing stories.

(C) She is a Valve employee.

(D) It's probably the first time she helps preparing for a conference.

解析

如果 (A) 正確的話，那她應該不會那麼 nervous，而 (C)，從 HQ 在台北以及 email address 裡的 htc.com 都可以知道是 HTC 的員工。剩下兩個答案，先看 (B)：email 一開始稱讚她 press release 寫得不錯，好像 OK。再來看 (D)：文章裡講到她很 nervous 還有 with your performance and your capability, we are confident that 你 在 conference preparation 上會 do a great job。明顯的，(D) 是比較好的答案。更何況 press release 寫得好，不見得 stories 就會寫得好，畢竟這兩類作品性質差很大。

195. When will Bin meeting with Allison?

(A) 10/19

(B) 11/5

(C) 11/12

(D) 11/19

在 email 的句 6 裡提到 … exactly two weeks before the event，而第一篇文章裡也說了 On Nov. 19, HTC and Valve will be…，所以答案是 (B) 11/5。這類的題目，只要你已經有了心理的準備，就變得很簡單，但是如果沒有預期到這類的題目，前前後後不論找幾遍，都回答不出來。

Questions 196 - 200 refer to the following letter and cost estimation document.

Reba McEntire
38 Ford St.
San Marcos, Tx 78666

EasyJet Claim Office
EasyJet Airline
1 EasyJet Plaza,
Orlando, FL 32801

Dear Sir/Madam,

1. I am writing with regard to my badly damaged luggage during my trip from San Jose to Austin.
2. I was traveling from Mineta San Jose Airport to Austin-Bergstrom Airport on EasyJet flight EJ2857 on April 3.
3. Upon picking up my luggage from the baggage claim area, I noticed that two wheels were missing and the top handle was detached from it.

4. I immediately reported it to the EasyJet office at the Bergstrom Airport and properly filled out the damaged baggage claim form.

5. I already had my baggage checked at a local luggage retailer, Howard Limited, to see if it's repairable.

6. They feel that only the two missing wheels could be fully repaired but the handle would be tough to fix and thus they would suggest a replacement.

7. Please see the enclosed copy of estimate for more detail.

8. I would like to request that EasyJet reimburse me for the cost of a new luggage as shown in the estimate.

9. Also, on that date, because of the damaged luggage, I wasn't able to take any public transportation from the airport and had to take a taxi.

10. I would also ask EasyJet to reimburse me for the $50 taxi fare.

Yours sincerely,

Reba McEntire

文章解析

1. 為了 (with regard to) badly damaged luggage 寫這封信，during my trip from San Jose to Austin 只是說明時間點而已。

2. 講清楚哪個航班，哪個時間從 San Jose Airport 搭機到 Austin Airport，裡面的 Mineta 和 Bergstrom 只是機場名字而已。

3. 如果 baggage claim area 不認識，就是下飛機後那個有轉盤，旅客領行李的地方。領到行李後發現 two wheels were missing 還有 the top handle 也 detached 了，detached 不懂，反正不是好事。看看例句：You can detach the blue copy of the form and keep it for your reference (or record). 你可以 detach 藍色 copy 然後作為你自己的參考 (或記錄)。再看一句：If necessary, the lizard will detach its tail to try to get away. 必要時蜥蜴會 detach 它的尾巴來試著逃掉。這樣對 detach 就有 FU 了，再回到原句念一次，如果 handle 不懂，請你到 Google 圖片蒐尋找一下 door handle，再來邊看著圖片邊念 door handle 就可以了。

4. 這句只是 I reported it (to the EasyJet office) and filled out the (damaged baggage claim) form 而已。

5. 已找了個 local luggage retailer 看看怎麼修？

6. 只有 missing wheels 可以修好而 handle 沒法修了，乾脆換掉比較划算。

7. 附上 copy of estimate 上面又有 detail(你可以查看)。

8. 要求退還預估單裡 a new luggage 的錢。

9. 當天因為這個 damaged luggage，沒法搭 publuc transportation，只能搭 taxi。

10. 也請退還計程車錢。

1. Howard Limited: Authorized Delsey Retailer

43 Oran St. Austin, Tx 78745

2. Estimate of Repair Date: April 6

Item to be repaired:　　Delsey Helium Aero 29 luggage

Repairs to be done:　　Replace two wheels and reattach handle

Estimated cost:　　　 $ 30 (please see notes below)

3. Notes: The two wheels can be fully repaired, but it would not be possible to securely reattach the handle because the handle attachment pad was too severely damaged.

4. The cost to replace it with the same model is $ 140.

文章解析

1. 反正就是個 authorized 的 Delsy Retailer，給個 authorized 例句：With extra budget authorized by the top management, the team goes ahead and hires more engineers. 既然是 extra budget 當然需要被高層管理 authorized，才能使用。你要賣一些高品質高價的品牌，往往都需要這些品牌的 authorization，這樣對 authorize 授權有 FU 了嗎？順道提一下 authority：權力、職權，另外有權力有職權的 authority 當然就是當權者、官方、政府機關。接下來的地址不需要看，就算考了，回來再看都來的及

2. 給了 4 個訊息：估價的日期、估價的東西、需要修理的清單及預估的價錢。價錢的部分還有註釋如下。

3. 這句話很長，架構上可以先以 but 做分界，but 之前的部分只是説

two wheels can be repaired 很容易吧！but 後面的就真的又臭又長，事實上卻不難，在這一句裡，注意到沒？有個 because，所以這部分又可以用 because 切開成兩半，because 之前其實也只是 it would not be possible to reattach the handle 而已，because 後面的部分只是解釋因為 the handle attachement pad was too severely damaged 而已，如果 handle attachment pad 不懂，是不是覺得其實就是個 pad，而 handle attachment 只是說明什麼樣的 pad，如果 pad 不懂，iPad 總聽說過吧！iPad 是個平板電腦，當然 pad 就是個板子、墊子了，再來講一下 attachment，還記得前面講過了 detach 是分開，那 attach 呢？大家應該都記過 email 吧，email 裡經常會有附件，attachment 在 email 上面就是附件，所以這裡的 handle attachement pad 當然就是個用來把 handle attach 上去的一個 pad，懂了嗎？

4. 簡化這句就是 The cost is $140.。刪掉的部分：to replace it with the same modle 指示加強說明什麼樣的 cost 而已。

196. What is the purpose of the letter?
    (A) To report a damaged item.
    (B) To complain about a baggage service.
    (C) To request a refund.
    (D) To claim some expenses.

解析

先看 (A)：信中有沒有 report a damaged item 當然有，就是那個 luggage，但是最重要的重點嗎？當然不是，以偏概全錯！再看 (B)：有 complain about the baggage service 好像有又好像沒有，baggage

有沒有壞掉？有！但是她的 complaint 是給航空公司，不是針對 baggage claim 所以也是錯！剩下 (C) 和 (D)，從剩下的兩個答案來比較一下，很明顯差別就在 refund 和 expense 這兩個字上面，refund 很簡單，去百貨公司或賣場買了東西以後，覺得不滿意，就回到原賣場要求退貨當然退貨以後，賣場就要 refund 錢給你，這樣 refund 就懂了，再來講 expense，假設你去出差，回來以後是不是要把所有相關收據拿來報帳，也就是要跟公司 file an expense report，expense 費用、支出懂了吧！那以這封信而言說的是 refund 還是 expense？答案當然是 (C)。

197. Why did Ms. McEntire visit Howard Limited?
    (A) To check for a new suitcase.
    (B) To complain about the damaged luggage.
    (C) To inquire about an estimation for repair work.
    (D) To pay a bill.

解析

為什麼會去 Howard Limited？
這題很簡單吧！(D) 可以先殺掉，再來 (B) 也不用看了，剩下 (A) 和 (C) 就算你因為不認識 inquire 不知道 (C) 比較對，也可以看出 (A) 比較錯吧！答案是 (C)，這裡的 inquire 當作 ask 就可以了。

198. What company made the damaged luggage?
    (A) Delsey
    (B) Howard Limited
    (C) EasyJet
    (D) San Marcos

這個 damaged luggage 是哪家公司製作的？

Howard Limited 只是估價，EasyJet 是航空公司，而 San Marcos 文章裡根本沒出現，看到了估價單裡的 Item to be repaired: Delsey Helium Aero 29 luggage 所以答案是 (A) Delsey，簡單吧！

199. Why did Ms. McEntire enclosed a document?
    (A) To provide a physical evidence of the damaged luggage
    (B) To prove that the luggage had been repaired
    (C) To support her claim for the reimbursement
    (D) To suggest EasyJet a better way of handling luggage

解析

為什麼 Ms. McEntire enclosed 一個文件？

在這裡先簡單的解釋一下 enclose/enclosement 和 attach/attachment 的差別，enclose 顧名思義就是包起來，attach 前面講過了附上、繫上、裝上之類的意思，看出差別了嗎？簡單地說 enclosed 一定是信件，因為只有信件才能 enclose something，而 attach/attachment 一定是 email，因為 email 才會 attach something。再來該看題目了。答案裡的 (B) 可以先刪掉，luggage 的 handle 不值得修，所以絕對不會 had been repaired 已經修好了，再看 (A)，如果要 provide 這類 damaged luggage 的 physical evidence 照片最好吧，不會是估價單，也是錯！再來是 (D)：估價單裡有 suggest a better way of handling luggage 也沒有，錯！答案是 (C)：給個估價單，讓專業的廠商來證明無法檢修必須換新。

200. How much is the total amount of reimbursement asked by Ms. McEntire?

(A) $ 30

(B) $ 140

(C) $ 170

(D) $ 190

解析

總共要求多少錢？

估價單裡有 replace luggage 的 $140，不過還記得她要求 taxi 的費用嗎？再加 $50 所以答案是 (D) $ 190。

最後的叮嚀

首先把我強調過的重點再說一次：一開始練習聽力時，要先把原稿念一次，先確認腦子裡面沒有中文都能夠一念就懂，如果句子裡面有單字，把單字查過以後，再把句子念個幾次，確認不需要中文都可以了解意思後，不看原稿的聽，Part 3 和 Part 4 就先念一句、聽一句，最後整段對話一口氣聽完，如果還是有些部分沒法聽懂，針對聽不懂的句子再次地唸完後聽，但是不論如何，最後都是要一口氣地把整段的對話聽完。只要你能照這方式練習下來，英國腔、澳洲腔都不會是問題。

記得考聽力的時候，一聽就要懂，只要腦子出現中文，聽的時候就會卡卡的，考試一定考不好！當你練習聽力到腦子都沒有中文的時候，就要接下來練習閱讀時也不需要中文！這點真的比較難，不過你一樣可以把單字、文法甚至閱讀的考題的題目念個幾次，念到對句子有直接的感覺，一念就懂，從短句子開始練習，練習到一念就懂，慢慢地來加強。接下來你就會感覺到有些句子真的不需要中文就會懂，如果你念懂以後，還是又想要翻中文，你就會發現其實腦子把念懂的英文句子翻成中文，只是會拖慢你的閱讀速度，只是讓你在已經了解的句子上面浪費時間而已。你可以從單字考題、文法考題的句子裡先練習，一念就有感覺、一念就懂，慢慢發現這好處以後，就會成為你在進一步練習的動力，而且也會發現在閱讀時如果可以捨棄中文，直接了解英文，對閱讀速度，會有很大的幫助。

再來談一下聽力考試時一個很重要的應試技巧，那就是：<u>深呼吸！</u>考過聽力的同學應該都會有個體驗，考聽力好累喔！聽力考試的特點就是，只要你一恍神，一題就沒了！整個聽力考試過程都需要全神貫注，專心一致的應考。

以新多益聽力考試而言，總共 45 分鐘，說實話，一般人很難聚精會神整整 45 分鐘，整個考試過程總會有恍神的時候！那該怎麼辦？三個字：**深呼吸！**新多益聽力 Part 1 最簡單，只要你遵照我說的方式來練習聽力，Part 1 一般問題不大，多數情況下，你只要聽完前三個答案，就已經知道正確答案了，如果前三個答案都不好，那正確答案一定是 (D)，所如果你在聽到 (A) 或 (B) 時，已經知道答案，立刻深呼吸一兩次，調整一下自己的心情，讓自己放鬆一下，以輕鬆的心情去聽剩下的答案，只是再確認沒問題而已。聽過前三個都不好的答案，也同樣的深呼吸一兩次，用輕鬆一點的心情去確認 (D) 是最好的答案。

同樣的，在考 Part 2 時，也是如此，唯一的差別只是 Part 2 只有三個答案，記得適時的深呼吸放鬆心情，才能有精力去面對 Part 3 和 Part 4 的聽力考題。這個技巧要找時間練習一下，讓深呼吸成為一種習慣，也好讓自己有足夠的精神，不至於在最後 Part 3 和 Part 4 的緊要關頭因為恍神而失分。

再來談一下我最怕學生在考過新多益以後跟我將的一句話：「我把閱讀題目都做完了，我在最後的幾分鐘裡，把雙篇閱讀題目答完！」此時我心裡想的是，這下成績不會太高了！

正式的新多益考試有個特點：所有題目一律按照難易度，在出題上都是由簡單到困難，七個部分都一樣。大家都知道閱讀最後的 20 題是雙篇文章，所以最後的兩大題雙篇閱讀（也就是總共四篇文章），是閱讀裡面最難的文章和題目，尤其是最後一篇。換句話說這最後兩組雙篇文章，最花時間去讀、去解題，尤其是最後一組，單就這一組兩篇文章、5 題題目，保守估計一般考生需要花十分鐘以上才能好好地把題目做完。

現在請你回想一下我一直強調的新多益出題特點，往往你可以輕易地選出兩個不對的答案，然後在剩下的兩個答案裡找出比較對，或是比較錯的答案。如果你沒有九成以上的把握，就回去原文章找一下，注意一下因為你已經把文章看過，多少應該知道到哪裡找。一般而言，不到 30 秒鐘就可以確認你的答案是否正確？需不需要更改？花十分鐘去讀最後一組的雙篇閱讀，不如把這十分鐘花在確認答案上面，保守估計你可以確定 20 題的答案。你覺得回答最後最難的五題比較重要，還是確認 20 題都可以答對比較有效率？

我一直跟學生強調，我寧可你最後面的五題、十題的雙篇文章沒有做，也要你確保前面的 95 或 90 題能夠好好地回答，如果你能好好地把前面的題目做好，甚至最後的 15 題沒答都沒關係！我真的要強調一下這個很重要，卻是其他人沒有提出的觀念：寧可後面的五題、十題、十五題沒時間作答，也要確定把前面的 90 題、85 題好好的作對！當然如果你的閱讀能力很強，能夠快、狠、準，能夠有時間好好地把最後五題、十題做完，當然更好，我只是要你記得，把前面的題目做好、作對，遠比把題目做完更加重要許多！

考前最後關頭的注意事項

再來要提醒所有新多益考生，在考前最後的時間，做幾份新多益官方全真試題，因為只有這份考題會遵照正式考題，把所有七大部分的題目，一律由簡單到困難來出題。你一定要做個幾份官方考題，才能真正體會出這種按難易度區分考題的特性與應考方式，例如，前面提到的寧可題目沒做完，也要確認前面的題目都能做對的重點，只有用官方考題，你才可以體會到這種應視方式的好處，這才是真正的準備新多益考試。

前面講的聽力考試技巧：深呼吸！用官方考題就會體會到由易漸難的情況下，你該如何調整呼吸、調適心情來面對聽力。試過閱讀考題，你就會知道為什麼寧可要你把前面的題目做好，也不要要求自己把題目做完的重要性！一般坊間新多益測驗，都沒有把題目按照難易度編排，你就很難體會這個最重要的關鍵！

希望大家在看完這本書後，能對新多益考試甚至英文學習有個更棒的認知和體驗，知道如何能有效地準備新多益考試進而拿到理想的高分，最後祝大家：輕鬆學英文、新多益拿高分！

LISTENING

Part 1

No.	ANSWER (A B C D)
1	Ⓐ Ⓑ Ⓒ Ⓓ
2	Ⓐ Ⓑ Ⓒ Ⓓ
3	Ⓐ Ⓑ Ⓒ Ⓓ
4	Ⓐ Ⓑ Ⓒ Ⓓ
5	Ⓐ Ⓑ Ⓒ Ⓓ
6	Ⓐ Ⓑ Ⓒ Ⓓ
7	Ⓐ Ⓑ Ⓒ Ⓓ
8	Ⓐ Ⓑ Ⓒ Ⓓ
9	Ⓐ Ⓑ Ⓒ Ⓓ
10	Ⓐ Ⓑ Ⓒ Ⓓ

Part 2

No.	ANSWER (A B C D)	No.	ANSWER (A B C D)
11	Ⓐ Ⓑ Ⓒ Ⓓ	21	Ⓐ Ⓑ Ⓒ Ⓓ
12	Ⓐ Ⓑ Ⓒ Ⓓ	22	Ⓐ Ⓑ Ⓒ Ⓓ
13	Ⓐ Ⓑ Ⓒ Ⓓ	23	Ⓐ Ⓑ Ⓒ Ⓓ
14	Ⓐ Ⓑ Ⓒ Ⓓ	24	Ⓐ Ⓑ Ⓒ Ⓓ
15	Ⓐ Ⓑ Ⓒ Ⓓ	25	Ⓐ Ⓑ Ⓒ Ⓓ
16	Ⓐ Ⓑ Ⓒ Ⓓ	26	Ⓐ Ⓑ Ⓒ Ⓓ
17	Ⓐ Ⓑ Ⓒ Ⓓ	27	Ⓐ Ⓑ Ⓒ Ⓓ
18	Ⓐ Ⓑ Ⓒ Ⓓ	28	Ⓐ Ⓑ Ⓒ Ⓓ
19	Ⓐ Ⓑ Ⓒ Ⓓ	29	Ⓐ Ⓑ Ⓒ Ⓓ
10	Ⓐ Ⓑ Ⓒ Ⓓ	30	Ⓐ Ⓑ Ⓒ Ⓓ
31	Ⓐ Ⓑ Ⓒ Ⓓ	
32	Ⓐ Ⓑ Ⓒ Ⓓ	
33	Ⓐ Ⓑ Ⓒ Ⓓ	
34	Ⓐ Ⓑ Ⓒ Ⓓ	
35	Ⓐ Ⓑ Ⓒ Ⓓ	
36	Ⓐ Ⓑ Ⓒ Ⓓ	
37	Ⓐ Ⓑ Ⓒ Ⓓ	
38	Ⓐ Ⓑ Ⓒ Ⓓ	
39	Ⓐ Ⓑ Ⓒ Ⓓ	
40	Ⓐ Ⓑ Ⓒ Ⓓ	

Part 3

No.	ANSWER (A B C D)	No.	ANSWER (A B C D)	No.	ANSWER (A B C D)
41	Ⓐ Ⓑ Ⓒ Ⓓ	51	Ⓐ Ⓑ Ⓒ Ⓓ	61	Ⓐ Ⓑ Ⓒ Ⓓ
42	Ⓐ Ⓑ Ⓒ Ⓓ	52	Ⓐ Ⓑ Ⓒ Ⓓ	62	Ⓐ Ⓑ Ⓒ Ⓓ
43	Ⓐ Ⓑ Ⓒ Ⓓ	53	Ⓐ Ⓑ Ⓒ Ⓓ	63	Ⓐ Ⓑ Ⓒ Ⓓ
44	Ⓐ Ⓑ Ⓒ Ⓓ	54	Ⓐ Ⓑ Ⓒ Ⓓ	64	Ⓐ Ⓑ Ⓒ Ⓓ
45	Ⓐ Ⓑ Ⓒ Ⓓ	55	Ⓐ Ⓑ Ⓒ Ⓓ	65	Ⓐ Ⓑ Ⓒ Ⓓ
46	Ⓐ Ⓑ Ⓒ Ⓓ	56	Ⓐ Ⓑ Ⓒ Ⓓ	66	Ⓐ Ⓑ Ⓒ Ⓓ
47	Ⓐ Ⓑ Ⓒ Ⓓ	57	Ⓐ Ⓑ Ⓒ Ⓓ	67	Ⓐ Ⓑ Ⓒ Ⓓ
48	Ⓐ Ⓑ Ⓒ Ⓓ	58	Ⓐ Ⓑ Ⓒ Ⓓ	68	Ⓐ Ⓑ Ⓒ Ⓓ
49	Ⓐ Ⓑ Ⓒ Ⓓ	59	Ⓐ Ⓑ Ⓒ Ⓓ	69	Ⓐ Ⓑ Ⓒ Ⓓ
50	Ⓐ Ⓑ Ⓒ Ⓓ	60	Ⓐ Ⓑ Ⓒ Ⓓ	70	Ⓐ Ⓑ Ⓒ Ⓓ

Part 4

No.	ANSWER (A B C D)	No.	ANSWER (A B C D)	No.	ANSWER (A B C D)
71	Ⓐ Ⓑ Ⓒ Ⓓ	81	Ⓐ Ⓑ Ⓒ Ⓓ	91	Ⓐ Ⓑ Ⓒ Ⓓ
72	Ⓐ Ⓑ Ⓒ Ⓓ	82	Ⓐ Ⓑ Ⓒ Ⓓ	92	Ⓐ Ⓑ Ⓒ Ⓓ
73	Ⓐ Ⓑ Ⓒ Ⓓ	83	Ⓐ Ⓑ Ⓒ Ⓓ	93	Ⓐ Ⓑ Ⓒ Ⓓ
74	Ⓐ Ⓑ Ⓒ Ⓓ	84	Ⓐ Ⓑ Ⓒ Ⓓ	94	Ⓐ Ⓑ Ⓒ Ⓓ
75	Ⓐ Ⓑ Ⓒ Ⓓ	85	Ⓐ Ⓑ Ⓒ Ⓓ	95	Ⓐ Ⓑ Ⓒ Ⓓ
76	Ⓐ Ⓑ Ⓒ Ⓓ	86	Ⓐ Ⓑ Ⓒ Ⓓ	96	Ⓐ Ⓑ Ⓒ Ⓓ
77	Ⓐ Ⓑ Ⓒ Ⓓ	87	Ⓐ Ⓑ Ⓒ Ⓓ	97	Ⓐ Ⓑ Ⓒ Ⓓ
78	Ⓐ Ⓑ Ⓒ Ⓓ	88	Ⓐ Ⓑ Ⓒ Ⓓ	98	Ⓐ Ⓑ Ⓒ Ⓓ
79	Ⓐ Ⓑ Ⓒ Ⓓ	89	Ⓐ Ⓑ Ⓒ Ⓓ	99	Ⓐ Ⓑ Ⓒ Ⓓ
80	Ⓐ Ⓑ Ⓒ Ⓓ	90	Ⓐ Ⓑ Ⓒ Ⓓ	100	Ⓐ Ⓑ Ⓒ Ⓓ

READING

Part 5

No.	ANSWER (A B C D)	No.	ANSWER (A B C D)
101	Ⓐ Ⓑ Ⓒ Ⓓ	111	Ⓐ Ⓑ Ⓒ Ⓓ
102	Ⓐ Ⓑ Ⓒ Ⓓ	112	Ⓐ Ⓑ Ⓒ Ⓓ
103	Ⓐ Ⓑ Ⓒ Ⓓ	113	Ⓐ Ⓑ Ⓒ Ⓓ
104	Ⓐ Ⓑ Ⓒ Ⓓ	114	Ⓐ Ⓑ Ⓒ Ⓓ
105	Ⓐ Ⓑ Ⓒ Ⓓ	115	Ⓐ Ⓑ Ⓒ Ⓓ
106	Ⓐ Ⓑ Ⓒ Ⓓ	116	Ⓐ Ⓑ Ⓒ Ⓓ
107	Ⓐ Ⓑ Ⓒ Ⓓ	117	Ⓐ Ⓑ Ⓒ Ⓓ
108	Ⓐ Ⓑ Ⓒ Ⓓ	118	Ⓐ Ⓑ Ⓒ Ⓓ
109	Ⓐ Ⓑ Ⓒ Ⓓ	119	Ⓐ Ⓑ Ⓒ Ⓓ
110	Ⓐ Ⓑ Ⓒ Ⓓ	120	Ⓐ Ⓑ Ⓒ Ⓓ
121	Ⓐ Ⓑ Ⓒ Ⓓ	131	Ⓐ Ⓑ Ⓒ Ⓓ
122	Ⓐ Ⓑ Ⓒ Ⓓ	132	Ⓐ Ⓑ Ⓒ Ⓓ
123	Ⓐ Ⓑ Ⓒ Ⓓ	133	Ⓐ Ⓑ Ⓒ Ⓓ
124	Ⓐ Ⓑ Ⓒ Ⓓ	134	Ⓐ Ⓑ Ⓒ Ⓓ
125	Ⓐ Ⓑ Ⓒ Ⓓ	135	Ⓐ Ⓑ Ⓒ Ⓓ
126	Ⓐ Ⓑ Ⓒ Ⓓ	136	Ⓐ Ⓑ Ⓒ Ⓓ
127	Ⓐ Ⓑ Ⓒ Ⓓ	137	Ⓐ Ⓑ Ⓒ Ⓓ
128	Ⓐ Ⓑ Ⓒ Ⓓ	138	Ⓐ Ⓑ Ⓒ Ⓓ
129	Ⓐ Ⓑ Ⓒ Ⓓ	139	Ⓐ Ⓑ Ⓒ Ⓓ
130	Ⓐ Ⓑ Ⓒ Ⓓ	140	Ⓐ Ⓑ Ⓒ Ⓓ

Part 6

No.	ANSWER (A B C D)	No.	ANSWER (A B C D)
141	Ⓐ Ⓑ Ⓒ Ⓓ	151	Ⓐ Ⓑ Ⓒ Ⓓ
142	Ⓐ Ⓑ Ⓒ Ⓓ	152	Ⓐ Ⓑ Ⓒ Ⓓ
143	Ⓐ Ⓑ Ⓒ Ⓓ	153	Ⓐ Ⓑ Ⓒ Ⓓ
144	Ⓐ Ⓑ Ⓒ Ⓓ	154	Ⓐ Ⓑ Ⓒ Ⓓ
145	Ⓐ Ⓑ Ⓒ Ⓓ	155	Ⓐ Ⓑ Ⓒ Ⓓ
146	Ⓐ Ⓑ Ⓒ Ⓓ	156	Ⓐ Ⓑ Ⓒ Ⓓ
147	Ⓐ Ⓑ Ⓒ Ⓓ	157	Ⓐ Ⓑ Ⓒ Ⓓ
148	Ⓐ Ⓑ Ⓒ Ⓓ	158	Ⓐ Ⓑ Ⓒ Ⓓ
149	Ⓐ Ⓑ Ⓒ Ⓓ	159	Ⓐ Ⓑ Ⓒ Ⓓ
150	Ⓐ Ⓑ Ⓒ Ⓓ	160	Ⓐ Ⓑ Ⓒ Ⓓ

Part 7

No.	ANSWER (A B C D)	No.	ANSWER (A B C D)	No.	ANSWER (A B C D)
161	Ⓐ Ⓑ Ⓒ Ⓓ	171	Ⓐ Ⓑ Ⓒ Ⓓ	181	Ⓐ Ⓑ Ⓒ Ⓓ
162	Ⓐ Ⓑ Ⓒ Ⓓ	172	Ⓐ Ⓑ Ⓒ Ⓓ	182	Ⓐ Ⓑ Ⓒ Ⓓ
163	Ⓐ Ⓑ Ⓒ Ⓓ	173	Ⓐ Ⓑ Ⓒ Ⓓ	183	Ⓐ Ⓑ Ⓒ Ⓓ
164	Ⓐ Ⓑ Ⓒ Ⓓ	174	Ⓐ Ⓑ Ⓒ Ⓓ	184	Ⓐ Ⓑ Ⓒ Ⓓ
165	Ⓐ Ⓑ Ⓒ Ⓓ	175	Ⓐ Ⓑ Ⓒ Ⓓ	185	Ⓐ Ⓑ Ⓒ Ⓓ
166	Ⓐ Ⓑ Ⓒ Ⓓ	176	Ⓐ Ⓑ Ⓒ Ⓓ	186	Ⓐ Ⓑ Ⓒ Ⓓ
167	Ⓐ Ⓑ Ⓒ Ⓓ	177	Ⓐ Ⓑ Ⓒ Ⓓ	187	Ⓐ Ⓑ Ⓒ Ⓓ
168	Ⓐ Ⓑ Ⓒ Ⓓ	178	Ⓐ Ⓑ Ⓒ Ⓓ	188	Ⓐ Ⓑ Ⓒ Ⓓ
169	Ⓐ Ⓑ Ⓒ Ⓓ	179	Ⓐ Ⓑ Ⓒ Ⓓ	189	Ⓐ Ⓑ Ⓒ Ⓓ
170	Ⓐ Ⓑ Ⓒ Ⓓ	180	Ⓐ Ⓑ Ⓒ Ⓓ	190	Ⓐ Ⓑ Ⓒ Ⓓ
				191	Ⓐ Ⓑ Ⓒ Ⓓ
				192	Ⓐ Ⓑ Ⓒ Ⓓ
				193	Ⓐ Ⓑ Ⓒ Ⓓ
				194	Ⓐ Ⓑ Ⓒ Ⓓ
				195	Ⓐ Ⓑ Ⓒ Ⓓ
				196	Ⓐ Ⓑ Ⓒ Ⓓ
				197	Ⓐ Ⓑ Ⓒ Ⓓ
				198	Ⓐ Ⓑ Ⓒ Ⓓ
				199	Ⓐ Ⓑ Ⓒ Ⓓ
				200	Ⓐ Ⓑ Ⓒ Ⓓ

LISTENING

Part 1

No.	ANSWER
1	A B C D
2	A B C D
3	A B C D
4	A B C D
5	A B C D
6	A B C D
7	A B C D
8	A B C D
9	A B C D
10	A B C D

Part 2

No.	ANSWER	No.	ANSWER	No.	ANSWER
11	A B C D	21	A B C D	31	A B C D
12	A B C D	22	A B C D	32	A B C D
13	A B C D	23	A B C D	33	A B C D
14	A B C D	24	A B C D	34	A B C D
15	A B C D	25	A B C D	35	A B C D
16	A B C D	26	A B C D	36	A B C D
17	A B C D	27	A B C D	37	A B C D
18	A B C D	28	A B C D	38	A B C D
19	A B C D	29	A B C D	39	A B C D
10	A B C D	30	A B C D	40	A B C D

Part 3

No.	ANSWER	No.	ANSWER	No.	ANSWER
41	A B C D	51	A B C D	61	A B C D
42	A B C D	52	A B C D	62	A B C D
43	A B C D	53	A B C D	63	A B C D
44	A B C D	54	A B C D	64	A B C D
45	A B C D	55	A B C D	65	A B C D
46	A B C D	56	A B C D	66	A B C D
47	A B C D	57	A B C D	67	A B C D
48	A B C D	58	A B C D	68	A B C D
49	A B C D	59	A B C D	69	A B C D
50	A B C D	60	A B C D	70	A B C D

Part 4

No.	ANSWER	No.	ANSWER	No.	ANSWER
71	A B C D	81	A B C D	91	A B C D
72	A B C D	82	A B C D	92	A B C D
73	A B C D	83	A B C D	93	A B C D
74	A B C D	84	A B C D	94	A B C D
75	A B C D	85	A B C D	95	A B C D
76	A B C D	86	A B C D	96	A B C D
77	A B C D	87	A B C D	97	A B C D
78	A B C D	88	A B C D	98	A B C D
79	A B C D	89	A B C D	99	A B C D
80	A B C D	90	A B C D	100	A B C D

READING

Part 5

No.	ANSWER	No.	ANSWER	No.	ANSWER
	A B C D		A B C D		A B C D
101	Ⓐ Ⓑ Ⓒ Ⓓ	111	Ⓐ Ⓑ Ⓒ Ⓓ	121	Ⓐ Ⓑ Ⓒ Ⓓ
102	Ⓐ Ⓑ Ⓒ Ⓓ	112	Ⓐ Ⓑ Ⓒ Ⓓ	122	Ⓐ Ⓑ Ⓒ Ⓓ
103	Ⓐ Ⓑ Ⓒ Ⓓ	113	Ⓐ Ⓑ Ⓒ Ⓓ	123	Ⓐ Ⓑ Ⓒ Ⓓ
104	Ⓐ Ⓑ Ⓒ Ⓓ	114	Ⓐ Ⓑ Ⓒ Ⓓ	124	Ⓐ Ⓑ Ⓒ Ⓓ
105	Ⓐ Ⓑ Ⓒ Ⓓ	115	Ⓐ Ⓑ Ⓒ Ⓓ	125	Ⓐ Ⓑ Ⓒ Ⓓ
106	Ⓐ Ⓑ Ⓒ Ⓓ	116	Ⓐ Ⓑ Ⓒ Ⓓ	126	Ⓐ Ⓑ Ⓒ Ⓓ
107	Ⓐ Ⓑ Ⓒ Ⓓ	117	Ⓐ Ⓑ Ⓒ Ⓓ	127	Ⓐ Ⓑ Ⓒ Ⓓ
108	Ⓐ Ⓑ Ⓒ Ⓓ	118	Ⓐ Ⓑ Ⓒ Ⓓ	128	Ⓐ Ⓑ Ⓒ Ⓓ
109	Ⓐ Ⓑ Ⓒ Ⓓ	119	Ⓐ Ⓑ Ⓒ Ⓓ	129	Ⓐ Ⓑ Ⓒ Ⓓ
110	Ⓐ Ⓑ Ⓒ Ⓓ	120	Ⓐ Ⓑ Ⓒ Ⓓ	130	Ⓐ Ⓑ Ⓒ Ⓓ

No.	ANSWER	No.	ANSWER
	A B C D		A B C D
131	Ⓐ Ⓑ Ⓒ Ⓓ	141	Ⓐ Ⓑ Ⓒ Ⓓ
132	Ⓐ Ⓑ Ⓒ Ⓓ	142	Ⓐ Ⓑ Ⓒ Ⓓ
133	Ⓐ Ⓑ Ⓒ Ⓓ	143	Ⓐ Ⓑ Ⓒ Ⓓ
134	Ⓐ Ⓑ Ⓒ Ⓓ	144	Ⓐ Ⓑ Ⓒ Ⓓ
135	Ⓐ Ⓑ Ⓒ Ⓓ	145	Ⓐ Ⓑ Ⓒ Ⓓ
136	Ⓐ Ⓑ Ⓒ Ⓓ	146	Ⓐ Ⓑ Ⓒ Ⓓ
137	Ⓐ Ⓑ Ⓒ Ⓓ	147	Ⓐ Ⓑ Ⓒ Ⓓ
138	Ⓐ Ⓑ Ⓒ Ⓓ	148	Ⓐ Ⓑ Ⓒ Ⓓ
139	Ⓐ Ⓑ Ⓒ Ⓓ	149	Ⓐ Ⓑ Ⓒ Ⓓ
140	Ⓐ Ⓑ Ⓒ Ⓓ	150	Ⓐ Ⓑ Ⓒ Ⓓ

Part 6

No.	ANSWER	No.	ANSWER
	A B C D		A B C D
151	Ⓐ Ⓑ Ⓒ Ⓓ	161	Ⓐ Ⓑ Ⓒ Ⓓ
152	Ⓐ Ⓑ Ⓒ Ⓓ	162	Ⓐ Ⓑ Ⓒ Ⓓ
153	Ⓐ Ⓑ Ⓒ Ⓓ	163	Ⓐ Ⓑ Ⓒ Ⓓ
154	Ⓐ Ⓑ Ⓒ Ⓓ	164	Ⓐ Ⓑ Ⓒ Ⓓ
155	Ⓐ Ⓑ Ⓒ Ⓓ	165	Ⓐ Ⓑ Ⓒ Ⓓ
156	Ⓐ Ⓑ Ⓒ Ⓓ	166	Ⓐ Ⓑ Ⓒ Ⓓ
157	Ⓐ Ⓑ Ⓒ Ⓓ	167	Ⓐ Ⓑ Ⓒ Ⓓ
158	Ⓐ Ⓑ Ⓒ Ⓓ	168	Ⓐ Ⓑ Ⓒ Ⓓ
159	Ⓐ Ⓑ Ⓒ Ⓓ	169	Ⓐ Ⓑ Ⓒ Ⓓ
160	Ⓐ Ⓑ Ⓒ Ⓓ	170	Ⓐ Ⓑ Ⓒ Ⓓ

Part 7

No.	ANSWER	No.	ANSWER	No.	ANSWER
	A B C D		A B C D		A B C D
171	Ⓐ Ⓑ Ⓒ Ⓓ	181	Ⓐ Ⓑ Ⓒ Ⓓ	191	Ⓐ Ⓑ Ⓒ Ⓓ
172	Ⓐ Ⓑ Ⓒ Ⓓ	182	Ⓐ Ⓑ Ⓒ Ⓓ	192	Ⓐ Ⓑ Ⓒ Ⓓ
173	Ⓐ Ⓑ Ⓒ Ⓓ	183	Ⓐ Ⓑ Ⓒ Ⓓ	193	Ⓐ Ⓑ Ⓒ Ⓓ
174	Ⓐ Ⓑ Ⓒ Ⓓ	184	Ⓐ Ⓑ Ⓒ Ⓓ	194	Ⓐ Ⓑ Ⓒ Ⓓ
175	Ⓐ Ⓑ Ⓒ Ⓓ	185	Ⓐ Ⓑ Ⓒ Ⓓ	195	Ⓐ Ⓑ Ⓒ Ⓓ
176	Ⓐ Ⓑ Ⓒ Ⓓ	186	Ⓐ Ⓑ Ⓒ Ⓓ	196	Ⓐ Ⓑ Ⓒ Ⓓ
177	Ⓐ Ⓑ Ⓒ Ⓓ	187	Ⓐ Ⓑ Ⓒ Ⓓ	197	Ⓐ Ⓑ Ⓒ Ⓓ
178	Ⓐ Ⓑ Ⓒ Ⓓ	188	Ⓐ Ⓑ Ⓒ Ⓓ	198	Ⓐ Ⓑ Ⓒ Ⓓ
179	Ⓐ Ⓑ Ⓒ Ⓓ	189	Ⓐ Ⓑ Ⓒ Ⓓ	199	Ⓐ Ⓑ Ⓒ Ⓓ
180	Ⓐ Ⓑ Ⓒ Ⓓ	190	Ⓐ Ⓑ Ⓒ Ⓓ	200	Ⓐ Ⓑ Ⓒ Ⓓ

英語學習 —生活·文法·考用—

定價：NT$369元/HK$115元
規格：320頁/17＊23cm/MP3

定價：NT$380元/HK$119元
規格：320頁/17＊23cm/MP3

定價：NT$349元/HK$109元
規格：352頁/17＊23cm

定價：NT$380元/HK$119元
規格：288頁/17＊23cm/MP3

定價：NT$329元/HK$103元
規格：352頁/17＊23cm

定價：NT$349元/HK$109元
規格：304頁/17＊23cm

定價：NT$380元/HK$119元
規格：352頁/17＊23cm

定價：NT$369元/HK$115元
規格：304頁/17＊23cm/MP3

定價：NT$380元/HK$119元
規格：304頁/17＊23cm/MP3

Leader 026

突破新多益 800：滿分名師的教學密笈

作　　者　TC Hung（洪子健）
發 行 人　周瑞德
企劃編輯　陳欣慧
執行編輯　陳韋佑
校　　對　饒美君、魏于婷
封面構成　高鍾琪

內頁構成　華漢電腦排版有限公司
印　　製　大亞彩色印刷製版股份有限公司
初　　版　2015 年 9 月
定　　價　新台幣 499 元
出　　版　力得文化
電　　話　(02) 2351-2007
傳　　真　(02) 2351-0887
地　　址　100 台北市中正區福州街 1 號 10 樓之 2
E－m a i l　best.books.service@gmail.com

港澳地區總經銷　泛華發行代理有限公司
地　　　　址　香港新界將軍澳工業邨駿昌街 7 號 2 樓
電　　　　話　(852) 2798-2323
傳　　　　真　(852) 2796-5471

國家圖書館出版品預行編目資料

突破新多益 800：滿分名師的教學密笈 / 洪子健
著. -- 初版. -- 臺北市：力得文化, 2015.09
　　面；　公分. -- (Leader ; 26)
　　ISBN 978-986-91914-5-6(平裝附光碟片)

　　1.多益測驗

805.1895　　　　　　　　　　　　104016794